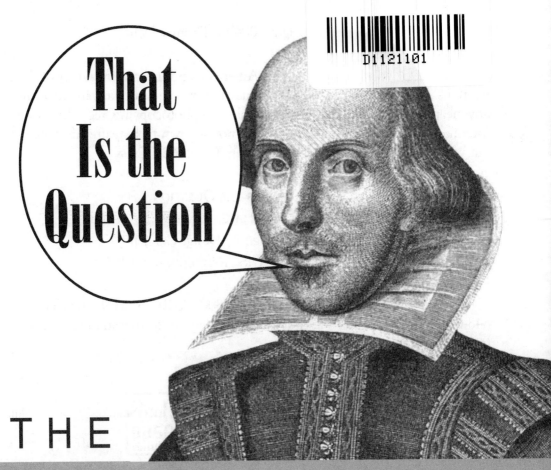

That
Is the
Question

THE
Ultimate
SHAKESPEARE
Quiz Book

THOMAS DELISE

New Page Books
A Division of The Career Press, Inc.
Franklin Lakes, NJ

THAT IS THE QUESTION
EDITED AND TYPESET BY CLAYTON W. LEADBETTER
Cover design by DesignConcept
Printed in the U.S.A. by Book-mart Press

To order this title, please call toll-free 1-800-CAREER-1 (NJ and Canada: 201-848-0310) to order using VISA or MasterCard, or for further information on books from Career Press.

The Career Press, Inc., 3 Tice Road, PO Box 687,
Franklin Lakes, NJ 07417
www.careerpress.com
www.newpagebooks.com

Library of Congress Cataloging-in-Publication Data

Delise, Thomas, 1955-
   That is the question : the ultimate Shakespeare quiz book / by Thomas Delise.
      p. cm.
   Includes bibliographical references.
   ISBN 1-56414-734-7 (pbk.)
      1. Shakespeare, William, 1564-1616—Examinations, questions, etc. I. Title.

PR2987.D45 2004
822.3'3—dc22   2003070206

Dedication

To Christine,
my wife and the love of my life:
"As true a lover as ever sighed upon a midnight pillow"
and
Virginia Delise, my mother,
whose life-long love of books led me to Shakespeare.

Acknowledgments

I never really intended to write a book consisting of nearly 100 quizzes dealing with Shakespeare. Four years ago, the original goal was much smaller, but once immersed in the idea, there was always one more quiz idea that seemed to materialize, and ultimately, this book developed a life of its own. Finally, I had to force myself to stop because I think it could have gone on forever. Shakespeare is truly boundless.

Many people have provided their support in many ways during the past four years. Michael Lomonico, Norrie Epstein, David Allen White, and Ralph Alan Cohen were extremely generous in taking time to critique the book, and I will always be grateful to them for their kind endorsements. Michael answered many questions, and his *Shakespeare Book of Lists* served as a valuable resource. A workshop he ran at a conference in New York City was not only the spark that radically changed the way I taught Shakespeare, but also encouraged me to fully commit to this book. Norrie was always gracious, and her book *The Friendly Shakespeare* is a must-read for all Shakespeare fans. David continually showed enthusiastic support, and his *Shakespeare A-Z* is a necessary resource for all things Shakespeare. All Shakespeare lovers should plan a trip to Staunton, Virginia, to see Ralph's wonderful *Shenandoah Shakespeare* company "do it in the right light" at their spectacular Blackfriars Theatre.

Jim Demcheck offered enthusiastic support and stayed up into the wee hours of the morning correcting my mistakes and assuring me that somewhere there was someone who would want to read this book. Bill Heller was extremely helpful in his advice regarding all aspects of the publishing process. Robert Schreur was very kind in supplying advice and resources. Jim Matterer generously provided medieval woodcuts from his Website *Gode Cookery*.

My students in Liberty High and Century High in Sykesville, Maryland, taught me more about Shakespeare than any book I ever read or course I ever took. Their eagerness to learn and willingness to experiment with Shakespeare has been an inspiration to me.

Everyone on the staff at Career Press/New Page Books was extremely professional and supportive during the entire publication process. Michael Lewis, Michael Pye, and Kirsten Beucler patiently answered a thousand and one questions on all possible topics. Clayton Leadbetter was everything an author could ask for in an editor. Editing a book of this type was a difficult task, but Clayton was always patient, insightful, and dedicated to the integrity of the book.

My friends and colleagues, Steve and Katherine Shoup, Bruce Damasio, Lorene Livermore, Thom McHugh, and Jeff Sharp, provided support and encouragement.

My family, Mario and Virginia Delise, Karen Delise, Gary Delise, and Justin and Sarah Delise have provided life-long support in all I have ever done.

And most important of all, my Christine, who is, in all things, my better angel. I am deeply appreciative of her unfailing support during all the hours I spent in my office pouring over volumes of forgotten and unforgettable lore: "My heart is unto you knit."

Note to the Reader

In some cases, it was convenient and necessary to devise abbreviations for some play titles in the text. The following is a list of abbreviations used:

All's Well	*All's Well That Ends Well*
Ant & Cleo	*Antony and Cleopatra*
As You	*As You Like It*
Com Err	*The Comedy of Errors*
1 Henry IV	*Henry IV, Part One*
2 Henry IV	*Henry IV, Part Two*
1 Henry VI	*Henry VI, Part One*
2 Henry VI	*Henry VI, Part Two*
3 Henry VI	*Henry VI, Part Three*
John	*King John*
J. Caesar	*Julius Caesar*
Lear	*King Lear*
Love's LL	*Love's Labor's Lost*
Measure	*Measure For Measure*
Merchant	*The Merchant of Venice*
Merry Wives	*The Merry Wives of Windsor*
MN Dream	*A Midsummer Night's Dream*
Much Ado	*Much Ado About Nothing*
Rom & Jul	*Romeo and Juliet*
Tam Shrew	*The Taming of the Shrew*
Tempest	*The Tempest*
Timon	*Timon of Athens*
Titus	*Titus Andronicus*
Tr & Cr	*Troilus and Cressida*
Twelfth N	*Twelfth Night*
Two Gents	*The Two Gentlemen of Verona*
Two Noble	*The Two Noble Kinsmen*
Win Tale	*The Winter's Tale*

All text references throughout the book are from *The Riverside Shakespeare* (Houghton Mifflin, 1974).

Contents

Introduction

William Shakespeare is everywhere. His image, his characters, and quotes from his works can be found in countless movies, television shows, literary works, and advertisements. Type his name in any search engine and you will find thousands of Websites. Do the same for an auction site and you will find thousands of Shakespeare related items: books, films, bottle openers, coffee mugs, T-shirts, statues, letter openers, action figures, coins, stamps, and much more. New film adaptations of his plays are constantly being made, and the Hollywood version of his love life, *Shakespeare in Love*, was a critically acclaimed box office extravaganza.

But Shakespeare has given us much more than these trinkets. It has been commonly said that a new book about Shakespeare is published somewhere in the world every day, and millions of people go to theaters around the world to see his plays performed. He has given us wonderful tales filled with remarkable characters who are windows into our own souls. Characters such as Othello, who force us to realize that within each of us the better angel of our nature is always struggling for dominance with a subtle dark angel.

He has given us language of unsurpassed beauty, as well. After all, our language is a window through which others may peer into our souls, and as we listen to the moving speeches of Juliet and Hamlet and Falstaff, we can see into their heart's core. In addition, his mastery of the language is demonstrated by the many expressions which have crept into our modern speech. His language has become our language, and in his book *The Story of English*, Bernard Levin illustrates this quite adeptly:

> "If you cannot understand my argument, and declare 'It's Greek to me,'
> you are quoting Shakespeare; if you claim to be more sinned against than
> sinning, you are quoting Shakespeare; if you recall your salad days, you are
> quoting Shakespeare; if you act more in sorrow than in anger, if your wish
> is father to the thought, if your lost property has vanished into thin air, you
> are quoting Shakespeare; if you have refused to budge an inch or suffered
> from green-eyed jealousy, if you have played fast and loose, if you have
> been tongue-tied, a tower of strength, hoodwinked or in a pickle, if you
> have knitted your brows, made a virtue of necessity, insisted on fair play,
> slept not one wink, stood on ceremony, danced attendance (on your lord
> and master), laughed yourself into stitches, had short shrift, cold comfort
> or too much of a good thing, if you have seen better days or lived in a fool's
> paradise—why, be that as it may, the more fool you, for it is a foregone
> conclusion that you are (as good luck would have it) quoting Shakespeare;
> if you think it is early days and clear out of bag and baggage, if you think it
> is high time and that that is the long and short of it, if you believe the
> game is up and that truth will out even if it involves your own flesh and
> blood, if you lie low until the crack of doom because you suspect foul play,
> if you have your teeth set on edge (at one fell swoop) without rhyme or
> reason, then—to give the devil his due—if the truth were known (for

surely you have a tongue in your head) you are quoting Shakespeare; even if you bid me good riddance and send me packing, if you wish I were as dead as a door-nail, if you think I am an eyesore, a laughing stock, the devil incarnate, a stoney-hearted villain, bloody-minded or a blinking idiot, then—by Jove! Tut, tut! for goodness sake! what the dickens! but me no buts—it is all one to me, for you are quoting Shakespeare."

As a fan of Shakespeare I continually see the profound impact that Shakespeare has on modern audiences, but even more important for me, as a teacher of Shakespeare for more than a quarter of a century, I have seen my own students cry when we performed the murder of Desdemona in my classroom and laugh until they cried at the antics of Nick Bottom and his rude mechanicals as they perform before Duke Theseus in *A Midsummer Night's Dream*. Just last semester my freshman English class performed *Romeo and Juliet* for their parents and other students. As the Prince spoke the final lines of the play, "For never was a story of more woe,/Than this of Juliet, and her Romeo," all my young actors bowed their heads in frozen sorrow as the curtain slowly closed. The next morning, one of my students told me that in the audience at that final moment, his father cried.

In the mouths of 14-year-old students on stage for the first time in their lives, the words of William Shakespeare have the same power to move as when they are uttered by giants of the stage such as Olivier and Gielgud.

I have seen his power, and I believe.

Shakespeare is a twofold treasure of possibility for us all, expert and novice alike. First, he offers us the chance to see ourselves in him. As Anthony Burgess said, "To see his face we need only look in the mirror. He is ourselves, ordinary suffering humanity, fired by moderate ambitions, concerned with money, the victim of desire, all too mortal...We are all Will."

And then, after holding up the mirror to our faces, Shakespeare offers the opportunity for us to go along with him to the next level. As Stanley Wells put it, in *Shakespeare for All Time*, he is "...a writer who is aware, and makes his spectators aware, of the mystery of things, of man's impulse to seek, however unavailingly, for an understanding of how we came to be on this earth as well as how we should conduct ourselves now that we are here." In *Hamlet*, Ophelia said, "We know what we are, but know not what we may be" (4.5.43), but in this, maybe Shakespeare was wrong. If we are able to realize the power of Shakespeare, maybe we will not only know who we are, but we *will* know what we can be. Perhaps it is the opportunity to mine this nugget of hope, more than any other that he offers us, that enables his work to transcend time.

For many, the noted scholar Harold Bloom foremost among them, "The plays remain the outward limit of human achievement," and as such, they are commonly regarded with a seriousness approaching the worship of holy relics. I assure you, that will not be the attitude you will find in this book. The primary purpose here is to have fun with Shakespeare and to treat the works as living, breathing celebrations of humanity rather than as stuffy and unapproachable museum pieces. Whether you are a Shakespeare expert, or just some-one who read a few plays when he was in high school, there is something here for you. For the expert, there are little tidbits and facts that may have slipped your mind over the years.

For the rest, this book is a fun way to learn some interesting things about the man and his work, and hopefully, you will find it a pleasant way to get to know the works of the world's greatest writer, without having to wade through onerous books and articles that feature heavy technical analysis. And who knows? Maybe something in this book will inspire you to engage in a deeper exploration into some (if not all) of Shakespeare's works. I sincerely hope it does.

In *That Is the Question: The Ultimate Shakespeare Quiz Book*, each quiz deals with a specific topic and has a relevant quote selected from one of Shakespeare's works as a title. Most of the quizzes consist of 20 or 25 questions, and virtually all the quizzes are objective in nature; that is, most are either multiple choice or matching in format. This prevents the format and content from being too difficult and intimidating. Answers to all questions and grading scales are provided.

The quizzes are organized into six major sections:

I. Quoting Shakespeare (14 quizzes)—Focuses on identifying the works through quotes.

II. Shakespeare's Characters (15 quizzes)—Focuses on identifying the characters in the plays through quotes, descriptions, and so forth.

III. Shakespeare's Infinite Variety (19 quizzes)—Includes the topics of medicine, songs, sports, mythology, dreams, the supernatural, and many more.

IV. Film, Stage, and Literature (15 quizzes)—Focuses on film and stage performances, actors and actresses, other writers, and so on.

V. Individual Plays (18 quizzes)—Contains quizzes for 18 of Shakespeare's best-known plays.

VI. Just for Fun (14 quizzes)—Includes Shakespeare trivia, Shakespearean vocabulary, anagrams, a crossword puzzle, and more.

Remember, the ultimate goal here is to have fun. In the words of Stanley Wells, "[Shakespeare] is a source of aesthetic pleasure and intellectual stimulus to millions. There is no holding him back. He is in the water supply, and is likely to remain there until the pipes run dry." So open up this book, and take a good long drink—he will restore and refresh you. Then read and reread his works.

Section I

Quoting Shakespeare

Quiz 1

This Is the True Beginning: Identify the Play by the Opening Lines

Each of the following is the opening from one of Shakespeare's plays. Match the opening lines with the plays from the answer bank provided, and if you are really good, identify the speaker of the lines, as well.

All's Well	*Henry V*	*Love's LL*	*MN Dream*	*Tam Shrew*
Ant & Cleo	*1 Henry VI*	*Macbeth*	*Much Ado*	*Tempest*
Com Err	*3 Henry VI*	*Measure*	*Othello*	*Titus*
Hamlet	*J. Caesar*	*Merchant*	*Richard III*	*Tr & Cr*
1 Henry IV	*Lear*	*Merry Wives*	*Rom & Jul*	*Twelfth N*

1) "Who's there?"

2) "In sooth, I know not why I am so sad..."

3) "O for a Muse of fire, that would ascend
The brightest heaven of invention!"

4) "If music be the food of love, play on."

5) "When shall we three meet again in
Thunder, lightning, or in rain?"

6) "Sir Hugh, persuade me not; I will make a
Star Chamber matter of it."

7) "Let fame, that all hunt after in their lives,
Live regist'red upon our brazen tombs,
And then grace us in the disgrace of death..."

8) "Noble patricians, patrons of my right,
Defend the justice of my cause with arms."

9) "Tush, never tell me!"

10) "Now is the winter of our discontent."

11) "I thought the king had more affected the Duke
of Albany than Cornwall."

12) "So shaken as we are, so wan with care,
   Find we a time for frighted peace to pant
   And breathe short-winded accents of new broils
   To be commenc'd in stronds afar remote."

13) "Boatswain!"

14) "Proceed, Solinus, to procure my fall,
   And by the doom of death and woes and all."

15) "Now, fair Hippolyta, our nuptial hour
   Draws on apace."

16) "I'll pheeze you, in faith."

17) "I wonder how the king escap'd our hands."

18) "Nay, but this dotage of our general's
   o'erflows the measure."

19) "I learn in this letter that Don Pedro of
   Arragon comes this night to Messina."

20) "Hence! Home, you idle creatures, get you
   home: Is this a holiday?"

21) "In Troy, there lies the scene."

22) "In delivering my son from me, I bury a second husband."

23) "Escalus."

24) "Hung be the heavens with black, yield day to night!"

25) "Two households, both alike in dignity,
   In fair Verona, where we lay our scene..."

Quiz 2

What Do You Call the Play?: Identify the Play by a Quote

The plays of Shakespeare have generated many statements that are easily recognizable today. From the titles provided, can you identify the play where you can find the following famous quotes? Try to identify the speaker, as well, if you can. Each answer can be used only once.

Ant & Cleo	*1 Henry VI*	*Love's LL*	*MN Dream*	*Rom & Jul*
As You	*2 Henry VI*	*Macbeth*	*Much Ado*	*Tam Shrew*
Hamlet	*John*	*Measure*	*Othello*	*Tempest*
1 Henry IV	*J. Caesar*	*Merchant*	*Richard II*	*Twelfth N*
Henry V	*Lear*	*Merry Wives*	*Richard III*	*Win Tale*

1) "Once more into the breach, dear friends, once more;
   or close the wall up with our English dead!"

2) "Beware the ides of March."

3) "Grief fills the room up of my absent child,
   Lies in his bed, walks up and down with me,
   Puts on his pretty looks, repeats his words,
   Remembers me of all his gracious parts..."

4) "O! beware, my lord, of jealousy;
   It is the green-eyed monster which doth mock
   The meat it feeds on."

5) "A horse! a horse! my kingdom for a horse!"

6) "Good night, good night! parting is such sweet sorrow,
   That I shall say good night till it be morrow."

7) "We are such stuff
   As dreams are made on; and our little life
   Is rounded with a sleep."

8) "Be not afraid of greatness: some are born great, some
   achieve greatness, and some have greatness thrust upon 'em."

9) "O villain, villain, smiling, damned villain!
   My tables—meet it is I set it down
   That one may smile, and smile, and be a villain!"

10) "And here I prophesy: this brawl to-day
Grown to this faction in the Temple Garden,
Shall send between the Red Rose and the White
A thousand souls to death and deadly night."

11) "Life's but a walking shadow; a poor player
That struts and frets his hour upon the stage
And then is heard no more. It is a tale
Told by an idiot, full of sound and fury,
Signifying nothing."

12) "The quality of mercy is not strained,
It droppeth as the gentle rain from heaven
Upon the place beneath: it is twice blessed;
It blesseth him that gives and him that takes."

13) "Lord, what fools these mortals be!"

14) "When we are born, we cry that we are come
To this great stage of fools."

15) "The first thing we do, let's kill all the lawyers."

16) "This royal throne of kings, this scept'red isle,
This earth of majesty, this seat of Mars...
This blessed plot, this earth, this realm, this England."

17) "Wives may be merry, and yet honest too."

18) "I will be master of what is mine own.
She is my goods, my chattels; she is my house,
My household stuff, my field, my barn,
My horse, my ox, my ass, my anything."

19) "A fool, a fool! I met a fool in the forest,
A motley fool."

20) "Let Rome in Tiber melt, and the wide arch
Of the ranged empire fall! Here is my space.
Kingdoms are clay."

21) "From women's eyes this doctrine I derive:
They sparkle still the right Promethean fire;
They are the books, the arts, the academes,
That show, contain, and nourish all the world."

22) "We were as twinned lambs, that did frisk i' th' sun,
And bleat the one at th' other; what we changed
Was innocence for innocence; we knew not
The doctrine of ill-doing, nor dreamed
That any did."

23) "Shall I never see a bachelor of three-score again?"

24) "...shall there be gallows standing in England
when thou art king? and resolution thus fubb'd as
it is with the rusty curb of old father antic the law?
Do not thou, when thou art king, hang a thief."

25) "We must not make a scarecrow of the law,
Setting it up to fear the birds of prey,
And let it keep one shape till custom make it
Their perch and not their terror."

Quiz 3

I Would My Horse Had the Speed of Your Tongue:
Identify the Play by an Insult Used

Shakespeare created many wonderful characters who displayed sharp wit through their insulting remarks. Can you identify the plays where some of Shakespeare's more cutting comments may be found? Granted, this is a difficult task and getting even a few correct makes you quite a Shakespearean scholar, but it is fun to read them, nevertheless. Who knows, one day you might even be able to slip one into a conversation you have! Each play is used only once.

All's Well	1 Henry IV	Lear	Much Ado	Timon
As You	2 Henry IV	Love's LL	Pericles	Tr & Cr
Coriolanus	Henry V	Measure	Richard III	Twelfth N
Cymbeline	John	Merchant	Rom & Jul	Two Gents
Hamlet	J. Caesar	Merry Wives	Tam Shrew	Win Tale

1) "Frailty, thy name is woman."

2) "They have been at a great feast of languages, and stolen the scraps."

3) "'Tis fools such as you
That makes the world full of ill-favored children."

4) "It is certain that when he makes water, his urine is congealed ice."

5) "You are not worth the dust which the rude wind blows in your face."

6) "Away, you three inch fool!"

7) "Blush, blush, thou lump of foul deformity."

8) "More of your conversation would infect my brain."

9) "Either thou art ignorant by age,
    Or thou wert born a fool."

10) "He has not so much brain as ear wax."

11) "He's a most notable coward, and infinite and endless liar, an hourly promise-breaker, the owner of no one good quality."

12) "He never broke any man's head but his own, and that was against a post when he was drunk."

13) "Vile worm, thou wast o'erlooked even in thy birth."

14) "Do thou amend thy face, and I'll amend my life."

15) "You blocks, you stones, you worse than senseless things."

16) "If you spend word for word with me, I shall make your wit bankrupt."

17) "There is not so ugly a fiend of hell
    As thou shalt be."

18) "Were I like thee I'd throw myself away."

19) "I can never see him but I am heart-burned an hour after."

20) "Her beauty and her brain go not together."

21) "Thy food is such as hath been belch'd on by infected breath."

22) "When he is best, he is little worse than a man, and when he is worst he is little better than a beast."

23) "I will sooner have a beard grow in the palm of my hand than he shall get one off his cheek."

24) "Thy head is as full of quarrels as an egg is full of meat."

25) "I can hardly forbear hurling things at him."

Quiz 4

Thus Men May Grow Wiser Every Day: Identify the Play by a Wise Quote

The plays of Shakespeare are filled with statements that express wisdom about the human condition. Here you will find 25 examples from the many hundreds that could have been used. Each statement comes from a different play.

All's Well	2 Henry IV	Love's LL	MN Dream	Rom & Jul
Ant & Cleo	Henry VIII	Macbeth	Much Ado	Tempest
As You	John	Measure	Othello	Tr & Cr
Hamlet	J. Caesar	Merchant	Pericles	Twelfth N
1 Henry IV	Lear	Merry Wives	Richard II	Two Gents

1) "This above all; to thine own self be true."

2) "The web of our life is of a mingled yarn, good and ill together."

3) "So quick bright things come to confusion."

4) "Some innocents 'scape not the thunderbolt."

5) "Experience is by industry achieved,
And perfected by the swift course of time."

6) "The better part of valor is discretion."

7) "Young blood doth not obey an old decree."

8) "The world is still deceived with ornament."

9) "Heat not a furnace for your foe so hot that it do singe yourself."

10) "To mourn a mischief that is past and gone
Is the next way to draw new mischief on."

11) "Dost thou think, because thou art virtuous,
There shall be no more cakes and ale?"

12) "Better a little chiding than a great deal of heartbreak."

13) "'Tis time to fear when tyrants seem to kiss."

14) "There's no art to find the mind's construction in the face."

15) "'Tis one thing to be tempted...another thing to fall."

16) "Misery acquaints a man with strange bedfellows."

17) "How oft the sight of means to do ill deeds makes deeds ill done."

18) "Be patient, for the world is broad and wide."

19) "Mine honor is my life; both grow in one;
    Take honor from me and my life is done."

20) "O, how full of briers is this working-day world!"

21) "Past and to come seem best; things present worst."

22) "Modest doubt is called the beacon of the wise."

23) "There was never yet philosopher
    That could endure the toothache patiently."

24) "Keep thy foot out of brothels, thy hand out of plackets, thy pen from lender's books, and defy the foul fiend."

25) "The abuse of greatness is when it disjoins
    Remorse from power."

Quiz 5

This Bud of Love: Identify the Play by a Love Quote

Shakespeare's observations on love are some of the most beautiful and proverbial in the English language. Can you identify the plays in which the following comments about love can be found? For five of the plays listed in the answer bank, you will find two quotes each; all the others can be matched with only one.

All's Well	Henry VIII	Merchant	Tam Shrew
As You	J. Caesar	MN Dream	Tr & Cr
Hamlet	Lear	Much Ado	Twelfth N
2 Henry IV	Love's LL	Othello	Two Gents
3 Henry VI	Measure	Rom & Jul	Win Tale

1) "All lovers swear more performance than they are able."

2) "The course of true love never did run smooth."

3) "Love, and be silent."

4) "Alas, how love can trifle with itself!"

5) "Love is a familiar; Love is a devil. There is no evil angel but love."

6) "Is it not strange that desire should so many years outlive performance?"

7) "When love begins to sicken and decay,
   It useth an enforced ceremony."

8) "Base men being in love have then a nobility in their natures more than is native to them."

9) "Love is blind, and lovers cannot see the pretty follies that themselves commit."

10) "Love all, trust a few."

11) "Friendship is constant in all other things
    Save in the office and affairs of love."

12) "Believe not that the dribbling dart of love
    Can pierce a complete bosom."

13) "Hasty marriage seldom proveth well."

14) "Love thyself last; cherish those hearts that hate thee."

15) "O spirit of love, how quick and fresh thou art."

16) "Love is merely a madness."

17) "There lives within the very flame of love
    A kind of wick or snuff that will abate it."

18) "Prosperity's the very bond of love."

19) "To be wise and love
    Exceeds man's might; that dwells with gods above."

20) "Stony limits cannot hold love out."

21) "A lover's eyes will gaze an eagle blind.
    A lover's ear will hear the lowest sound."

22) "All hearts in love use their own tongues."

23) "The sight of lovers feedeth those in love."

24) "Love sought is good, but given unsought is better."

25) "Kindness in women, not their beauteous looks,
    Shall win my love."

Quiz 6

Will You Rhyme Upon't?: Complete the Play's Rhyming Couplet

Shakespeare is famous for his clever and beautiful rhymes. Below you will find some of the lines from the plays; most of them are closing couplets that he liked to use to end a scene. Can you supply the rhyming word that Shakespeare himself used?

1) "Come, side by side, together live and die,
   And soul with soul from France to heaven _____!"
   Henry VI, Part One (4.5.54)

2) "The weight of this sad time we must obey;
   Speak what we feel, not what we ought to _____."
   King Lear (5.3.324)

3) "If I can check my erring love, I will;
   If not, to compass her I'll use my _____."
   The Two Gentlemen of Verona (2.4.213)

4) "But I have that within which passeth show:
   These are but the trappings and the suits of _____."
   Hamlet (1.2.85)

5) "O, what may man within him hide,
   Though angel on the outward _____."
   Measure for Measure (3.2.271)

6) "O me! My uncle's spirit is in these stones.
   Heaven take my soul, and England keep my _____!"
   King John (4.3.9)

7) "True hope is swift, and flies on swallow's wings;
    Kings it makes gods, and meaner creatures _____."
    Richard III (5.2.23)

8) "I 'gin to be aweary of the sun,
    And wish the estate o' the world were now _____."
    Macbeth (5.5.48)

9) "I have't. It is engendered. Hell and night
    Must bring this monstrous birth to the world's _____."
    Othello (1.3.403)

10) "For gnarling sorrow hath less power to bite
    The man that mocks at it and sets it _____."
    Richard II (1.3.292)

11) "More should I question thee, and more I must,
    Though more to know could not be more to _____."
    All's Well That Ends Well (2.1.205)

12) "There sleeps Titania some time of the night,
    Lulled in these flowers with dances and _____."
    A Midsummer Night's Dream (2.1.253)

13) "Golden lads and girls all must
    As chimney sweepers, come to _____."
    Cymbeline (4.2.262)

14) "Uncle, adieu. O, let the hours be short
    Till fields and blows and groans applaud our _____."
    Henry IV, Part One (1.3.301)

15) "Get posts and letters, and make friends with speed,
    Never so few, and never yet more _____."
    Henry IV, Part Two (1.1.214)

16) "Cheerly to sea! The signs of war advance!
    No king of England, if not king of _____!"
    Henry V (2.2.192)

17) "I will your faithful feeder be,
    And buy it with your gold right _____."
    As You Like It (2.4.99)

18) "Fate, show thy force. Ourselves we do not owe;
    What is decreed must be, and be this _____."
    Twelfth Night (1.5.310)

19) "And after this let Caesar seat him sure,
   For we will shake him, or worse days _____."
   Julius Caesar (1.2.321)

20) "If in his death the gods have us befriended,
   Great Troy is ours, and our sharp wars are _____."
   Troilus and Cressida (5.9.9)

21) "All's well that ends well! still the fine's the crown;
   What e'er the course, the end is the _____."
   All's Well That Ends Well (4.4.35)

22) "Men must learn how with pity to dispense,
   For policy sits above _____."
   Timon of Athens (3.2.86)

23) "Come, let's away. When, Caius, Rome is thine,
   Thou art poor'st of all; then shortly art thou _____."
   Coriolanus (4.7.56)

24) "The world's a city full of straying streets,
   And death's the market-place, where each one _____."
   The Two Noble Kinsmen (1.5.15)

25) "As I have made ye one, lords, one remain;
   So I grow stronger, you more honor _____."
   Henry VIII (5.2.214)

Quiz 7

Say But the Word: Complete the Play's Quote

Let's see if you are a wordsmith of Shakespeare's caliber. Fill in the missing word for each of the following well-known quotes from the plays. Unlike the previous quiz, the missing words here are not rhymes.

1) "But, soft! What light through yonder window breaks?
It is the east, and Juliet is the _____."
Romeo and Juliet (2.2.1)

2) "Many a good hanging prevents a bad _____."
Twelfth Night (1.5.19)

3) "How sharper than a serpent's tooth it is
To have a thankless _____."
King Lear (1.4.288)

4) "Forbear to judge, for we are _____ all."
Henry VI, Part Two (3.3.31)

5) "I have not slept one _____."
Cymbeline (3.4.100)

6) "Small cheer and great welcome make a merry _____."
The Comedy of Errors (3.1.26)

7) "'Tis the _____ that makes the body rich."
The Taming of the Shrew (4.3.172)

8) "Why, then the world's mine _____,
Which I with sword will open."
The Merry Wives of Windsor (2.2.3)

9) "By the pricking of my thumbs,
Something _____ this way comes."
Macbeth (4.1.45)

10) "I count myself in nothing else so happy
As in a soul remembering my good _____."
Richard II (2.3.46)

11) "I like not fair terms and a villain's _____."
The Merchant of Venice (1.3.179)

12) "Bell, book, and _____ shall not drive me back.
    When gold and silver becks me to come on."
    King John (3.3.12)

13) "Out of this nettle, danger, we pluck this flower, _____."
    Henry IV, Part One (2.3.9)

14) "I am as poor as Job, my lord, but not so_____."
    Henry IV, Part Two (1.2.126)

15) "Nothing emboldens sin so much as _____."
    Timon of Athens (3.5.3)

16) "He wears his faith but as the fashion of his _____."
    Much Ado About Nothing (1.1.75)

17) "My _____ fell with my fortunes."
    As You Like It (1.2.252)

18) "A sad tale's best for _____; I have one
    Of sprites and goblins."
    The Winter's Tale (2.1.25)

19) "My _____ days,
    When I was green in judgment, cold in blood."
    Antony and Cleopatra (1.5.73)

20) "This fellow's wise enough to play the _____,
    And to do that well craves a kind of wit."
    Twelfth Night (3.1.60)

21) "Fling away _____.
    By that sin fell the angels."
    Henry VIII (3.2.440)

22) "Nature teaches beasts to know their _____."
    Coriolanus (2.1.6)

23) "'Tis mad idolatry
    To make the service greater than the _____."
    Troilus and Cressida (2.2.56)

24) "The law hath not been dead, though it hath _____."
    Measure for Measure (2.2.90)

25) "Woe to the land that's governed by a _____."
    Richard III (2.3.11)

Quiz 8

Why, How Now, Hamlet!: Complete the *Hamlet* Quote

Of all the plays of William Shakespeare, *Hamlet* **is certainly the most famous and most quoted. Fill in the missing word for each of the following well-known quotes.**

1) "A little more than kin, and less than _____." (1.2.65)

2) "Neither a borrower nor a _____ be." (1.3.75)

3) "There are more things in heaven and earth, Horatio,
   Than are dreamt of in your _____." (1.5.166)

4) "This is the very ecstasy of _____." (2.1.99)

5) "It is common for the younger sort
   To lack _____." (2.1.113)

6) "Brevity is the soul of _____." (2.2.90)

7) "More matter, with less _____." (2.2.95)

8) "To be _____, as this world goes, is to be one
   man picked out of ten thousand." (2.2.178)

9) "There is nothing either good or bad but _____ makes it so." (2.2.249)

10) "O God! I could be bounded in a nutshell, and count myself a king of infinite space,
    were it not that I have bad _____." (2.2.253)

11) "What a piece of work is a _____." (2.2.303)

12) "They say an old man is twice a _____." (2.2.385)

13) "Use every man after his desert, and who should 'scape _____?" (2.2.529)

14) "The play's the thing
    Wherein I'll catch the _____ of the king." (2.2.604)

15) "Get thee to a _____." (3.1.120)

16) "The glass of _____ and the mould of form." (3.1.153)

17) "Some must watch, while some must _____." (3.2.273)

18) "You would pluck out the heart of my _____." (3.2.365)

19) "Do you think I am easier to be played on than a _____?" (3.2.369)

20) "Assume a _____, if you have it not." (3.4.160)

21) "When sorrows come, they come not single spies,
    But in _____." (4.5.78)

22) "There's rosemary, that's for _____." (4.5.175)

23) "And where the offence is let the great _____ fall." (4.5.219)

24) "There's a _____ that shapes our ends,
    Rough-hew them how we will." (5.2.10)

25) "Good night, sweet prince,
    And flights of _____ sing thee to thy rest!" (5.2.359)

Quiz 9

To Be, or Not To Be: Complete the Hamlet Soliloquy

   Hamlet's "To be, or not to be" speech is undoubtedly the most famous speech in all of Shakespeare. From each pair, can you choose the correct word that Shakespeare used when composing this timeless contemplation on life and death?

To be, or not to be: that is the question:

1) Whether 'tis nobler in the **(heart/mind)** to suffer

2) The slings and **(arrows/spears)** of outrageous fortune,

3) Or to take arms against a **(stream/sea)** of troubles,
And by opposing end them? To die: to sleep;
No more; and by a sleep to say we end

4) The heart-ache and the thousand natural **(shocks/fears)**
That flesh is heir to, 'tis a consummation

5) **(Piously/Devoutly)** to be wish'd. To die, to sleep;
To sleep: perchance to dream: ay, there's the rub;
For in that sleep of death what dreams may come

6) When we have shuffled off this mortal **(foil/coil)**,
Must give us pause: there's the respect

7) That makes **(catastrophe/calamity)** of so long life;

8) For who would bear the **(whips/quips)** and scorns of time,
The oppressor's wrong, the proud man's contumely,

9) The **(fangs/pangs)** of despised love, the law's delay,
The insolence of office and the spurns

10) That **(patient/ancient)** merit of the unworthy takes,
When he himself might his quietus make

11) With a **(bright/bare)** bodkin? who would fardels bear,

12) To grunt and **(fret/sweat)** under a weary life,

13) But that the **(thought/dread)** of something after death,
The undiscover'd country from whose bourn

14) No **(seafarer/traveler)** returns, puzzles the will

15) And makes us rather bear those **(ills/cares)** we have
Than fly to others that we know not of?
Thus conscience does make cowards of us all;

16) And thus the native **(dew/hue)** of resolution

17) Is sicklied o'er with the pale cast of **(thought/hope)**,

18) And **(contemplations/enterprises)** of great pith and moment

19) With this regard their **(fortunes/currents)** turn awry,

20) And lose the name of **(action/motion)**.

Quiz 10

All the World's a Stage: Complete the *As You Like It* Soliloquy

Choosing the words that Shakespeare used, select the 20 correct words in this famous soliloquy by the notoriously melancholy character Jaques, from the glorious pastoral comedy *As You Like It.*

All the world's a stage,

1) And all the men and women merely (**players/actors**):
They have their exits and their entrances;

2) And one man in his (**time/life**) plays many parts,

3) His acts being seven (**stages/ages**). At first the infant,

4) Mewling and (**puking/sucking**) in the nurse's arms.
And then the whining school-boy, with his satchel

5) And shining morning face, creeping like (**cat/snail**)
Unwillingly to school. And then the lover,

6) (**Sighing/Burning**) like furnace, with a woeful ballad
Made to his mistress' eyebrow. Then a soldier,

7) Full of strange (**oaths/hopes**) and bearded like the pard,

8) (**Zealous/Jealous**) in honour, sudden and quick in quarrel,

9) Seeking the (**double/bubble**) reputation

10) Even in the cannon's mouth. And then the (**lawyer/justice**),

11) In fair round (**belly/stomach**) with good capon lined,

12) With (**eyes/mouth**) severe and beard of formal cut,

13) Full of wise saws and (**modern/ancient**) instances;
And so he plays his part. The sixth age shifts

14) Into the lean and slipper'd (**pantaloon/grandfather**),

15) With spectacles on nose and (**purse/pouch**) on side,
His youthful hose, well saved, a world too wide

16) For his (**trunk/shrunk**) shank; and his big manly voice,
Turning again toward childish treble, pipes

17) And whistles in his sound. Last (**scene/show**) of all,

18) That ends this (**strange/sad**) eventful history,

19) Is second (**foolishness/childishness**) and mere oblivion,

20) Sans teeth, sans eyes, sans (**smell/taste**), sans everything.

Quiz 11

Now Is the Winter of Our Discontent: Complete the *Richard III* Soliloquy

There has always been great debate regarding Shakespeare's portrayal of infamous King Richard III, and some disagree that he was as diabolical as Shakespeare presents him. Nevertheless, in the opening soliloquy of the play, Richard explains his evil intentions quite clearly. Choose the correct words to complete this famous soliloquy spoken by the evil Richard at the very beginning of the play that bears his name.

Now is the winter of our discontent

1) Made glorious summer by this **(star/sun)** of York;

2) And all the **(pain/clouds)** that lour'd upon our house

3) In the deep bosom of the **(ocean/planet)** buried.

4) Now are our **(doors/brows)** bound with victorious wreaths;
   Our bruised arms hung up for monuments;

5) Our stern alarums changed to **(mighty/merry)** meetings,
   Our dreadful marches to delightful measures.

6) Grim-visaged **(war/hate)** hath smooth'd his wrinkled front;
   And now, instead of mounting barbed steeds

7) To fright the **(hearts/souls)** of fearful adversaries,
   He capers nimbly in a lady's chamber

8) To the lascivious pleasing of a **(flute/lute)**.

9) But I, that am not shaped for sportive **(tricks/jests)**,

10) Nor made to **(court/woo)** an amorous looking-glass;
    I, that am rudely stamp'd, and want love's majesty

11) To **(dance/strut)** before a wanton ambling nymph;
    I, that am curtail'd of this fair proportion,

12) Cheated of **(feature/figure)** by dissembling nature,
    Deformed, unfinish'd, sent before my time

13) Into this breathing **(world/orb)**, scarce half made up,
    And that so lamely and unfashionable

14) That dogs bark at me as I **(halt/limp)** by them;

15) Why, I, in this **(soft/weak)** piping time of peace,
    Have no delight to pass away the time,

16) Unless to spy my **(reflection/shadow)** in the sun

17) And descant on mine own **(deformity/monstrosity)**:

And therefore, since I cannot prove a lover,

18) To **(entertain/endure)** these fair well-spoken days,

19) I am determined to prove a **(villain/devil)**

20) And hate the **(foolish/idle)** pleasures of these days.

Quiz 12

Here Is Part of My Rhyme: Complete the Sonnet Rhyme

The sonnets of Shakespeare are written in the form known as the English, or Shakespearean sonnet. Each of these rigidly structured poems ends with a rhyming couplet, which serves as a conclusion for the poem. See if you can complete each couplet with the same word that Shakespeare chose. For your reference, the sonnet number is in parentheses after the couplet.

1) Be not self-will'd, for thou art much too fair
   To be death's conquest and make worms thine _____   (#6)

2) But were some child of yours alive that time,
   You should live twice, in it and in my _____   (#17)

3) So long as men can breathe or eyes can see,
   So long lives this, and this gives life to _____   (#18)

4) Yet eyes this cunning want to grace their art,
   They draw but what they see, know not the _____   (#24)

5) But day doth daily draw my sorrows longer,
   And night doth nightly make grief's length seem _____   (#28)

6) For thy sweet love rememb'red such wealth brings,
   That then I scorn to change my state with _____   (#29)

7) But if the while I think on thee, dear friend,
   All losses are restor'd, and sorrows _____   (#30)

8) His beauty shall in these black lines be seen,
   And they shall live, and he in them still _____   (#63)

9) And him as for a map doth Nature store,
   To show false Art what beauty was of _____   (#68)

10) But thou art all my art, and dost advance
    As high as learning my rude _____   (#78)

11) There lives more life in one of your fair eyes
    Than both your poets can in praise _____   (#83)

12) Such is my love, to thee I so belong,
    That for thy right myself will bear all _____   (#88)

13) For sweetest things turn sourest by their deeds;
    Lilies that fester smell far worse than _____   (#94)

14) Yet seem'd it winter still, and, you away,
    As with your shadow I with these did _____   (#98)

15) For we which now behold these present days
    Have eyes to wonder, but lack tongues to _____   (#106)

16) And thou in this shalt find thy monument,
    When tyrants' crests and tombs of brass are _____ (#107)

17) Then give me welcome, next my heaven the best,
    Even to thy pure and most loving _____   (#110)

18) You are so strongly in my purpose bred
    That all the world besides methinks are _____   (#112)

19) Unless this general evil they maintain:
    All men are bad and in their badness _____   (#121)

20) To this I witness call the fools of Time,
    Which die for goodness, who have liv'd for _____   (#124)

21) And yet, by heaven, I think my love as rare
    As any she belied with false _____   (#130)

22) Make but my name thy love, and love that still,
    And then thou lovest me, for my name is _____   (#136)

23) Yet do not so, but since I am near slain,
    Kill me outright with looks, and rid my _____   (#139)

24) So shall thou feed on Death, that feeds on men,
    And death once dead, there's no more dying _____   (#146)

25) For I have sworn thee fair, and thought thee bright,
    Who art as black as hell, as dark as _____   (#147)

Quiz 13

'Tis Well Said Again: Identify the Play Where a Famous Phrase May Be Found

The brilliance of Shakespeare's use of language is evident in the large number of statements and images from his works that have become a part of our every day speech. Match the famous expression with the play in which you can find it. More than one quote may come from the same play.

As You	*2 Henry IV*	*Macbeth*	*Richard II*
Com Err	*John*	*Merchant*	*Rom & Jul*
Coriolanus	*J. Caesar*	*Merry Wives*	*Tempest*
Hamlet	*Love's LL*	*Othello*	*Two Gents*

1) "My own flesh and blood"

2) "It was Greek to me"

3) "As good luck would have it"

4) "He has eaten me out of house and home"

5) "Too much of a good thing"

6) "A fool's paradise"

7) "To make a virtue of necessity"

8) "Method in his madness"

9) "Throw cold water on it"

10) "The crack of doom"

11) "Play fast and loose"

12) "Elbow room"

13) "Misery acquaints a man with strange bedfellows"

14) "Pomp and circumstance"

15) "In my mind's eye"

16) "Cold comfort"

17) "A nine days wonder"

18) "A spotless reputation"

19) "It smells to heaven"

20) "A sorry sight"

21) "A foregone conclusion"

22) "To die by inches"

23) "Masters of their fates"

24) "Hearts of gold"

25) "Something in the wind"

Quiz 14

Our Revels Now Are Ended: Identify the Play by the Ending Lines

The following quotes are the last words uttered in some of Shakespeare's plays. Identify the play and the character who spoke the last words.

As You	1 Henry IV	Lear	Much Ado	Tam Shrew
Com Err	2 Henry IV	Love's LL	Othello	Tempest
Coriolanus	3 Henry VI	Macbeth	Richard II	Twelfth N
Cymbeline	John	Measure	Richard III	Two Gents
Hamlet	J. Caesar	Merchant	MN Dream	Win Tale

1) "Well, while I live I'll fear no other thing
   So sore as keeping safe Nerissa's ring."

2) "'Tis a wonder, by your leave, she will be tamed so."

3) "Give me your hands, if we be friends,
   And Robin shall restore amends."

4) "But that's all one, our play is done,
   And we'll strive to please you every day."

5) "My tongue is weary, when my legs are too, I will
   bid you good night.

6) "Myself will straight aboard, and to state
   This heavy act with heavy heart relate."

7) "Such a sight as this
   Becomes the field, but here shows much amiss.
   Go, bid the soldiers shoot."

8) "The oldest hath born most; we that are young
   Shall never see so much, not live so long."

9) "Now civil wounds are stopped, peace lives again:
   That she may long live here, God say amen!"

10) "...I am sure as many as have good beards or good
    faces or sweet breaths will, for my kind offer, when
    I make curtsy, bid me farewell."

11) "As you from crimes would pardon'd be,
      Let your indulgence set me free."

12) "Come, Proteus; 'tis your penance to hear
      The story of your loves discovered:
      That done, our day of marriage shall be yours;
      One feast, one house, one mutual happiness."

13) "So, bring us to our palace; where we'll show
      What's yet behind, that's meet you all should know."

14) "Nay, then, thus:
      We came into the world like brother and brother;
      And now let's go hand in hand, not one before the other."

15) "Think not on him till to-morrow:
      I'll devise thee brave punishments for him.
      Strike up, pipers."

16) "The woods of Mercury are harsh after the songs
      of Apollo. You that way; we this way."

17) "Though in this city he
      Hath widow'd and unchilded many a one,
      Which to this hour bewail the injury,
      Yet he shall have a noble memory.
      Assist."

18) "Lead us from hence, where we may leisurely
      Each one demand and answer to his part
      Perform'd in this wide gap of time since first
      We were dissever'd: hastily lead away."

19) "Nought shall make us rue,
      If England to itself do rest but true."

20) "I'll make a voyage to the Holy Land,
      To wash this blood off from my guilty hand:
      March sadly after; grace my mournings here;
      In weeping after this untimely bier."

21) "And in the temple of great Jupiter
      Our peace we'll ratify; seal it with feasts.
      Set on there! Never was a war did cease
      Ere bloody hands were wash'd, with such a peace."

22) "Within my tent his bones to-night shall lie,
    Most like a soldier, order'd honourably.
    So call the field to rest; and let's away,
    To part the glories of this happy day."

23) "Rebellion in this land shall lose his sway,
    Meeting the check of such another day:
    And since this business so fair is done,
    Let us not leave till all our own be won."

24) "Sound drums and trumpets! farewell sour annoy!
    For here, I hope, begins our lasting joy."

25) "So, thanks to all at once and to each one,
    Whom we invite to see us crown'd at Scone."

Section II

Shakespeare's Characters

Quiz 15

Have We Not Affections?: Identify the Significant Others

There are an abundance of lovers and married couples in the plays of Shakespeare. From the list of women that is provided, identify the "significant other" of the male characters from the plays. Keep in mind that if the male character becomes infatuated with a woman during the course of the play but ends up with another at the end, the "significant other" is the woman that "wins" the male character at the play's conclusion.

Anne Page	Desdemona	Hermione	Lavinia	Paulina
Audrey	Emilia	Hero	Mariana	Portia
Beatrice	Gertrude	Imogen	Miranda	Rosalind
Bianca	Helena	Julia	Nerissa	Silvia
Celia	Hermia	Katherina	Olivia	Viola

1) Orlando

2) Benedick

3) Petruchio

4) Bertram

5) Proteus

6) Angelo

7) Iago

8) Orsino

9) Lysander

10) Valentine

11) Claudius

12) Touchstone

13) Lucentio

14) Bassianus

15) Posthumus

16) Fenton

17) Sebastian

18) Othello

19) Gratiano

20) Claudio

21) Bassanio

22) Antigonus

23) Ferdinand

24) Oliver

25) Leontes

Quiz 16

Lord, What Fools: Identify the Fool

Shakespeare's plays contain many fools, jesters, clowns, and foolish characters. Some are very witty and display the knowledge of wise men. Others are just plain foolish. Identify the play in which you can find each of the funny men. More than one of the fools may be found in the same plays.

All's Well	Love's LL	Merry Wives	Tempest
As You	Macbeth	MN Dream	Tr & Cr
Com Err	Measure	Much Ado	Twelfth N
Hamlet	Merchant	Tam Shrew	Two Gents

1) Touchstone

2) Feste

3) Launcelot Gobbo

4) Speed

5) Nick Bottom

6) Dogberry

7) Lavache

8) Peter Elbow

9) Trinculo

10) Costard

11) Thersites

12) A wisecracking gravedigger

13) An unnamed drunken porter

14) The Dromio brothers

15) Launce

16) Parolles

17) Gremio

18) Abraham Slender

19) Bum Pompey

20) Don Adriano de Armado

Quiz 17

Where Are My Children?: Identify the Parent and Child

In the plays of Shakespeare, you will find a number of parents and their children. Some have very loving and normal relationships, others have relationships that are a bit more unusual. From the numbered names of the parents and the answer bank of their offspring (listed alphabetically), match the son or daughter with the appropriate mother or father.

Antipholus	Desdemona	Hermia	Lavinia	Ophelia
Bertram	Ferdinand	Hero	Lucentio	Orlando
Cordelia	Fleance	Imogen	Malcolm	Perdita
Coriolanus	Florizel	Jessica	Marina	Proteus
Cressida	Hamlet	Katherina	Miranda	Troilus

1) Countess of Rossillion

2) Rowland de Boys

3) Volumnia

4) Cymbeline

5) Polonius

6) King Lear

7) Duncan

8) Shylock

9) Egeus

10) Leonato

11) Brabantio

12) Pericles

13) Baptista Minola

14) Alonso

15) Titus Andronicus

16) Antonio

17) Priam

18) Leontes

19) Egeon

20) Gertrude

21) Vincentio

22) Calchas

23) Polixenes

24) Banquo

25) Prospero

Quiz 18

O, Odious Is the Name: Identify the Character With the Unusual Name

Shakespeare, like Charles Dickens a few hundred years later, had a knack for devising wonderful and unusual names for some of his characters. For each of the following characters, identify the play in which he or she appears. Note that the same play may correspond to more than one character listed, and some characters may appear in more than one play.

Com Err	Henry V	Merchant	Much Ado	Timon
2 Henry IV	Love's LL	Merry Wives	Rom & Jul	Twelfth N
2 Henry VI	Measure	MN Dream	Tempest	Win Tale

1) Mistress Overdone

2) Robin Starvling

3) Potpan

4) Peter Thump

5) Fang

6) Sir Toby Belch

7) Old Gobbo

8) Apemantus

9) Mopsa

10) Hugh Oatcake

11) Anthony Dull

12) Dr. Pinch

13) Ralph Mouldy

14) Abhorson

15) Sir Andrew Aguecheek

16) Peter Simple

17) Doll Tearsheet

18) Dogberry

19) Caliban

20) Mustardseed

21) Froth

22) Nym

23) Francis Feeble

24) James Soundpost

25) Dromio

Quiz 19

Double, Double, Toil and Trouble: Multiple Use of Character Names

The following are names that Shakespeare used for characters in more than one of his plays. Identify the plays where these characters appear. Each name is used in only two plays, unless there is a number in parentheses after the name (indicating the number of different plays where a character with that name appears).

1) Angelo

2) Antonio (5)

3) Bianca

4) Claudio

5) Claudius

6) Demetrius (3)

7) Emilia (4)

8) Escalus

9) Francisco

10) Gratiano

11) Helena

12) Juliet

13) Lucius (4)

14) Maria

15) Mariana

16) Portia

17) Sebastian

18) Stephano

19) Valentine (3)

20) Vincentio

Quiz 20

This Title Honors Me and Mine: Identify Characters by Their Title

Many of Shakespeare's characters have high and mighty titles. Can you match the character with his or her title?

Alonso	Escalus	Leontes	Orsino	Priam
Antiochus	Ferdinand	Leonato	Pericles	Tamora
Bertram	Fortinbras	Macbeth	Polixenes	Theseus
Cymbeline	Gertrude	Macduff	Prospero	Titania
Don Pedro	Hippolyta	Oberon	Solinus	Vincentio

1) Count of Rossillion

2) Duke of Ephesus

3) King of Britain

4) Prince of Norway

5) King of Navarre

6) Thane of Glamis

7) Prince of Arragon

8) Prince of Tyre

9) King of Naples

10) Prince of Verona

11) Queen of the Goths

12) Duke of Illyria

13) King of Sicilia

14) Thane of Fife

15) King of the Fairies

16) Duke of Athens

17) Governor of Messina

18) King of Antioch

19) Queen of Denmark

20) Duke of Milan

21) Queen of the Amazons

22) Duke of Vienna

23) King of Troy

24) Queen of the Fairies

25) King of Bohemia

Quiz 21

Our Parts So Poor: Identify the Play in Which a Minor Character Appears

Shakespeare's immense literary talent was able to breathe life into even some of his minor characters with small roles. Admittedly, not all of the minor characters listed here are memorable ones, but see if you can identify the play where each can be found. No more than one character from a play is used.

All's Well	1 Henry IV	Macbeth	Othello	Titus
Ant & Cleo	Henry V	Measure	Pericles	Tr & Cr
As You	Henry VIII	Merchant	Rom & Jul	Twelfth N
Com Err	Lear	MN Dream	Tam Shrew	Two Gents
Hamlet	Love's LL	Much Ado	Timon	Win Tale

1) Philostrate

2) Poins

3) Alice

4) Lafew

5) Fabian

6) Biondello

7) Dorcas

8) Holofernes

9) Seyton

10) Iras

11) Lucio

12) Montano

13) Solario

14) Voltemand

15) Oswald

16) Chiron

17) Eglamour

18) Luce

19) Ursula

20) Boult

21) Adam

22) Patience

23) Cassandra

24) Timandria

25) Sampson

Quiz 22

We Were the First, Part I: Identify the Female Character by Her First Words

Each of the following quotes are the first words uttered by female characters in some of Shakespeare's plays. Can you match the famous first words with the famous female speakers? Good luck!

Adriana	Gertrude	Julia	Miranda	Rosalind
Beatrice	Helena	Juliet	Olivia	Tamora
Cleopatra	Hermione	Katherina	Ophelia	Titania
Cressida	Imogen	Lady Macbeth	Perdita	Viola
Desdemona	Isabella	Maria	Portia	Volumnia

1) "By my troth, Nerissa, my little body is a-weary of this great world."

2) "Call you me fair? That fair again unsay. Demetrius loves your fair."

3) "I pray you, is Signoir Mountanto return'd from the wars or no?"

4) "What country, friends, is this?"

5) "If it be love indeed, tell me how much."

6) "Dissembling courtesy! How fine this tyrant Can tickle where she wounds!"

7) "I had thought, sir, to have held my peace until You had drawn oaths from him not to stay."

8) "How now, who calls?"

9) "What, jealous Oberon? Fairies, skip hence— I have forsaken his bed and his company."

10) "I pray you, sir, is it your will To make a stale of me amongst these mates?"

11) "Who were those that went by?"

12) "Sir, my gracious lord, To chide at your extremes it not becomes me."

13) "By my troth, Sir Toby, you must come in earlier a' nights."

14) "Dear Celia—I show more mirth than I am
mistress of, and would you yet I were merrier?"

15) "Neither my husband nor the slave return'd,
That in such haste I sent to seek his master."

16) "I pray you, daughter, sing, or express yourself in a more comfortable sort."

17) "Do you doubt that?"

18) "But say, Lucetta, now we are alone,
Wouldst thou then counsel me to fall in love?"

19) "Take the fool away."

20) "They met me in the day of
success; and I have learn'd by the perfect'st report,
They have more in them than mortal knowledge."

21) "My noble father,
I do perceive here a divided duty..."

22) "If by your art, my dearest father, you have
Put the wild waters in this roar, allay them."

23) "And have you nuns no further privileges?"

24) "Stay, Roman brethren! Gracious conqueror,
Victorious Titus, rue the tears I shed,
A mother's tears in passion for her son."

25) "Good Hamlet, cast thy nighted color off,
And let thine eye look like a friend on Denmark."

Quiz 23

We Were the First, Part II: Identify the Male Character by His First Words

As you were asked to match the women characters with their first words in the previous quiz, match these famous male characters with the first words they utter.

Angelo	Falstaff	Macbeth	Posthumus	Timon
Bertram	Feste	Mark Antony	Prospero	Titus Andronicus
Brutus	Hamlet	Othello	Puck	Toby Belch
Caliban	Iago	Petruchio	Romeo	Touchstone
Coriolanus	Lear	Polixenes	Shylock	Troilus

1) "A little more than kin, and less than kind."

2) "So foul and fair a day I have not seen."

3) "Verona, for awhile I take my leave
   To see my friends in Padua."

4) "Three thousand ducats, well."

5) "How now, spirit, whither wander you?"

6) "Now, Master Shallow, you'll complain of me to the King?"

7) "What a plague means my niece to take the death of her brother thus?"

8) "Hail, Rome, victorious in thy mourning weeds!"

9) "Is the day so young?"

10) "There's beggary in the love that can be reckon'd."

11) "Call here my varlet, I'll unarm again."

12) "Always obedient to your Grace's will,
    I come to know your pleasure."

13) "Attend the lords of France and Burgundy, Gloucester."

14) "'Tis better as it is."

15) "A soothsayer bids you beware the ides of March."

16) "Imprison'd is he, say you?"

17) "'Sblood, but you'll not hear me.
    If ever I did dream of such a matter,
    Abhor me."

18) "Please your Highness,
    I will from hence to-day."

19) "Thanks. What's the matter, you dissentious rogues,
    That rubbing the poor itch of your opinion
    Make yourselves scabs?"

20) "Be collected
    No more amazement. Tell your piteous heart
    There's no harm done."

21) "Mistress, you must come away to your father."

22) "And I in going madam, weep o'er my father's death anew; but I must attend his
    Majesty's command, to whom I am now in ward, evermore in subjection."

23) "There's wood enough within."

24) "Let her hand me! He that is well hang'd in this world needs to fear no colors."

25) "Nine changes of the wat'ry star hath been
    The shepherd's note since we have left our throne
    Without a burden."

Quiz 24

A Woman Is a Dish for the Gods: Identify the Female Character From a Quote

In this quiz you will find quotes taken from the speeches of Shakespeare's many memorable female characters. From the answer list provided, match each quote with the speaker. Each character may be used only once.

Anne Bullen	Cressida	Hermione	Katherina	Rosalind
Beatrice	Desdemona	Imogen	Lady Macbeth	Rosaline
Calpurnia	Emilia	Isabella	Miranda	Titania
Cleopatra	Gertrude	Julia	Ophelia	Viola
Cordelia	Helena	Juliet	Portia	Volumnia

1) "Give me my robe, put on my crown; I have
   Immortal longings in me."

2) "The lady doth protest too much, methinks."

3) "I swear again, I would not be a queen
   For all the world."

4) "My only love sprung from my only hate!
   Too early seen unknown, and known too late!"

5) "I see a woman may be made a fool,
   If she had not a spirit to resist."

6) "O wonder!
   How many goodly creatures are there here!
   How beauteous mankind is! O brave new world
   That has such people in't!"

7) "I had rather hear my dog bark at a
   crow than a man swear he loves me."

8) "...what visions have I seen!
   Methought I was enamor'd of an ass."

9) "'Tis not a year or two shows us a man:
   They are all but stomachs, and we all but food;
   They eat us hungerly, and when they are full
   They belch us."

10) "Here's the smell of the blood still: all the perfumes
    Of Arabia will not sweeten this little hand. Oh, oh, oh."

11) "O! woe is me,
    To have seen what I have seen, see what I see."

12) "I pray you, do not fall in love with me,
    For I am falser than vows made in wine."

13) "'Twere all one
    That I should love a bright particular star
    And think to wed it, he is so above me."

14) "Better it were a brother died at once
    Than that a sister, by redeeming him,
    Should die forever."

15) "The emperor of Russia was my father.
    Oh that he were alive, and here beholding
    His daughter's trial! That he did but see
    The flatness of my misery; yet with eyes
    Of pity, not revenge!"

16) "I may neither choose who I would, nor refuse who I dislike; so is the will of a living
    daughter curb'd by the will of a dead father."

17) "Unhappy that I am, I cannot heave
    My heart unto my mouth. I love your Majesty
    According to my bond, no more nor less."

18) "My master loves her dearly,
    And I (poor monster) fond as much on him;
    And she (mistaken) seems to dote on me.
    What will become of this?"

19) "When beggars die there are no comets seen;
    The heavens themselves blaze forth the death of princes."

20) "They say all lovers swear more performance than they are able and yet reserve an
    ability that they never perform, vowing more than the perfection often and dis-
    charging less than the tenth part of one."

21) "If my son were my husband, I should freelier rejoice in that absence wherein he
    won honor than in the embracements of his bed where he would show most love."

22) "My mother had a maid call'd Barbary;
      She was in love, and he she lov'd prov'd mad,
      And did forsake her. She had a song of "Willow"
      An old thing 'twas, but it express'd her fortune,
      And she died singing it. That song to-night
      Will not go from my mind."

23) "Be thou ashamed that I have took upon me
      Such an immodest raiment, if shame live
      In a disguise of love.
      It is the lesser blot, modesty finds,
      Women to change their shapes than men their minds."

24) "You are attaint with faults and perjury:
      Therefore if you my favor mean to get,
      A twelvemonth shall you spend, and never rest,
      But seek the weary beds of people sick."

25) "A father cruel and a stepdame false,
      A foolish suitor to a wedded lady
      That hath her husband banished."

Quiz 25

What a Piece of Work Is a Man!: Identify the Male Character From a Quote

Here you will find quotes taken from some of the speeches of Shakespeare's memorable male characters. From the list provided, identify the speakers.

Benedick	Henry V	Macbeth	Petruchio	Richard III
Bertram	Horatio	Mark Antony	Prospero	Shylock
Coriolanus	Hotspur	Othello	Puck	Timon
Falstaff	Julius Caesar	Orlando	Romeo	Valentine
Hamlet	King Lear	Orsino	Richard II	Wolsey

1) "When thou canst get the ring upon my finger, which never shall come off, and show me a child begotten of thy body that I am father to, then call me husband."

2) "My father charg'd you in his will to give me good education. You have train'd me like a peasant, obscuring and hiding from me all gentlemen-like qualities."

3) "Despising
   For you, the city thus I turn my back.
   There is a world elsewhere."

4) "O God! O God!
   How weary, stale, flat, and unprofitable
   Seem to me all the uses of this world.
   Fie on't!"

5) "By heaven methinks it were an easy leap
   To pluck bright honor from the pale-faced moon,
   Or dive into the bottom of the deep,
   Where fathom-line could never touch the ground,
   And pluck up drowned honor by the locks."

6) "Had I but served my God with half the zeal
   I served my king, He would not in mine age
   Have left me to mine enemies."

7) "But I am constant as the northern star,
   Of whose true-fixed and resting quality
   There is no fellow in the firmament."

8) "I am a man
   More sinned against than sinning."

9) "I am that merry wanderer of the night."

10) "Is this a dagger which I see before me,
    The handle toward my hand? Come, let me clutch thee."

11) "If you prick us, do we not bleed? If you tickle us, do we not laugh? If you poison us,
    do we not die? And if you wrong us, shall we not revenge?"

12) "Shall quips and sentences and these paper bullets of the brain awe a man from the
    career of his humor? No, the world must be peopled. When I said I would die a
    bachelor, I did not think I should live till I were married."

13) "When you shall these unlucky deeds relate,
    Speak of me as I am; nothing extenuate,
    Nor set down aught in malice. Then must you speak
    Of one that lov'd not wisely but too well..."

14) "For God's sake, let us sit upon the ground
    And tell sad stories about the death of kings."

15) "O! I am Fortune's fool."

16) "...me (poor man) my library
    Was dukedom enough."

17) "I am Misanthropos, and hate mankind."

18) "That man that hath a tongue, I say is no man,
   If with his tongue he cannot win a woman."

19) "There is no woman's sides
   Can bide the beating of so strong a passion
   As love doth give my heart; no woman's heart
   So big, to hold so much; they lack retention."

20) "Now cracks a noble heart. Good-night, sweet prince,
   And flights of angels sing thee to thy rest!"

21) "I am not only witty in myself, but the cause that wit is in other men."

22) "We few, we happy few, we band of brothers.
   For he today who sheds his blood with me shall be my brother."

23) "Friends, Romans, countrymen, lend me your ears;
   I come to bury Caesar, not to praise him.
   The evil that men do lives after them;
   The good is oft interred with their bones."

24) "My conscience hath a thousand several tongues,
   And every tongue brings in a several tale,
   And every tale condemns me for a villain."

25) "This is a way to kill a wife with kindness,
   And thus I'll cure her mad and headstrong humor."

Quiz 26

A Long Farewell to All My Greatness:
Identify the Characters by Their Dying Words

The following are the last words uttered by characters, both male and female, before their imminent deaths. Identify the speakers and the play in which they appear.

Aaron	Cleopatra	Henry IV	Juliet	Richard, Duke of York
Antony	Coriolanus	Hotspur	Lear	Richard II
Brutus	Desdemona	Iago	Macbeth	Richard III
Buckingham	Gertrude	Jack Cade	Mercutio	Romeo
Claudius	Hamlet	King John	Othello	Titus Andronicus

1) "The rest is silence."

2) "O I could prophesy,
But that the earthly and cold hand of death
Lies on my tongue. No, Percy, thou art dust,
And food for—"

3) "I kissed thee ere I killed thee. No way but this—
Killing myself, to die upon a kiss."

4) "Yea, noise? then I'll be brief. O happy dagger!
This is thy sheath; there rust, and let me die."

5) "Mount, mount, my soul! Thy seat is up on high;
Whilst my gross flesh sinks downward, here to die."

6) "If one good deed in all my life I did,
I do repent it from my very soul."

7) "Farewell, good Strato—Caesar, now be still;
I killed not thee with half so good a will."

8) "Demand me nothing. What you know, you know.
From this time forth I never will speak word."

9) "The drink, the drink! I am poisoned."

10) "...a Roman, by a Roman
Valiantly vanquished. Now my spirit is going,
I can no more."

11) "Do you see this? Look on her! Look! her lips!
    Look there, look there!"

12) "My heart hath one poor string to stay it by,
    Which holds but till thy news be uttered;
    And then all this thou seest is but a clod
    And module of confounded royalty."

13) "A horse! A horse! my kingdom for a horse!"

14) "Here's to my love! O true apothecary!
    The drugs are quick. Thus with a kiss I die."

15) "O yet defend me, friends! I am but hurt."

16) "Nobody—I myself. Farewell.
    Commend me to my kind lord. O, farewell."

17) "But bear me to that chamber, there I'll lie,
    In that Jerusalem shall Harry die."

18) "What should I stay—"

19) "...A plague a' both your houses!
    They have made worms' meat of me. I have it,
    And soundly too. Your houses!"

20) "Come lead me, officers, to the block of shame.
    Wrong hath but wrong, and blame the due of blame."

21) "Open the gate of mercy, gracious God!
    My soul flies through these wounds to seek out thee."

22) "...Before my body
    I throw my warlike shield. Lay on, Macduff,
    And damned be him that first cries, 'Hold, enough!'"

23) "Why there they are, both baked in this pie,
    Whereof their mother hath daintily fed,
    Eating the flesh that she herself hath bred.
    'Tis true, 'tis true; witness my knife's sharp point."

24) "...O that I had him,
    With six Aufidiuses, or more, his tribe,
    To use my lawful sword!"

25) "Iden, farewell, and be proud of thy victory. Tell Kent from me, she hath lost her best man, and exhort all the world to be cowards; for I, that never fear'd any, am vanquished by famine, not by valor."

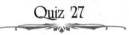

Quiz 27

Which Is the Villain?: Identify the Villain by the Quote

Everyone loves a good villain, and Shakespeare is well known for creating some wonderful ones. Although the characters listed may not be the epitome of villainy, the quote selected certainly reflects villainous thoughts or intents. From their own words, identify the villains.

Aaron	Claudius	Edmund	Macbeth
Angelo	Cloten	Iago	Richard III
Antiochus	Don John	Iachimo	Shylock
Antonio	Duke of Cornwall	Lady Macbeth	Tamora
Caliban	Duke Frederick	Leontes	Tybalt

1) "Come, you spirits
That tend on mortal thoughts, unsex me here,
And fill me from the crown to the toe, top-full
Of direst cruelty!"

2) "O! my offense is rank, it smells to heaven;
It hath the primal eldest curse upon't,
A brother's murder!"

3) "I have done a thousand dreadful things
As willingly as one would kill a fly,
And nothing grieves me heartily indeed,
But that I cannot do ten thousand more."

4) "I will lay you ten thousand ducats to your ring that, commend me to the court
   where your lady is, with no more advantage than the opportunity of a second
   conference, and I will bring from thence that honor of hers which you imagine so
   reserved."

5) "Find out thy brother, wheresoe'er he is;
   Seek him with the candle; bring him dead or living
   Within this twelvemonth, or turn thou no more
   To seek a living in our territory."

6) "Redeem thy brother
   By yielding up thy body to my will,
   Or else he must not only die the death,
   But thy unkindness shall his death draw out
   To ling'ring sufferance."

7) "Lest it see more, prevent it. Out, vile jelly! Where is thy lustre now?"

8) "...I cannot be said to be a flattering honest man, it must not be denied but I am a
   plain-dealing villain. I am trusted with a clog; therefore I have decreed not to sing in
   my cage. If I had my mouth, I would bite; if I had my liberty, I would do my liking."

9) "For when my outward action doth demonstrate
   The native act and figure of my heart
   In complement extern, 'tis not long after
   But I will wear my heart on my sleeve
   For daws to peck at: I am not what I am."

10) "And therefore since I cannot prove a lover
    To entertain these fair well-spoken days,
    I am determined to prove a villain
    And hate the idle pleasures of these days."

11) "He hath found the meaning,
    For which we mean to have his head.
    He must not live to trumpet forth my infamy
    Nor tell the world [I] doth sin
    In such a loathed manner;
    And therefore instantly this prince must die,
    For by his fall my honor must keep high."

12) "Patience perforce with willful choler meeting
    Makes my flesh tremble in their different greeting.
    I will withdraw, but this intrusion shall,
    Now seeming sweet, convert to bitt'rest gall."

13) "With that suit upon my back will I ravish her; first kill him, and in her eyes...He on the ground, my speech of insultment ended on his dead body, and when my lust hath dined...to the court I'll knock her back, foot her home again."

14) "You taught me language, and my profit on't
    Is, I know how to curse: the red plague rid you,
    For learning me your language."

15) "For mine own good
    All causes shall give way. I am in blood
    Stepp'd in so far that, should I wade no more,
    Returning were as tedious as go o'er.
    Strange things I have in head, that will to hand,
    Which must be acted ere they may be scann'd."

16) "I hate him for he is a Christian...
    If I can catch him once upon the hip,
    I will feed fat the ancient grudge I bear him.
    ...Cursed be my tribe
    If I forgive him."

17) "Ne'er let my heart know merry cheer indeed
    Till all the Andronici be made away.
    Now will I hence to seek my lovely Moor,
    And let my spleenful sons this trull deflow'r."

18) "...carry
    This female bastard hence, and that thou bear it
    To some remote and desert place quite out
    Of our dominions, and that there thou leave it
    Without more mercy to its own protection."

19) "Here lies your brother,
    No better than the earth he lies upon,
    If he were that which now he's like—that's dead,
    Whom I with this obedient steel, three inches of it,
    Can lay to bed forever."

20) "To both these sisters have I sworn my love;
    Each jealous of the other, as the stung
    Are of the adder. Which of them shall I take?
    Both? one? or neither? Neither can be enjoy'd
    If both remain alive."

Quiz 28

What Art Thou That Talk'st of Kings and Queens?: Identify the Kings and Queens in the Plays

Shakespeare's history plays provide memorable portrayals of some actual rulers of England. Granted, not all the portrayals are historically accurate, but they certainly are entertaining. Test your knowledge of Shakespeare's kings and queens.

1) Eleanor of Aquitaine was the mother of which of Shakespeare's title kings?

    A. Henry VIII   B. Henry V   C. John   D. Richard II

2) Which of Shakespeare's title kings was the son of the famous warrior Edward, the Black Prince?

    A. Richard II   B. John   C. Henry IV   D. Henry VI

3) Margaret of Anjou was the queen of which king?

    A. Richard II   B. Richard III   C. Henry IV   D. Henry VI

4) Jane Shore was the mistress of which king?

    A. Richard III   B. Edward IV   C. Henry IV   D. Henry VIII

5) From which king did Richard III usurp the crown?

    A. Henry IV   B. Henry VI   C. Edward IV   D. Edward V

6) Richard III married which of the following women?

    A. Lady Bona   B. Blanche of Spain
    C. Anne Neville   D. Katharine Swynford

7) He became king immediately after the death of Richard III.

    A. James I   B. Charles I   C. Henry VII   D. Henry VIII

8) She was the first wife and queen of Henry VIII.

    A. Anne Boleyn   B. Katherine Howard
    C. Katherine of Aragon   D. Anne of Cleves

9) Richard III was the brother of which other English king?

    A. Edward IV   B. Edward V   C. Henry VI   D. Henry VII

10) Which of the English queens portrayed by Shakespeare was the first commoner to become queen?

    A. Anne Boleyn   B. Elizabeth Woodville
    C. Margaret of Anjou   D. Anne Neville

11) Which king was the brother of King Richard I (the "Lionhearted")?

    A. Richard II   B. Henry IV   C. Henry VI   D. John

12) Which king was killed at the Battle of Bosworth Field?

    A. Richard II   B. Richard III   C. Edward V   D. Henry VI

13) Which of the kings named Henry was Henry Bolingbroke?

    A. Henry IV   B. Henry V   C. Henry VI   D. Henry VIII

14) Which English king's portrait is believed to be the first to reflect a true likeness of him and show us what he may actually have looked like in real life?

    A. Henry IV   B. Henry V   C. Richard II   D. Richard III

15) Which of Shakespeare's kings said, "Uneasy lies the head that wears a crown"?

    A. Henry IV   B. Richard III   C. King John   D. Henry VI

16) Which of the queens was described in one of the histories as a "She wolf of France"?

    A. Eleanor of Aquitaine   B. Catherine of Valois
    C. Margaret of Anjou   D. Anne of Cleves

17) Who was the mother of Richard III?

    A. Elizabeth Woodville   B. Margaret of Anjou
    C. Duchess of York   D. Bona of Savoy

18) According to Shakespeare, Philip Faulconbridge in *King John* was the bastard son of which king?

    A. John   B. Richard I   C. Philip II of France   D. Henry III

19) Which of the following kings died at the youngest age?

    A. Henry V   B. Richard III   C. King John   D. Edward IV

20) Of the following, who was NOT the son of a king of England?

    A. Henry V   B. Richard III   C. Henry VI   D. King John

Quiz 29

We Shall Speak of You: Identify the Character Mentioned or Addressed

Listed here you will find speeches from characters who are either directly addressing another character or speaking about another character. From the list provided, can you identify the character who is being addressed or spoken about? Good luck!

Anne Neville	Coriolanus	Hamlet	King Lear	Polonius
Beatrice	Desdemona	Hermia	Macbeth	Proteus
Brutus	Falstaff	Juliet	Ophelia	Richard III
Cleopatra	Prince Hal	Katherina	Pinch	Earl of Warwick

1) "His life was gentle, and the elements
   So mixed in him that Nature might stand up
   And say to all the world, 'This was a man!'"

2) "I know thee not, old man. Fall to thy prayers.
   How ill white hairs becomes a fool and jester!"

3) "Thou wretched, rash, intruding fool, farewell!
   I took thee for thy better."

4) "Thou setter up and plucker down of kings."

5) "Age cannot wither her, nor custom stale
   Her infinite variety; other women cloy
   The appetites they feed, but she makes hungry
   Where she most satisfies..."

6) "Yet I do fear thy nature;
   It is too full o' the milk of human kindness
   To catch the nearest way; thou wouldst be great,
   Art not without ambition; but without
   The illness should attend it."

7) "O, when she is angry, she is keen and shrewd!
   She was a vixen when she went to school;
   And though she be but little, she is fierce."

8) "He was a thing of blood, whose every motion
   Was timed with dying cries."

9) "She speaks poniards, and every word stabs: if her breath were as terrible as her terminations, there were no living near her; she would infect to the north star."

10) "It seems she hangs upon the cheek of night
    Like a rich jewel in an Ethiop's ear;
    Beauty too rich for use, for earth too dear!"

11) "My nearest and dearest enemy."

12) "Take heed of yonder dog!
    Look when he fawns he bites; and when he bites,
    His venom tooth will rankle to the death.
    Have not to do with him, beware of him.
    Sin death, and hell have set their marks on him."

13) "...a hungry, lean-faced villain,
    A mere anatomy, a mountebank,
    A threadbare juggler, and a fortune-teller,
    A needy, hollow-eyed, sharp-looking wretch,
    A living-dead man."

14) "I rather would entreat thy company
    To see the wonders of the world abroad
    Than, living dully sluggardized at home,
    Wear out thy youth with shapeless idleness."

15) "We are not the first
    Who with the best meaning have incurred the worst.
    For thee oppressed king, I am cast down,
    Myself else could out from false Fortune's frown.
    Shall we not see these daughters and these sisters?"

16) "She loved me for the dangers I had passed,
    And I loved her that she did pity them.
    This only is the witchcraft I have used."

17) "Do not for ever with thy vailed lids
    Seek for thy noble father in the dust.
    Thou know'st 'tis common, all that lives must die,
    Passing through nature to eternity."

18) "Get thee to a nunn'ry, why would'st thou be a breeder of sinners?"

19) "Mates, maid, how you mean that? No mates for you
    Unless you were of gentler, milder mould."

20) "Was ever woman in this humor wooed?
    Was ever woman in this humor won?
    I'll have her, but I will not keep her long."

Section III

Shakespeare's
Infinite Variety

Quiz 30

To Peruse Him by Items: Identify the Play by the Item in It

Each of the items listed figure prominently in the events of one of Shakespeare's plays. Can you identify the play where you will find the item? Choose your answer from the list of plays provided. Each play can be used only once.

Ant & Cleo	*Henry V*	*MN Dream*	*Titus*
As You	*3 Henry VI*	*Othello*	*Tr & Cr*
Com Err	*Macbeth*	*Pericles*	*Twelfth N*
Cymbeline	*Merchant*	*Tam Shrew*	*Two Gents*
Hamlet	*Merry Wives*	*Tempest*	*Two Noble*

1) A love potion called Love-in-Idleness

2) A laundry basket

3) A floating dagger

4) A jester's skull

5) A handkerchief embroidered with strawberries

6) Yellow stockings

7) A paper crown

8) A banquet that magically appears and disappears

9) Gold, silver, and lead caskets

10) Tennis balls

11) Love notes nailed to trees

12) An asp in a basket of figs

13) A ladder made of rope to be used for an elopement

14) A copy of Ovid's *Metamorphoses*

15) A gold necklace that is misdelivered

16) A mole on a woman's left breast

17) A chest containing a woman washed ashore after a storm

18) A sleeve and a glove exchanged as love tokens

19) Food and a file

20) A lute broken over a suitor's head

Quiz 31

Particular Additions: Identify the Play by a Description

Shakespeare's plays are filled with a variety of interesting characters, allusions, and details. From the answer bank, can you identify the play where you can find the following? Each answer can be used only once.

All's Well	Henry V	Merchant	Rom & Jul
Ant & Cleo	1 Henry VI	Merry Wives	Tam Shrew
As You	John	Othello	Tempest
Com Err	Love's LL	Pericles	Two Gents
Cymbeline	Measure	Richard III	Win Tale

1) The only mention of America

2) Three female characters disguised as males

3) Two husbands who kill their wives on stage

4) A heroine who is the only human female character in the play

5) The only stepmother to appear in Shakespeare's plays

6) The only character who is a native Russian

7) England ruled by four kings

8) The Garter Inn

9) A chorus that introduces each of the five acts in the play

10) The daughter of a recently deceased physician named Gerard de Narbonne

11) A nun named Francesca

12) A woman who tears up her sweetheart's letter to her and then kisses the pieces

13) A character who wishes that he was a glove

14) A group of men who disguise themselves as Russians in order to play a prank

15) A character who knocks down the priest with a punch during his own wedding ceremony

16) A duke who leads a group of men who live "like the old Robin Hood of England."

17) An English king who sings on his deathbed

18) The Battle of Actium

19) Scenes set in a brothel in Mytilene

20) Stage directions that say "Enter fiends...they walk and speak not...they bang their heads...they depart."

Quiz 32

The Game's Afoot: Identify the Play by the Opening Situation

Each of the following situations describes the action developing at the beginning of one of Shakespeare's plays. Identify the play from the answer bank provided. Each answer will be used only once.

All's Well	Hamlet	Lear	MN Dream	Tam Shrew
Ant & Cleo	1 Henry IV	Love's LL	Much Ado	Tempest
As You	Henry V	Macbeth	Othello	Titus
Com Err	1 Henry VI	Measure	Richard II	Twelfth N
Coriolanus	J. Caesar	Merchant	Richard III	Two Gents

1) A king and his three companions have decided to retire for three years to study philosophy.

2) A man is told that, unless he can pay a large ransom by the end of the day, he will be executed.

3) Sentinels are discussing the recent sighting of a ghost.

4) One character is accusing another of double-crossing him.

5) A young man ready to embark on a voyage playfully teases his lovesick friend who is refusing to leave his love.

6) Romans are in the process of selecting a new emperor.

7) Two arguing noblemen appear before their king and demand a trial by combat to settle their disagreement.

8) A duke decides to abdicate his position to his deputy and observe the morality of his city disguised as a monk.

9) A man is unsuccessfully attempting to explain why he is depressed.

10) A group of people are on a ship in a raging storm.

11) Two men attempt to stop a celebration taking place in the streets in honor of a conquering hero.

12) Two churchmen are worried about internal politics and desire the king to go to war with France.

13) A couple is discussing their impending nuptial when they are interrupted by a father who is angry at his daughter.

14) A practical joke is being played on a drunken tinker.

15) A mother bids farewell to her son, who is traveling to the court of a king in poor health.

16) Witches are planning to meet with a character.

17) A young woman is washed ashore after a shipwreck.

18) Soldiers are expressing concern that their leader is neglecting his duties.

19) A character is ruminating over his physical deformity.

20) A king is concerned about internal problems and desires to go to the Holy Land to do penance.

21) A messenger arrives with news that a group of friendly soldiers are arriving for a visit after a victory in battle.

22) The funeral of a king is taking place and astrological omens of disaster are present.

23) Citizens are upset because of a shortage of grain, and they feel the city's nobles are hoarding it.

24) A young man is expressing frustration over the way his older brother is treating him.

25) A king is dividing his kingdom among his daughters.

Quiz 33

A Pretty Plot, Well Chosen To Build Upon:
Identify the Play by Plot Development

Shakespeare's plays consist of many interesting plot wrinkles. Can you identify the play where you can find each of the following plot developments? Each answer is used only once.

Ant & Cleo	J. Caesar	MN Dream	Rom & Jul
Hamlet	Lear	Much Ado	Timon
Henry V	Macbeth	Othello	Twelfth N
1 Henry IV	Merchant	Pericles	Two Noble
1 Henry VI	Merry Wives	Richard III	Win Tale

1) A character is stabbed while spying from behind an arras.

2) An Indian boy is the cause of a marital dispute.

3) A misanthrope goes off to live in isolation.

4) A character dies when he is thrown from his horse.

5) A battle is fought on St. Crispin's Day.

6) A group of robbers is robbed of their ill-gotten gains.

7) A "statue" of a woman "comes to life."

8) A quarantined monk is unable to deliver a letter, leading to tragic consequences.

9) A drunken brawl angers a general.

10) A king rages in a storm with his fool.

11) A prince woos a young lady for his comrade.

12) Two married women play practical jokes on a lecherous man who attempts to woo them simultaneously.

13) Opposing factions pluck red and white roses from a garden.

14) A woman impersonates a lawyer to save a man's life.

15) A man is led to believe that he cannot be harmed by any man born of woman.

16) A poet is mistaken for an assassin and killed by an angry mob.

17) A man woos a woman over the coffin of her husband, who he killed.

18) A young woman is separated from her twin brother in a storm at sea.

19) A king has an incestuous relationship with his daughter.

20) A group of military leaders have a drunken party aboard a ship.

Quiz 34

It Is a Sweet Comedy: Questions on the Comedies

Shakespeare's comedies are filled with insults, slapstick, delightful puns, bawdy jokes, cross-dressing, stock comic characters, and hilarious comic situations. In other words, they are just like many of our sitcoms of today. See how much you know about the comedies of Shakespeare by answering these questions.

1) Which is the only comedy that is set entirely in England?

    A. *The Comedy of Errors*   B. *The Taming of the Shrew*
    C. *Love's Labor's Lost*   D. *The Merry Wives of Windsor*

2) In which comedy does a man's beloved tell him that he must work in a hospital for a year before she will consider marrying him?

    A. *The Two Gentlemen of Verona*   B. *Love's Labor's Lost*
    C. *The Merchant of Venice*   D. *All's Well That Ends Well*

3) In which play does a servant disguise himself as his master's father?

    A. *All's Well That Ends Well*   B. *As You Like It*
    C. *The Taming of the Shrew*   D. *Twelfth Night*

4) Which comedy features two sets of identical twins who are separated in a shipwreck?

    A. *The Two Gentlemen of Verona*   B. *The Comedy of Errors*
    C. *The Merry Wives of Windsor*   D. *Much Ado About Nothing*

5) Which two comedies feature a convention known as "the bed trick," in which two women conspire to get a man to sleep with one of them thinking that it is another?

    A. *Measure for Measure* and *All's Well That Ends Well*
    B. *The Two Gentlemen of Verona* and *Twelfth Night*
    C. *The Merchant of Venice* and *Love's Labor's Lost*
    D. *The Taming of the Shrew* and *The Merry Wives of Windsor*

6) What are the names of the title characters from *The Two Gentlemen of Verona*?

    A. Proteus and Thurio   B. Thurio and Eglamour
    C. Proteus and Valentine   D. Eglamour and Valentine

7) Which comedy has a lead character who also appears in two of Shakespeare's history plays?

    A. *Much Ado About Nothing*   B. *The Merry Wives of Windsor*
    C. *Troilus and Cressida*   D. *Measure for Measure*

8) Who is NOT a suitor of Bianca in *The Taming of the Shrew*?

    A. Lucentio   B. Hortensio   C. Gremio   D. Vincentio

9) In which play is a love potion placed in the eyes of young lovers with comic results?

    A. *A Midsummer Night's Dream*   B. *As You Like It*
    C. *Measure for Measure*   D. *All's Well That Ends Well*

10) In which play is a man ordered to marry a woman named Kate Keepdown?

    A. *Measure for Measure*   B. *As You Like It*
    C. *All's Well That Ends Well*   D. *The Two Gentlemen of Verona*

11) Which play has the alternate title of *What You Will*?

    A. *As You Like It*   B. *Love's Labor's Lost*
    C. *Twelfth Night*   D. *Much Ado About Nothing*

12) In which play do comical characters perform a play in which they take the roles of traditional medieval heroes known as the Nine Worthies?

    A. *A Midsummer Night's Dream*   B. *Love's Labor's Lost*
    C. *Troilus and Cressida*   D. *The Comedy of Errors*

13) In which comedy will you find the Ford family?

    A. *Measure for Measure*   B. *Twelfth Night*
    C. *The Merry Wives of Windsor*   D. *The Comedy of Errors*

14) Which of the comedies has the most songs?

    A. *Love's Labor's Lost*   B. *As You Like It*

    C. *Much Ado About Nothing*   D. *Twelfth Night*

15) Which is the only comedy that contains no songs?

    A. *The Comedy of Errors*   B. *Troilus and Cressida*

    C. *Measure for Measure*   D. *The Merchant of Venice*

16) Who is NOT a suitor of Mistress Anne Page in *The Merry Wives of Windsor?*

    A. Fenton   B. Dr. Caius   C. Hugh Evans   D. Abraham Slender

17) Although she does not actually appear in the play in which she is mentioned, Leah is the wife of which character?

    A. Leonato in *Much Ado About Nothing*

    B. Shylock in *The Merchant of Venice*

    C. Baptista Minola in *The Taming of the Shrew*

    D. Duke Senior in *As You Like It*

18) In most portraits, Shakespeare is depicted in various stages of hair loss. In which comedy will you find the following humorous statement regarding baldness: "What he hath scanted men in hair he hath given them in wit"?

    A. *Love's Labor's Lost*   B. *The Comedy of Errors*

    C. *Twelfth Night*   D. *Troilus and Cressida*

19) What is the name of the Merchant of Venice?

    A. Shylock   B. Gratiano   C. Salerio   D. Antonio

20) Which play uses the small village with the quaint name of Frogmore as the setting in a scene?

    A. *The Merry Wives of Windsor*   B. *The Comedy of Errors*

    C. *All's Well That Ends Well*   D. *A Midsummer Night's Dream*

21) Which comedy contains the longest Latin word in existence, *honorificabilitudinitatibus*, meaning something like "the state of being loaded with honors or worthiness"?

    A. *The Taming of the Shrew*   B. *All's Well That Ends Well*

    C. *Love's Labor's Lost*   D. *Twelfth Night*

22) Which play's title is a reference to Christ's Sermon on the Mount?

    A. *Measure for Measure*   B. *All's Well That Ends Well*

    C. *The Winter's Tale*   D. *Love's Labor's Lost*

23) The famous line "Who ever lov'd that lov'd not at first sight?" was originally penned by Christopher Marlowe, a contemporary of Shakespeare. In which play does Shakespeare "borrow" this line?

A. *The Merchant of Venice*   B. *The Taming of the Shrew*
C. *As You Like It*   D. *Troilus and Cressida*

24) Which play mentions Nell, a fat cook who never actually appears in the play, but whose body parts are humorously described in detail as parts of the globe?

A. *Much Ado About Nothing*   B. *The Comedy of Errors*
C. *Measure for Measure*   D. *As You Like It*

25) In which play will you find a character who takes the disguise of a mythological creature, Herne, the hunter?

A. *A Midsummer Night's Dream*   B. *As You Like It*
C. *Troilus and Cressida*   D. *The Merry Wives of Windsor*

Quiz 35

The Complot of This Timeless Tragedy: Questions on the Tragedies

Shakespeare's experimental style results in tragedies that are a diverse group of plays. On the one hand is the horribly brutal *Titus Andronicus*, and on the other hand there is the deeply moving *Hamlet*. Somewhere in between fall the others. The tragedies are the ones that are most often covered in high school classes, so many people should do well with this quiz!

1) Which character in the tragedies was born on Lammas Day, August 1?

A. Juliet   B. Brutus   C. Hamlet   D. Cordelia

2) Who of the following does NOT die as a result of being poisoned?

A. Regan in *King Lear*   B. Juliet in *Romeo and Juliet*
C. Gertrude in *Hamlet*   D. Romeo in *Romeo and Juliet*

3) Tullus Aufidius is the name of the archrival of which Shakespearean tragic hero?

A. Mark Antony   B. Cymbeline   C. Timon   D. Coriolanus

4) Which of the following title characters commits suicide?

A. Othello   B. Hamlet   C. Macbeth   D. Lear

5) At the very beginning of *Antony and Cleopatra*, to which woman is Mark Antony married?

A. Cleopatra   B. Lavinia   C. Fulvia   D. Octavia

6) Which of the following female characters commits suicide in one of the tragedies?

A. Lavinia in *Titus Andronicus*   B. Portia in *Julius Caesar*
C. Virgilia in *Coriolanus*   D. Cordelia in *King Lear*

7) Which of the following male characters does NOT commit suicide in one of the tragedies?

A. Cassius   B. Mark Antony   C. Romeo   D. Iago

8) In *Titus Andronicus*, which book does Lavinia use to help identify her attackers?

A. Ovid's *Metamorphoses*   B. The *King James Bible*
C. Homer's *Iliad*   D. Virgil's *Aeneid*

9) In which play will you find references to devils named Flibbertigibber, Frateretto, Modo, Mahu, and Smulkin?

A. *King Lear*   B. *Hamlet*   C. *Romeo and Juliet*   D. *Timon of Athens*

10) The English literary critic, poet, and playwright John Dryden wrote a play titled *All for Love*, which is a very loose adaptation of which Shakespearean tragedy?

A. *Othello*   B. *Macbeth*   C. *King Lear*   D. *Antony and Cleopatra*

11) Which character kills his own son for disobeying him?

A. Duke of Gloucester in *King Lear*   B. Coriolanus in *Coriolanus*
C. Titus in *Titus Andronicus*   D. Enobarbus in *Antony and Cleopatra*

12) Which tragedy uses a chorus to introduce the play?

A. *Coriolanus*   B. *Antony and Cleopatra*
C. *Romeo and Juliet*   D. *Timon of Athens*

13) In which of the following tragedies will you NOT find a ghost?

A. *Macbeth*   B. *King Lear*   C. *Hamlet*   D. *Julius Caesar*

14) In which tragedy will you find a drunken porter who supplies comic relief?

A. *Coriolanus*   B. *Antony and Cleopatra*
C. *Timon of Athens*   D. *Macbeth*

15) The last written words of Charles Dickens are a quotation from Shakespeare: "These violent delights have violent ends." In which tragedy will you find this quote?

A. *Romeo and Juliet*   B. *Titus Andronicus*   C. *King Lear*   D. *Othello*

16) Which character is duped into cutting off his hand to send in a vain attempt to ransom his sons?

A. Titus in *Titus Andronicus*   B. Earl of Gloucester in *King Lear*
C. Coriolanus in *Coriolanus*   D. Pompey in *Antony and Cleopatra*

17) Which tragic character finds himself in conflict with a race named the Volscians?

A. Macbeth   B. Titus Andronicus   C. Coriolanus   D. Mark Antony

18) Which character in the tragedies refers to himself as "Misanthrope"?

A. King Lear   B. Timon   C. Iago   D. Macbeth

19) Which title character only speaks approximately 150 lines in the play in which he appears?

A. Titus Andronicus   B. Romeo   C. Coriolanus   D. Julius Caesar

20) The only known illustration of one of Shakespeare's plays, created in his own time, depicts which play?

A. *Romeo and Juliet*   B. *King Lear*
C. *Titus Andronicus*   D. *Antony and Cleopatra*

21) Some scholars believe that which of the following was written to flatter James I?

A. *Macbeth*   B. *Hamlet*   C. *Julius Caesar*   D. *King Lear*

22) Of the ten tragedies, how many are at least partially set in what is today Italy?

A. 5   B. 6   C. 7   D. 8

23) In which tragedy do we find a title character giving instructions much like a director to a group of actors?

A. *Julius Caesar*   B. *King Lear*   C. *Othello*   D. *Hamlet*

24) In the plays that are considered to be Shakespeare's four great tragedies, in which will you find the least number of deaths of named or speaking characters?

A. *Hamlet*   B. *Macbeth*   C. *Othello*   D. *King Lear*

25) Which character's dead body is ordered left to wild beasts because her life was "devoid of pity"?

A. Goneril in *King Lear*   B. Lady Macbeth in *Macbeth*
C. Tamora in *Titus Andronicus*   D. Cleopatra in *Antony and Cleopatra*

Quiz 36

Is Not This Something More Than Fantasy?: Questions on the Romances

A *romance* is a tale that contains elements of comedy and tragedy, and they are believed to be the works of Shakespeare's final period. His romances share common themes, complex staging, and *symbolic* rather than *realistic* characterization. Unfortunately, other than *The Tempest*, the romances are largely avoided by many readers. However, they do make interesting reading for those who are inclined to take them with a grain of salt. If you haven't read all of them, maybe some of these questions will stimulate a desire to do so.

1) The title character Cymbeline is king of which land?

    A. Britain   B. Rome   C. Mesopotamia   D. Gaul

2) In which play does the medieval poet John Gower appear as the Chorus?

    A. *Pericles*   B. *The Two Noble Kinsmen*
    C. *Cymbeline*   D. *The Winter's Tale*

3) Which play is the basis for W.H. Auden's poem sequence *The Sea and the Mirror*?

    A. *Pericles*   B. *Cymbeline*   C. *The Tempest*   D. *The Winter's Tale*

4) In which play will you find that NO characters die?

    A. *Cymbeline*   B. *The Tempest*
    C. *The Winter's Tale*   D. *The Two Noble Kinsmen*

5) For which of the following did Shakespeare use Chaucer's *Canterbury Tales* as a source?

    A. *Pericles*   B. *The Winter's Tale*
    C. *Cymbeline*   D. *The Two Noble Kinsmen*

6) In which play will you find a doctor named Cornelius, who supplies a potion that produces a death-like slumber to a character who thinks it is poison?

    A. *Cymbeline*   B. *The Winter's Tale*
    C. *The Tempest*   D. *The Two Noble Kinsmen*

7) The plot of which play encompasses 16 years—the longest time span in any of Shakespeare's plays?

    A. *The Tempest*   B. *Cymbeline*   C. *The Winter's Tale*   D. *Pericles*

8) Although it is commonly categorized as a romance by modern editors, which of the following was listed by the editors of The First Folio, the first publication of the complete works of Shakespeare, as a tragedy?

    A. *The Winter's Tale*   B. *The Two Noble Kinsmen*
    C. *Pericles*   D. *Cymbeline*

9) One of the names of the title characters in *The Two Noble Kinsmen* is Arcite. What is the name of the other noble kinsman?

    A. Valerius   B. Gerrold   C. Artesius   D. Palamon

10) Which one of the following characters was NOT thought to be dead by other characters in the play at one time or another?

    A. Imogen in *Cymbeline*   B. Hermione in *The Winter's Tale*
    C. Thaisa in *Pericles*   D. Emilia in *The Two Noble Kinsmen*

11) In which play will you find fishermen named Pilch and Patch-breech?

    A. *The Tempest*   B. *Pericles*   C. *Cymbeline*   D. *The Winter's Tale*

12) In which romance will you find two different men, each of whom is conspiring to kill his own brother?

    A. *The Two Noble Kinsmen*   B. *Cymbeline*
    C. *The Tempest*   D. *Pericles*

13) Giulio Romano (Gilulio Pippi), an Italian painter and architect, is the only Renaissance artist mentioned in Shakespeare's works. In which play is Giulio mentioned?

    A. *The Winter's Tale*   B. *Pericles*
    C. *The Tempest*   D. *Cymbeline*

14) Which romance includes characters which can also be found in one of Shakespeare's comedies?

    A. *The Winter's Tale*   B. *Pericles*
    C. *The Two Noble Kinsmen*   D. *Cymbeline*

15) Which is the only play in which Britain is at war with Rome?

    A. *The Two Noble Kinsmen*   B. *Cymbeline*
    C. *The Winter's Tale*   D. *Pericles*

16) The allegorical figure Time appears in which play to inform the audience of the passing of years?

    A. *Cymbeline*   B. *The Winter's Tale*
    C. *The Tempest*   D. *The Two Noble Kinsmen*

17) Which play ends with an epilogue delivered by an anonymous actor who is anxious about the audience's reaction to the play they have just watched?

    A. *The Two Noble Kinsmen*   B. *The Winter's Tale*
    C. *The Tempest*   D. *Cymbeline*

18) In which play is a young woman kidnapped by pirates and then sold to a brothel?

    A. *The Two Noble Kinsmen*   B. *Cymbeline*
    C. *The Winter's Tale*   D. *Pericles*

19) In which play will you find a villain named Cloten?

A. *Pericles*
C. *Cymbeline*
B. *The Two Noble Kinsmen*
D. *The Tempest*

20) In which play will you find the vagabond petty thief Autolycus?

A. *Cymbeline*
C. *The Tempest*
B. *The Winter's Tale*
D. *The Two Noble Kinsmen*

Quiz 37

It Is a Kind of History: Questions on the Histories

Unfortunately, many readers are scared away by Shakespeare's history plays, and that is a shame. The plays are filled with action and well-developed characters such as Prince Hal, Falstaff, and Richard III. Although his histories don't necessarily stick close to the truth in every case, they do make for interesting reading. If you are not familiar with many of the history plays, hopefully these questions will whet your appetite for more!

1) Joan of Arc appears as a character in which play?

A. *Henry V*
C. *Henry VI, Part Two*
B. *Henry VI, Part One*
D. *Henry VI, Part Three*

2) In which play is the famous battle of Agincourt depicted?

A. *Henry V*   B. *Richard II*   C. *Richard III*   D. *Henry IV, Part One*

3) The historical figure John of Gaunt appears as a character in which play?

A. *Henry V*
C. *Henry VI, Part Two*
B. *Henry IV, Part One*
D. *Richard II*

4) Which play portrays events that took place during the Hundred Years' War?

A. *King John*   B. *Henry V*   C. *Richard III*   D. *Henry VIII*

5) Which play portrays events that took place during the Wars of the Roses?

A. *Henry VIII*
C. *Henry IV, Part Two*
B. *Henry VI, Part Three*
D. *Richard II*

6) Sir John Talbot was the doomed hero of which play?

A. *Richard III*
C. *Henry VIII*
B. *King John*
D. *Henry VI, Part One*

7) Which king was of the House of York?

A. *Richard III*   B. *Richard II*   C. *Henry V*   D. *Henry IV*

8) In which play does the infamous Richard, Duke of Gloucester (the future Richard III) first appear?

A. *Henry VI, Part One*   B. *Henry VI, Part Two*
C. *Henry VI, Part Three*   D. *Richard III*

9) The Jerusalem Chamber is a room in Westminster Palace. In which play does an important event take place in this room?

A. *Henry VIII*   B. *Richard II*
C. *Henry VI, Part Three*   D. *Henry IV, Part Two*

10) Which play contains the famous deposition scene that shows a monarch forced to abdicate his crown?

A. *King John*   B. *Henry VIII*   C. *Richard II*   D. *Henry VI, Part Three*

11) Which old friend of Henry V is later executed, by order of Henry, for stealing when serving in the army in France?

A. Pistol   B. Nym   C. Bardolph   D. Peto

12) According to Shakespeare, who was the murderer of King Henry VI?

A. George, Duke of Clarence   B. Richard, Duke of Gloucester
C. Edward IV   D. John of Lancaster

13) What was the name of the son of King Henry VI?

A. Edward   B. Richard   C. William   D. Arthur

14) In which play will you find a prophet by the name of Peter of Pomfret?

A. *King John*   B. *Richard II*   C. *Richard III*   D. *Henry VIII*

15) In which history play do we learn of the death of Falstaff—quite possibly Shakespeare's greatest comic creation?

A. *Henry IV, Part Two*   B. *Henry V*
C. *Henry VI, Part One*   D. *Henry VI, Part Two*

16) Which was the rival house to the House of York in the Wars of the Roses?

A. Stuart   B. Hanover   C. Tudor   D. Lancaster

17) Which English monarch is portrayed on stage as an infant at the end of *Henry VIII?*

A. Elizabeth   B. James I   C. Mary   D. Edward VI

18) Which play contains a famous scene where the king looks into a mirror to contemplate the loss of his crown?

A. *Henry IV, Part Two*   B. *Richard II*
C. *Henry VI, Part Three*   D. *King John*

19) Which of the history plays makes use of the classical convention of a chorus?

A. *King John*   B. *Henry IV, Part One*
C. *Henry V*   D. *Henry VI, Part One*

20) In which play do we witness the banishment of Henry Bolingbroke?

A. *Richard II*   B. *Henry IV, Part One*
C. *Henry IV, Part Two*   D. *Henry VI, Part One*

21) Which play depicts events in the Battle of Shrewsbury?

A. *Henry IV, Part One*   B. *Henry IV, Part Two*
C. *Richard II*   D. *Henry VI, Part Three*

22) The rebellion led by Jack Cade is depicted in which play?

A. *Richard II*   B. *Henry VI, Part One*
C. *Henry VI, Part Two*   D. *Henry VI, Part Three*

23) Which king meets his death when he is poisoned by a monk?

A. Richard II   B. Henry IV   C. Henry VI   D. John

24) *All Is True* is an alternate title for which history play?

A. *Richard III*   B. *King John*   C. *Henry V*   D. *Henry VIII*

25) Which character in the history plays had the nickname "kingmaker" because of his influence in setting up and bringing down kings?

A. Henry Stafford, Duke of Buckingham   B. Richard Neville, Earl of Warwick
C. Richard Plantagenet, Duke of York   D. Edmund Beaufort, Duke of Somerset

Quiz 38

At First and Last the Hearty Welcome:
Firsts and Lasts Associated With Shakespeare

There are many illustrious firsts and lasts associated with William Shakespeare and his works. How many of them can you identify?

1) Which was the first of William Shakespeare's works to appear in print?
   A. *Venus and Adonis*   B. *The Rape of Lucrece*
   C. The sonnets   D. *The Passionate Pilgrim*

2) Which was the first of Shakespeare's plays to appear in print?
   A. *Henry VI, Part One*   B. The *Comedy of Errors*
   C. *Titus Andronicus*   D. *As You Like It*

3) *Quartos* were usually either unauthorized versions that often mangled the author's work, or they were published by the acting companies themselves to supercede the unauthorized versions. Which of Shakespeare's plays, published in quarto, was the first to bear his name on the title page as the author?
   A. *Love's Labor's Lost*   B. *The Two Gentlemen of Verona*
   C. *Much Ado About Nothing*   D. *The Merry Wives of Windsor*

4) Which is generally believed to be the first tragedy that Shakespeare wrote?
   A. *Julius Caesar*   B. *Macbeth*   C. *Hamlet*   D. *Titus Andronicus*

5) The first reference, in print, to William Shakespeare as a writer was a scathing criticism written by who?
   A. Ben Jonson   B. Robert Greene   C. Thomas Dekker   D. John Webster

6) Which play was placed first in The First Folio of 1623?
   A. *The Comedy of Errors*   B. *The Taming of the Shrew*
   C. *The Tempest*   D. *The Two Gentlemen of Verona*

7) Sir Laurence Olivier made his Shakespearean film debut in an adaptation of which of the following?
   A. *As You Like It*   B. *Romeo and Juliet*   C. *Julius Caesar*   D. *Love's Labor's Lost*

8) Who was the first to appear in film as Hamlet?
   A. Ellen Terry   B. Sarah Bernhardt   C. Laurence Olivier   D. John Barrymore

9) The first "talkie" film adaptation of one of Shakespeare's works was made of which play?

A. *Macbeth*   B. *As You Like It*
C. *A Midsummer Night's Dream*   D. *The Taming of the Shrew*

10) The earliest surviving full-length motion picture—long lost but eventually rediscovered—was a 55-minute, five-reel version of which of Shakespeare's plays?

A. *The Tempest*   B. *Hamlet*   C. *King Lear*   D. *Richard III*

11) Which of the plays was the first to be partially recorded on film?

A. *King Lear*   B. *Henry VIII*   C. *King John*   D. *Richard II*

12) Famed Japanese film director Akira Kurosawa's first and least known adaptation of a Shakespearean play was titled *The Bad Sleep Well*. On which play is this film based?

A. *Hamlet*   B. *Othello*   C. *Coriolanus*   D. *Titus Andronicus*

13) The first recorded performance of an actress on the English stage was that of Margaret Hughes on December 8, 1660. Coincidentally, she performed in one of Shakespeare's plays on that date. What role did she play?

A. Juliet   B. Desdemona   C. Ophelia   D. Rosalind

14) What was the last Shakespearean film role of Sir Laurence Olivier?

A. Shylock   B. Prospero   C. King Lear   D. Leontes

15) Which play is generally believed to be the last that Shakespeare wrote without a collaborator?

A. *Henry VIII*   B. *The Tempest*   C. *The Two Noble Kinsmen*   D. *Pericles*

16) Which comedy is generally believed to be the last that Shakespeare wrote?

A. *All's Well That Ends Well*   B. *Troilus and Cressida*
C. *The Merchant of Venice*   D. *Measure for Measure*

17) Which writer was the first to initiate the authorship controversy and suggest that it was someone other than William Shakespeare who wrote the plays most credit him with today?

A. Nicholas Rowe   B. Northrup Frye   C. Delia Bacon   D. Thomas Osgood

18) Which of the history plays is the last one that Shakespeare wrote?

A. *King John*   B. *Richard III*   C. *Henry VIII*   D. *Henry V*

19) Of the plays commonly considered to be Shakespeare's four greatest tragedies, which was the first to be written?

A. *Hamlet*   B. *King Lear*   C. *Othello*   D. *Macbeth*

20) The Shakespeare Jubilee in Stratford, organized by David Garrick, was a celebration of William Shakespeare and his work, and as such, it is considered to be the first Shakespeare Festival ever held. In which year did the Shakespeare Jubilee take place?

    A. 1754   B. 1769   C. 1798   D. 1816

21) Which was the last play to be performed in the original Globe Theatre?

    A. *Hamlet*   B. *The Winter's Tale*   C. *Twelfth Night*   D. *Henry VIII*

22) Which was the first play to be performed for the official opening of the reconstructed Globe Theatre in 1997?

    A. *Romeo and Juliet*   B. *The Merchant of Venice*
    C. *Henry V*   D. *The Tempest*

23) Who of the following is considered to be the first editor of Shakespeare's works?

    A. Nicholas Rowe   B. Alfred Harbage   C. Samuel Johnson   D. A.L. Rowse

24) Which of Shakespeare's fellow actors was the first to play the major roles such as *Othello, Macbeth,* and *Hamlet?*

    A. Will Kempe   B. Richard Burbage   C. Robert Armin   D. Edward Alleyn

25) In 1938 the BBC broadcast the first full-length Shakespearean production on television. It was a production of which play?

    A. *Hamlet*   B. *As You Like It*   C. *Julius Caesar*   D. *Richard III*

Quiz 39

O, Horrible, O, Horrible, Most Horrible!: Identify the Play Where the Horrible Event Can Be Found

In a number of Shakespeare's plays, horrible and brutal events occur. Identify the play with the horrible plot developments listed below. More than one nasty event may be found in the same play.

Ant & Cleo	*3 Henry VI*	*Lear*	*Pericles*	*Titus*
Hamlet	*John*	*Macbeth*	*Richard III*	*Tr & Cr*
1 Henry VI	*J. Caesar*	*Othello*	*Tempest*	*Win Tale*

1) A woman's children are baked into a pie and served to her.

2) A man's eyeballs are plucked out of his head and crushed underfoot.

3) An infant is condemned to death by exposure by her own father.

4) A woman commits suicide by "swallowing fire."

5) A man has his brother drowned in a butt of malmsey (wine).

6) Horses devour one another after their master is murdered.

7) A woman is raped and then her hands and tongue are cut off so she cannot identify her attackers.

8) A young boy, earlier threatened with having his eyes put out by a hot iron, jumps to his death.

9) Two women commit suicide by allowing a poisonous snake to bite them.

10) A man is torn to pieces by a bear.

11) A man is brutally murdered by being stabbed 33 times.

12) The ghost of a king visits his son to reveal he was murdered by his brother.

13) In a war, 21 of a man's sons are killed.

14) A man smothers his innocent wife to death.

15) A man's wife and all his children are wiped out because he fled a tyrant.

16) A woman is burned at the stake.

17) A father kills his son, and a son kills his father.

18) A king has an incestuous relationship with his daughter.

19) The dead body of a valiant warrior is tied to a horses tail and dragged shamefully around the battlefield.

20) A creature that is half man and half fish plots a murderous revolt.

Quiz 40

This Supernatural Soliciting: Identify the Play Where the Supernatural Occurs

Shakespeare's plays are filled with magic, witchcraft, ghosts, gods, and goddesses. Identify the play, from the list provided, in which you can find the examples of supernatural activity. More than one supernatural event may be found in the same play.

As You	2 Henry VI	MN Dream	Tempest
Cymbeline	J. Caesar	Pericles	Win Tale
1 Henry VI	Macbeth	Richard III	

1) The goddess of witchcraft, Hecate, appears in the play.

2) More ghosts can be found in this play than any other.

3) Spirits in the shape of dogs are conjured up to chase villains.

4) The king and queen of the fairies and an elfish sprite interfere with the lives of humans.

5) Three witches brew a disgusting potion.

6) The ghost of a murdered woman haunts the husband who killed her.

7) A ghost promises to meet one of his assassins at Philippi.

8) Characters include a conjurer named Roger Bolingbroke and a witch named Margery Jordan.

9) A fire from heaven is sent by the gods to destroy two characters.

10) The parts of the goddesses Iris, Juno, and Ceres are played by spirits in a masque.

11) The god of marriage, Hymen, appears.

12) Joan of Arc conjures up fiends.

13) Diana, the Roman goddess of chastity, appears to a character in a vision.

14) A spirit trapped in a tree is freed by a magician.

15) A king orders the oracle of Apollo at Delphi to be consulted concerning his wife's fidelity.

16) A mischievous fairy conjures the head of an ass to appear on an unsuspecting bumpkin.

17) A spirit named Asnath is conjured up.

18) A character claims that a spell was placed on him, which withered his arm.

19) Jupiter, the king of the gods, gives a young man a cryptic prophecy on a tablet.

20) The mutilated ghost of a murdered man appears at a banquet to torment the man who ordered his murder.

Quiz 41

All the Places That the Eye of Heaven Visits: Identify the Play by the Setting

From the list of settings supplied, choose the setting that best corresponds to each of the following plays.

Agincourt	Cyprus	An unnamed island	Phillipi
Forest of Arden	Egypt	Messina	Scotland
Athens	Elsinore	Milan	Troy
Belmont	Ephesus	Navarre	Verona
Bohemia	Illyria	Padua	Vienna

1) *Hamlet*

2) *As You Like It*

3) *Twelfth Night*

4) *Macbeth*

5) *Love's Labor's Lost*

6) *A Midsummer Night's Dream*

7) *Troilus and Cressida*

8) *Much Ado About Nothing*

9) *Othello*

10) *Romeo and Juliet*

11) *The Taming of the Shrew*

12) *Julius Caesar*

13) *Henry V*

14) *The Comedy of Errors*

15) *Antony and Cleopatra*

16) *Measure for Measure*

17) *The Merchant of Venice*

18) *The Winter's Tale*

19) *The Two Gentlemen of Verona*

20) *The Tempest*

Quiz 42

Away, the Gentles Are at Their Game: Games and Sports in the Plays

All cultures have had their various forms of recreation, and the people of Shakespeare's time were no different. Many of their sports and games were similar to ones we play today; others are no longer played at all. Here are references in the works of Shakespeare to the various games that were common in his time. How many can you identify?

1) In *The Merry Wives of Windsor* (4.5), Falstaff says, "I never prospered/since I forswore myself at primero." What is *primero*?

   A. Dice game   B. Card game   C. Board game   D. Jousting game

2) In Hamlet's famous "to be, or not to be" soliloquy, he says, "Ay, there's the rub." (3.1) The use of the word *rub* is actually a reference to which game?

   A. Tennis   B. Rugby   C. Football   D. Bowling

3) Which is the only play where you will find two characters playing chess?

   A. *Hamlet*   B. *The Merchant of Venice*
   C. *The Tempest*   D. *Pericles*

4) In *Henry V* (1.2), the Dauphin sends an insulting gift to King Henry V. What is this sports-related gift?

   A. Bowling balls   B. Backgammon set C. Tennis balls   D. Croquet set

5) In which play will you find a wrestling match with a highly regarded wrestler named Charles?

   A. *As You Like It*   B. *All's Well That Ends Well*
   C. *The Merry Wives of Windsor*   D. *The Comedy of Errors*

6) In which play will you find a character named John Rugby?

   A. *1 Henry IV*   B. *Richard II*
   C. *Measure for Measure*   D. *The Merry Wives of Windsor*

7) Billards, a variation of the game known to us today as *billiards*, is mentioned in only which play?

   A. *Much Ado About Nothing*   B. *Antony and Cleopatra*
   C. *Twelfth Night*   D. *Richard III*

8) Sackerson was a famous participant in which popular sport of Shakespeare's time?

   A. Football   B. Rugby   C. Bear-baiting   D. Archery

9) The term *hazard*, used many times in Shakespeare's plays, is associated with which game?

    A. Dice   B. Horseshoes   C. Bowling   D. Cards

10) A *foil* is a necessary piece of equipment for which sport?

    A. Archery   B. Rugby   C. Fencing   D. Falconry

11) Which character was described by another in the play as one who "is given to sports, wildness, and much company"?

    A. Falstaff   B. Mark Antony   C. Caliban   D. Orlando

12) In which play does a character insult another by calling him a "base football player"?

    A. *Coriolanus*   B. *King Lear*   C. *Henry IV, Part Two*   D. *Macbeth*

13) In Shakespeare's time, if a person "plays at tables," which game would he be playing?

    A. Backgammon   B. Table tennis   C. Tennis   D. Chess

14) A popular game in Shakespeare's time involved throwing shaped pieces of wood at a stake in the ground. What was it called? (Hint: Hamlet mentions this game in the grave digging scene.)

    A. Riband   B. Yare   C. Pith   D. Loggats

15) In *Antony and Cleopatra*, Octavius Caesar is upset with Mark Antony because he has reports that Antony is spending his time drinking and engaging in which activity?

    A. Hunting   B. Fishing   C. Bowling   D. Sailing

16) A supposedly innocent fencing match turns murderous in which play?

    A. *Macbeth*   B. *Titus Andronicus*   C. *Coriolanus*   D. *Hamlet*

17) In *Love's Labor's Lost* (5.2.544), Novum is mentioned. What type of a game is Novum?

    A. Cards   B. Jousting   C. Dice   D. Board game

18) In a number of Shakespeare's plays he makes reference to a special type of dramatic entertainment that was performed at court and involved elaborate scenery and spectacle. What were these entertainments called?

    A. Drolls   B. Flourishes   C. Masques   D. Jubilees

19) In *Henry VI, Part 3*, it was stated that the daily exercise of Edward, Earl of March and later King Edward IV, was which sport?

    A. Hunting   B. Archery   C. Falconry   D. Jousting

20) In *Measure for Measure* (1.2.190), Lucio mentions the game of tick-tack in a sexually suggestive way. Tick-tack, in Shakespeare's time, most resembled which game of today?

    A. Tic-tac-toe   B. Backgammon   C. Old Maid   D. Horseshoes

Quiz 43

How Many Goodly Creatures Are There Here!: Creatures in the Plays

References to all kinds of creatures abound in the works of Shakespeare. He mentions various types of animals, birds, reptiles, insects, and many other living things. Choose the name of the creature that answers the question or completes the statement.

1) Which creature was an emblem to represent the infamous King Richard III?

    A. Tiger   B. Boar   C. Serpent   D. Hawk

2) In *The Merchant of Venice*, Shylock's daughter, Jessica, trades the ring her mother had given to her father for which creature?

    A. Dog   B. Cat   C. Parrot   D. Monkey

3) The inn where Sebastian and Antonio plan to meet in *Twelfth Night* is the name of which creature?

    A. Elephant   B. Zebra   C. Ram   D. Porcupine

4) In *A Midsummer Night's Dream*, the impish Puck places the head of which animal on the shoulders of the ham actor, Nick Bottom?

    A. Ape   B. Baboon   C. Jackass   D. Hyena

5) In a famous scene in *Hamlet* (2.2), Hamlet satirically asks Polonius to describe the shape of a cloud. Hamlet mentions the cloud being shaped as three creatures. Which of the following does he NOT compare it to?

    A. Camel   B. Weasel   C. Lion   D. Whale

6) Shakespeare seems to have disliked a particular animal. In *All's Well That Ends Well* (4.3.237), a character "could endure any thing before but" which animal?

    A. Dog   B. Cat   C. Rat   D. Horse

7) What is the legendary creature, mentioned by Shakespeare, that is deadly to mortals who meet its gaze?

    A. Basilisk   B. Phoenix   C. Porpentine   D. Pajock

8) Which of the following was a term used in Shakespeare's time to refer to bats?

    A. Cockatrice   B. Chanticleer   C. Cormorant   D. Rere-mice

9) In Shakespeare's time, which of the following creatures was believed to have a life-span several times as long as a man?

    A. Rooster   B. Oyster   C. Lion   D. Crow

10) In *Henry IV, Part One* (2.1.147), Shakespeare used the word *moldwarp* to refer to which creature?

    A. Ant   B. Mole   C. Hedgehog   D. Spider

11) *The Winter's Tale* contains what may be Shakespeare's most famous stage direction—to "Exit, pursued by a..." what?

    A. Cockatrice   B. Dragon   C. Bear   D. Leopard

12) Which bird was featured on the Shakespeare family coat of arms?

    A. Falcon   B. Phoenix   C. Owl   D. Eagle

13) In *Henry V* (1.2.187), what are described as "creatures that by a rule in nature teach the act of order to a peopled kingdom"?

    A. Ants   B. Honeybees   C. Spiders   D. Fish

14) In *Twelfth Night* (2.4.22), what "must be caught with tickling"?

    A. Trout   B. Pigeon   C. Kitten   D. Crab

15) "Look like th' innocent flower,
    But be the _____ under 't." *Macbeth* (1.5.65)

    A. Serpent   B. Scorpion   C. Spider   D. Dragon

16) "If that the earth could teem with woman's tears,
    Each drop she falls would prove a _____ ." *Othello* (4.1.244)

    A. Deer   B. Phoenix   C. Porpoise   D. Crocodile

17) "There is a special providence in the fall of a _____." *Hamlet* (5.2.219)

    A. Mouse   B. Sparrow   C. Minnow   D. Beetle

18) "She is your treasure, she must have a husband;
    I must dance barefoot on her wedding day,
    And, for your love to her, lead _____ in hell."
    The Taming of the Shrew (2.1.32)

    A. Swine   B. Donkeys   C. Apes   D. Rats

19) "I am but mad north-northwest: when the wind is southerly
    I know a _____ from a handsaw." *Hamlet* (2.2.378)

    A. Halibut   B. Hippopotamus   C. Hedgehog   D. Hawk

20) "Mark what mercy his mother shall bring from him: there is no more mercy in him than there is milk in a male _____." *Coriolanus* (5.4.27)

    A. Viper   B. Wolf   C. Tiger   D. Baboon

Quiz 44

Sir, 'Tis My Occupation: The World of Work in Shakespeare

The world of work in Shakespeare's time consisted of some jobs which are still performed in our world today, although our technological world has also made some of them obsolete. See if you can match up the job description from the alphabetized list of occupations below. For your reference, a play where you may find the occupation mentioned is provided after the description.

Apothecary	Collier	Drovier	Miller	Sawyer
Brazier	Comfit-maker	Fuller	Milliner	Steward
Chandler	Cutler	Joiner	Ostler	Tinker
Cobbler	Drawer	Mercer	Provost	Warrener

1) Candymaker; confectioner. *1 Henry IV* (3.1.248)

2) One whose trade is to cleanse cloth. *Henry VIII* (1.2.33)

3) One who oversees the running of an estate. *Twelfth N* (2.3.73)

4) One whose occupation is to grind corn to meal. *Titus* (2.1.86)

5) One who sells drugs for medicinal uses. *2 Henry VI* (3.3.17)

6) The keeper of a prison; warden or jailer. *Measure* stage directions (1.2.115)

7) A gamekeeper. *Merry Wives* (1.4.27)

8) A digger or seller of coals; also one who sells charcoal. *Twelfth N* (3.4.117)

9) A dealer in fabrics. *Measure* (4.3.10)

10) A waiter. *Merry Wives* (2.2.159)

11) One who works with brass. *Henry VIII* (5.3.41)

12) One whose occupation is to make knives. *Merchant* (5.1.149)

13) A maker of wooden furniture. *MN Dream* (1.1.64)

14) A man who deals in fancy articles. *Win Tale* (4.4.192)

15) One who mends shoes. *J. Caesar* (1.1.11)

16) One who cuts lumber for building. *2 Henry VI* stage directions (4.2.30)

17) The person who has the care of horses at an inn. *1 Henry IV* (2.1.3)

18) A cattle dealer. *Much Ado* (2.1.194)

19) One who mends pots and pans. *MN Dream* (1.2.61)

20) One who makes or sells candles. *1 Henry IV* (3.3.46)

Quiz 45

Tales of Woeful Ages Long Ago: Mythological References in the Plays

Shakespeare made many references in his work to characters and places in Greek and Roman mythology. Can you match each description with a name or item from the list provided? For your reference, the play where you may find the allusion is provided after the description.

Amazon	Cerberus	Icarus	Narcissus	Prometheus
Argus	Charon	Janus	Nemesis	Proteus
Ariachne	Diana	Leander	Niobe	Pygmalion
Bacchus	Hydra	Mercury	Pegasus	Tarquin
Centaurs	Hymen	Minerva	Phaethon	Thisbe

1) He flew too close to the sun, melting his wax wings and falling to his death. *1 Henry VI* (4.6.55)

2) The winged horse of Perseus. *Tam Shrew* (4.4.5)

3) The 100-eyed monster watchman for the Greek gods. *Love's LL* (3.1.199)

4) She killed herself when she discovers the dead body of her beloved Pyramus. *MN Dream* (1.2.12)

5) Youth of exceptional beauty who fell in love with his own reflection. *Venus and Adonis* (161)

6) Greek god of marriage. *Timon* (4.3.383)

7) Three-headed dog that guarded the entrance into Hades. *2 Henry IV* (2.4.168)

8) Greek goddess of wisdom. *Tam Shrew* (1.1.84)

9) Goddess of chastity and the moon. *Merchant* (1.2.107)

10) Titan who stole the sacred fire from heaven and gave it to man. *Titus* (2.1.17)

11) Of a race of fierce women who fought the Greeks. *John* (5.2.155)

12) Youth who nightly swam the Hellespont to visit his lover, Hero. *Much Ado* (5.2.30)

13) She was turned into a spider by the gods for comparing her weaving skills with those of Minerva. *Tr & Cr* (5.2.152)

14) Sculptor whose statue of a young woman comes to life. *Measure* (2.3.43)

15) Race of creatures that were half man and half horse. *Titus* (5.2.203)

16) Roman messenger of the gods who wore winged sandals. *1 Henry IV* (4.1.106)

17) Multiheaded beast killed by Hercules. *1 Henry IV* (5.4.25)

18) Avenging her insults, Apollo and Artemis kill her sons and turn her into stone, but her statue continues to weep. *Hamlet* (1.2.149)

19) He stole his father's (Apollo) sun chariot, which he could not control, and was struck dead by Zeus. *3 Henry VI* (1.4.33)

20) Boatman who ferried the dead across the River Styx to the Elysian Fields. *Tr & Cr* (3.2.10)

21) Old Man of the Sea; constantly changing shape to avoid capture. *3 Henry VI* (3.2.192)

22) Goddess of avenging justice in Greek mythology. *1 Henry VI* (4.7.78)

23) Son of the last king of Rome; he raped Lucrece. *Macbeth* (2.1.55)

24) Greek god of wine. *Love's LL* (4.3.336)

25) Double-faced god of the Romans. *Merchant* (1.1.50)

Quiz 46

I'll Tell You My Dream: Dream References in Shakespeare

In many of Shakespeare's plays you will find characters describing their dreams. From the quotes and descriptions, can you identify the character whose dream is described?

Andromache	Brabantio	George, Duke of Clarence	Posthumus
Antigonus	Caliban	Humphrey, Duke of Gloucester	Romeo
Balthasar	Calpurnia	Hermia	Shylock
Banquo	Cinna	Lady Macbeth	Titania
Cardinal Beauford	Cleopatra	Nick Bottom	Tullus Aufidius

1) "I dreamt my lady came and found me dead...
And breath'd such life with kisses in my lips
That I reviv'd and was an emperor."

2) "I dreamt to-night that I did feast with Caesar,
And things unluckily charge my fantasy."

3) "I dreamt last night of the three weird sisters:
To you they have show'd some truth."

4) "Ay me, for pity! what a dream was here!
...Methought a serpent ate my heart away,
And you sate smiling at his cruel prey."

5) "...I have dreamt
Of bloody turbulence, and this whole night
Hath nothing been but shapes and forms of slaughter."

6) "Sometimes a thousand twangling instruments
Will hum about mine ears; and sometimes voices,
That if I then had wak'd after long sleep,
Will make me sleep again, and then in dreaming,
The clouds methought would open, and show riches
Ready to drop upon me, that when I wak'd
I cried to dream again."

7) "...Thou hast beat me out
Twelve several times, and I have nightly since
Dreamt of encounters 'twixt thyself and me;
We have been together in my sleep,
Unbuckling helms, fisting each other's throat,
And wak'd half dead with nothing."

8) "Look to my house. I am right loath to go;
     There is some ill a-brewing towards my rest,
     For I did dream of money-bags to-night."

9) "O, I have pass'd a miserable night,
     So full of fearful dreams, of ugly sights,
     ...I saw a thousand fearful wracks;
     A thousand men that fishes gnawed upon."

10) "...I did dream to-night
     The Duke was dumb and could not speak a word."

11) "I have had a dream, past the wit of man to say what dream it was.
     Man is but an ass if he go about t' expound this dream.
     Methought I was—there is no man can tell what."

12) "As I did sleep under this yew tree here,
     I dreamt my master and another fought,
     And that my master slew him."

13) "Sleep, thou hast been a grandsire and begot
     A father to me; and thou hast created
     A mother and two brothers. But O scorn!
     Gone! They went hence so soon as they were born."

14) "My troublous dreams this night doth make me sad.
     Methought this staff of mine office-badge in court
     Was broke in twain...
     And on the pieces of the broken wand
     Were plac'd the heads of Edmund, Duke of Somerset,
     And William de la Pole, first Duke of Suffolk."

15) "I dreamt there was an Emperor Antony.
     O, such another sleep, that I might see
     But such another man!"

16) "...what visions have I seen!
     Methought I was enamor'd of an ass!"

17) "Come poor babe.
     I have heard (but not believ'd) the spirits o' th' dead
     May walk again. If such thing be, thy mother
     Appear'd to me last night; for ne'er was a dream
     So like waking."

18) "Out, damn'd spot! out I say! One—two—why then 'tis time to do't. Hell is murky. Fie, my lord, fie, a soldier, and afeard? What need we fear who knows it, when none can call our pow'r to accompt? Yet who would have thought the old man to have had so much blood in him?"

19) "She dreamt to-night she saw my statue
    Which, like a fountain with an hundred spouts,
    Did run pure blood; and many lusty Romans
    Came smiling and did bathe their hands in it."

20) "Strike on the tinder, ho!
    Give me a taper! Call up all my people!
    This accident is not unlike my dream,
    Belief of it oppresses me already.
    Light, I say, light!"

Quiz 47

He Hath Songs for Man or Woman: Songs in Shakespeare

Many songs can be found in the plays of Shakespeare. From the list provided, match the name of the play with the following list of songs. Some plays correspond with more than one song.

As You	Henry VIII	Merchant	Othello	Two Gents
Cymbeline	Love's LL	MN Dream	Tempest	Two Noble
Hamlet	Measure	Much Ado	Twelfth N	Win Tale

1) "Who is Silvia?"

2) "When daisies pied"

3) "You spotted snakes"

4) "Under the greenwood tree"

5) "Come away, death"

6) "Take, O take those lips away"

7) "Fear no more the heat o' the sun"

8) "When daffodils begin to peer"

9) "Where the bee sucks"

10) "Orpheus with his lute"

11) "Roses, their sharp spines being gone"

12) "Tell me where is fancy bred?"

13) "The Willow Song"

14) "To-morrow is Saint Valentine's day"

15) "Pardon, goddess of the night"

16) "O mistress mine! Where are you roaming?"

17) "Full fathom five"

18) "It was a lover and his lass"

19) "Hark, hark, the lark"

20) "Sigh, no more, ladies"

Quiz 48

Doctor, Cast the Water of My Land, Find Her Disease: Shakespeare and the World of Medicine

Test your knowledge of the medical world in Shakespeare!

1) Which of the following family members of William Shakespeare was a medical doctor?
   A. His son-in-law Thomas Quiney   B. His son-in-law John Hall
   C. His brother Gilbert   D. His uncle Henry

2) An apothecary appears in only one of Shakespeare's plays. Which one?
   A. *Titus*   B. *Hamlet*   C. *Lear*   D. *Rom & Jul*

3) Which of the following characters is the daughter of the doctor Gerard de Narbonne?
   A. Portia in *Merchant*   B. Sylvia in *Two Gents*
   C. Helena in *All's Well*   D. Rosaline in *Love's LL*

4) According to Shakespeare, which historical character was deaf in his left ear?
   A. King Henry IV   B. King John   C. Julius Caesar   D. Mark Antony

5) Which of Shakespeare's characters claims that he suffers from "hysterica passio," an overwhelming feeling of physical distress and suffocation?

    A. King Lear   B. Macbeth   C. Othello   D. Hamlet

6) Which of the following characters is bound and placed in a dark room—a common remedy for those in Shakespeare's time who were thought to be insane—as a practical joke?

    A. Touchstone in *As You*   B. Malvolio in *Twelfth N*
    C. Falstaff in *Merry Wives*   D. Vincentio in *Tam Shrew*

7) In which play will you find a doctor by the name of Cerimon?

    A. *Pericles*   B. *Win Tale*   C. *Timon*   D. *Ant & Cleo*

8) In which comedy will you find the foolish Doctor Caius?

    A. *Love's LL*   B. *Two Gents*   C. *Measure*   D. *Merry Wives*

9) Doctor William Butts is the only historical doctor to appear in one of Shakespeare's plays. Doctor Butts was the doctor of which English monarch?

    A. Richard II   B. Richard III   C. Henry VI   D. Henry VIII

10) In which play will you find two speaking characters who are doctors?

    A. *Coriolanus*   B. *Othello*   C. *Macbeth*   D. *Tr & Cr*

11) In which play will you find a doctor named Cornelius?

    A. *Com Err*   B. *Cymbeline*   C. *Coriolanus*   D. *Timon*

12) In Shakespeare's time, which of the following organs was thought to be the source of blood formation and connected with courage and cowardice?

    A. Heart   B. Kidney   C. Liver   D. Skin

13) In *Othello*, as the evil Iago watches Cassio and Desdemona politely and affection-ately converse, he says, "Yet again your fingers to your lips? Would they were clyster-pipes for your sake" (2.1.177). What medical procedure utilized clyster-pipes?

    A. Amputation   B. Stitching wounds
    C. Preparing potions   D. Administering enemas

14) Which play ends with an epilogue in which the speaker bequeaths his diseases to the audience?

    A. *Tr & Cr*   B. *All's Well*   C. *Measure*   D. *Merchant*

15) Which of Shakespeare's plays contains the most references to syphilis?

    A. *Rom & Jul*   B. *Measure*   C. *Timon*   D. *Win Tale*

16) Which condition was known in Shakespeare's time as "the king's evil" because it was believed to be cured by the touch of a king?

    A. Diarrhea   B. Scrofula   C. Psoriasis   D. Constipation

17) In *Julius Caesar*, which character is described as having "the falling sickness" (epilepsy) and suffers a seizure during the course of the play?

    A. Julius Caesar   B. Brutus   C. Cassius   D. Octavius

18) Which character utters the following terrible curse against his daughter: "Into her womb convey sterility./ Dry up in her the organs of increase."

    A. Titus Andronicus   B. Cymbeline   C. Coriolanus   D. King Lear

19) Which of the following Shakespearean characters dies of "the malady of France" (syphilis)?

    A. Mistress Overdone in *Measure*   B. Mistress Quickly in *Henry V*
    C. Hermione in *Win Tale*   D. The Countess of Rossillion in *All's Well*

20) In *Romeo and Juliet*, the tragic consequences at the end of the play result when an outbreak of what disease prevents Friar John from delivering Friar Lawrence's letter to Romeo?

    A. Influenza   B. Tuberculosis   C. Plague   D. Leprosy

21) In which play will you find a king who is dying of a "fistula" at the beginning of the play, but is cured by the play's heroine?

    A. *As You*   B. *All's Well*   C. *Much Ado*   D. *Love's LL*

22) In Shakespeare's time, all matter was believed to consist of one of four elements: earth, air, fire, and water. In the human body it was believed that air took the form of which of the following:

    A. Blood   B. Phlegm   C. Black bile   D. Yellow bile

23) According to Iago in *Othello*, what malady keeps him awake the night he alleges that Cassio declared his love for Desdemona in his sleep?

    A. Headache   B. Earache   C. Toothache   D. Constipation

24) In Shakespeare's time, it was believed that sadness, anger, gaiety, and envy emanated from which part of the body?

    A. Pancreas   B. Brain   C. Stomach   D. Spleen

25) In *Troilus and Cressida*, Shakespeare refers to which disease by the phrase "the Neapolitan bone-ache?"

    A. Cancer   B. Syphilis   C. Rheumatism   D. Arthritis

Section IV

Film, Stage, and Literature

Quiz 49

This Wide and Universal Theatre: Shakespeare in Film

The influence of Shakespeare can be found in many films—even those that are not direct adaptations of his plays. Some of these questions deal with adaptations of Shakespeare's plays, others simply with references to Shakespeare in film.

1) Famed Japanese film director Akira Kurosawa's *Throne of Blood* (1957) is an adaptation of which Shakespearean play?

    A. *King Lear*   B. *Macbeth*   C. *Romeo and Juliet*   D. *Richard III*

2) Which Shakespearean film was made by Laurence Olivier in an effort to boost morale during World War II?

    A. *Richard III*   B. *Henry V*   C. *As You Like It*   D. *Hamlet*

3) In 1967, Orson Welles directed a film that was a combination of four Shakespearean plays: *1 Henry IV, 2 Henry IV, Henry V,* and *Merry Wives.* What was the title of this film?

    A. *A Touch of Evil*   B. *The Third Man*   C. *Chimes at Midnight*   D. *The Trial*

4) The 1971 film adaptation of *Macbeth*, directed by Roman Polanski, was produced by a Motion Picture Company better known for its magazine of the same name. What was its name?

    A. Life Film Company   B. Esquire Cinema
    C. Reader's Digest Productions   D. Playboy Pictures

5) After the death of Macbeth and the crowning of Malcolm, an unique twist occurs at the end of Polanski's 1971 film adaptation of *Macbeth*: A character is seen making a visit to the three witches. Which character makes this visit?

    A. Macduff   B. Ross   C. Fleance   D. Donalbain

6) Which film adaptation of *Hamlet* opens with a voice-over that states "this is the story about a man who cannot make up his mind"?

    A. Olivier's (1948)   B. Richardson's (1969)
    C. Zeffirelli's (1990)   D. Branagh's (1996)

7) *Put money in Thy Purse: The Filming of Orson Welles's Othello* (1952) was the first complete volume devoted to the making of a Shakespearean film by a single author. Who wrote it?

    A. Orson Welles   B. Micheal Machiammoir
    C. Suzanne Cloutier   D. Michael Laurence

8) In 1982, Woody Allen made a film that was titled loosely after one of Shakespeare's plays. Allen's title for his film was based on which play?

    A. *Love's Labor's Lost*   B. *A Midsummer Night's Dream*
    C. *The Merchant of Venice*   D. *The Two Gentlemen of Verona*

9) In the 1995 film adaptation of *Richard III*, directed by Richard Loncraine and starring Sir Ian McKellen in the title role, the lyrics to the opening song are from a poem titled "The Passionate Shepherd to His Love" by one of Shakespeare's contemporaries. Who is the author of this poem?

    A. Ben Jonson   B. John Lyly   C. Christopher Marlowe D. John Fletcher

10) Peter Weir's 1989 *Dead Poet's Society*, starring Robin Williams, contains performance scenes from which play?

    A. *A Midsummer Night's Dream*   B. *The Tempest*
    C. *As You Like It*   D. *Twelfth Night*

11) In the 1944 film adaptation of *Henry V* directed by Laurence Olivier, the film opens with Olivier portraying what actor colleague of Shakespeare?

    A. Edward Alleyn   B. Henry Condell   C. John Heminges   D. Richard Burbage

12) In *The Filth and the Fury*, a documentary of punk band The Sex Pistols, Johnny Rotten mentions his fascination with which Shakespearean character?

    A. Iago   B. Othello   C. Hamlet   D. Richard III

13) In *Free Enterprise*, a pair of trekkies confront life and love, and a silly William Shatner (the original Captain Kirk) performs a rap version of which play?

    A. *Julius Caesar*   B. *Hamlet*   C. *Richard III*   D. *Henry V*

14) In *Last Action Hero*, directed by John McTiernan, Arnold Schwarzenegger quotes a famous speech from which play?

    A. *As You Like It*   B. *Hamlet*   C. *Macbeth*   D. *Romeo and Juliet*

15) In *Reefer Madness*, a cult anti-drug propaganda film from 1936, quoting from which play leads to immorality in teens?

    A. *Macbeth*   B. *Richard III*   C. *Romeo and Juliet* D. *Henry IV, Part One*

16) The title of Alfred Hitchcock's thriller *North by Northwest*, starring Cary Grant, is taken from which of Shakespeare's plays?

    A. *Hamlet*   B. *Timon of Athens* C. *Coriolanus*   D. *Measure for Measure*

17) In *A Midsummer Night's Dream* (1999), directed by Michael Hoffman, other performers are rehearsing while the Mechanicals are waiting for word from the Duke. One group of players is rehearsing the Greek tragedy Oedipus Rex and another pair of players are rehearsing a scene from which of Shakespeare's plays?

    A. *Lear*   B. *Othello*   C. *Henry IV, Part One* D. *Twelfth Night*

18) Which play has spawned the most film versions?

    A. *Hamlet*   B. *Romeo and Juliet*
    C. *A Midsummer Night's Dream*   D. *Macbeth*

19) Near the beginning of the film *Shakespeare in Love*, a play written by Shakespeare is being performed before the Queen. What is the title of that play?

    A. *Troilus and Cressida*   B. *The Merry Wives of Windsor*
    C. *Much Ado About Nothing*   D. *The Two Gentlemen of Verona*

20) Which film adaptation adds a character called the Holy Father?

    A. Welles's *Othello* (1952)   B. Olivier's *Richard III* (1955)
    C. Welles's *Macbeth* (1948)   D. Olivier's *Hamlet* (1948)

21) In the film *Shakespeare in Love*, an unpleasant young fellow named John Webster is shown feeding mice to a cat and informing the authorities that a woman is performing (illegally) on the stage. This character represents an actual person from Shakespeare's time. What was the occupation of the real John Webster?

    A. Scientist   B. Politician   C. Playwright   D. Spy

22) In the 1980 film *Fame*, directed by Alan Parker and starring Irene Cara, which play figures prominently in audition sequences?

    A. *Twelfth Night*   B. *Romeo and Juliet* C. *King Lear*   D. *Othello*

23) In the 1973 film *Theatre of Blood*, Edward Lionheart is a Shakespearean actor who goes on a killing spree to obtain revenge against his critics in gruesome and amusing ways that would make Shakespeare proud. Who stars as Edward Lionheart in this film?

    A. Boris Karloff   B. Bela Lugosi   C. Jack Palance   D. Vincent Price

24) In Franco Zeffirelli's 1968 film adaptation of *Romeo and Juliet*, what is the estimated amount of original language from Shakespeare's text that is retained?

    A. 35%   B. 45%   C. 65%   D. 85%

25) *Shakespeare Wallah* (1965), directed by James Ivory, deals with a family-run Shakespeare troupe's financial difficulties in which country?

    A. India   B. South Africa   C. Australia   D. New Zealand

Quiz 50

You Precious Winners All: Academy Awards for Shakespeare

Here are some questions that deal with Shakespearean films that have had Academy Award nominations and winners. Test your knowledge of Hollywood's best and brightest stars in their performances of Shakespeare.

1) Which actress was nominated, but did not win an Academy Award for her portrayal of Ophelia in Laurence Olivier's 1948 *Hamlet*?

    A. Jean Simmons   B. Eileen Herlie   C. Claire Bloom   D. Vivien Leigh

2) Marlon Brando was nominated for an Academy Award in 1953 for his portrayal of which Shakespearean character?

    A. Macbeth   B. Richard III   C. Iago   D. Mark Antony

3) Which director was nominated for an Academy Award for his 1968 Adaptation of *Romeo and Juliet,* which was also nominated for Best Picture and won two Academy Awards?

    A. Franco Zeffirelli   B. Roman Polanski
    C. Stuart Burge   D. John Gielgud

4) What was the first foreign film to win an Academy Award for Best Picture?

    A. Svend Gade's 1920 *Hamlet*   B. Olivier's 1944 *Henry V*
    C. Paul Czinner's 1936 *As You Like It*   D. Olivier's 1948 *Hamlet*

5) Which of the following was NOT nominated for Best Picture?

    A. Max Reinhardt and William Dieterle's 1935 *A Midsummer Night's Dream*
    B. Joseph Mankiewicz's 1953 *Julius Caesar*
    C. Orson Welles's 1948 *Macbeth*
    D. George Cukor's 1936 *Romeo and Juliet*

6) For which film did Kenneth Branagh receive Academy Award nominations for Best Actor and Best Director?

    A. *Hamlet*   B. *Much Ado About Nothing*
    C. *Henry V*   D. *Love's Labor's Lost*

7) How many Academy Awards did *Shakespeare in Love* win in 1998?

    A. 6   B. 7   C. 8   D. 9

8) In the 1998 film *Shakespeare in Love,* who won an Academy Award for Best Actress for her role as Viola?

    A. Gwyneth Paltrow   B. Kate Winslet
    C. Helena Bonham Carter   D. Imogen Stubbs

9) In George Cukor's 1936 *Romeo and Juliet*, which actor received an Academy Award nomination for Best Supporting Actor for his portrayal of Tybalt?

    A. John Barrymore   B. Douglas Fairbanks
    C. Alex Jennings   D. Basil Rathbone

10) In the 1998 film *Shakespeare in Love*, who won an Academy Award for Best Supporting Actress for her role as Queen Elizabeth?

    A. Kate Blanchard   B. Glenn Close   C. Judi Dench   D. Julie Christie

11) George Cukor's 1936 *Romeo and Juliet* was nominated for how many Academy Awards?

    A. 2   B. 3   C. 4   D. 5

12) Who was nominated as Best Actress, but did not win, for her role as Juliet in George Cukor's 1936 *Romeo and Juliet*?

    A. Edna May Oliver   B. Norma Shearer
    C. Elisabeth Bergner   D. Freda Jackson

13) Kenneth Branagh's 1989 *Henry V* was nominated for three Academy Awards and won an Oscar for which one?

    A. Best Actor   B. Best Costume Design
    C. Best Original Screenplay   D. Best Supporting Actor

14) Which of the following films did NOT result in a Best Actor nomination for Laurence Olivier?

    A. *As You Like It*   B. *Hamlet*   C. *Henry V*   D. *Othello*

15) Ronald Colman won a Best Actor award in *A Double Life* (1948) for his portrayal of an actor who becomes dangerously consumed by his role as which Shakespearean character?

    A. Macbeth   B. Caliban   C. Othello   D. Hamlet

16) Who was nominated but did not win an Academy Award for Best Supporting Actor for his portrayal of Iago in Stuart Burge's 1965 *Othello*, which starred Laurence Olivier in the title role?

    A. Ian Holm   B. Ralph Richardson
    C. Jose Ferrer   D. Frank Findlay

17) Max Reinhardt and William Dieterle's 1935 *A Midsummer Night's Dream* was nominated for three Academy Awards. Which of the following are the two it won?

    A. Best Original Screenplay and Best Costume Design
    B. Best Cinematography and Best Film Editing
    C. Best Supporting Actress and Best Supporting Actor
    D. Best Original Musical Score and Best Director

18) She was nominated for an Academy Award for Best Supporting Actress for her portrayal of Desdemona in Stuart Burge's 1965 *Othello*, which starred Laurence Olivier in the title role.

A. Joyce Redmond   B. Joan Plowright
C. Vanessa Redgrave   D. Maggie Smith

19) Who was nominated for Best Supporting Actor for *Shakespeare in Love*?

A. Ben Affleck   B. Colin Firth   C. Geoffrey Rush   D. Anthony Sher

20) *Shakespeare in Love* was nominated for all of the following Academy Awards, and won all EXCEPT which one?

A. Best Original Screenplay   B. Best Director
C. Best Costume Design   D. Best Art Direction

21) Famed Japanese film director Akira Kurosawa was nominated for Best Director for which Shakespearean film adaptation?

A. *Ran*   B. *Throne of Blood*
C. *The Bold Sleep Well*   D. *Spider's Web Castle*

22) Which of these Shakespearean film adaptations was nominated for the most Academy Awards?

A. Al Pacino's 1996 *Looking for Richard*
B. Trevor Nunn's 1995 *Twelfth Night*
C. Franco Zeffirelli's 1966 *The Taming of the Shrew*
D. Kenneth Branagh's 1993 *Much Ado About Nothing*

23) In *The Goodbye Girl* (1977), Richard Dreyfuss won an Academy Award for Best Actor for his portrayal of an actor cast in which Shakespearean role?

A. Lear's Fool   B. Prospero   C. Richard III   D. Hotspur

24) Which of the following Shakespearean film adaptations did NOT receive any Academy Award nominations?

A. Julie Taymor's 1999 *Titus*   B. Kenneth Branagh's 1996 *Hamlet*
C. Richard Loncraine's 1995 *Richard III*   D. Stuart Burge's 1970 *Julius Caesar*

25) What is the only Shakespearean film adaptation in which all four leading actors were nominated for Academy Awards?

A. Olivier's 1948 *Hamlet*
B. Stuart Burge's 1965 *Othello*
C. Baz Luhrmann's 1996 *William Shakespeare's Romeo and Juliet*
D. Franco Zeffirelli's 1966 *The Taming of the Shrew*

Quiz 51

The Best Actors in the World, Part I: Actors in Shakespearean Film

Many wonderful actors have relished playing Shakespearean characters. Identify the actors and their roles from the following films based on the plays of Shakespeare.

1) In the 1935 film adaptation of *A Midsummer Night's Dream*, directed by Max Reinhardt and William Dieterle, who played the role of Puck?

  A. Mickey Rooney   B. Ian Hunter   C. Victor Jory   D. Joe E. Brown

2) In the 1936 film adaptation of *Romeo and Juliet*, directed by George Cukor, what 40-year-old actor starred as a teenage Romeo?

  A. Clark Gable   B. Leslie Howard   C. Dick Powell   D. Reginald Denny

3) In the 1935 film adaptation of *A Midsummer Night's Dream*, directed by Max Reinhardt and William Dieterle, Dick Powell played which role?

  A. Lysander   B. Demetrius   C. Oberon   D. Peter Quince

4) In Orson Welles's 1948 film adaptation of *Macbeth*, who played the role of Malcolm?

  A. Dan O'Herlihy   B. Ian McKellen
  C. Roddy McDowell   D. Ralph Richardson

5) In Laurence Olivier's 1948 *Hamlet*, who played the role of Osric?

  A. Basil Sydney   B. Anthony Quayle   C. Christopher Lee   D. Peter Cushing

6) In the 1953 film adaptation of *Julius Caesar*, directed by Joseph Mankiewicz, who played the role of Cassius?

  A. John Gielgud   B. Edmond O'Brien   C. James Mason   D. Louis Calhern

7) In the 1955 film adaptation of *Richard III*, directed by and starring Laurence Olivier in the title role, who played the role of the Duke of Buckingham?

  A. Cedric Hardwicke   B. Ralph Richardson
  C. John Gielgud   D. Russell Thorndike

8) In the 1966 film adaptation of *The Taming of the Shrew*, directed by Franco Zeffirelli, which role was played by Michael York?

  A. Tranio   B. Lucentio   C. Hortensio   D. Baptista

9) In his 1967 film *Chimes at Midnight*, which role did Orson Welles play?

  A. Henry IV   B. Prince Hal   C. Falstaff   D. Bardolph

10) In the 1968 film adaptation of *Romeo and Juliet*, directed by Franco Zeffirelli, who played the role of the Prologue and the Epilogue?

  A. John Gielgud   B. Ralph Richardson
  C. Ian McKellen   D. Laurence Olivier

11) In the 1969 *Hamlet*, directed by Tony Richardson and starring Nicol Williamson in the title role, who played the role of Claudius?

  A. Anthony Hopkins   B. Bob Hoskins
  C. Jose Ferrer   D. James Earl Jones

12) In the 1970 film adaptation of *Julius Caesar*, directed by Stuart Burge, who played the role of Mark Antony?

  A. Robert Vaughn   B. Richard Chamberlain
  C. Charlton Heston   D. Robert Wagner

13) In the 1971 film adaptation of *Macbeth*, directed by Roman Polanski, who starred as Macbeth?

  A. Jon Finch   B. Hugh O'Brien   C. James Coburn   D. Ian McKellen

14) In Michael Eliot's 1984 *King Lear*, starring Laurence Olivier in the title role, who played the role of the Fool?

  A. John Heard   B. Robert Lindsay   C. William Hurt   D. John Hurt

15) In the 1989 film adaptation of *Henry V*, directed by and starring Kenneth Branagh in the title role, who plays the role of the Chorus?

  A. Derek Jacobi   B. Brian Blessed   C. Richard Briers   D. Ian Holm

16) In the 1991 Franco Zeffirelli film adaptation of *Hamlet*, starring Mel Gibson in the title role, which role was played by Paul Scofield?

  A. Claudius   B. Ghost   C. Polonius   D. Marcellus

17) In Peter Greenaway's 1991 *Prospero's Books*, an adaptation of *The Tempest*, who played the role of Prospero?

  A. Kenneth Branagh   B. David Carradine
  C. Ian McKellen   D. John Gielgud

18) In Kenneth Branagh's 1993 film adaptation of *Much Ado About Nothing*, who stars as Don Pedro, the Prince of Arragon?

  A. Keanu Reeves   B. Richard Briers
  C. Denzel Washington   D. Robert Sean Leonard

19) In the 1995 film adaptation of *Othello*, directed by Oliver Parker, who played the role of Othello?

A. Wesley Snipes   B. Laurence Fishburne
C. Louis Gosset, Jr.   D. Cuba Gooding, Jr.

20) In Kenneth Branagh's 1996 *Hamlet*, who played the role of the gravedigger?

   A. David Slade   B. Jack Lemmon   C. Bill Murray   D. Billy Crystal

21) In the 1996 film adaptation of *Twelfth Night*, directed by Trevor Nunn, which role was played by Ben Kingsley?

   A. Orsino   B. Feste   C. Sir Toby Belch   D. Antonio

22) Who starred as William Shakespeare in the Academy Award winning film *Shakespeare in Love*?

   A. Geoffrey Rush   B. Joseph Fiennes   C. Anthony Sher   D. Rupert Everett

23) In the 1999 film adaptation of *A Midsummer Night's Dream*, directed by Michael Hoffman, who played the role of Nick Bottom?

   A. Kevin Kline   B. Christian Bale   C. David Straithairn   D. Stanley Tucci

24) In Kenneth Branagh's 2000 film adaptation of *Love's Labor's Lost*, which role is played by Nathan Lane?

   A. Don Armado   B. Berowne   C. Costard   D. Moth

25) In Michael Almereyda's 2000 film adaptation of *Hamlet*, set on modern-day Wall Street, who played the role of Hamlet?

   A. Ethan Hawke   B. Kyle MacLachlan   C. Sam Shepard   D. Matt Damon

124   That Is the Question

Quiz 52

The Best Actors in the World, Part II: Actors in Shakespearean Film

So, how did you do on Part I? Here's another chance to display your knowledge of the many wonderful actors who have relished playing Shakespearean characters. Once again, identify the actors and their roles from the following films based on the plays of Shakespeare.

1) In Sam Taylor's 1929 *The Taming of the Shrew*, who of the following played the role of Petruchio?
- A. Tyrone Power
- B. Douglas Fairbanks
- C. Errol Flynn
- D. Geoffrey Wardell

2) In the 1935 film adaptation of *A Midsummer Night's Dream*, directed by Max Reinhardt and William Dieterle, what role did James Cagney play?
- A. Peter Quince
- B. Oberon
- C. Nick Bottom
- D. Demetrius

3) In the 1936 film adaptation of *Romeo and Juliet*, directed by George Cukor, what role was played by John Barrymore?
- A. Tybalt
- B. Lord Capulet
- C. Benvolio
- D. Mercutio

4) In Laurence Olivier's 1948 *Hamlet*, who played the role of Claudius?
- A. Basil Sydney
- B. Felix Aylmer
- C. Terence Morgan
- D. John Gielgud

5) In the 1953 film version of *Julius Caesar*, directed by Joseph Mankiewicz, who played the role of Mark Antony?
- A. James Mason
- B. John Gielgud
- C. Richard Burton
- D. Marlon Brando

6) In Laurence Olivier's 1955 *Richard III*, what role was played by Cedric Hardwicke?
- A. Duke of Buckingham
- B. King Edward IV
- C. Duke of Clarence
- D. Earl of Richmond

7) In Orson Welles's 1967 *Chimes at Midnight*, what role was played by John Gielgud?
- A. Prince Hal
- B. Hotspur
- C. Henry IV
- D. Bardolph

8) In the 1968 film version of *Romeo and Juliet*, directed by Franco Zeffirelli, who played the role of Romeo?
- A. Michael York
- B. Derek Jacobi
- C. Leonard Whiting
- D. Paul Hardwick

9) In the 1970 film adaptation of *Julius Caesar*, directed by Stuart Burge, who played the role of Brutus?
- A. Richard Johnson
- B. Jason Robards
- C. Derek Godfrey
- D. Lee Marvin

10) In the 1973 film version of *The Merchant of Venice*, directed by John Sichel, what role was played by Laurence Olivier?

    A. Shylock   B. Antonio   C. Bassanio   D. the Duke

11) In the 1974 film version of *Antony and Cleopatra*, directed by Jon Scoffield and Trevor Nunn, who starred as Mark Antony?

    A. Richard Johnson   B. Corin Redgrave   C. Patrick Stewart   D. Adrian Noble

12) In Kenneth Branagh's 1989 film version of *Henry V*, which role was played by Paul Scofield?

    A. Bardolph   B. Fluellen   C. Duke of Exeter   D. King of France

13) In the 1991 Franco Zeffirelli film adaptation of *Hamlet* starring Mel Gibson in the title role, who played the role of Claudius?

    A. Ian Holm   B. Alan Bates
    C. Richard Attenborough   D. Jack Lemmon

14) In Kenneth Branagh's 1993 film adaptation of *Much Ado About Nothing*, who stars as Dogberry?

    A. John Candy   B. John Lithgow   C. Michael Keaton   D. Steve Martin

15) In the 1995 film adaptation of *Othello*, directed by Oliver Parker, who played the role of Iago?

    A. Michael Maloney   B. Kenneth Branagh
    C. John Turturro   D. Nathaniel Parker

16) In the 1995 film version of *Richard III* directed by Richard Loncraine and starring Ian McKellen as the title character, which role was played by Robert Downey, Jr.?

    A. James Tyrrel   B. Clarence   C. Earl Rivers   D. Buckingham

17) In Kenneth Branagh's 1996 film adaptation of *Hamlet*, what role is played by Robin Williams?

    A. Yorick   B. Voltemand   C. Osric   D. Reynaldo

18) In Kenneth Branagh's 1996 film adaptation of *Hamlet*, who played the role of Marcellus?

    A. Charlton Heston   B. Richard Briers   C. Brian Blessed   D. Jack Lemmon

19) In Baz Luhrmann's 1996 *William Shakespeare's Romeo and Juliet*, starring Leonardo DiCaprio and Claire Danes in the title roles, who played the role of Tybalt?

    A. John Leguizamo   B. Pete Postlethwaite
    C. Harold Perrineau   D. Paul Sorvino

20) In Al Pacino's 1996 *Looking for Richard*, he was the Duke of Buckingham.

    A. Alec Baldwin   B. Aidan Quinn   C. Kevin Conway   D. Kevin Spacey

21) In the 1996 film adaptation of *Twelfth Night*, directed by Trevor Nunn, who played the role of Malvolio?

    A. Richard E. Grant B. Toby Stephens C. Nigel Hawthorne D. Mel Smith

22) In the 1998 film *Shakespeare in Love*, who played the role of the famous Elizabethan actor, Ned Alleyn?

    A. Ben Affleck   B. Colin Firth   C. Martin Clunes   D. John Leguizamo

23) In director Julie Taymor's 1999 *Titus*, who starred as Titus?

    A. Anthony Hopkins   B. Ian McKellen
    C. Matthew Rhys   D. Billy Bob Thornton

24) In the 1999 film adaptation of *A Midsummer Night's Dream*, directed by Michael Hoffman, what role was played by Rupert Everett?

    A. Theseus   B. Peter Quince C. Oberon   D. Puck

25) In Michael Almereyda's 2000 film adaptation of *Hamlet*, set on modern-day Wall Street, who played the role of Polonius?

    A. Michael Douglas B. Bill Murray C. Dan Aykroyd   D. Patrick Stewart

Quiz 53

Let Her Shine as Gloriously, Part I: Actresses in Shakespearean Film

Distinguished actresses throughout history have been as equally enamored of Shakespearean roles as their male counterparts. This quiz and the one that follows test your knowledge about actresses and their roles in Shakespearean film adaptations.

1) In the 1929 film adaptation of *The Taming of the Shrew*, Douglas Fairbanks played the role of Petruchio. Who played opposite him in the role of Katherina, the Shrew?

    A. Mary Pickford B. Janet Gaynor C. Louise Dresser   D. Gloria Swanson

2) She played Rosalind, opposite Laurence Olivier as Orlando, in Paul Czinner's 1936 *As You Like It*.

    A. Gladys George B. Elisabeth Bergner C. Merle Oberon   D. Irene Dunn

3) She played the role of Gertrude in Laurence Olivier's 1948 *Hamlet*.

    A. Signe Hasso   B. Shelley Winters C. Eileen Herlie   D. Linda Darnell

4) In the 1948 film adaptation of *Macbeth*, directed by and starring Orson Welles in the title role, who played the role of Lady Macbeth?

A. Agnes Moorehead   B. Ethel Barrymore
C. Jeanette Nolan   D. Celeste Holm

5) In the 1953 film adaptation of *Julius Caesar*, directed by Joseph Mankiewicz, who played the role of Calpurnia?

A. Deborah Kerr   B. Greer Garson   C. Leslie Caron   D. Susan Hayward

6) In the 1955 film adaptation of *Richard III*, directed by and starring Laurence Olivier in the title role, who played the role of Anne Neville?

A. Elsa Lanchester   B. Gloria Grahame   C. Claire Trevor   D. Claire Bloom

7) In Orson Welles's 1967 *Chimes at Midnight*, who played the role of Doll Tearsheet?

A. Margaret Rutherford   B. Jeanne Moreau
C. Loretta Young   D. Vivien Leigh

8) In the 1968 film adaptation of *Romeo and Juliet*, directed by Franco Zeffirelli, who played the role of Juliet?

A. Sarah Miles   B. Olivia Hussey   C. Helen Hayes   D. Ali McGraw

9) In the 1969 *Hamlet*, directed by Tony Richardson and starring Nicol Williamson in the title role, who played the role of Ophelia?

A. Julie Harris   B. Tuesday Weld   C. Marianne Faithfull   D. Susan Fleetwood

10) In the 1970 film adaptation of *Julius Caesar*, directed by Stuart Burge, who played the role of Portia?

A. Marsha Mason   B. Anne Bancroft   C. Diana Rigg   D. Jill Bennett

11) In the 1971 film adaptation of *Macbeth*, directed by Roman Polanski, who played the role of Lady Macbeth?

A. Dyan Cannon   B. Barbara Harris   C. Francesca Annis   D. Ellen Burstyn

12) In Jonathan Miller's 1973 *The Merchant of Venice* starring Laurence Olivier as Shylock, who performed as the character Portia?

A. Joan Plowright   B. Louise Purnell   C. Anna Carteret   D. Vanessa Redgrave

13) In Michael Elliot's 1984 *King Lear*, who played the role of Cordelia?

A. Mary Steenburgen   B. Anna Calder-Marshall
C. Terri Garr   D. Sandy Dennis

14) In the 1989 film adaptation of *Henry V*, directed by and starring Kenneth Branagh in the title role, who plays the role of Mistress Quickly?

  A. Judi Dench   B. Rosemary Harris C. Dame Edith Evans D. Jessica Tandy

15) In the 1991 Franco Zeffirelli film adaptation of *Hamlet*, starring Mel Gibson in the title role, who played the role of Ophelia?

  A. Kyra Sedgwick B. Deborah Conway C. Helen Hunt D. Helen Bonham-Carter

16) In Peter Greenaway's *1991 Prospero's Books*, a film adaptation of *The Tempest*, who of the following starred as Miranda?

  A. Christine Lahti   B. Isabelle Pasco
  C. Anjelica Huston   D. Penelope Anne Miller

17) In Kenneth Branagh's 1993 film adaptation of *Much Ado About Nothing*, who stars as Beatrice?

  A. Kate Beckinsale B. Mercedes Ruehl C. Mira Sorvino D. Emma Thompson

18) In the 1995 film adaptation of *Richard III*, directed by Richard Loncraine and starring Sir Ian McKellen in the title role, who played the role of Anne Neville?

  A. Kathleen Quinlan   B. Juliet Binoche
  C. Kristin Scott Thomas   D. Gloria Stuart

19) In Kenneth Branagh's 1996 film adaptation of *Hamlet*, who stars as Ophelia?

  A. Kate Winslet B. Angelina Jolie C. Juliette Binoche D. Emily Watson

20) In Al Pacino's 1996 *Looking for Richard*, who played the role of doomed Anne Neville?

  A. Barbara Everett B. Kate Burton C. Winona Ryder D. Penelope Allen

21) Who starred as Juliet, opposite Leonardo DiCaprio as Romeo, in Baz Luhrmann's 1996 *William Shakespeare's Romeo and Juliet*?

  A. Claire Danes B. Joan Allen C. Toni Collette D. Angelina Jolie

22) In the 1996 film adaptation of *Twelfth Night*, directed by Trevor Nunn, who played the role of Olivia?

  A. Kate Hudson   B. Marisa Tomei
  C. Imogen Stubbs   D. Helena Bonham Carter

23) In director Julie Taymor's 1999 *Titus*, who starred as Tamora, Queen of the Goths?

  A. Pam Grier B. Jessica Lange C. Lainie Kazan D. Diane Ladd

24) In the 1999 film adaptation of *A Midsummer Night's Dream*, directed by Michael Hoffman, who played the role of Titania?

  A. Sophie Marceau B. Michelle Pfeiffer C. Kim Bassinger D. Lindsay Duncan

25) In Michael Almereyda's 2000 *Hamlet*, set on modern-day Wall Street, who played the role of Ophelia?

    A. Julianne Moore   B. Diane Venora   C. Julia Stiles   D. Julie Waters

Quiz 54

Let Her Shine as Gloriously, Part II: Actresses in Shakespearean Film

Did you pass Part I with flying colors? Test your wisdom about more Shakespearean actresses in this quiz.

1) In the 1935 film adaptation of *A Midsummer Night's Dream*, directed by Max Reinhardt and William Dieterle, who played the role of Hermia?

    A. Claudette Colbert   B. Bette Davis
    C. Carole Lombard   D. Olivia de Havilland

2) Which actress played the role of Celia in Paul Czinner's 1936 *As You Like It*?

    A. Gladys George   B. Sophie Stewart   C. Merle Oberon   D. Irene Dunn

3) In the 1936 film adaptation of *Romeo and Juliet*, directed by George Cukor, who starred as Juliet?

    A. Virginia Mayo   B. Merle Oberon   C. Norma Shearer   D. Greta Garbo

4) Who was Mistress Quickly in Olivier's 1944 *Henry V*?

    A. Freda Jackson   B. Gene Tierney   C. Angela Lansbury   D. Ann Blyth

5) Who played the role of Ophelia in Laurence Olivier's 1948 film version of *Hamlet*?

    A. Joan Plowright   B. Vivian Leigh   C. Jean Simmons   D. Dame Edith Evans

6) In Orson Welles's 1952 film adaptation of *Othello*, who played the role of Desdemona?

    A. Geraldine Page   B. Thelma Ritter   C. Anna Magnani   D. Suzanne Cloutier

7) In the 1953 film adaptation of *Julius Caesar*, directed by Joseph Mankiewicz, who played the role of Portia?

    A. Audrey Hepburn   B. Deborah Kerr   C. Vivien Leigh   D. Susan Hayward

8) In Stuart Burge's 1965 adaptation of *Othello*, starring Laurence Olivier in the title role, who played Desdemona?

    A. Judi Dench   B. Joyce Redmond   C. Patricia Neal   D. Maggie Smith

9) In Franco Zeffirelli's 1966 *The Taming of the Shrew*, starring Richard Burton, who played the role of the shrewish Katherina?

    A. Vanessa Redgrave   B. Natalie Wood   C. Elizabeth Taylor   D. Peggy Ashcroft

10) In Franco Zeffirelli's 1966 *The Taming of the Shrew*, starring Richard Burton, who played the role of Bianca?

    A. Lesley Anne Warren   B. Natasha Pyne
    C. Lynn Redgrave   D. Samantha Eggar

11) Who of the following did NOT appear in Peter Hall's 1968 film adaptation of *A Midsummer Night's Dream*?

    A. Judi Dench   B. Barbara Jefford   C. Diana Rigg   D. Estelle Parsons

12) In the 1969 *Hamlet*, directed by Tony Richardson and starring Nicol Williamson in the title role, who played the role of Gertrude?

    A. Judy Parfitt   B. Cloris Leachman   C. Lee Grant   D. Shelley Winters

13) In Peter Brook's 1971 film adaptation of *King Lear*, starring Paul Scofield in the title role, who played Goneril?

    A. Irene Worth   B. Liv Ullmann   C. Louise Fletcher   D. Janet Suzman

14) In the 1972 film adaptation of *Antony and Cleopatra*, directed by Charlton Heston, who starred as Cleopatra, opposite Heston's Antony?

    A. Valerie Perrine   B. Isabelle Adjani   C. Hildegarde Neil   D. Patricia Neal

15) In the 1978 film version of the Royal Shakespeare Company's *Macbeth*, directed by Trevor Nunn and starring Ian McKellen in the title role, who starred as Lady Macbeth?

    A. Vanessa Redgrave   B. Glenda Jackson   C. Ellen Burstyn   D. Judi Dench

16) In the 1989 film adaptation of *Henry V*, directed by and starring Kenneth Branagh in the title role, who plays the role of Katharine, the Princess of France and future wife of Henry V?

    A. Mary Steenburgen   B. Emma Thompson
    C. Anna Paquin   D. Helen Hunt

17) In the 1991 Franco Zeffirelli film adaptation of *Hamlet*, starring Mel Gibson in the title role, who played the role of Queen Gertrude?

    A. Glenda Jackson   B. Mare Winningham

    C. Glenn Close   D. Kathy Bates

18) In Kenneth Branagh's 1993 film adaptation of *Much Ado About Nothing*, who stars as Hero?

    A. Juliette Binoche   B. Marisa Tomei   C. Julia Stiles   D. Kate Beckinsale

19) In the 1995 film adaptation of *Othello*, directed by Oliver Parker and starring Laurence Fishburne in the title role, who played the role of Desdemona?

    A. Cate Blanchett   B. Irene Jacob   C. Joan Cusack   D. Julianne Moore

20) In the 1995 film adaptation of *Richard III*, directed by Richard Lancraine and starring Sir Ian McKellen in the title role, who played the role of Queen Elizabeth?

    A. Meryl Streep   B. Jennifer Tilly   C. Anna Paquin   D. Annette Bening

21) In the 1996 film adaptation of *Twelfth Night*, directed by Trevor Nunn, who played the role of Viola?

    A. Imogen Stubbs   B. Imelda Staunton   C. Julia Stiles   D. Gwyneth Paltrow

22) Who played Queen Gertrude in Kenneth Branagh's 1996 *Hamlet*?

    A. Maggie Smith   B. Julie Christie   C. Faye Dunaway   D. Ann-Margaret

23) In director Julie Taymor's 1999 *Titus*, who starred as Lavinia, the mutilated daughter of Titus?

    A. Geraldine McEwan   B. Anna Patrick   C. Laura Fraser   D. Anna Paquin

24) In the 1999 film adaptation of *A Midsummer Night's Dream*, directed by Michael Hoffman, what role was played by Calista Flockhart?

    A. Puck   B. Hermia   C. Helena   D. Hippolyta

25) In Kenneth Branagh's 2000 *Love's Labor's Lost*, she played the role of the Princess of France.

    A. Alicia Silverstone   B. Stefania Rocca   C. Emily Mortimer   D. Minnie Driver

Quiz 55

Derived From Honorable Loins: Shakespearean Film Offshoots

The works of Shakespeare have inspired many interesting, and in some cases, rather far-fetched films. Can you identify the offshoots of Shakespeare's plays?

1) Directed by Patrick McGoohan and starring Richie Havens, *Catch My Soul: Santa Fe Satan* (1973) is a rock opera adaptation of which of Shakespeare's plays?

    A. *Titus Andronicus*　　　B. *Macbeth*　　　C. *Measure for Measure*　　　D. *Othello*

2) Director William Wellman's western *Yellow Sky* (1948) starring Gregory Peck, Anne Baxter, and Richard Widmark, was an adaptation of which Shakespeare play?

    A. *Cymbeline*　　　B. *Pericles*　　　C. *Antony and Cleopatra*　　　D. *The Tempest*

3) Which of Shakespeare's plays served as a source of the 1990's film, *10 Things I Hate About You?*

    A. *The Comedy of Errors*　　　　　　B. *A Midsummer Night's Dream*
    C. *The Taming of the Shrew*　　　　　D. *The Two Gentlemen of Verona*

4) The science fiction movie classic *Forbidden Planet*, directed by Fred McLeod Wilcox and starring Walter Pidgeon, Anne Francis, and Leslie Neilson, is an adaptation of which play?

    A. *The Tempest*　　B. *Troilus and Cressida*　　C. *Antony and Cleopatra*　　D. *Cymbeline*

5) The Francis Ford Coppola film *The Godfather, Part III* (1990) is a cinematic offshoot of which of Shakespeare's plays?

    A. *Henry V*　　　B. *King Lear*　　　C. *Hamlet*　　　D. *Othello*

6) The 1989 film *Men of Respect*, directed by William Reilly and starring John Turturro, Peter Boyle, and Rod Steiger, is influenced by which play?

    A. *King Lear*　　　B. *Henry VIII*　　　C. *Julius Caesar*　　　D. *Macbeth*

7) In Kenneth Branagh's 1996 *A Midwinter's Tale* (a.k.a. *In the Bleak Midwinter*), an out-of-work actor struggles to save an old church by mounting a production of which play?

    A. *A Midsummer Night's Dream*　　　B. *Hamlet*
    C. *The Winter's Tale*　　　　　　　　D. *Cymbeline*

8) The 1956 *Jubal*, starring Glenn Ford, Ernest Borginine, and Rod Steiger, is a Western reworking of which play?

    A. *Othello*　　　B. *Richard II*　　　C. *Richard III*　　　D. *Hamlet*

9) The 1988 film *Big Business*, starring Bette Midler and Lily Tomlin, is influenced by which play?

A. *As You Like It*
C. *All's Well That Ends Well*

B. *Twelfth Night*
D. *The Comedy of Errors*

10) *Broken Lance* (1954), a western directed by Edward Dmytryk and starring Spencer Tracy, Robert Wagner, and Richard Widmark, follows the basic plot of which play?

A. *King Lear*   B. *Othello*   C. *Macbeth*   D. *Julius Caesar*

11) Which of the following films is a modernization of the two Henry IV plays?

A. *Carnival*   B. *Where the Heart Is*   C. *My Own Private Idaho*   D. *L.A. Story*

12) Disney's *The Lion King* is a cinematic offshoot of which play?

A. *Hamlet*   B. *King Lear*   C. *King John*   D. *Henry V*

13) The 1959 film *An Honourable Murder* is a modernization of which play?

A. *Macbeth*   B. *Titus Andronicus*   C. *Othello*   D. *Julius Caesar*

14) Set in the farmlands of the American Midwest and starring Michelle Pfeiffer, Jessica Lange, and Jason Robards, Jocelyn Moorhouse's 1997 *A Thousand Acres* is a modern adaptation of which play?

A. *Cymbeline*   B. *The Winter's Tale*   C. *As You Like It*   D. *King Lear*

15) *All Night Long* (1961), starring Richard Attenborough and Patrick McGoohan, was set in a London jazz club and featured jazz greats Dave Brubek, Charlie Mingus, and many others. This film was directed by Basil Dearden and was a modernization of which play?

A. *Twelfth Night*   B. *As You Like It*   C. *Othello*   D. *Cymbeline*

16) In *The Dresser*, directed by Peter Yates, Albert Finney stars as the mentally exhausted leader of a Shakespeare company, in wartime Britain, performing which play?

A. *Coriolanus*   B. *Henry V*   C. *King Lear*   D. *1 Henry IV*

17) *King Lear* (1987), directed by Jean-Luc Godard, was a very unique take on Shakespeare's tragedy. It starred Burgess Meredith as Don Learo, Woody Allen as the Fool, and Norman Mailer as the Great Writer. Who starred as William Shakespeare, Jr. V in this film?

A. Tom Courtney   B. Peter Sellars   C. Alec Guiness   D. Peter Finch

18) Written and directed by Tom Stoppard, *Rosencrantz and Guildenstern Are Dead* (1990) shows the point of view of the two title characters (from Shakespeare's *Hamlet*). Tim Roth starred as Rosencrantz. Who starred as Guildenstern?

A. Gary Oldman   B. Richard Dreyfuss   C. Dustin Hoffman   D. Jeremy Irons

19) In Serbian and Polish with English subtitles, *Fury is a Woman* (1961) is an offshoot of which play?

A. *The Taming of the Shrew*
C. *King Lear*

B. *Macbeth*
D. *Much Ado About Nothing*

20) *Strange Illusion* (1945) is director Edgar G. Ulmer's attempt to turn which of Shakespeare's plays into *film noir*?

A. *Macbeth*   B. *Cymbeline*   C. *Hamlet*   D. *Timon of Athens*

Quiz 56

The Two Hours' Traffic of Our Stage: Shakespeare on the Stage

This quiz deals with just a few of the countless performances of Shakespeare, the productions inspired by his works, and the many wonderful actors and actresses that have performed his memorable roles on the stages of theaters throughout the world.

1) Which play was the source for the 1938 Rodgers and Hart musical *The Boys From Syracuse*?

A. *As You Like It*   B. *The Comedy of Errors*
C. *Twelfth Night*   D. *The Two Gentlemen of Verona*

2) *Hamlet*, directed by John Gielgud, was the longest-running Shakespeare play on Broadway. Who starred as Hamlet?

A. Laurence Olivier   B. John Gielgud
C. Richard Burton   D. Ralph Richardson

3) *West Side Story* became a smash Broadway hit in 1957. Who starred in the role of Maria?

A. Natalie Wood   B. Rita Moreno   C. Chita Rivera   D. Carol Lawrence

4) Who wrote the music and lyrics for *West Side Story*?

A. Leonard Bernstein and Stephen Sondheim
B. Danny Apolinar and Hal Hester
C. Richard Rodgers and Lorenz Hart
D. Andrew Lloyd Webber and Tim Rice

5) While John Gielgud and Laurence Olivier alternated in the roles of Romeo and Mercutio in the 1935 production of *Romeo and Juliet* at the New Theatre, who played the role of Juliet?

A. Judith Anderson   B. Maggie Smith   C. Judi Dench   D. Peggy Ashcroft

6) Edwin Booth, the leading American actor of his day, first won acclaim for which Shakespearean role?

A. Richard III   B. Iago   C. Iachimo   D. Macbeth

7) In 1978, in New York City's Delacorte Theater in Central Park, Raul Julia was cast in the role of Petruchio opposite which actress's Kate in *The Taming of the Shrew*?

A. Blythe Danner   B. Judi Dench   C. Meryl Streep   D. Sinead Cusack

8) Which American actor, director, and producer of stage and film directed a controversial *Macbeth* in 1936, with an all-black cast, that was set in Haiti and featured a gigantic mask as Banquo's ghost?

    A. Orson Welles   B. Cecil B. DeMille   C. John Gielgud   D. Laurence Olivier

9) Who is believed by most to be the first black actor to play the role of Othello?

    A. James Earl Jones   B. Paul Robeson   C. Sidney Poiter   D. Ira Aldridge

10) Which accomplished Shakespearean actress achieved stardom at age 23, playing Desdemona opposite Paul Robeson's Othello?

    A. Judith Anderson   B. Peggy Ashcroft   C. Vivien Leigh   D. Katherine Cornell

11) Which play has a reputation, especially among theater people, for being cursed?

    A. *Titus Andronicus*   B. *Hamlet*   C. *Macbeth*   D. *Othello*

12) What famous musician played the role of Bottom in *Swingin' the Dream*, a 1939 Broadway musical that was a jazz adaptation of *A Midsummer Night's Dream*?

    A. Louis Armstrong   B. Muddy Waters   C. Chick Webb   D. Jelly Roll Morton

13) Renowned 18th-century actor David Garrick made his proper London debut in October 1741 in the role of which character?

    A. Hamlet   B. Richard III   C. Prince Hal   D. Othello

14) A leading Shakespearean actor and producer of the latter 19th century, who was the first actor to be knighted?

    A. Edmund Kean   B. Henry Irving   C. Maurice Evans   D. Edwin Booth

15) At age 14, Laurence Olivier won rave reviews for playing which role?

    A. Prince Arthur in *King John*   B. Rosalind in *As You Like It*
    C. Fleance in *Macbeth*   D. Katherina in *The Taming of the Shrew*

16) In a 1963 production in Stratford, Ontario, Duke Ellington wrote a score for which play?

    A. *Timon of Athens*   B. *Troilus and Cressida*
    C. *All's Well That Ends Well*   D. *The Comedy of Errors*

17) About which famous actor did Samuel Taylor Coleridge make this statement: "to see him act, is like reading Shakespeare by flashes of lightning"?

    A. J.P. Kemble   B. Colley Cibber   C. Edmund Kean   D. Edwin Booth

18) The play *Your Own Thing* is a musical inspired by which of Shakespeare's plays?

    A. *Love's Labor's Lost*   B. *The Taming of the Shrew*
    C. *Twelfth Night*   D. *Measure for Measure*

19) Billed as "the play Shakespeare would have finished if he'd had the time," *The Popular Mechanicals* is derived from which of Shakespeare's plays?

    A. *The Two Noble Kinsmen*   B. *A Midsummer Night's Dream*
    C. *The Two Gentlemen of Verona*   D. *Henry IV, Part One*

20) Which famous actress's first Shakespearean performance was at age 8, in the role of the little doomed prince in *The Winter's Tale*?

    A. Judi Dench   B. Ellen Terry   C. Judith Anderson   D. Peggy Ashcroft

21) Which play is the source of Cole Porter's musical *Kiss Me, Kate* which opened at the New Century Theatre on December 30, 1948, and ran for 1,070 performances?

    A. *The Taming of the Shrew*   B. *All's Well That Ends Well*
    C. *Henry V*   D. *As You Like It*

22) While playing the role of Hamlet, which actor used a specially designed wig that used hydraulics to make the hair stand on end in terror at the appearance of the ghost?

    A. Henry Irving   B. Colley Cibber   C. Charles Kemble   D. David Garrick

23) The famous 18th-century Irish actor Charles Macklin was most noted for his portrayal of which Shakespearean character?

    A. Titus Andronicus   B. Nick Bottom   C. Henry V   D. Shylock

24) Who was the world-famous novelist prominent in the fund-raising project to restore Shakespeare's birthplace? (He even played the role of Shallow, in a production of *The Merry Wives of Windsor*, to raise money for the project.)

    A. Thomas Hardy   B. Mark Twain
    C. Charles Dickens   D. Nathaniel Hawthorne

25) He is the American theatrical producer who was the founder of the New York Shakespeare Festival.

    A. Sam Wanamaker   B. Joseph Papp   C. Trevor Nunn   D. Orson Welles

Quiz 57

Stars Give Light to Thy Fair Way!: Shakespeare and Star Trek

Gene Roddenberry and the other series creators, screenwriters, and actors of the many Star Trek series have displayed a love for Shakespeare by using quotes from his works as titles and in the various episodes. Test your knowledge of Shakespeare in outer space by answering the following questions about the original *Star Trek* series (OST), *Star Trek: The Next Generation* (NG), *Deep Space Nine* (DS9), *Voyager*, and the *Star Trek* full length films.

1) Which actor from the original series was an understudy for Christopher Plummer in the title role of *Henry V* in a Stratford (Canada) production and won critical acclaim for his portrayal of the role when Plummer became ill?

    A. William Shatner　　　　　　B Leonard Nimoy
    C. James Doohan　　　　　　　D. DeForest Kelley

2) Which actor from the *Next Generation* series was a performing member of the Royal Shakespeare Company?

    A. Jonathan Frakes　　B. John de Lancie　　C. Michael Dorn　　　D. Patrick Stewart

3) In the film *Star Trek IV: The Voyage Home*, McCoy quotes a line from which play when he exclaims, "Angels and ministers of grace, defend us"?

    A. *Hamlet*　　　　B. *Macbeth*　　　　C. *Coriolanus*　　　　D. *King Lear*

4) The title of the OST episode #11, "Dagger of the Mind," is taken from which of Shakespeare's plays?

    A. *Hamlet*　　　B. *Romeo & Juliet*　　C. *Macbeth*　　　D. *Titus*

5) The title of the OST episode #13, "The Conscience of the King," is taken from which of Shakespeare's plays?

    A. *Richard III*　　B. *Hamlet*　　　C. *Henry V*　　　D. *King Lear*

6) In OST episode #13, "The Conscience of the King," the episode opens with an acting troupe named the Karidian Company of Actors performing an Arcturian version of which of Shakespeare's plays?

    A. *The Comedy of Errors*　B. *Richard II*　C. *Macbeth*　　　　D. *The Tempest*

7) The title of OST episode #68, "Wink of an Eye," is taken from the following Shakespearean passage: "every wink of an eye some new grace will be born." In which play will you find this statement?

    A. *Romeo and Juliet*　　B. *Richard III*　　C. *Henry IV, Part One*　D. *The Winter's Tale*

8) In OST episode #71, "Whom Gods Destroy," a character named Marta (who is a patient in a mental institution) quotes and claims to have written which of Shakespeare's sonnets?

    A. "Shall I Compare Thee to a Summer's Day?" (#18)
    B. "When In Disgrace With Fortune and Men's Eyes" (#29)
    C. "So Are You to My Thoughts as Food to Life" (#75)
    D. "My Mistress' Eyes Are Nothing Like the Sun" (#130)

9) The title of the OST episode #78, "All Our Yesterdays," is taken from which play?

    A. *Hamlet*   B. *Macbeth*   C. *King Lear*   D. *Othello*

10) The plot of the original *Star Trek* episode *Elaan of Troyius* most closely resembles the plot of which play?

    A. *Much Ado About Nothing*   B. *The Taming of the Shrew*
    C. *The Tempest*   D. *Twelfth Night*

11) In the NG episode #3, "The Naked Now," the android Data *loosely* quotes from *The Merchant of Venice*. Which of the following is the word that Data used to complete the quote: "If you prick us do we not _____"?

    A. bleed   B. cry   C. malfunction   D. leak

12) In the NG episode #58, "The Defector," Data performs a scene on the holodeck from which of Shakespeare's plays?

    A. The scene in *King Lear* where Lear wanders in the storm
    B. The scene in *The Tempest* where Prospero conjures the storm that causes a shipwreck
    C. The scene in *Henry V* where Henry mingles with troops before the battle of Agincourt
    D. The scene in *Richard III* where Richard is defeated at the Battle of Bosworth Field

13) The title of NG episode #65 "The Sins of the Fathers" is taken from which play?

    A. *King Lear*   B. *Titus Andronicus*
    C. *The Merchant of Venice*   D. *Henry IV, Part Two*

14) In the NG episode #70, "The Most Toys," Picard believes that Data is dead and reads from Shakespeare when he says, "'A was a man, take him for all in all,/ I shall not look upon his like again." In which play will you find this quote?

    A. *Hamlet*   B. *Othello*   C. *Coriolanus*   D. *King Lear*

15) In NG episode #72, "Ménage a Troi," Captain Picard must show himself as the devoted lover of Lwaxana Troi, and to do so, he quotes numerous lines from the works of Shakespeare, one of which is "When I have plucked thy rose,/ I cannot give it vital growth again,/ It needs must wither." From which work is this statement taken?

    A. *Romeo and Juliet*   B. *Othello*
    C. *The Taming of the Shrew*   D. *Love's Labor's Lost*

16) In the NG episode "Time's Arrow" (#126-127), Picard and his crew tell their San Francisco landlady they are actors rehearsing (and they later rehearse a scene) for which play?

   A. *The Two Gentlemen of Verona*   B. *The Comedy of Errors*
   C. *A Midsummer Night's Dream*   D. *Much Ado About Nothing*

17) In the beginning of the NG episode "Emergence" (#175), Data is prevented from performing the final scene of a play when he is interrupted by the Orient Express. Which play is he performing? (Hint: In both the play and the episode there is an emphasis on "strange new world").

   A. *As You Like It*   B. *Timon of Athens*   C. *The Winter's Tale*   D. *The Tempest*

18) The title of DS9 episode #157, "Once More Into the Breach," is take from which play?

   A. *Richard III*   B. *King John*   C. *Henry IV, Part One*   D. *Henry V*

19) The title of DS9 episode #60, "Heart of Stone," is take from which play?

   A. *As You Like It*   B. *Twelfth Night*   C. *Macbeth*   D. *Richard II*

20) The title of Voyager episode #80, "Mortal Coil," is take from which play?

   A. *Hamlet*   B. *Othello*   C. *The Tempest*   D. *Richard III*

21) The title of the OST movie, *Star Trek VI: The Undiscovered Country*, is taken from which play?

   A. *The Merchant of Venice*   B. *Othello*   C. *Hamlet*   D. *Macbeth*

In the OST movie *Star Trek VI: The Undiscovered Country*, Klingon General Chang (played by the accomplished Shakespearean actor Christopher Plummer) loves to quote Shakespeare, and he utters many of them throughout the film. For the following four questions, match each of Chang's quotes with the play where you will find it.

22) "Parting is such sweet sorrow."   A. *Hamlet*

23) "Cry 'havoc' and let slip the dogs of war."   B. *Julius Caesar*

24) "How long will a man lie in space ere he rot?" (paraphrase)   C. *Richard II*

25) "Let us sit upon the ground   D. *Romeo and Juliet*
    And tell sad stories of the death of kings."

Quiz 58

O, for a Muse of Fire: Titles of Other Works Derived From Shakespeare

   Many writers throughout the world have been greatly influenced by the works of Shakespeare, and as a result, they have quoted him, particularly in the titles they have chosen. Below you will find a short quote from one of Shakespeare's works. From the quote, identify the phrase that has been used as a title of another work. If you are really good, identify the author, as well. (More than one author may have chosen a title from the passage shown, and more than one author may have used the same quote for a title, so other answers than those listed in the answer key may be possible.)

1) "Life is as tedious as a twice told tale
   Vexing the dull ear of a drowsy man."
   King John (3.4.108)

2) "The ears are senseless that should give us hearing,
   To tell him his commandment is fulfilled,
   That Rosencrantz and Guildenstern are dead."
   Hamlet (5.2.369)

3) "By the pricking of my thumbs,
   Something wicked this way comes."
   Macbeth (4.1.45)

4) "I must comfort the weaker vessel, as doublet
   and hose ought to show itself courageous to
   petticoat."
   As You Like It (2.4.5)

5) "And your large speeches may your deeds approve,
   That good effects may spring from words of love."
   King Lear (1.1.184)

6) "Now is the winter of our discontent
   Made glorious summer by this son of York."
   Richard III (1.1.1)

7) "'Tis not so deep as a well, nor so wide as a church door; but 'tis enough, 'twill serve."
   Romeo and Juliet (3.1.96)

8) "O, wonder!
   How many goodly creatures are there here!
   How beauteous mankind is! O brave new world,
   That has such people in't!"
   The Tempest (5.1.181)

9) "O my lords,
   As you are great, be pitifully good:
   Who cannot condemn rashness in cold blood?"
   Timon of Athens (3.5.51)

10) "Dost thou think, because thou art virtuous, there shall be no more cakes and ale?"
   Twelfth Night (2.3.114)

11) "The quality of mercy is not strained.
   It droppeth as the gentle rain from heaven
   Upon the place beneath."
   The Merchant of Venice (4.1.184)

12) "My tables,—meet it is I set it down,
   That one may smile, and smile, and be a villain."
   Hamlet (1.5.107)

13) "The moon is down, I have not heard the clock."
   Macbeth (2.1.2)

14) "Under the greenwood tree,
   Who loves to lie with me,
   And turn his merry note
   Unto the sweet bird's throat."
   As You Like It (2.5.1)

15) "I will get Peter Quince to write a ballad of this dream; it shall be called Bottom's
   Dream, because it hath no bottom."
   A Midsummer Night's Dream (4.1.214)

16) CLEOPATRA: I'll set a bourn how far to be beloved.
   MARK ANTONY: Then must thou needs find out new heaven, new earth.
   Antony and Cleopatra (1.1.16)

17) "Come away, come away, death,
   And in sad cypress let me be laid;
   Fly away, fly away, breath;
   I am slain by a fair cruel maid."
   Twelfth Night (2.4.51)

18) "My mistress' eyes are nothing like the sun.
   Coral is far more red than her lips' red;
   If snow be white, why then her breasts are dun;
   If hairs be wires, black wires grow on her head."
   "Sonnet 130"

19) "The tongues of mocking wenches are as keen
     As is the razor's edge invisible,
     Cutting a smaller hair than may be seen,
     Above the sense of sense."
     Love's Labor's Lost (5.2.256)

20) "It is a tale
     Told by an idiot, full of sound and fury,
     Signifying nothing."
     Macbeth (5.5.26)

Quiz 59

An Advocate for an Imposter!: Is the Quote Shakespeare or Someone Else?

The works of Shakespeare have produced many memorable quotes and phrases. However, as a result of his fame, Shakespeare often receives credit for statements that were made by others. Can you pick out the Shakespearean from the "imposters"? And can you identify the source of the non-Shakespeare quotes? (Hint: There are 13 by Shakespeare and the rest from other sources.)

1) "Authority forgets a dying king."

2) "To reign is worth ambition though in hell;
    Better to reign in hell than serve in heaven."

3) "Small cheer and great welcome makes a merry feast."

4) "He lives in fame that died in virtue's cause."

5) "I like not fair terms and a villain's mind."

6) "Dost thou love life? Then squander not time; for that's the stuff life is made of."

7) "Things without all remedy
    Should be without regard: what's done is done."

8) "Tell me thy company, and I'll tell thee what thou art."

9) "Striving to better, oft we mar what's well."

10) "Oh, what a tangled web we weave
     When first we practice to deceive."

11) "Revenge should have no bounds."

12) "Was this the face that launched a thousand ships,
     And burnt the topless towers of Ilium?"

13) "How hard it is to hide the sparks of nature!"

14) "How poor are they that have not patience!
     What wound did ever heal but by degrees?"

15) "Out, out, brief candle!"

16) "Never send to know for whom the bell tolls; it tolls for thee."

17) "None but the brave deserves the fair."

18) "Knowledge is power."

19) "Men have died from time to time, and worms have eaten them, but not for love."

20) "Who steals my purse steals trash."

21) "To err is human, to forgive divine."

22) "These violent delights have violent ends."

23) "'Tis true we are in great danger;
     The greater therefore should our courage be."

24) "Tender is the night."

25) "It is a far, far better thing that I do, than I have ever done; it is a far, far better rest
     that I go to, than I have ever known."

Quiz 60

It May Be You Have Mistaken Him: Is It Shakespeare or the Bible?

As mentioned in the previous quiz, Shakespeare's fame has resulted in confusing his statements with those that originated in other sources. Can you tell which of the following statements originated from Shakespeare and which originated from the Bible? (Hint: There are 13 by Shakespeare, and the others are from the Bible.)

1) "No beast so fierce but knows some touch of pity."

2) "Great men are not always wise."

3) "As he thinketh in his heart, so he is."

4) "Much is the force of heaven-bred poesy."

5) "'Tis not enough to help the feeble up,
But to support him after."

6) "What is the city but the people?"

7) "Where no law is, there is no transgression."

8) "It is an heretic that makes the fire, not she which burns in't."

9) "It is not enough to speak, but to speak true."

10) "Better is a poor and a wise child than an old and foolish king."

11) "Consider the lilies of the field, how they grow; they toil not, neither do they spin."

12) "I must be cruel, only to be kind."

13) "They have sown the wind, and they shall reap the whirlwind."

14) "Every subject's duty is the king's; but every subject's soul is his own."

15) "Wisdom and goodness to the vile seem vile."

16) "Greater love hath no man than this, that a man lay down his life for his friends."

17) "Physician, heal thyself."

18) "Death hath no more dominion over him."

19) "He that is proud eats up himself; pride is his own glass, his own trumpet, his own chronicle."

20) "Many are called, but few are chosen."

21) "Light, seeking light, doth light of light beguile."

22) "Let us eat and drink; for tomorrow we shall die."

23) "'Tis the mind that makes the body rich."

24) "Many waters cannot quench love, neither can the floods drown it."

25) "Not all the water in the rough rude sea
Can wash the balm from an anointed king."

Quiz 61

Forgive the Comment That My Passion Made:
Other Writers' Comments About Shakespeare

Shakespeare's fame has caused many people to make comments about him, and not all are flattering. Here you will find comments about Shakespeare from his peers, his fellow writers. Selecting from the list of authors provided, match the statement with the writer who expressed it. Each name may be used only once.

Matthew Arnold	T.S. Eliot	John Keats	Mickey Spillane
James Barrie	Robert Graves	D.H. Lawrence	Leo Tolstoy
Samuel Coleridge	Ben Jonson	Henry Miller	Mark Twain
Charles Dickens	William Hazlitt	Samuel Pepys	Voltaire
John Dryden	Samuel Johnson	George Bernard Shaw	Virginia Woolf

1) "He was not of an age, but for all time!"

2) "Shakespeare is a drunken savage with some imagination whose plays can please only in London and Canada."

3) "Many of his words, and more than a few of his phrases, are scarce intelligible...and he often obscures his meaning by his words."

4) "If the public likes you, you're good. Shakespeare was a common down-to-earth writer in his day."

5) This writer stated that *Hamlet* was "certainly an artistic failure."

6) "To know the force of human genius we should read Shakespeare; to see the insignificance of human learning we may study his commentators."

7) "I know not, sir, whether Bacon wrote the works of Shakespeare, but if he did not it seems to me that he missed the opportunity of his life."

8) "Even the less known plays are written at a speed that is quicker than anybody else's quickest...Why then should anyone else attempt to write?"

9) "The life of Shakespeare is a fine mystery, and I tremble every day lest something should turn up."

10) This writer thought that A *Midsummer Night's Dream* was "the most insipid ridiculous play that I ever saw in my life."

11) "His drama is the mirror of life."

12) "People simply do not read Shakespeare any more, nor the Bible either. They read 'about' Shakespeare. The critical literature that has built up about his name and works is vastly more fruitful and stimulating than Shakespeare himself."

13) "With the single exception of Homer, there is no eminent writer, not even Sir Walter Scott, whom I despise as entirely as I despise Shakespeare when I measure up my mind against his. It would be a positive relief to dig him up and throw stones at him."

14) "I believe the souls of 500 Sir Isaac Newtons would go to the making up of a Shakespeare or a Milton."

15) This writer found Shakespeare "absurd, incomprehensible, and inartistic" and was amused at his tragic endings where "half a dozen corpses" would be "dragged out by the legs."

16) "I keep saying Shakespeare, Shakespeare, you are as obscure as life is."

17) "Shakespeare led a life of allegory; his works are the comments on it."

18) "When I read Shakespeare I am struck with wonder that such trivial people should muse and thunder in such lovely language...And Hamlet—how boring, how boring to live with so mean and self-conscious blowing and snoring."

19) "The remarkable thing about Shakespeare is that he really is very good, in spite of all the people who say he is very good."

20) This writer warned his wife not to read *Gulliver's Travels*, *Don Quixote*, or Shakespeare's plays, because they contained "grossness."

Quiz 62

All the Peers Are Here at Hand:
Theatrical and Literary Contemporaries of Shakespeare

In the following list you will find theatrical and literary contemporaries of Shakespeare. Can you match the person who best fits each description?

Edward Alleyn	Henry Condell	Henry Cary	Christopher Marlowe
Robert Armin	John Fletcher	Ben Jonson	Sir Philip Sidney
Francis Bacon	John Heminges	William Kempe	Edmund Spenser
Francis Beaumont	Philip Henslowe	Thomas Kyd	Edmund Tilney
Richard Burbage	Raphael Holinshed	Francis Langley	John Webster

1) He was a theatrical entrepreneur and owner of the Rose Theatre. He left behind an account book, referred to as the *Diary*, which is responsible for much of what is known about the theater of Shakespeare's time.

2) He was part owner of the Globe Theatre and the lead actor in Shakespeare's company who first played some of Shakespeare's greatest roles: Hamlet, Macbeth, and many more.

3) He was a comic actor in Shakespeare's company (he left the company in 1599) who specialized in improvisation, physical clowning, dancing, and the playing of musical instruments. He was also famous for performing a morris dance from London to Norwich, a distance of nearly 100 miles.

4) His function as Master of the Revels (1579–1610) was to provide entertainment for the court, license plays, and to serve as a government censor.

5) Along with being a celebrated playwright in his own right, he coauthored three plays with Shakespeare: *Henry VIII*, *The Two Noble Kinsmen*, and the lost *Cardenio*.

6) He was the author of such plays as *Every Man in His Humour*, *Volpone*, and *The Alchemist*. He also wrote a memorial poem about Shakespeare for The First Folio.

7) He was a fellow acting company member and friend of Shakespeare who teamed with John Heminges to produce The First Folio in 1623.

8) He was the author of an influential revenge tragedy, *The Spanish Tragedy*, and a lost play, *Ur-Hamlet*, which was probably a source for Shakespeare's *Hamlet*.

9) He was a Jacobean dramatist famous for his bloody tragedies, the two most famous of which are *The Duchess of Malfi* and *The White Devil*.

10) He was a theatrical entrepreneur and the builder and owner of the Swan Theatre.

11) He was a poet and author of *The Faerie Queene*, which celebrated the reign of Queen Elizabeth and influenced Shakespeare.

12) He teamed with John Fletcher to form a highly successful playwriting team, in the early Jacobean period, that produced 15 plays. His most notable works are *The Knight of the Burning Pestle* (1608) and *Philaster* (1610).

13) He was the author of *Chronicles of England, Scotland, and Ireland* which served as an invaluable source for the writers of the Elizabethan and Jacobean periods. This work was a source for Shakespeare's *Macbeth*, *King Lear*, *Cymbeline*, and the English history plays.

14) He was the Lord Chamberlain from 1583 until his death in 1596. He assumed patronage of Shakespeare's company (at the time, Derby's Men), and the company was renamed the Chamberlain's Men at that time.

15) He was the lead actor in the Lord Admiral's Men—the chief rival to Shakespeare's company—and performed some of Christopher Marlowe's major roles.

16) His *Arcadia* (published 1590) and *Asptrophel and Stella* (published 1591) influenced the plays and sonnets of Shakespeare. He was killed while serving in the Low Countries in 1586.

17) He was an actor who specialized in the more sophisticated comic roles such as Touchstone, Feste, and the Fool in *King Lear*.

18) He was an influential playwright who was the author of *Tamburlaine*, (1587), *The Jew of Malta* (1589), *Dr. Faustus* (1592), and *Edward II* (1592). He was stabbed to death under mysterious circumstances in 1592 at the age of 29.

19) He was a fellow acting company member and friend of Shakespeare who became the business manager for the company.

20) He is considered to be the greatest English philosopher of the Renaissance; his most highly regarded literary achievement is the *Essays*.

Quiz 63

Art Thou Base, Common and Popular?: Shakespeare in Pop Culture

The popularity of his work is not just a fad; Shakespeare is part of us. References to his works and his name are permanently woven into our culture—in advertising, films, television programs, cartoons, newspapers, book titles, music, and magazines. Type his name into an Internet auction site and you will find a seemingly endless variety of Shakespeare paraphernalia such as bottle openers, ties, mugs, stamps, statues, T-shirts, and bookmarks. In the following questions, you will find just a few examples of his wide appeal and influence.

1) One of America's popular TV series starred a nonhuman character, but few realize that this character originated in a series of 28 short stories in which the character would recite Shakespeare and speak Latin. What was the name of the character?

    A. My Mother the Car   B. Bugs Bunny   C. Scooby Doo   D. Mr. Ed

2) In which superhero's study was a bust of Shakespeare with a hinged head that, when pulled back, revealed a secret button?

    A. Superman   B. Batman   C. Spiderman   D. The Shadow

3) *Macbird!*, a play by Barbara Garson, is a parody of *Macbeth* and is also a spoof on the political career of which American President?

    A. Richard Nixon   B. Dwight Eisenhower
    C. Lyndon Johnson   D. Harry Truman

4) In the ABC TV series *Moonlighting*, which starred Cybill Shepherd and Bruce Willis, an episode titled "Atomic Shakespeare" (November 25, 1986) spoofed which of Shakespeare's plays?

    A. *The Comedy of Errors*
    B. *A Midsummer Night's Dream*
    C. *The Taming of the Shrew*
    D. *Love's Labor's Lost*

5) In an episode of *Gilligan's Island* titled "The Producers" (October 3, 1966), the castaways perform a musical version of which of Shakespeare's plays?

    A. *Hamlet*
    B. *King Lear*
    C. *Macbeth*
    D. *Romeo and Juliet*

6) Who is the creator of the *Sandman* comic book series that features the supernatural Lord Morpheus, who makes a Faustian bargain with William Shakespeare that is the focus of two of his tales: "A Midsummer Night's Dream" and "The Tempest"?

    A. Geoff Johns   B. Brian Azzarello   C. Brian Michael Bendis   D. Neil Gaiman

7) Which is an actual title of a *Simpsons* episode?

    A. *MacBart*   B. *Much Apu About Nothing*
    C. *Lisa's Labor's Lost*   D. *All's Well That Ends Krusty*

8) He was the host for the 1979 PBS series *Meeting of Minds*, which brought together Hamlet, Othello, Romeo, Shakespeare, and the Dark Lady of the Sonnets for a discussion on the nature of love.

    A. Walter Cronkite B. Dick Cavitt   C. Alistair Cooke   D. Steve Allen

9) In "Shakespeare's Ghost Writer," published in *Superman Comics* in 1947, Clark Kent, Lois Lane, and Jimmy Olsen wind up in Shakespeare's England. While there, Superman ghostwrites which play for the real Shakespeare?

    A. *Macbeth*   B. *Hamlet*   C. *Richard III*   D. *Henry V*

10) In which children's show will you find a character named William Shakespeare Wolf?

    A. Yogi Bear   B. Sesame Street
    C. Beany and Cecil   D. Electric Company

11) In an episode of "Peabody's Improbable History" from *The Adventures of Rocky and Bullwinkle* (February 1962), Sherman and Mr. Peabody travel to Shakespeare's time when he is struggling with writer's block over a play tentatively titled "Romeo and Zelda." During the episode, he is accused by another author of stealing his work. Which author makes this accusation?

    A. Christopher Marlowe   B. Francis Bacon
    C. Earl of Oxford   D. Sir Walter Raleigh

12) In episode #79 of *The Cosby Show* (October 22, 1987), titled "Shakespeare," Theo Huxtable and Cockroach are studying Shakespeare for a school assignment while a professor friend (played by Christopher Plummer) visits the family. Lines from which play are performed?

    A. *Julius Caesar*   B. *Othello*
    C. *The Comedy of Errors*   D. *Much Ado About Nothing*

13) In which of the following films does Kevin Costner play a character who is called Shakespeare and who acts out scenes from *Macbeth*?

    A. *Waterworld* (1995)   B. *A Perfect World* (1993)
    C. *The Postman* (1997)   D. *No Way Out* (1987)

14) The 1983 film *Strange Brew*, starring Rick Moranis and Dave Thomas, is a loose (*very* loose) spin-off of which of Shakespeare's plays?

    A. *Macbeth*   B. *Richard III*
    C. *A Midsummer Night's Dream*   D. *Hamlet*

15) In the "Brush Up Your Shakespeare" episode (September 15, 1973) of *Goober and the Ghost Chasers*, the Partridge kids are forced to cancel a concert when the ghost of which Shakespearean character haunts the hall?

    A. Hamlet's father   B. Hamlet   C. Falstaff   D. Macbeth

16) In episodes #65 and #66 of the original *Batman* TV series, starring Adam West as Batman and Burt Ward as Robin, the caped crusaders encounter a super-criminal played by the renowned Shakespearean actor Maurice Evans, and the two shows are filled with quotes from the Bard. What was the name of the villain played by Evans?

    A. False Face   B. The Puzzler   C. The Mad Hatter   D. Egghead

17) Which of the following novels involves Jessica Pruitt, an American actress in Venice, who goes back in time to meet Shakespeare and his patron, the Earl of Southampton, who have come to the Italian city to escape the plague?

    A. *Shylock's Daughter* (1987) by Erica Jong
    B. *The Quality of Mercy* (1989) by Faye Kellerman
    C. *The Daughter of Time* (1951) by Josephine Tey
    D. *The Shakespeare Girl* (1983) by Mollie Hardwick

18) The song "Brush Up Your Shakespeare" can be found in which musical?

    A. *Guys and Dolls*   B. *The Boys From Syracuse*
    C. *Kiss Me, Kate*   D. *South Pacific*

19) Produced in the 1950s, what was "Shakespeare 'Howls'"?

    A. A board game based on Shakespeare's comedies
    B. A series of children's books based on Shakespeare's comedies
    C. A set of cocktail napkins featuring humorous cartoons and Shakespearean quotes
    D. A book of humorous poems with Shakespeare's characters as speakers

20) *Gertrude and Claudius* (2000) is a prequel to *Hamlet* that tells the story of the title characters from the time of Gertrude's marriage to Hamlet's father up to the second scene of Shakespeare's play. Who is the author of this novel?

    A. John Irving   B. John Dos Passos   C. John Wideman   D. John Updike

Section V

Individual Plays

Quiz 64

We Have Kiss'd Away Kingdoms and Provinces: The Play *Antony and Cleopatra*

Antony and Cleopatra is regarded by some as the greatest love story ever told, and the Romantic poet and Shakespearean scholar Samuel Taylor Coleridge considered it to be Shakespeare's "most wonderful play." Many have agreed with him. Let's see what you know about it.

1) Along with Antony and Octavius, which of the following is the third member of the Triumvirate that rules the Roman Empire at the beginning of the play?

    A. Lepidus   B. Agrippa   C. Ventidius   D. Dolabella

2) What is the name of Antony's wife at the beginning of the play?

    A. Octavia   B. Lavinia   C. Fulvia   D. Alexas

3) Before Antony, who of the following was the lover of Cleopatra?

    A. Sextus Pompey   B. Enobarbus   C. Octavius   D. Julius Caesar

4) Which of the following is an eunuch who serves Cleopatra?

    A. Philo   B. Gallus   C. Thidias   D. Mardian

5) In the beginning of the play, why are some of Antony's soldiers upset with him?

    A. His love for Cleopatra is interfering with his duties as a Roman leader.
    B. Antony's drunkenness prevents him from ruling effectively.
    C. They feel that Antony is disrespectful to Octavius.
    D. Antony has not paid his men for months.

6) Antony's brother allies himself with who of the following to lead an uprising against Octavius?

    A. Enobarbus   B. Fulvia   C. Octavia   D. Sextus Pompey

7) Upon leaving Egypt to return to Rome, what does Antony send to Cleopatra as a gift?

    A. A pearl   B. A bracelet shaped like an asp
    C. A diamond   D. A necklace

8) Who proposes that Antony marry Octavia, in order to establish peace between Caesar and Antony?

    A. Agrippa   B. Lepidus   C. Octavius   D. Dolabella

9) An Egyptian soothsayer predicts that which character will outlive Cleopatra?

    A. Antony   B. Octavius   C. Charmian   D. Octavia

10) What does Charmian suggest that Cleopatra do to end Antony's anger against her?

    A. Pretend she doesn't know that Antony is angry
    B. Send him word that she has killed herself
    C. Apologize to him and pay more attention to him
    D. Bribe his lieutenants to plead with Antony to forgive her

11) While the Roman triumvirs are feasting in celebration aboard Pompey's ship, who suggests to Pompey that they kill them and thereby make Pompey the most powerful man alive?

    A. Menas   B. Menecrates   C. Scarus   D. Varrus

12) Which best describes the prediction made by the Soothsayer to Antony?

    A. As long as Antony remains in Rome, he will be overshadowed by Caesar.
    B. Caesar is plotting with Octavia against Antony.
    C. Cleopatra will try to kill him unless he returns to her.
    D. Antony will be defeated in a battle with Pompey.

13) What does Cleopatra contribute to Antony's battle with Caesar?

    A. A fleet of 60 ships   B. An army of 10,000 soldiers
    C. Gold to pay the troops   D. Horses for Antony's land forces

14) How does Antony react to the news of Enobarbus's desertion?

    A. He curses Enobarbus's disloyalty and vows never to trust anyone again.
    B. He vows to kill Enobarbus after he defeats Caesar.
    C. It doesn't surprise him because he never trusted Enobarbus.
    D. He blames himself for corrupting Enobarbus.

15) How does Antony react when Cleopatra deserts him in the sea battle?

    A. He is glad because he was afraid for her safety.
    B. He follows her and leads his troops in a retreat.
    C. He thinks it was a wise military strategy.
    D. He thinks Cleopatra is in love with Octavius and has betrayed him.

16) What does Antony request of Caesar after losing the battle to him?

    A. To be allowed to live alone in exile in Greece
    B. To resign from power and live as an average citizen in Rome
    C. To be allowed to live in Egypt with Cleopatra
    D. To be allowed to kill himself

17) Who does Antony order to kill him?

    A. Enobarbus   B. Mardian   C. Diomedes   D. Eros

18) What does Caesar intend to do with Cleopatra after Antony's death?

A. Marry her
B. Keep her on display in Rome
C. Kill her
D. Send her into exile

19) How does Cleopatra kill herself?

A. She stabs herself with a dagger.
B. She jumps from the top of her monument.
C. She drowns herself in the Nile.
D. She lets herself be bitten by poisonous snakes.

20) By the end of the play, who is the only one to remain alive?

A. Charmian   B. Iras   C. Dolabella   D. Enobarbus

Quiz 65

O Wonderful, Wonderful, Most Wonderful: The Play *As You Like It*

As You Like It is a glorious pastoral comedy, and the wonderful Rosalind may well be Shakespeare's most endearing female character. See how much you know about this play by answering the following questions. Good luck!

1) In which country can you find the Forest of Arden, where this play is set?

A. England   B. France   C. Netherlands   D. Austria

2) Who is the devoted old servant who flees with Orlando into the Forest of Arden?

A. Le Beau   B. Jaques   C. Adam   D. Dennis

3) Why is Orlando upset with his brother Oliver in the beginning of the play?

A. Oliver ignores the provisions for Orlando in their late father's will.
B. Oliver and Orlando are in love with the same woman.
C. Oliver has taken away Orlando's favorite servant.
D. Oliver has thrown their other brother out of the house.

4) What is Rosalind's relation to the Duke Frederick?

    A. Cousin   B. Daughter   C. Niece   D. No relation

5) Which character from the play is noted for his melancholy disposition?

    A. Orlando   B. Adam   C. Duke Senior   D. Jaques

6) What is the name of the man who Oliver hires to kill Orlando in a wrestling match?

    A. Dennis   B. Le Beau   C. Amiens   D. Charles

7) What token does Rosalind give Orlando for winning the wrestling match?

    A. Ring   B. Necklace   C. Slipper   D. Silk sash

8) Who is sent by Duke Frederick to bring Orlando back to the court dead or alive?

    A. Le Beau   B. Dennis   C. Oliver   D. Charles

9) What is the name that Rosalind uses when she disguises herself as a man?

    A. Ganymede   B. Geryon   C. Guido   D. Gorin

10) What does Orlando do in the forest to prove his love for Rosalind?

    A. He writes love poems to her and burns them so their ashes will soar to heaven.
    B. He attaches love poems to arrows and shoots them into the sky.
    C. He puts love poems in bottles and floats them down a stream.
    D. He pins love poems to the trees in the forest.

11) Which character delivers the famous "All the world's a stage" speech?

    A. Adam   B. Orlando   C. Jaques   D. Rosalind

12) Which of the following characters falls in love with a woman impersonating a man?

    A. Audrey   B. Phebe   C. Aliena   D. Celia

13) How does the disguised Rosalind offer to cure Orlando of his lovesickness?

    A. She will whip him each time he expresses his love for Rosalind.
    B. She will pretend to be his love and reject his courtship.
    C. She matches him up with a more suitable woman.
    D. She will show him the undesirable side of Rosalind.

14) In the play, what is the occupation of Oliver Martext?

    A. Shepherd   B. Magistrate   C. Vicar   D. Outlaw

15) From which animal does Orlando save Oliver?

    A. Bear   B. Tiger   C. Boar   D. Lioness

16) Which character decides to become a hermit at the end of the play?

    A. Oliver   B. Touchstone   C. Duke Frederick   D. Duke Senior

17) What is the name of the second son of Roland de Bois?

    A. Jaques   B. Louis   C. Damien   D. Dennis

18) Who marries Touchstone at the end of the play?

    A. Audrey   B. Aliena   C. Celia   D. Rosalind

19) Who marries Phebe at the end of the play?

    A. Corin   B. Silvius   C. William   D. Jaques

20) Which character delivers the epilogue at the end of the play?

    A. Duke Senior   B. Orlando   C. Rosalind   D. Touchstone

Quiz 66

Pardon's the Word to All: The Play *Cymbeline*

Cymbeline is a play that contains motifs from romantic literature that contribute to produce an almost fairy-like atmosphere. The play has not been widely performed in the 20th century, but it does have a number of intriguing elements, not the least of which is the attractive character of Imogen.

1) Why is Cymbeline angry at the beginning of the play?

    A. Because the Romans are preparing to invade Britain
    B. Because the Queen refuses to control Cloten
    C. Because Imogen has married Posthumus Leonatus
    D. Because the British people are complaining about high taxes

2) What is Cloten's relation to Imogen?

    A. Cousin   B. Brother   C. Half brother   D. Stepbrother

3) What is the name of the doctor in this play?

    A. Cornelius   B. Philarmonus   C. Morgan   D. Cadwal

4) What does the Queen ask the doctor to give her?

    A. Sleeping potion   B. Aphrodisiac   C. Poison   D. Herb to control temper

5) Why was Posthumus Leonatus given his first name?

    A. He was named after a Roman captain who saved his mother's life.
    B. His father died before he was born.
    C. It was the name of a brother who died before he was born.
    D. The play never gives a reason for his first name.

6) What present does Posthumus give Imogen before he goes into exile?

    A. Love poem   B. Bracelet   C. Diamond ring   D. Necklace

7) To which country does Posthumus go after he is ordered exiled?

    A. France   B. Denmark   C. Scotland   D. Italy

8) Who is responsible for kidnapping the sons of Cymbeline 20 years earlier?

    A. Pisanio   B. Philario   C. Caius Lucius   D. Belarius

9) Who makes a bet with Posthumus that he can seduce Imogen?

    A. Aviragus   B. Cloten   C. Iachimo   D. Philarmonus

10) Why does war break out between Britain and Rome in this play?

    A. Cymbeline refused to pay tribute to Rome.
    B. Britain attacked a Roman outpost in Wales.
    C. Cymbeline executed a Roman messenger.
    D. Rome invaded France, which was an ally of Britain.

11) How does Iachimo sneak into Imogen's bedroom?

    A. He hides in a trunk that he has delivered to her room.
    B. He disguises himself as a female servant.
    C. He uses a hidden door in the room that is unknown to Imogen.
    D. He bribes a servant to leave the door unlocked.

12) The mole that Iachimo observes on Imogen while she is sleeping is located on which part of her body?

    A. Back of her neck   B. Thigh   C. Breast   D. Left shoulder blade

13) After believing that she has been unfaithful to him, Posthumus sends a letter telling Imogen to meet him in which place?

    A. Dover   B. Milford Haven   C. London   D. Cameliard

14) Which is the name of Posthumus's servant, who he orders to kill Imogen?

    A. Philario   B. Cornelius   C. Philarmonus   D. Pisanio

15) While in disguise, Imogen takes what name?

    A. Fidele   B. Polydore   C. Morgan   D. Cadwal

16) What is the ultimate fate of Cloten?

    A. Posthumus kills him in a battle between the Romans and Britons.
    B. He is ordered to be executed by Cymbeline at the end of the play.
    C. He is killed and beheaded by Guiderius.
    D. He asks to be executed for his crimes, but is pardoned by Cymbeline.

17) Which of the following is a son of Cymbeline?

    A. Belarius   B. Sicilius Leonatus   C. Arviragus   D. Cloten

18) In a prison, Posthumus falls asleep and has a vision involving which of the following?

    A. The god Mars and the goddess Venus   B. His father, mother, and brothers
    C. Imogen, Cloten, and Iachimo   D. British soldiers killed in battle

19) Who of the following is rescued from Roman capture by Belarius, Arviragus, and Guiderius?

    A. Cymbeline   B. Imogen   C. The Queen   D. Posthumus

20) Which of the following announcements concludes the play?

    A. The Queen is to be executed for her treachery.
    B. Posthumus is declared to be the heir to the British throne.
    C. Cymbeline declares his intention to renew efforts to conquer Rome.
    D. Cymbeline announces an alliance with the Romans once again.

Quiz 67

Now Cracks a Noble Heart: The Play *Hamlet*

Hamlet is undoubtedly Shakespeare's best known play, and it is an action-packed tale filled with murder, insanity, sword fights, pirates, and even a ghost. Test your knowledge of this timeless and tragic masterpiece that attempts to probe the ultimate questions of life and death.

1) Who does Polonius send to spy on his son, Laertes?

    A. Voltemand   B. Cornelius   C. Francisco   D. Reynaldo

2) Which was the poison used by Claudius to kill Hamlet's father, the King of Denmark?

    A. Hemlock   B. Hebona   C. Burdock   D. Baneberry

3) In which city was Hamlet studying before he had to return to Denmark for his father's funeral?

    A. Paris   B. Wittenberg   C. Berlin   D. London

4) How many times does the ghost of Hamlet's father appear in this play?

    A. 1   B. 2   C. 3   D. 4

5) In Act I, Claudius grants permission for Laertes to travel to which country?

    A. Germany   B. Poland   C. France   D. England

6) According to Polonius, what role did he once perform in a play?

    A. Julius Caesar   B. Dr. Faustus   C. Romeo   D. Brutus

7) What is the name of the play that Hamlet asks the visiting players to perform before the court?

    A. *The Isle of Dogs*   B. *The White Devil*
    C. *Death in the Orchard*   D. *The Murder of Gonzago*

8) What is Hamlet's satirical name for the play that is to be performed for the court?

    A. *The Graveyard*   B. *The Mousetrap*   C. *Murder Most Foul*   D. *Fatal Vision*

9) Fortinbras is from which country?

    A. Norway   B. Sweden   C. Poland   D. France

10) What does Polonius believe is the cause of Hamlet's "lunacy"?

    A. Grief   B. Anger   C. Jealousy   D. Love

11) What is the name of the dead court jester to whose skull Hamlet speaks in the graveyard scene?

    A. Hopfrog   B. Fortunato   C. Yorick   D. Melachon

12) To whom does Hamlet say, "I must be cruel, only to be kind"?

    A. Ophelia   B. Gertrude   C. Laertes   D. Polonius

13) Claudius makes arrangements with which country for the death of Hamlet?

    A. Norway   B. France   C. Spain   D. England

14) How does Ophelia die?

    A. Takes poison   B. Stabs herself   C. Falls off a cliff   D. Drowns

15) Who is the judge in the fencing match between Hamlet and Laertes?

    A. Horatio   B. Osric   C. Reynaldo   D. Voltemand

16) Excluding the ghost, who is already dead, how many named characters die during the course of events in the play?

    A. 6   B. 7   C. 8   D. 9

17) Of the deceased referred to in the previous question, how many are killed directly by Hamlet's hands?

    A. 3   B. 4   C. 5   D. 6

18) Under the pretext of awarding Hamlet a prize for his dueling skill, what object does Claudius drop in Hamlet's drink?

    A. Pearl   B. Diamond   C. Ruby   D. Emerald

19) What is the name of Hamlet's father?

    A. Corambis   B. Uther   C. Elsinore   D. Hamlet

20) Who speaks the final lines in the play?

    A. Hamlet   B. Horatio   C. Fortinbras   D. Marcellus

Quiz 68

Company, Villainous Company: The Play *Henry IV, Part One*

Although *Henry IV, Part One* is classified as one of Shakespeare's history plays, it contains raucous comedy, woven around Sir John Falstaff, who is generally regarded as Shakespeare's greatest comic creation. Test your knowledge of the wonderful play by answering the following questions.

1) At what tavern do Falstaff and friends congregate?

    A. The Pearl and Swine   B. The White Hart
    C. The Witches' Brew   D. The Boar's Head

2) Where does the final battle of the play take place?

    A. Gaultree Forest   B. Shrewsbury   C. Bosworth Field   D. Towton

3) Prince Hal's father, Henry IV, became the king of England by deposing which monarch?

    A. Edward III   B. Richard II   C. Henry III   D. John

4) Why does Prince Hal say he is spending so much time with Falstaff?

    A. To lower expectations, so that when he becomes king, he will be more impressive
    B. To trick Hotspur into underestimating him
    C. To learn Falstaff's secrets of thievery
    D. To escape his father, whom he hates

5) What is Hotspur's given name?

    A. Henry Percy   B. Walter Percy   C. Walter Blount   D. Henry Blount

6) John of Lancaster is what relation to Hal?

    A. Older brother   B. Cousin   C. Younger brother   D. Nephew

7) What is the nationality of Owen Glendower?

    A. Scottish   B. Irish   C. French   D. Welsh

8) In the tavern, Hal and Falstaff engage in a role-playing game where they assume the identities of which people?

    A. Prince Hal and Hotspur   B. Prince Hal and Henry IV
    C. Hotspur and Owen Glendower   D. Hotspur and Henry IV

9) How does Hotspur's family justify their rebellion against Henry IV?

    A. They say that Henry is a cruel and unjust king.
    B. They say that Henry has wasted England's wealth on personal expenses.
    C. They say that Henry usurped the throne.
    D. They say that Henry is ungrateful for their role in helping him attain the throne.

10) Which character is the butt of jokes because of his prominent red nose?

    A. Peto   B. Bardolph   C. Poins   D. Gadshill

11) Which character boasted that he could conjure up spirits to do his bidding?

    A. Glendower   B. Douglas   C. Falstaff   D. Hotspur

12) While Falstaff and his cronies plan to rob a group of travelers, with whom does Hal conspire to rob the robbers, as a joke?

    A. Peto   B. Bardolph   C. Poins   D. Gadshill

13) When King Henry IV hears news of Hotspur's success in battle, he wishes that

    A. Hotspur had been killed
    B. Hotspur had not been so successful
    C. Hotspur was his son instead of Prince Hal
    D. Hotspur had been more ruthless with his enemies

14) News of conflict within his country forces King Henry IV to abandon which plan?

    A. An invasion of France   B. A crusade to the Holy Land
    C. Rebuilding England's economy   D. Mending his relationship with Hal

15) Hotspur refuses to hand over captured prisoners to the king unless Henry IV ransoms which man?

    A. Mortimer   B. Walter Blunt   C. Richard Vernon   D. Thomas Percy

16) Who is the hostess of the tavern that Falstaff and his cronies frequent?

    A. Doll Tearsheet   B. Eleanor Rigby   C. Lucille Potter   D. Mistress Quickly

17) What is the name of Hotspur's wife?

    A. Nell   B. Jane   C. Elizabeth   D. Kate

18) Mortimer marries the daughter of which character?

    A. Douglas   B. Glendower   C. Thomas Percy   D. Richard Scroop

19) Why is Hotspur's father unable to join the final battle?

    A. He died a few days earlier.   B. He was attacked by the Scots.
    C. He was too ill.   D. He was late arriving at the scene.

20) When Hal examines Falstaff's pistol case at the final battle, what is the only item that he finds in it?

    A. Money to bribe the enemy if he is captured
    B. A half-eaten turkey leg
    C. A bottle of wine
    D. A broken, rusty dagger

Quiz 69

A Little Touch of Harry in the Night: The Play *Henry V*

Henry V is Shakespeare's patriotic celebration of his nation's foremost hero king, and it is one of his most popular history plays. How much do you know about it?

1) Who of the following is a brother of Henry V?

    A. Edward, Duke of York   B. Richard, Earl of Salisbury
    C. Ralph, Earl of Westmoreland   D. Humphrey, Duke of Gloucester

2) Who of the following is an uncle of Henry V?

    A. Duke of Exeter   B. Duke of Bedford   C. Duke of York   D. Duke of Clarence

3) Who of the following is NOT involved in the plot to assassinate Henry V prior to his departure for France?

    A. Richard, Earl of Cambridge   B. Henry, Lord Scroop
    C. Sir John Bates   D. Sir Thomas Grey

4) To whom was the Hostess (formerly Mistress Quickly) engaged before she married Pistol?

    A. Bardolph   B. Nym   C. Falstaff   D. Poins

5) What is Bardolph's military rank?

    A. Ensign   B. Corporal   C. Lieutenant   D. Captain

6) According to Pistol and Nym, what broke the heart of Falstaff and caused his death?

    A. After becoming king, Henry V rejected him.
    B. Mistress Quickly refused to marry him and married Pistol instead.
    C. His cowardice is revealed by Henry V and he was filled with shame.
    D. Justice Shallow was going to have him arrested.

7) What is the name of the French herald who carries messages from the French to Henry V?

    A. Le Bon   B. Grandpre   C. Le Fer   D. Mountjoy

8) What is the insulting gift that is sent to Henry by the Dauphin?

    A. A white rose   B. Oysters   C. Tennis balls   D. Cheap ale

9) What is the name of the French king who rules during the course of this play?

    A. Philip III   B. Louis XIV   C. Henri IV   D. Charles VI

10) Upon first landing in France, Henry V and his army lay siege to which city?

    A. Calais   B. Harfleur   C. Rouen   D. Paris

11) Which of the following captains in Henry V's army is Welsh?

    A. Macmorris   B. Fluellen   C. Jamy   D. Gower

12) What is the name of the woman who attends the Princess of France, Catherine, and tries to teach her English in the event that she must marry Henry V?

    A. Alice   B. Margaret   C. Michelle   D. Marie

13) Henry V orders the execution of which old friend for stealing from a French church?

    A. Pistol   B. Nym   C. Bardolph   D. Poins

14) Which best describes the attitude of the Dauphin and the other French lords towards the English troops prior to the Battle of Agincourt?

    A. Grudging respect   B. Open fear   C. Pity for their plight   D. Mocking contempt

15) The night before the Battle of Agincourt, Henry V asks God not to punish his soldiers for which of the following?

 A. Henry's brutality in the previous battle.
 B. His execution of English soldiers for stealing from French citizens.
 C. His father usurping the throne.
 D. Waging a war against the French without a religious purpose.

16) Who of the following expresses a wish for reinforcements just before the Battle of Agincourt, causing Henry V to deliver his famed "St. Crispin's Day" speech?

 A. Earl of Westmoreland   B. Earl of Salisbury
 C. Earl of Huntingdon   D. Earl of Warwick

17) Who of the following requests and is granted the honor of leading the English vanguard against the French?

 A. Duke of Exeter B. Duke of York   C. Fluellen   D. Earl of Warwick

18) Which of the following actions of the French angers Henry V and results in his order to slit the throats of all the French prisoners captured by his men in battle?

 A. The French repeatedly send him insulting messages.
 B. The English prisoners captured in the battle are murdered.
 C. The French state that an invasion of England has begun.
 D. The English pages guarding the luggage are murdered.

19) Who of the following dies in the Battle of Agincourt?

 A. Sir Thomas Erpingham   B. Fluellen
 C. John, Duke of Bedford   D. Edward, Duke of York

20) In his last speech of the play, Pistol states that he plans to return to England and do what?

 A. Enter a monastery   B. Run Mistress Quickly's tavern
 C. Become a thief and a pimp   D. Become an actor

Quiz 70

This Was the Most Unkindest Cut of All: The Play *Julius Caesar*

Julius Caesar, one of Shakespeare's Roman plays, is a play commonly taught in American high schools. How much do you remember from this popular tragedy? Make your English teacher proud!

1) In the beginning of the play, the Romans are celebrating Julius Caesar's victory over which enemy?

    A. Sons of Pompey B. Pompey   C. Sons of Crassus   D. Crassus

2) On which day of the month does the Ides of March fall?

    A. March 1   B. March 10   C. March 15   D. March 31

3) Who was the wife of Julius Caesar in this play?

    A. Portia   B. Lavinia   C. Julia   D. Calpurnia

4) Which Roman festival is being celebrated as the play begins?

    A. Bacchanalia   B. Fornacalia   C. Lupercalia   D. Saturnalia

5) In the beginning of the play, two tribunes are trying to stop the celebration of Caesar's victory. One of the tribunes is Murellus. Who is the other?

    A. Dardanius   B. Flavius   C. Varrus   D. Volumnius

6) What was Octavius Caesar's relationship to Julius Caesar?

    A. Son   B. Nephew   C. Cousin   D. Adopted heir

7) Julius Caesar was known to have which disease?

    A. Tuberculosis   B. Epilepsy   C. Diabetes   D. Asthma

8) What is Brutus's main motive in deciding to become involved in the assassination of Caesar?

    A. Jealousy of Caesar's power and popularity
    B. Fear that Caesar will become king and abuse his power
    C. Fear that Caesar's health makes him unacceptable as a leader
    D. Fear that Caesar is not a strong leader and will let others influence him

9) How are Brutus and Cassius related?

    A. Brothers-in-law   B. Brothers   C. Cousins   D. Uncle and nephew

10) Which character reports that he rescued Caesar from drowning in the Tiber River?

    A. Mark Antony   B. Brutus   C. Cassius   D. Casca

11) Which conspirator "reinterprets" the threatening dream of Caesar's wife and convinces him to go to the Senate House on the day of the assassination?

    A. Cassius   B. Marcus Brutus   C. Decius Brutus   D. Cinna

12) Who of the following writes a letter to Caesar warning him of the conspirators?

    A. Popilius Lena   B. Titinius   C. Cicero   D. Artemidorus

13) Which is NOT one of the conspirators involved in the assassination of Julius Caesar?

    A. Cicero   B. Trebonius   C. Caius Ligarius   D. Metullus Cimber

14) Who is the first conspirator to stab Caesar?

    A. Cassius   B. Casca   C. Brutus   D. Cinna

15) Who is NOT a member of the triumvirate set up to rule Rome after Caesar's death?

    A. Publius   B. Mark Antony   C. Octavius   D. Lepidus

16) Which character in this play dies on his birthday?

    A. Julius Caesar   B. Cinna, the poet   C. Brutus   D. Cassius

17) In his funeral oration for Caesar, which word does Mark Antony sarcastically repeat to describe Brutus and the other conspirators?

    A. Cowardly   B. Ambitious   C. Honorable   D. Bloody

18) Which character holds the sword so that Brutus can run on it and commit suicide?

    A. Volumnius   B. Clitus   C. Strato   D. Dardanius

19) Near what place does the final battle in the play occur?

    A. Pharsalia   B. Philippi   C. Sardis   D. Xanthius

20) At the end of the play, who states that Brutus was the "noblest Roman of them all"?

    A. Octavius   B. Lepidus   C. Young Cato   D. Mark Antony

Quiz 71

Nothing Will Come of Nothing: The Play *King Lear*

King Lear is considered to be one of Shakespeare's four great tragedies, along with **Hamlet, Macbeth,** and **Othello.** Test your knowledge of this intense and profound tragedy by answering the following questions.

1) Why does King Lear get angry with Cordelia and banish her in the first scene of the play?

    A. She refuses a proposed marriage to the Duke of Burgundy.
    B. She refuses to express her love for Lear as strongly as her sisters.
    C. She is upset with the share of the kingdom that is assigned to her by Lear.
    D. She argues with Lear about the banishment of Kent.

2) Cordelia marries the king of which country?

    A. Spain   B. Portugal   C. France   D. Norway

3) Who is the villainous bastard son of the Earl of Gloucester?

    A. Edgar   B. Edmund   C. Oswald   D. Curan

4) Who of the following does Lear banish from his country for defending Cordelia?

    A. Kent   B. Gloucester   C. Fool   D. Edgar

5) Which suitor of Cordelia refuses to marry her after she is disinherited?

    A. Burgundy   B. Kent   C. Edmund   D. King of France

6) Who is the husband of Goneril?

    A. Duke of Tintagel   B. Duke of Leister   C. Duke of Albany   D. Duke of Cornwall

7) Because Kent threatens and insults Oswald (a servant of Goneril), how is he punished by Cornwall?

    A. His right hand is cut off.   B. He is placed in the dungeon.
    C. He receives 50 lashes with a whip.   D. He is placed in the stocks.

8) When Edgar first becomes a fugitive, after he has been set up by Edmund, he assumes which disguise?

    A. Doctor   B. Shepherd   C. Jester   D. Beggar

9) Why does Cornwall punish Gloucester by blinding him?

    A. Because Gloucester helped Lear escape him
    B. Because his wife loves Gloucester's son
    C. Because Gloucester insulted him
    D. Because he hates Gloucester's goodness

10) Who kills the Duke of Cornwall?

    A. Edgar   B. One of his servants   C. Kent   D. Duke of Albany

11) In his speeches, Edgar mentions the names Flibbertigibbit, Smulkin, Modo, and Mahu. These names refer to which of the following?

    A. Angels   B. Pagan gods   C. Devils   D. Stars

12) Who makes plans to have Edmund kill the Duke of Albany?

    A. Goneril   B. Regan   C. Edgar   D. Kent

13) How does Regan die?

    A. Stabed by Edmund   B. Suicide
    C. Poisoned by Goneril   D. Stabbed by her husband

14) How does Goneril die?

    A. Thrown off a cliff by Edmund
    B. Suicide by stabbing
    C. Killed by the invading French army
    D. Killed by her servant, Oswald

15) Edmund convinces Gloucester that which character is trying to seize his estates?

    A. Edgar   B. Duke of Albany C. Duke of Cornwall   D. Lear

16) In the midst of his insanity, Lear conducts a mock trial, during which he accuses which of the following?

    A. Cordelia and Kent   B. Edmund and Gloucester
    C. Goneril and the Duke of Cornwall   D. Regan and Goneril

17) During the course of the play, Lear states his age. How old is he?

    A. 65   B. 70   C. 75   D. 80

18) As he lies dying, what is the last action Edmund attempts to make?

    A. To kill Edgar   B. To ask for forgiveness
    C. To save Cordelia and Lear from death   D. To drag himself to the seaside

19) What is the alias taken by Kent when he disguises himself to attend on Lear?

    A. Tom   B. Helicanus   C. Pandosto   D. Caius

20) Who becomes the ruler of Britain at the end of the play?

    A. Kent   B. Edgar   C. Duke of Albany   D. Gloucester

Quiz 72

This Dead Butcher and His Fiend-like Queen: The Play *Macbeth*

Macbeth is another one of Shakespeare's plays that is commonly taught in American high schools. The play has witches, a ghost, battles, madness, and brutal murders. What more could you want? How much of the gory details do you remember?

1) At the beginning of the play, the Scots are at war with which country?

     A. Sweden   B. Norway   C. England   D. Ireland

2) Duncan rewards Macbeth for his loyalty by giving him which title?

     A. Thane of Glamis   B. Thane of Cawdor
     C. Prince of Cumberland   D. Prince of Forres

3) What is the name of Macbeth's father?

     A. Macbeth   B. Fergus   C. Angus   D. Sinel

4) Who is the Thane of Fife?

     A. Banquo   B. Macduff   C. Lennox   D. Donalbain

5) What is the name of the Scottish traitor that Macbeth "unseamed...from the nave to the chaps"?

     A. Thane of Cawdor   B. Caithness   C. Macdonwald   D. Elgin

6) With whom is Macbeth traveling when he first meets the witches?

     A. Banquo   B. Duncan   C. Lennox   D. Ross

7) Where was the location of Macbeth's castle?

     A. Forres   B. Scone   C. Perth   D. Inverness

8) Which is NOT one of the apparitions conjured up for Macbeth by the witches in Act IV?

     A. A floating dagger   B. A bloody child
     C. A child crowned, with a tree in his hand   D. An armed head

9) Who discovers the body of the murdered Duncan?

     A. Lennox   B. Ross   C. Macduff   D. The Porter

10) What present does Duncan send Lady Macbeth when he arrives at Macbeth's castle?

     A. Necklace   B. Diamond   C. Ring   D. Brooch

11) What is the name of Banquo's son?

    A. Edgar   B. Bethoc   C. Fleance   D. Kenneth

12) After the murder of Duncan, Donalbain flees to which country?

    A. England   B. Wales   C. Ireland   D. France

13) What was the traditional place where Scottish kings were crowned? (Macbeth is crowned there.)

    A. Hebrides   B. Dundee   C. Lothian   D. Scone

14) Which is NOT an ingredient in the potion that the witches brew in Act IV?

    A. Sailor's thumb   B. Eye of newt   C. Toe of frog   D. Tooth of wolf

15) How many kings appear in the Show of Kings conjured up by the witches in Act IV?

    A. 8   B. 10   C. 12   D. 14

16) Who tells Macbeth, "The queen, my lord, is dead" (5.5.16)?

    A. The Doctor   B. Seyton   C. A Gentlewoman   D. Lennox

17) What is the name of the wood that comes to Dunsinane Hill, fulfilling a prophecy of the witches?

    A. Elgin   B. Lothian   C. Birnam   D. Dundee

18) Who tells Macbeth that he "was from his mother's womb/ Untimely ripp'd" (5.8.15)?

    A. Fleance   B. Ross   C. Malcolm   D. Macduff

19) Who of the following is killed in battle by Macbeth?

    A. Ross   B. Angus   C. Young Siward   D. Old Siward

20) Who becomes king after the death of Macbeth?

    A. Malcolm   B. Donalbain   C. Seyton   D. Fleance

Quiz 73

I Like Not Fair Terms and Villain's Mind: The Play *The Merchant of Venice*

The Merchant of Venice is an intriguing play because Shylock, originally regarded as a diabolical villain, is now regarded with a great deal of sympathy. In fact, he is perceived to be a victim of cruel prejudice, while some view the Christians in the play as the real villains. Was Shakespeare himself sympathetic to Shylock's plight? We'll never truly know, but let's see how much you know about the details of this thought-provoking masterpiece.

1) What explanation does Antonio give for being sad at the beginning of the play?

    A. His youngest brother recently died in a shipwreck.

    B. He owes a great deal of money to Shylock.

    C. He says he does not know why he is sad.

    D. He has been rejected by a woman whom he deeply loves.

2) According to his explanation to Antonio, to what does Bassanio attribute the deep debts he has accumulated?

    A. His extravagant lifestyle

    B. His failed business ventures

    C. His father died deeply in debt

    D. He was cheated out of his fortune by Jews

3) Which is NOT a reason Shylock gives for his hatred of Antonio?

    A. Antonio has repeatedly insulted Shylock.

    B. Antonio was rude to Shylock's wife before her death.

    C. Antonio harms Shylock's business by lending money without interest.

    D. Antonio hates Jews.

4) A prospective suitor of Portia must select one of three caskets: gold, silver, or lead. If he selects the one with the portrait of Portia, he wins her hand. Who or what is responsible for this "unique" courting ritual?

    A. It was a condition of the will of Portia's recently deceased father.

    B. It was a test designed by Portia to ensure that her future husband truly loved her.

    C. It was a custom of the Italian city where Portia lived.

    D. Shakespeare never explains in the play how this situation originated.

5) Which of the following is NOT a condition to which a prospective suitor of Portia must agree before selecting one of the caskets?

    A. Not to reveal which casket he chose to anyone

    B. Never to woo a maid in way of marriage

    C. To leave immediately

    D. To donate a large sum to an Italian orphanage

6) Which of the following statements is inscribed on the silver casket?

A. "Who chooseth me must give and hazard all he hath."
B. "Who chooseth me shall get as much as he deserves."
C. "Who chooseth me shall gain what many men desire."
D. "Who chooseth me must give all that he doth desire."

7) Which of Portia's suitors chooses the gold casket?

A. Prince of Morocco   B. Prince of Arragon
C. LeBon, the French lord   D. Falconbridge, the English lord

8) Launcelot Gobbo leaves the household of Shylock to serve who?

A. Gratiano   B. Antonio   C. Solerio   D. Bassanio

9) Who of the following is a friend to Shylock?

A. Leonardo   B. Tubal   C. Balthasar   D. Stephano

10) According to Bassanio, who "speaks an infinite deal of nothing" and is "too wild, too rude, and bold of voice"?

A. Lorenzo   B. Shylock   C. Gratiano   D. Solanio

11) How much does Shylock lend Antonio (in ducats)?

A. 3,000   B. 5,000   C. 10,000   D. 20,000

12) What is the name of Shylock's daughter?

A. Jessica   B. Leah   C. Nerissa   D. Lovisa

13) With whom does Shylock's daughter elope?

A. Solanio   B. Salerio   C. Leonardo   D. Lorenzo

14) What is the name of Portia's cousin, who gives her a letter of introduction as a "doctor of laws"?

A. Balthasar   B. Bellario   C. Montferrat   D. Montresor

15) Which best describes Antonio's behavior in court as Shylock demands his pound of flesh?

A. He begs Shylock for his life.
B. He begs the court to intervene on his behalf.
C. He displays resigned acceptance of his fate.
D. He curses Shylock and vows revenge from the grave.

16) What technicality in Shylock's bond allows Portia, disguised as a lawyer, to prevent him from taking a pound of Antonio's flesh?

A. The bond was not signed by Shylock.
B. The bond allows for a pound of flesh but does not allow for any blood to be taken.
C. The notary of the bond, Daniel, failed to put his seal on the bond.
D. Jewish law prohibits a bond of this type.

17) Which best describes the sentence that all agree is to be imposed upon Shylock by the court?

    A. He is banished and must turn over his estate to Antonio.
    B. He is ordered to turn over his entire estate to his daughter and her husband.
    C. He must surrender his estate to Antonio and become his servant.
    D. Half his estate goes to Antonio, and he must pay a fine and become a Christian.

18) What is Shylock's reaction to the court's sentence?

    A. He says he does not feel well and asks to leave.
    B. He begs Antonio and the court for forgiveness.
    C. He refuses to accept the decision and is arrested.
    D. He rushes at Antonio and tries to take the pound of flesh.

19) What does Bassanio give the law clerk (Portia, in disguise) as a reward for saving Antonio's life?

    A. Shylock's dagger.   B. The money originally due to Shylock.
    C. The ring that Portia gave him.   D. A partnership in his uncle's law firm.

20) What news does Antonio receive at the end of the play?

    A. Three of the ships that were thought to have been lost have arrived in port.
    B. Shylock has committed suicide.
    C. Shylock has repented and entered a monastery.
    D. The lover who rejected him now wishes to marry him.

Quiz 74

If We Shadows Have Offended: The Play *A Midsummer Night's Dream*

Although some critics have treated **A Midsummer Night's Dream** rather unkindly, it remains one of Shakespeare's most beloved and regularly performed plays. Filled with fairies, magic, clowns, and young lovers, how can you not be swept away in midsummer madness?

1) Who brings a complaint against Hermia to Theseus in the beginning of the play?
   A. Oberon   B. Lysander   C. Egeus   D. Helena

2) Who tells Demetrius that Hermia and Lysander are planning to elope?
   A. Egeus   B. Theseus   C. Helena   D. Hippolyta

3) Hippolyta, the beloved of Theseus, is Queen of which race?
   A. Babylonians   B. Amazons   C. Pygmies   D. Spartans

4) What does Oberon want that Titania refuses to give him?
   A. An Indian boy   B. Her servant girl   C. A magic wand   D. A magic potion

5) By what other name is Puck also known?
   A. Robin Loxley   B. Robin O'Day   C. Robin Goodfellow   D. Robin Elfwood

6) Who is NOT one of the fairy attendants of Titania?
   A. Peaseblossom   B. Mustardseed   C. Cobweb   D. Hobnail

7) Which of the young lovers is first affected by the love potion?
   A. Demetrius   B. Lysander   C. Hermia   D. Helena

8) Characters in the play make fun of which physical attribute of Hermia?
   A. Hair   B. Complexion   C. Height   D. Weight

9) Who is the Master of Revels for Theseus?
   A. Philostrate   B. Egeus   C. Moth   D. Starveling

10) What is the profession of Nick Bottom?
   A. Joiner   B. Carpenter   C. Tinker   D. Weaver

11) Who is the director of the play performed before Theseus?
   A. Nick Bottom   B. Tom Snout   C. Peter Quince   D. Francis Flute

12) With which of the clowns, or "rude mechanicals," does Titania fall in love?

    A. Nick Bottom   B. Tom Snout   C. Peter Quince   D. Francis Flute

13) What is Helena's reaction when she finds both Lysander and Demetrius courting her?

    A. She enjoys it thoroughly.
    B. She thinks they are both mocking her.
    C. She can't make up her mind which she prefers.
    D. She feels guilty about taking Lysander from Hermia.

14) When Bottom awakens from his ordeal with the fairies, he thinks his experience was a dream. What does he want to do with this dream?

    A. Return to the woods to see if it was real
    B. Tell it to his children and grandchildren
    C. Have Quince write a ballad about it
    D. Make believe it never happened

15) Which of the clowns plays part of the wall in the play before Theseus and the lovers?

    A. Snug   B. Snout   C. Flute   D. Bottom

16) While watching the clowns perform their play, which character says, "This is the silliest stuff that ever I heard" (5.1.210)?

    A. Hippolyta   B. Theseus   C. Lysander   D. Helena

17) Why does the Master of the Revels try to talk Theseus out of seeing the play of the "rude mechanicals"?

    A. He does not like Peter Quince.   B. He prefers another group.
    C. He thinks the play is too short.   D. He thinks it's badly performed.

18) The "rude mechanicals" perform a play that is based on which Greek myth?

    A. Hero and Leander   B. Leda and the Swan
    C. Venus and Adonis   D. Pyramus and Thisbe

19) At the end of the play, a Bergomask is performed by the clowns. What is a Bergomask?

    A. Song   B. Dance   C. Dumb show   D. Puppet show

20) Who speaks the epilogue at the end of the play?

    A. Oberon   B. Titania   C. Puck   D. Theseus

A Kind of Merry War: The Play *Much Ado About Nothing*

Much Ado About Nothing is one of Shakespeare's most amusing comedies, but you will find a touch of evil and a few rather unsettling moments in this popular play, as well. However, as in most typical Shakespearean comedies, it ends with multiple weddings. See how much you know about this play by answering the following questions.

1) What is the relationship between Beatrice and Hero?

    A. Sisters   B. Aunt and niece   C. Cousins   D. No blood relation

2) This play is set on which island?

    A. Elba   B. Crete   C. Cyprus   D. Sicily

3) What is Don Pedro's position?

    A. Prince of Arragon   B. Governor of Messina
    C. Prince of Morocco   D. Governor of Genoa

4) Who proposes marriage to Beatrice before she accepts Benedick's proposal?

    A. Don Pedro   B. Don John   C. Borachio   D. Balthasar

5) What is Don John's relationship to Don Pedro?

    A. Brother   B. Half brother   C. Cousin   D. Uncle and nephew

6) Which of the following is Don John's first attempt to create trouble?

    A. He tries to steal Hero away from Claudio by spreading lies about him.
    B. He tries to provoke a fight between Benedick and Claudio.
    C. He tries to convince Claudio that Don Pedro is wooing Hero for himself.
    D. He tries to convince Leonato that Don Pedro is a poor leader.

7) Most of Dogberry's humor comes from which of the following techniques?

    A. Malapropism   B. Irony   C. Clever wit   D. Puns

8) Who is the headborough, a petty constable who was second-in-command to Dogberry?

    A. Balthasar   B. George Seacoal   C. Verges   D. Hugh Oatcake

9) Who calls Dogberry "an ass"?

    A. Leonato   B. Borachio   C. Don John   D. Conrade

10) As part of an evil plan to discredit Hero, who makes love to Margaret near Hero's bedroom window, to make it appear that Hero is cheating on Claudio the night before their planned wedding?

    A. George Seacoal   B. Antonio   C. Conrade   D. Borachio

11) After Claudio publicly rejects Hero on what was to be their wedding day, what is the plan that is proposed by the Friar?

    A. To send Hero to a nunnery to atone for her sin
    B. To send out the guard to investigate the charges against Hero
    C. To pretend that Hero is dead until they can reveal her innocence
    D. That Benedick should disguise himself, to join Don John's group and find out the truth

12) Who overhears Don John's henchmen describing their role in the plot to discredit Hero?

    A. Dogberry   B. Dogberry's watchmen   C. Verges   D. Ursula

13) Which of the following is NOT true?

    A. Beatrice admits that she once gave her heart to Benedick.
    B. At the beginning of the play, both Beatrice and Benedick state they will never marry.
    C. At first, Leonato believes the accusations that Claudio makes about Hero's infidelity.
    D. Leonato banishes Margaret for her role in Don John's plan to discredit Hero.

14) Who of the following in NOT involved in the plot to trick Beatrice and Benedick into admitting their love for each other?

    A. Dogberry   B. Leonato   C. Don Pedro   D. Claudio

15) Which of the following does NOT occur in the play?

    A. Don John is captured.
    B. Leonato rewards Dogberry for uncovering Don John's plot.
    C. Benedick and Claudio fight a duel in which Claudio is wounded.
    D. Don Pedro seems sad at the end of the play.

16) Who of the following shows remorse for his role in the plot to shame Hero?

    A. Don John   B. Borachio   C. Conrade   D. Balthasar

17) When Claudio believes that Hero is dead and innocent, Leonato says he will forgive him if he carries out certain actions. Which is NOT one of the actions stipulated by Leonato?

    A. To marry his brother's daughter, who looks just like Hero
    B. To write her an epitaph, declaring her innocence
    C. To sing an epitaph at her tomb, declaring her innocence
    D. To agree never to marry and spend his life praying for Hero

18) After Hero is publicly disgraced, what does Beatrice demand that Benedick do to prove his love for her?

A. Kill Don John   B. Break off his friendship with Don John
C. Kill Claudio   D. Break off his friendship with Claudio

19) What is the name of the Friar who conducts the double wedding at the end of the play?

     A. Lodowick   B. Laurence   C. Francis   D. John

20) Beatrice and Benedick finally admit their love for each other and agree to get married when they are publicly confronted with what evidence?

     A. Love poems they wrote for one another
     B. Hero's statement that she overheard them declare their love for one another
     C. The friar's statement that Benedick asked him to marry them
     D. Leonato's statement that Benedick asked him for Beatrice's hand

Quiz 76

O! Beware My Lord of Jealousy: The Play *Othello*

Othello is one of Shakespeare's great tragedies and remains a cautionary tale regarding the dangers of jealousy. The play is most memorable, however, for the charming, roguish, frightening, and evil Iago.

1) How old is Iago?

     A. 20   B. 28   C. 33   D. 40

2) What position is held by Desdemona's father, Brabantio?

     A. Senator   B. Governor   C. Duke   D. Magistrate

3) Which is the uncle of Desdemona?

     A. Brabantio   B. Duke of Venice   C. Montano   D. Gratiano

4) Which character admits that he has a problem handling alcohol?

     A. Cassio   B. Iago   C. Montano   D. Roderigo

5) After they leave Venice, where does Othello and his fleet land?

    A. Morocco   B. Turkey   C. Cyprus   D. Sicily

6) Who is the first to reveal the treachery of Iago to the others?

    A. Desdemona   B. Emilia   C. Cassio   D. Othello

7) What position is held by Iago at the beginning of the play?

    A. Ensign   B. Sergeant   C. Lieutenant   D. Captain

8) Which woman is in love with Cassio?

    A. Desdemona   B. Emilia   C. Innogen   D. Bianca

9) According to Iago, what is the "green-eyed monster"?

    A. Women   B. Prejudice   C. Jealousy   D. Youth

10) In Act I, who accuses Othello of using witchcraft or black magic?

    A. Iago   B. Roderigo   C. Brabantio   D. The Duke of Venice

11) According to what he tells Roderigo in Act I, why does Iago hate Othello?

    A. Othello gave Cassio a promotion that Iago desired.
    B. He thinks Othello had an affair with his wife.
    C. He dislikes Othello because of his race.
    D. He does not give any reason to Roderigo.

12) Which two are killed by Iago's own hand?

    A. Roderigo and Cassio   B. Roderigo and Emilia
    C. Cassio and Emilia   D. Emilia and Othello

13) According to Othello, who gave his mother the handkerchief embroidered with strawberries that was his first gift to Desdemona?

    A. His father   B. An Egyptian charmer
    C. A dying soldier   D. A Greek prophet

14) The actions of which enemy nation force Othello and his army to leave Venice?

    A. Gaul   B. Egypt   C. Turkey   D. Lybia

15) What is the name of the inn where Iago tells Roderigo to meet him in Act I?

    A. Bell and Candle B. Sailor's Sigh   C. Centaur   D. Sagittary

16) Who first finds the handkerchief after Desdemona accidentally drops it?

    A. Iago   B. Cassio   C. Bianca   D. Emilia

17) Iago suggests that Othello kill Desdemona using which method?

A. Smother her in bed   B. Poison her wine
C. Stab her in bed   D. Torture her to death

18) Which is NOT used as evidence by Iago to suggest that Desdemona is unfaithful?

   A. Desdemona keeps pleading to Othello to restore Cassio's rank.
   B. Iago overheard Cassio talking in his sleep about his love for Desdemona.
   C. Iago saw a love letter Cassio had written to Desdemona.
   D. Cassio had Desdemona's handkerchief.

19) Who is the only character to know that Iago hates Othello before the last scene of the play?

   A. Emilia   B. Roderigo   C. Cassio   D. Brabantio

20) Othello describes himself as a(n) _____ murderer.

   A. Honorable   B. Despicable   C. Reluctant   D. Unnatural

Quiz 77

Cheated of Feature by Dissembling Nature: The Play *Richard III*

Richard III is a fascinating historical and literary figure. Some regard him as one of the more infamous rulers in history; others regard him as a man who "fortune hath cruelly scratched" and believe that his nefarious reputation can be greatly attributed to Shakespeare's play and is unjustified by historical fact. In any case, the play is an interesting one.

1) Before he became king, Richard held which title?

   A. Duke of Gloucester   B. Earl of March   C. Duke of York   D. Prince of Wales

2) Which of the following became the wife of Richard III?

   A. Elizabeth York   B. Elizabeth Woodville
   C. Anne Neville   D. Cecily Neville

3) Who is the brother of Queen Elizabeth (the wife of Edward IV)?

   A. Earl Rivers   B. Earl of Surrey   C. Sir Walter Herbert   D. Earl of Oxford

4) What are the names of the two sons of Edward IV?

   A. Edward and Henry   B. Edward and Arthur
   C. Richard and Henry   D. Edward and Richard

5) Who does Richard hire to kill his nephews, the young princes in the tower?

   A. Sir Walter Blunt   B. Sir James Tyrrel
   C. Sir Robert Brakenbury   D. Sir Thomas Vaughan

6) Who is the main accomplice who helps Richard obtain the throne of England?

    A. Duke of Norfolk   B. Duke of Buckingham

    C. Lord Hastings   D. Lord Stanley

7) Although given a role in the play by Shakespeare, which of the following characters was actually dead during the time in history depicted?

    A. Queen Margaret   B. Cardinal Bourchier

    C. Lord Hastings   D. Earl Rivers

8) What was the name of the mistress of King Edward IV?

    A. Margaret Plantagenet   B. Cecily Neville

    C. Jane Shore   D. Joan De Pucelle

9) What does Richard III ask John Morton, the Bishop of Ely, to bring him from his garden?

    A. Roses   B. Tomatoes   C. Strawberries   D. Sunflowers

10) Who of the following was NOT a supporter of Richard III?

    A. Catesby   B. Lovell   C. Lord Stanley   D. Ratcliffe

11) Before marrying Edward IV, Queen Elizabeth had been married to Lord Grey. Who of the following is a son of Queen Elizabeth by her first husband?

    A. Sir Thomas Vaughan   B. Earl of Oxford

    C. Sir William Brandon   D. Marquess of Dorset

12) How does Richard discredit Edward's heir and convince the people to make him king instead?

    A. He convinces everyone that Edward's heir is too young to rule.

    B. He arranges that the heirs of Edward are declared illegitimate.

    C. He gathers supporters who then overthrow Edward's heir.

    D. He has the heirs of Edward killed so they cannot rule.

13) After the death of his wife, who does Richard attempt to marry?

    A. Cecily Neville   B. Elizabeth, daughter of Edward

    C. Margaret Plantagenet   D. Anne Neville

14) Who does Richard accuse of bewitching and withering his arm?

    A. Jane Shore   B. Queen Margaret

    C. Earl Rivers   D. George, Duke of Clarence

15) Who was the father-in-law of Anne Neville?

    A. Earl of Warwick   B. Marquess of Dorset

    C. King Henry VI   D. Lord Grey

16) Who plans to marry Elizabeth of York after Richard has died?
   A. Earl of Richmond   B. George, Duke of Clarence
   C. Duke of Norfolk   D. Edward Plantagenet

17) Which of the following is NOT a ghost that visits Richard III the night before his death?
   A. King Henry VI   B. King Edward IV   C. Buckingham   D. Hastings

18) Whose son is held hostage by Richard, prior to the Battle of Bosworth Field, as assurance for his loyalty?
   A. Duke of Norfolk   B. Earl of Surrey   C. Lord Stanley   D. Sir James Blunt

19) Who becomes King Henry VII after the death of Richard III?
   A. Earl of Oxford   B. Earl of Richmond   C. Marquess of Dorset   D. Duke of Norfolk

20) In which year is Richard killed?
   A. 1402   B. 1436   C. 1452   D. 1485

Quiz 78

For Never Was a Story of More Woe: The Play *Romeo and Juliet*

Romeo and Juliet is the timeless story of doomed love that has delighted and fascinated readers for centuries. It continues to be a staple of the high school classroom and has inspired film, ballet, and operatic offshoots.

1) How old is Juliet during the play?
   A. 12   B. 13   C. 14   D. 15

2) With whom is Romeo in love before he sets eyes upon Juliet?
   A. Helena   B. Livia   C. Gabriella   D. Rosaline

3) Who is the nephew of Lady Capulet?
   A. Escalus   B. Tybalt   C. Benvolio   D. Balthasar

4) Juliet's father ordered her to marry which man?
   A. Paris   B. Abram   C. Escalus   D. Lord Gregory

5) What was the name of the friar unable to deliver Friar Laurence's letter to Romeo because he was shut up in quarantine during a plague outbreak?
   A. Thomas   B. Francis   C. John   D. Lodowick

6) After killing Tybalt, Romeo flees to which city?
   A. Mantua   B. Padua   C. Venice   D. Florence

7) The action in *Romeo and Juliet* comprises how much time?

   A. 2 days   B. 5 days   C. 2 weeks   D. 3 weeks

8) Who makes the following statement: "Earth has swallowed all my hopes but she;/ She is the hopeful lady of my earth"? (1.2.14)

   A. Romeo   B. Paris   C. The nurse   D. Lord Capulet

9) Believing that Juliet is dead, who does Romeo kill in the Capulet's tomb?

   A. Tybalt   B. Benvolio   C. Petruchio   D. Paris

10) Why does Tybalt first challenge Romeo to a duel?

   A. He is offended that Romeo shows up at the Capulet ball.
   B. He is offended that Romeo loves his cousin.
   C. He is offended that Romeo bites his thumb at him.
   D. Tybalt does not challenge Romeo to a duel; he challenges Mercutio.

11) Which character delivers the famous and bawdy Queen Mab speech?

   A. Tybalt   B. Benvolio   C. Mercutio   D. Gregory

12) Which is the nephew of Lord Montague?

   A. Escalus   B. Tybalt   C. Benvolio   D. Mercutio

13) Which of the characters has a birthday on Lammas Day—August 1st?

   A. Juliet   B. Romeo   C. Mercutio   D. The nurse

14) The beautiful and haunting last lines of this play are "For never was a story of more woe/ than this of Juliet and her Romeo." Who speaks these lines?

   A. The chorus   B. Friar Laurence   C. Lord Capulet   D. Prince Escalus

15) At the end of the play, Montague and Capulet declare that they will honor the memory of Romeo and Juliet through which means?

   A. They will have a poem written which will tell their story.
   B. They will erect golden statues of the young lovers.
   C. They will have a feast to honor the lovers once every year.
   D. They will help Prince Escalus end all feuds in Verona.

16) What does Juliet place by her bedside as she takes the sleeping potion?

   A. Bible   B. Dagger   C. Portrait of Romeo   D. Tybalt's ring

17) Who is the last person to see Juliet alive?

   A. Friar Laurence   B. Romeo   C. The nurse   D. Lady Capulet

18) Why doesn't Romeo's mother accompany her husband to the tomb in the final act?

A. She was searching for Romeo.   B. She was ill with grief over Romeo's exile.
C. She died of grief over Romeo's exile.   D. She is still angry with the Capulets.

19) Friar Laurence gives Juliet a potion that will make her appear to be dead. For how many hours will the effect of this potion last?

A. 12   B. 24   C. 36   D. 42

20) Who tells Romeo that Juliet is dead?

A. Benvolio   B. Friar Laurence   C. Lord Montague   D. Balthasar

Quiz 79

Pluck My Magic Garment From Me: The Play *The Tempest*

The Tempest is a wonderful play filled with magic, villains, and young lovers. Some scholars believe that it is Shakespeare's farewell to the theatrical world. We probably will never know Shakespeare's intentions for this play, but let's see what you know about the magical mystery tour that is *The Tempest*.

1) How long have Prospero and his daughter Miranda been on the island where the play is set?

A. 5 years   B. 7 years   C. 10 years   D. 12 years

2) Who is the "honest old councillor" who aided Prospero and Miranda when they were banished?

A. Adrian   B. Francisco   C. Stephano   D. Gonzalo

3) Who is the King of Naples?

A. Alonso   B. Antonio   C. Ferdinand   D. Adrian

4) Before he was usurped by his brother, Prospero was Duke of which Italian city?

A. Padua   B. Milan   C. Venice   D. Florence

5) Who was the brother who usurped Prospero's kingdom?

A. Alonso   B. Francisco   C. Antonio   D. Ferdinand

6) Ferdinand is the son of which character?

A. Antonio   B. Gonzalo   C. Alonso   D. Sebastian

7) Where was Ariel imprisoned until Prospero freed him?

A. In a cave under the sea   B. In a cloven pine
C. In a boulder by the sea   D. In a blade of grass

8) Alonso is returning from the wedding of his daughter when Prospero conjures the tempest that strands his ship on the island. Although she does not actually appear in the play, what is the name of Alonso's daughter?

    A. Claribel   B. Annabel   C. Hermione   D. Dorinda

9) The description of Caliban that is given makes him half man and half what other creature?

    A. Dog   B. Lizard   C. Toad   D. Fish

10) Caliban worships him as a god because he gave him an alcoholic drink.

    A. Sebastian   B. Stephano   C. Alonso   D. Antonio

11) Who does Antonio persuade to try to kill Alonso as he lies sleeping?

    A. Trinculo   B. Gonzalo   C. Sebastian   D. Adrian

12) What is the reason that Prospero gives for why he enslaved Caliban?

    A. Caliban tried to rape Miranda.
    B. Caliban tried to kill Prospero and rule the island.
    C. Caliban tried to kill Ariel.
    D. Caliban stole Prospero's books and tried to create evil spells.

13) Which character does Caliban originally think is one of Prospero's tormenting spirits?

    A. Stephano   B. Trinculo   C. Boatswain   D. Gonzalo

14) How old was Miranda when she first arrived on the island?

    A. 3 years old   B. 5 years old   C. 8 years old   D. 10 years old

15) During the magic banquet (3.3) Ariel assumes the shape of which creature?

    A. Dragon   B. Wolf   C. Bat   D. Harpy

16) What is the name of Caliban's mother?

    A. Bellona   B. Sycorax   C. Setebos   D. Argier

17) Which of the following does NOT occur in *The Tempest*?

    A. Stephano and Triculo engage in a drunken duel, and Triculo is wounded.
    B. Prospero gives up his magic.
    C. Ariel is given his freedom.
    D. Prospero tests Ferdinand's love for Miranda by forcing him to carry wood.

18) What is the last order that Prospero gives Ariel?

    A. To imprison Caliban in a cave, as punishment for his evil plots
    B. To arrange the marriage of Ferdinand and Miranda
    C. To provide calm seas for the return of the ships to Italy
    D. To bless the island for all future visitors

19) By the end of the play, all of the following statements are true except one. Which one is NOT true?

    A. Caliban admits he was foolish to think his drunken companions were gods.
    B. Prospero plans to return to his Italian kingdom.
    C. Gonzalo decides to stay on the island and form a utopian community there.
    D. Prospero decides not to seek vengeance against those who wronged him.

20) Which character speaks an epilogue at the end of the play?

    A. Ariel   B. Prospero   C. Miranda   D. Caliban

Quiz 80

Laugh Yourself Into Stitches: The Play *Twelfth Night*

Twelfth Night **is one of Shakespeare's most highly regarded comedies. Test your knowledge of this hilarious and thought-provoking play by answering the following questions. Good luck!**

1) Sebastian and Viola are from which city?

    A. Messaline   B. Ephesus   C. Florence   D. Trieste

2) How does Viola come to be at Orsino's court?

    A. She saw him, fell in love with him, and went to woo him.
    B. She and her brother are shipwrecked and separated.
    C. She is given bad directions by a thief who plans to rob her.
    D. She is just traveling aimlessly, mourning the death of her father.

3) What is Sir Toby Belch's relation to Olivia?

    A. Cousin   B. Nephew   C. Uncle   D. Brother

4) What is Malvolio's position in Olivia's household?

    A. Tutor   B. Steward   C. Butler   D. Cook

5) What is Sir Toby's greatest vice?

    A. Food of all types   B. Tobacco   C. Lying   D. Alcoholic beverages

6) Who of these is NOT one of Orsino's servants?

    A. Fabian   B. Valentine   C. Cesario   D. Curio

7) Why does Feste calls Olivia a fool?

    A. She will not accept Orsino.
    B. She will not allow parties and singing in her house.
    C. She doesn't want to have children, and pass on her beauty.
    D. She mourns her brother, when he's in heaven.

8) Before serving Olivia, Feste served which of the following?

    A. Sir Toby Belch   B. Sir Andrew Aquecheek
    C. Orsino   D. Olivia's father

9) Why is Antonio a wanted man in Illyria?

    A. He stole valuable jewels from Orsino.   B. He killed Orsino's cousin in a duel.
    C. He committed piracy against Illyria.   D. He is a spy for the enemy of Illyria.

10) Who forges the letter that Malvolio thinks is from Olivia?

    A. Feste   B. Maria   C. Sir Toby   D. Sir Andrew

11) What does Antonio give to Sebastian when they separate in Illyria?

    A. His purse   B. His hat   C. A jewel   D. A letter

12) When does Viola first realize that Olivia loves "Cesario"?

    A. When she invites "Cesario" back after their second meeting
    B. When she sends "Cesario" the ring
    C. When Olivia asks if "Cesario" loves her
    D. When Olivia asks questions to test "Cesario's" eligibility

13) Who challenges "Cesario" to a duel?

    A. Sebastian   B. Sir Toby   C. Sir Andrew   D. Fabian

14) The letter that is left to dupe Malvolio recommends that he display all of the following when wooing Olivia EXCEPT what?

    A. Smiles   B. Yellow stockings   C. Red velvet, plumed hat   D. Cross garters

15) As what does Feste disguise himself when he speaks with the imprisoned Malvolio?

    A. Curate   B. Jailer   C. School teacher   D. Magistrate

16) Which character is involved in the scheme to bait Malvolio with the fake letter?

    A. Valentine   B. Curio   C. Sebastian   D. Fabian

17) Who does Maria plan to marry at the end of the play?

    A. Feste   B. Antonio   C. Sir Andrew   D. Sir Toby

18) Who wounds Sir Toby in a fight?

    A. Sebastian   B. Antonio   C. Sir Andrew   D. Orsino

19) Who is NOT in love with Olivia at one point in the play?

    A. Sir Andrew   B. Malvolio   C. Antonio   D. Orsino

20) The chorus of the ending song that Feste sings is:

    A. "The rain it raineth every day"
    B. "A thousand, thousand sighs to save"
    C. "Youth's a stuff will not endure"
    D. "Farewell dear heart, since I needs be gone"

Quiz 81

A Sad Tale's Best for Winter: The Play *The Winter's Tale*

Along with **The Tempest,** Shakespeare's **The Winter's Tale** is a triumph of the dramatic form scholars have come to call the "romance." Like *Othello,* it is a play about the discrepancy between appearance and reality and the horrible consequences that can result when one is not astute enough to know the difference. However, unlike *Othello,* it has a happy ending (even though, in the play, it takes many years for it to arrive).

1) Which kingdoms are ruled by Leontes and Polixenes?

    A. Leontes is king of Athens, and Polixenes is king of Cyprus.
    B. Leontes is king of Cyprus, and Polixenes is king of Athens.
    C. Leontes is king of Bohemia, and Polixenes is king of Sicilia.
    D. Leontes is king of Sicilia, and Polixenes is king of Bohemia.

2) Why is Polixenes in the kingdom of Leontes at the beginning of the play?

    A. To make arrangements for a military treaty between the two kingdoms
    B. To arrange economic agreements between the two kingdoms
    C. Visiting, because they have been friends since childhood
    D. Taking refuge, because the ship on which he was traveling was damaged in a storm

3) What is the name of the young son of Leontes?

    A. Dion   B. Mamillius   C. Cleomenes   D. Ventidius

4) Who is the husband of Paulina at the beginning of the play?

    A. Antigonus   B. Archidamus   C. Camillo   D. Polixenes

5) As the play opens, Polixenes has been the guest of Leontes for what period of time?

    A. 1 month   B. 3 months   C. 6 months   D. 9 months

6) Who does Leontes order to poison Polixenes?

    A. Camillo   B. Cleomenes   C. Dion   D. Mamillius

7) To determine whether or not Hermione is guilty of adultery, Leontes sends messengers to the oracle of which deity at Delphos?

    A. Jupiter   B. Venus   C. Apollo   D. Juno

8) How does Paulina attempt to convince Leontes that the child, born to Hermione while she was in prison, is his daughter?

    A. She says that Hermione was never alone with Polixenes.
    B. She says that Polixenes is happily married.
    C. She says that the child physically resembles Leontes.
    D. She says that Hermione is morally incapable of adultery.

9) Who delivers the written declaration of the oracle to Leontes?

    A. Camillo and Dion   B. Cleomenes and Dion
    C. Camillo and Archidamus   D. Cleomenes and Antigonus

10) Which of the following is NOT a statement in the scroll received from the oracle?

    A. "Hermione is chaste, Polixenes is blameless."
    B. "Hermione will sleep, and her daughter will be lost."
    C. "Camillo is a true subject, Leontes is a jealous tyrant."
    D. "The King shall live without an heir, if that which is lost is not found."

11) Who appears to Antigonus in a dream the night before he abandons Perdita in the wilderness on a foreign shore?

    A. Mamillius   B. Paulina   C. Leontes   D. Hermione

12) How does Antigonus die?

    A. Killed by a bear
    B. By falling ill shortly after returning home
    C. In a stormy shipwreck during his return voyage
    D. Of a broken heart, after he is forced to abandon Hermione's daughter

13) At the beginning of Act 4, Time, as a Chorus, announces the passing of how many years?

    A. 14   B. 15   C. 16   D. 17

14) After she is abandoned, Perdita is found and raised by whom?

    A. A farmer   B. A peddler   C. A tinker   D. A shepherd

15) Florizel, the son of Polixenes, takes what alias as he woos Perdita?

    A. Cadwal   B. Doricles   C. Lodowick   D. Sebastian

16) Who can be described as a singing peddler and a thief?

    A. Mopsa   B. Dorcas   C. Autolycus   D. Giacomo

17) Who suggests that Florizel and Perdita flee to the kingdom of Leontes to get married?

    A. Camillo   B. Autolycus   C. Mopsa   D. Dorcas

18) As Florizel prepares to flee with Perdita, he is disguised by exchanging clothes with whom?

    A. A sailor   B. An old shepherd C. Mopsa   D. Autolycus

19) Leontes has sworn never to marry again until who gives him permission to do so?

    A. Polixenes   B. Paulina   C. Perdita   D. Mamillius

20) Who does Paulina marry at the end of the play?

    A. Cleomenes   B. Archidamus   C. Dion   D. Camillo

Section VI

Just for Fun

Quiz 82

Wild and Whirling Words: Shakespearean Vocabulary

The works of Shakespeare are filled with many interesting and fun words. Some are archaic and obsolete today, but see if you can pick out the correct definition for each. Good luck!

1) Clodpole:
   A. Bedroom   B. Quarreler   C. Dunce   D. Wrinkled apple

2) Bodkin:
   A. Fool   B. Dagger   C. Rude fellow   D. Gossip

3) Welkin:
   A. Sky   B. Day   C. Officer   D. Noose

4) Carbuncle:
   A. Harlot   B. Meal   C. Song   D. Ruby

5) Fardel:
   A. Simpleton   B. Bully   C. Gulp   D. Burden

6) Sooth:
   A. Dainty   B. Truth   C. Beardless   D. Grimy

7) Prig:
   A. Prison   B. Friend   C. Thief   D. Slob

8) Gibbet:
   A. Intestines   B. Gallows   C. Collar   D. Spear

9) Malapert:
   A. Sneaky person   B. Demon   C. Hawk   D. Rude person

10) Foppery:
   A. Foolishness   B. Infection   C. Preparation   D. Disdain

11) Smatch:
   A. Small portion   B. Smack   C. Kiss   D. Taste

12) Ouph:

    A. Grunt   B. Disaster   C. Laugh   D. Elf

13) Catch:

    A. Song   B. Disease   C. Jailer   D. Constable

14) Bugbear:

    A. Insect   B. Stubborn   C. Goblin   D. Politician

15) Perchance:

    A. Dice game   B. Perhaps   C. Hasty   D. Crude

16) Recreant:

    A. Coward   B. Lawless   C. Deputy   D. Meal

17) Grammarcy:

    A. A park   B. Thank you   C. Enough   D. Alas

18) Quest:

    A. Explorer   B. Constable   C. Jury   D. Soldier

19) Mickle:

    A. Dejected   B. Interruption   C. Great   D. Plow

20) Pickthank:

    A. Informer   B. Frenchman   C. Politician   D. Peasant

21) Whirligig:

    A. A tornado   B. A hurricane   C. A drinking song   D. A top

22) Moiety:

    A. Portion   B. Religion   C. Multicolored   D. Mischief

23) Wight:

    A. Wheel   B. Drawer   C. Person   D. Fairy

24) Matin:

    A. Buzzard   B. Star   C. Morning   D. Sea

25) Sith:

    A. Stitch   B. Since   C. Also   D. Alas

Quiz 83

I Smell a Device: Literary Features and Terms Used by Shakespeare

As most excellent writers do, William Shakespeare employed many different literary devices and literary features in his works. In the answer bank, you will find some of the devices he used; see if you can match them with the examples or descriptions provided.

Alliteration	Blazon	Dramatic irony	Metonymy	Prolepsis
Allusion	Caesura	Hyperbole	Onomatopoeia	Simile
Anachronism	Chiasmus	Invective	Oxymoron	Soliloquy
Anagnorisis	Doggerel	Metaphor	Paradox	Synecdoche

1) A denunciation of a person by using derogatory epithets, as in *Henry IV, Part One*, when Prince Hal calls Falstaff "this bed presser, this horseback-breaker, this huge hill of flesh." *Henry IV, Part One* (2.4.242)

2) It makes an explicit comparison between two distinctly different things using a word of comparison such as *like* or *as*, as in comparing a schoolboy "creeping like snail/ Unwillingly to school." *As You Like It* (2.7.146)

3) Two terms used together that are contraries in ordinary usage, as in "Feather of lead, bright smoke, cold fire, sick health." *Romeo and Juliet* (1.1.180)

4) A rhetorical exaggeration, as in "His legs bestride the ocean; his reared arm crested the world." *Antony and Cleopatra* (5.2.82)

5) Trivial or bad poetry, often characterized by a monotonous rhythm, as in the poetry of the "rude mechanicals" in *A Midsummer Night's Dream*.

6) Use of words that seem to imitate the sounds they refer to, as in "Sometimes a thousand twanging instruments/ Will hum about mine ears." *The Tempest* (3.2.137)

7) A listing of a beloved's admirable physical qualities in a love poem, as mocked in "Sonnet 130."

8) A figure of speech in which two terms are repeated in reverse order, as in "I wasted time, and now doth time waste me." *Richard II* (5.5.49)

9) A figure of speech in which something is described prematurely in terms that are not yet applicable, as in "I am dead, Horatio." *Hamlet* (5.2.333)

10) A part of something is used to signify the whole, as in York addressing Bolingbroke as, "banished and forbidden legs." *Richard II* (2.3.90)

11) Discrepancy between what a character knows about his situation and what the audience knows about it, as in Duncan's remarks about the welcoming appearance of the castle in which he is about to be murdered. *Macbeth* (1.6.1-3)

12) A pause within a line of verse.

13) Repetition of similar sounds (usually initial consonants) within any sequence of words, as in "Borne on the bier with white and bristly beard." "Sonnet 12"

14) The representation of something as existing or occurring at some other than its proper time, as in the mention of a clock in *Julius Caesar* (2.1.192).

15) An expression that appears puzzling or self-contradictory, as in "the truest poetry is the most feigning." *As You Like It* (3.3.19)

16) A comparison made between two distinctly different things without a word used to assert the comparison, as in "the bubble reputation." *As You Like It* (2.7.152)

17) A dramatic speech uttered by a single character alone on the stage, as in Richard III's speech which begins the play that bears his name.

18) An indirect reference to something that the author expects the reader to recognize, as in the many references to Roman mythology made by Shakespeare.

19) The turning point at which a protagonist discovers the true state of which he had been unaware, as in Othello's recognition that Desdemona was not unfaithful.

20) A figure of speech that substitutes one thing for another with which it has become closely associated, as in "the quick and the dead" to refer to people. *Hamlet* (5.1.126)

Quiz 84

The Articles Collected From His Life: Biography of William Shakespeare

Although not much is definitively known about the life of William Shakespeare, we actually do know more about him than most of the writers of his time. Much of what is printed about him today is speculation and surmise, but the questions below do pertain to the known facts of the life of this remarkable author.

1) In which English village was Shakespeare born?

    A. Snitterfield   B. Shrewsbury   C. Tewkesbury   D. Stratford

2) Which was the maiden name of Shakespeare's wife, Anne?

    A. Sadler   B. Hathaway   C. Fields   D. Whatley

3) Which was the maiden name of Shakespeare's mother, Mary"

    A. Arden   B. Avon   C. Lowin   D. Dowden

4) How many children did Shakespeare's parents, John and Mary, have?

    A. 2   B. 4   C. 6   D. 8

5) How many children did William and Anne Shakespeare have?

    A. 1   B. 2   C. 3   D. 4

6) In which year was William Shakespeare was born?

    A. 1552   B. 1558   C. 1560   D. 1564

7) In which year did William Shakespeare die?

    A. 1611   B. 1616   C. 1623   D. 1631

8) What is the name of the river that flows through William Shakespeare's hometown?

    A. Avon   B. Thames   C. Severn   D. Trent

9) Which is the day that is commonly attributed to be William Shakespeare's birthday?

    A. April 23   B. May 23   C. June 23   D. July 23

10) How many of Shakespeare's children survived him?

    A. None   B. 1   C. 2   D. 3

11) Which one of the following survived William Shakespeare?

    A. His mother   B. His father   C. His wife   D. His brother

12) Which is believed to have been the primary occupation of William Shakespeare's father?

   A. Butcher   B. Tinker   C. Glover   D. Wine merchant

13) What controversial item was the only specific thing left by William Shakespeare to his wife in his will?

   A. The second best bed   B. A copy of *The Rape of Lucrece*
   C. 50 bushels of wool   D. A deed to only the eastern half of his house

14) How many signatures of William Shakespeare have survived?

   A. None   B. 1   C. 3   D. 6

15) Who were the two fellow actors and friends of Shakespeare responsible for the publication of The First Folio, the first published collection of Shakespeare's works?

   A. Richard and Cuthbert Burbage   B. John Heminges and Henry Condell
   C. Augustine Philips and John Sly   D. Robert Armin and William Ostler

16) How many grandchildren did William Shakespeare have?

   A. 4   B. 5   C. 6   D. 7

17) Which of the following is the creator of the portrait of Shakespeare which appears in The First Folio of 1623?

   A. Richard Burbage   B. John Chandos   C. Martin Droeshout   D. Edward Boyden

18) Who of the following was a dramatist of the Restoration period who sometimes claimed (especially when drinking) to be the illegitimate son of William Shakespeare?

   A. Francis Beaumont   B. William D'avenant
   C. John Dryden   D. John Webster

19) What is the name of the street where the birthplace of William Shakespeare is located?

   A. High Street   B. Bridge Street   C. Church Street   D. Henley Street

20) In 1607, Edmund, the youngest brother of William Shakespeare, died at age 27. What seems to have been the occupation of Edmund Shakespeare?

   A. Farmer   B. Actor   C. Sailor   D. Minister

21) What was the profession of John Hall, William Shakespeare's son-in-law?

   A. Lawyer   B. Vintner   C. Medical doctor   D. Butcher

22) What is the name of the church where William Shakespeare is buried?

   A. Holy Trinity   B. Westminster Abbey
   C. Canterbury Cathedral   D. St. Giles

23) Which of the following statements about Shakespeare is the one that can be substantiated with documented evidence?

    A. He was a witness in a lawsuit.   B. He left his hometown for London in 1592.
    C. He was caught poaching deer.   D. He went to the local grammar school.

24) Which of the following was NOT the name of one of Shakespeare's sisters?

    A. Joan   B. Margaret   C. Alice   D. Anne

25) Which of the following was the name of Shakespeare's son-in-law?

    A. William Campbell   B. Thomas Quiney   C. William Catesby   D. Nathan Field

Quiz 85

I Have a Sonnet Will Serve the Turn: Sonnets and Other Poetry

    In addition to the immortal plays for which he is now most famous, William Shakespeare also wrote sonnets and narrative poems which were regarded as a higher literary form than the plays and were extremely popular in his own time. Test your knowledge of these poems by answering the questions below.

1) In which country did the sonnet form originate?

    A. England   B. Italy   C. France   D. Spain

2) How many sonnets did Shakespeare write?

    A. 110   B. 154   C. 200   D. 340

3) How many lines are in a sonnet?

    A. 14   B. 16   C. 18   D. 20

4) Which is the verse pattern used to write a sonnet?

    A. Heroic couplets   B. Anapestic trimeter
    C. Trochaic tetrameter   D. Iambic pentameter

5) How many syllables are in a line of a sonnet?

   A. 8   B. 10   C. 12   D. 14

6) Which pattern expresses the rhyme scheme of a Shakespearean sonnet?

   A. ABBA ABBA CDCD CD   B. AABB CCDD EEFF GG
   C. ABAB CDCD EFEF GG   D. Has no rhyme

7) To whom did William Shakespeare dedicate the sonnets?

   A. Mr. W.H.   B. Queen Elizabeth C. Earl of Essex   D. his wife

8) Which of the following is NOT addressed by Shakespeare's sonnets?

   A. A fair youth   B. A dark-haired lady   C. A child   D. A rival poet

9) Of all Shakespeare's sonnets, which word is most often used as the last word of the poem?

   A. Me   B. Thee   C. Day   D. Light

10) Which play begins with a sonnet?

   A. *Love's Labor's Lost*   B. *Romeo and Juliet*
   C. *The Two Gentlemen of Verona*   D. *As You Like It*

11) The line "the mortal moon hath her eclipse endured" in Sonnet 107 is believed by some scholars to allude to the death of which of the following?

   A. His wife   B. His mother   C. His mistress   D. Queen Elizabeth

12) Which famous author made the following statement about Shakespeare's sonnets: "With this key, Shakespeare unlocked his heart"?

   A. John Keats   B. William Blake
   C. Samuel Taylor Coleridge   D. William Wordsworth

13) Which of the following works attributed to Shakespeare appears as a coda at the end of the Sonnets when they were first published in quarto in 1609?

   A. *The Passionate Pilgrim*   B. *A Funeral Elegy*
   C. *A Lover's Complaint*   D. *The Phoenix and the Turtle*

14) Which poetic work did William Shakespeare himself refer to as the "first heir of my invention"?

   A. *Venus and Adonis*   B. *The Rape of Lucrece*
   C. the Sonnets   D. *A Lover's Complaint*

15) Which of the following poems attributed to Shakespeare is the shortest?

   A. *Venus and Adonis*   B. *The Phoenix and the Turtle*
   C. *The Rape of Lucrece*   D. *A Lover's Complaint*

16) Which was the patron to whom Shakespeare dedicated the poems *Venus and Adonis* and *The Rape of Lucrece*?

    A. Henry Wriothesley, Earl of Southampton   B. Henry Hunsdon, Lord Chamberlain
    C. Robert Devereaux, Earl of Essex   D. Queen Elizabeth

17) How is Adonis killed in *Venus and Adonis*?

    A. Gored by the tusk of a boar   B. Drowns while chasing a boar
    C. Killed by the jealous god, Ares   D. Commits suicide

18) In *Venus and Adonis*, when the dead body of Adonis melts away, what springs up in its place?

    A. A red rose   B. A mulberry tree   C. A bubbling spring   D. A purple flower

19) Which creature pulls the chariot of Venus in *Venus and Adonis*?

    A. Sea horses   B. Fiery horses   C. Doves   D. Eagles

20) In which poem will you find a woman sitting by a river and tearing up love letters and throwing gift jewels into the water?

    A. *The Phoenix and the Turtle*   B. *Funeral Elegy*
    C. *A Lover's Complaint*   D. *The Passionate Pilgrim*

21) Which is a collection of 20 short, amorous, and somewhat erotic poems published in 1599 and commonly attributed to Shakespeare?

    A. *The Phoenix and the Turtle*   B. *Funeral Elegy*
    C. *A Lover's Complaint*   D. *The Passionate Pilgrim*

22) Which is the rhyme pattern used by Shakespeare in *The Rape of Lucrece*?

    A. Rhyme royal   B. Double rhyme   C. Heroic couplets   D. Tercets

23) In Shakespeare's narrative poem *The Rape of Lucrece*, who rapes Lucrece?

    A. Tarquin   B. Collatine   C. Giacomo   D. Junius

24) Who is the Roman statesman who is the husband of Lucrece?

    A. Tarquin   B. Collatine   C. Giacomo   D. Junius

25) What is the ultimate fate of Lucrece in *The Rape of Lucrece*?

    A. Killed by her rapist
    B. Killed by her husband
    C. Commits suicide by stabbing herself
    D. Goes to a nunnery where she dies years later

Quiz 86

The Numbers True: Statistical Shakespeare

Okay, here's one for all you bean counters and number crunchers out there! Everyone likes to dabble with statistics every now and then, so here's a Shakespeare quiz which focuses on numerical analysis. Although line and word counts may vary based on the edition, resulting in slight numeric differences, these questions still apply.

1) Which play has the most lines?

    A. *Coriolanus*   B. *Hamlet*   C. *As You*   D. *Richard III*

2) Which play has the fewest lines?

    A. *MN Dream*   B. *Tempest*   C. *Com Err*   D. *Two Gents*

3) After Hamlet's 1,422 lines, which Shakespearean character has the next largest role?

    A. Mark Antony in *Ant & Cleo*   B. Coriolanus in *Coriolanus*
    C. King Lear in *Lear*   D. Richard III in *Richard III*

4) In which of the following plays does the title character <u>NOT</u> speak the most lines?

    A. *Othello*   B. *Henry V*   C. *Coriolanus*   D. *Timon*

5) In all the plays of Shakespeare, which female character has the most lines?

    A. Cleopatra in *Ant & Cleo*   B. Rosalind in *As You*
    C. Portia in *Merchant*   D. Juliet in *Rom & Jul*

6) In all the plays of Shakespeare, which female character ranks second for most lines?

    A. Cleopatra in *Ant & Cleo*   B. Rosalind in *As You*
    C. Portia in *Merchant*   D. Juliet in *Rom & Jul*

7) In number of lines, which is the shortest of Shakespeare's tragedies?

    A. *Timon*   B. *Titus*   C. *J. Caesar*   D. *Macbeth*

8) Which of the following has the fewest lines written in verse?

    A. *As You*   B. *Merry Wives*   C. *Much Ado*   D. *Win Tale*

9) On average, what percentage of lines in a typical play by Shakespeare are rhymed?

    A. 10%   B. 25%   C. 40%   D. 60%

10) In four of Shakespeare's plays, a female character has the largest part (in words). Who of the following does NOT have the largest part in the play in which she appears?

    A. Helena in *All's Well*   B. Portia in *Merchant*

C. Cleopatra in *Ant & Cleo*   D. Imogen in *Cymbeline*

11) What percentage of lines in a typical play by William Shakespeare are written in blank verse?

    A. 45%   B. 55%   C. 65%   D. 75%

12) Which play has the highest percentage of rhyming lines?

    A. *MN Dream*   B. *Love' s LL*   C. *Macbeth*   D. *Twelfth N*

13) How many plays were included in The First Folio (the first published collection of William Shakespeare's works)?

    A. 36   B. 38   C. 40   D. 42

14) Of all the plays in The First Folio, how many were being published for the first time?

    A. 6   B. 10   C. 12   D. 18

15) Which play is divided into the most scenes?

    A. *Hamlet*   B. *Coriolanus*   C. *Ant & Cleo*   D. *2 Henry IV*

16) Which of the following roles contains more than 1,000 lines?

    A. Falstaff in *Merry Wives*   B. Henry V in *Henry V*
    C. Timon in *Timon*   D. Benedick in *Much Ado*

17) Which of the following tragedies has the highest percentage of rhyming lines?

    A. *Lear*   B. *Othello*   C. *Hamlet*   D. *Rom & Jul*

18) Which play has the most unique individual words?

    A. *Tam Shrew*   B. *Richard II*   C. *Henry V*   D. *Hamlet*

19) Of the almost 900,000 words penned by Shakespeare, what is the total number of different words that he used?

    A. 8,961   B. 16,222   C. 29,066   D. 35,218

20) Ranging through all of Shakespeare's works, with the exception of *Pericles* and the non-dramatic poems, one biblical scholar has identified quotations from or references to how many books in the Bible?

    A. 12   B. 22   C. 32   D. 42

Quiz 87

This Wooden O: The Theater of Shakespeare

There has always been a great deal of interest in the theaters of Shakespeare's time, and that interest was intensified in 1989 with the official uncovering of the foundations of the Rose Theater and Shakespeare's Globe Theater. Test your knowledge of the theaters of Shakespeare's time by answering the following questions.

1) Which of the following is now believed to be the first playhouse constructed in England?
   A. Curtain   B. Swan   C. Rose   D. Red Lion

2) What was the London suburb where the Globe Theatre was located?
   A. Knightsbridge   B. Southwark   C. Cripplegate   D. Cheapside

3) It was the name given to the people who paid a penny to stand in the area in the front of the stage of the Globe to watch a performance.
   A. Canaries   B. Gatherers   C. Strumpets   D. Groundlings

4) Which is generally considered the best estimate of the Globe Theatre's seating capacity?
   A. 1,000   B. 2,500   C. 3,500   D. 5,000

5) In which year was the first Globe Theater built?
   A. 1585   B. 1592   C. 1599   D. 1605

6) Of all the playhouses that existed during Shakespeare's lifetime, there currently exists a drawing of the interior of only one. Which is it?
   A. Rose   B. Fortune   C. Swan   D. Curtain

7) The Globe Theatre was built with the timber from the dismantling of which theater?
   A. Blackfriars   B. The Theatre   C. Red Lion   D. Hope

8) Who was the carpenter primarily responsible for the building of the Globe and Fortune playhouses?
   A. Peter Street   B. Cuthbert Burbage   C. Hamnet Sadler   D. Thomas Pope

9) Aside from the Globe, of which other theater was Shakespeare part owner?
   A. Blackfriars   B. Whitechapel   C. Paris Gardens   D. Fortune

10) Which man's notes offer the only preserved eyewitness accounts of Shakespeare on the professional stage?
   A. Wenceslaus Hollar   B. Thomas Lodge
   C. Dr. Simon Forman   D. Ben Jonson

11) What was the name given to the area underneath the stage that was often used to represent the underworld?

    A. France   B. Spain   C. Purgatory   D. Hell

12) Which playhouse was closest in proximity to the Globe Theatre?

    A. Rose   B. Curtain   C. Whitefriars   D. Blackfriars

13) What was the name given to the area of the playhouse where the dressing rooms and storage rooms were located.

    A. The heavens   B. Inner below   C. Tiring house   D. Gentlemen's Rooms

14) What is believed to be the starting time of the performances in the outdoor theaters of Shakespeare's time?

    A. 10 a.m.   B. 12 p.m.   C. 2 p.m.   D. 4 p.m.

15) Which of Shakespeare's plays was being performed when the first Globe Theatre burned to the ground on June 29, 1613?

    A. *Henry V*   B. *Henry VIII*   C. *Hamlet*   D. *Julius Caesar*

16) What is believed to be the minimum price of admission at open-air playhouses during Shakespeare's time?

    A. A sixpence   B. 1 shilling   C. 1 farthing   D. 1 penny

17) In the theater of Shakespeare's time, what was the function of a "book-holder"?

    A. He served as the acting company's accountant.
    B. He was responsible for censuring and licensing the plays.
    C. He held the prompt-book to remind actors of their lines and cues.
    D. He assigned the roles to the actors.

18) Shakespeare was part owner, or "housekeeper," of the Globe Theatre, and as such, he originally owned how much of an interest in the playhouse?

    A. 10%   B. 25%   C. 50%   D. 75%

19) In which year was the second Globe torn down?

    A. 1624   B. 1644   C. 1688   D. 1702

20) In which year was the original location of the Globe Theatre determined?

    A. 1776   B. 1860   C. 1924   D. 1989

21) Although it is depicted as circular in drawings of the time, evacuation of the Globe site in 1989 proved that the playhouse had how many sides?

    A. 8   B. 10   C. 14   D. 20

22) Which American actor formed the Globe Playhouse Trust in 1970 that ultimately led to the reconstruction of the Globe Theatre, near the site of the original, in 1997?

     A. Kirk Douglas   B. Wallace Beery   C. Sam Wanamaker   D. Robert Mitchum

23) Which play was performed at the official opening of Shakespeare's Globe in 1997?

     A. *Hamlet*   B. *As You Like It*   C. *Henry V*   D. *The Tempest*

24) Which of the following was an indoor playhouse?

     A. Blackfriars   B. Fortune   C. Newington Butts   D. Swan

25) Shakespeare was a member of which acting company that called the Globe Theatre home?

     A. The Admiral's Men   B. The Lord Chamberlain's Men
     C. The Queen's Men   D. The Lord Mayor's Men

Quiz 88

Behold the Poor Remains, Part I: Shakespearean Odds and Ends

How about some leftovers? Below is a potpourri of questions that defied inclusion in a specific quiz; nevertheless, they are interesting and should be in this book somewhere. So here they are—try your luck with these tidbits of Shakespeare!

1) In an episode of a well-known television series, William Shakespeare returns to the 20th century and becomes a television writer. In which series did this scenario occur?

     A. *Star Trek*   B. *The Outer Limits*
     C. *Alfred Hitchcock Presents*   D. *The Twilight Zone*

2) Which was President Abraham Lincoln's favorite play?

     A. *Macbeth*   B. *The Comedy of Errors*   C. *Hamlet*   D. *Henry IV, Part One*

3) Which future United States President played the part of Desdemona in *Othello* while he served in the infantry?

     A. Zachary Taylor   B Ulysses S. Grant
     C. Theodore Roosevelt   D. Dwight D. Eisenhower

4) Beethoven's Piano Sonata no. 17 is also known by the title of one of Shakespeare's plays because Beethoven once stated that a clue to the meaning of the sonata could be found in reading the play. To which play was Beethoven referring?

     A. *The Tempest*   B. *The Winter's Tale*   C. *As You Like It*   D. *King Lear*

5) In the earliest published version of *Hamlet*, the famous line "To be or not to be, that is the question," does not end with the word "question." With which word does it ends?

     A. Idea   B. Thought   C. Point   D. Answer

6) Which is the best approximation of the number of copies of The First Folio that still survive today?

   A. 23   B. 230   C. 530   D. 1230

7) In *Othello*, a simple handkerchief plays an important role. Interestingly enough an English king that Shakespeare wrote about is credited with the invention of the handkerchief. Which one?

   A. Richard II   B. King John   C. Henry VI   D. Henry VIII

8) Which famous writer's work served as sources for Shakespeare's *Romeo and Juliet*, *Troilus and Cressida*, *The Two Noble Kinsmen*, and *A Midsummer Night's Dream*?

   A. Cervantes   B. Marlowe   C. Bacon   D. Chaucer

9) Ten of which planet's 15 moons are named after Shakespearean characters?

   A. Saturn   B. Mars   C. Jupiter   D. Uranus

10) Which 19th-century composer proposed for his epitaph Macbeth's statement that life "is a tale told by an idiot, full of sound and fury, and signifying nothing" (5.5.26)?

   A. Hector Berlioz   B. Johannes Brahms
   C. Frederic Chopin   D. Piotr Ilyitch Tchaikovsky

11) To which play did T.S. Eliot refer as "one of the stupidest and most uninspired plays ever written," and Tennessee Williams as "one of the most ridiculous"?

   A. *A Midsummer Night's Dream*   B. *Love's Labor's Lost*
   C. *Titus Andronicus*   D. *All's Well That Ends Well*

12) Although it may be considered an odd choice today, who played the role of Iago in the 1953 Philco Televison Playhouse production of *Othello*?

   A. Dean Martin   B. Frank Sinatra   C. Karl Madden   D. Walter Matthau

13) Who proclaimed that Shakespeare was "for an afternoon, but not for all time" and coined the term "bardolater" to describe the typical Shakespeare worshiper?

   A. Oscar Wilde   B. George Bernard Shaw
   C. Ernest Hemingway   D. F. Scott Fitzgerald

14) In 1794, which of the following men forged a variety of documents he claimed were written by Shakespeare, including a letter from Shakespeare to his wife, with a lock of the writer's hair?

   A. Nicholas Rowe   B. Edmund Malone
   C. William Henry Ireland   D. A.L. Rowse

15) Which two characters appear in four different plays—the most of any characters?

   A. Bardolph and Margaret of Anjou   B. Pistol and Mistress Quickly
   C. Doll Tearsheet and Falstaff   D. Henry V and Henry VI

16) Which author fictionally recreated the sex life of Shakespeare and seemed to attribute his genius to syphilis?

    A. Phillip Burton   B. Anthony Burgess
    C. Stephanie Crowell   D. Robert Nye

17) Which play has parts for only two women who, between them, have fewer than 10 lines?

    A. *Julius Caesar*   B. *2 Henry IV*   C. *Coriolanus*   D. *Timon of Athens*

18) In which city will you find the Folger Shakespeare Library?

    A. Washington, D.C.   B. Seattle, WA   C. Philadelphia, PA   D. Chicago, IL

19) Which highly regarded English poet kept a portrait of Shakespeare in his study beside him while he wrote, hoping that Shakespeare would spark his creativity?

    A. John Keats   B. Lord Byron
    C. Percy Shelley   D. Samuel Taylor Coleridge

20) In J.D. Salinger's *The Catcher in the Rye*, the protagonist, Holden Caufield, says, "What I'll have to do is, I'll have to read that play." To which play was Holden referring?

    A. *Macbeth*   B. *King Lear*   C. *Hamlet*   D. *Othello*

21) Which character does not die in the play that bears his name?

    A. Coriolanus   B. Cymbeline   C. Timon of Athens   D. Titus Andronicus

22) Which of the following plays did not appear in The First Folio of 1623?

    A. *Henry VIII*   B. *Timon of Athens*   C. *Coriolanus*   D. *Pericles*

23) Which play was included in The First Folio of 1623 but was accidentally omitted from the table of contents?

    A. *The Taming of the Shrew*   B. *Troilus and Cressida*
    C. *Titus Andronicus*   D. *The Two Gentlemen of Verona*

24) In which two plays do friars orchestrate plans that involve the fake death of a young woman?

    A. *Romeo and Juliet* and *Cymbeline*
    B. *All's Well That Ends Well* and *Much Ado About Nothing*
    C. *Cymbeline* and *All's Well That Ends Well*
    D. *Much Ado About Nothing* and *Romeo and Juliet*

25) In *The Taming of the Shrew*, what is the name of Petruchio's dog?

    A. Balthasar   B. Faustus   C. Troilus   D. Peto

Quiz 89

Behold the Poor Remains, Part II: Shakespearean Odds and Ends

If the previous quiz was not enough, here are some more odds and ends. Try your hand with these.

1) Who referred to Shakespeare as a "monster" and commented about the "few pearls" to be discovered in his "enormous dung heap"?

   A. Voltaire   B. Catherine the Great   C. Charles Baudelaire   D. John Adams

2) What is the name of the brother and sister team who compiled prose renditions of the comedies and tragedies and entitled them *Tales From Shakespeare?*

   A. Charles and Mary Lamb   B. William and Dorothy Wordsworth
   C. Samuel and Ann Coleridge   D. Charles and Margaret Dodgson

3) The earliest surviving fragment of Charles Dickens is a *burlesque* (a humorous mockery) of which Shakespearean play?

   A. *Macbeth*   B. *Hamlet*   C. *Othello*   D. *Richard III*

4) He coined the word *Shakesperoids* to refer to those who consider every word of Shakespeare to be sacred.

   A. James Fenimore Cooper   B. Mark Twain
   C. F. Scott Fitzgerald   D. James Thurber

5) In a 1937 Columbia Network radio adaptation of *Henry IV*, what role was performed by Humphrey Bogart?

   A. Prince Hal   B. Hotspur   C. Falstaff   D. Henry IV

6) Which of the plays is named after an English holiday?

   A. *All's Well That Ends Well*   B. *Measure for Measure*
   C. *Twelfth Night*   D. *The Winter's Tale*

7) Which of the following editors was responsible for producing *The Family Shakespeare*, a collection of Shakespeare's works that omitted "those words and expressions...which cannot with propriety be read aloud in the family" or "by a gentleman to a company of ladies"?

   A. Richard Brinsley Sheridan   B. Samuel Ireland
   C. Samuel Johnson   D. Thomas Bowdler

8) What was the name of the bull and bear baiting arena on the Southwark side of the Thames, near the Globe? (It is mentioned in *Henry VIII*.)

   A. Piccadilly Circus   B. Whitefriars   C. Paris Gardens   D. The White Hart

9) It seems that Falstaff was not the first choice for the name of the hilarious and cowardly fat knight that has become so well known to audiences through the ages. What is the name that Shakespeare first used for this character?

    A. Sir George Seacoal   B. Sir Harvey Hightower
    C. Sir John Oldcastle   D. Sir Cecil Lummox

10) Some believe that, in addition to the plays and poems commonly credited to him, Shakespeare also made a literary contribution to which other famous work?

    A. The King James Bible   B. The coronation speech of King James
    C. The Magna Carta   D. *Don Quixote*

11) Which play depicts the events of the Battle of Tewkesbury?

    A. *Richard III*   B. *3 Henry VI*   C. *King John*   D. *2 Henry IV*

12) Which person has been associated with more major productions of *Hamlet*, either as an actor or director, than any other in the 20th century?

    A. Laurence Olivier   B. John Gielgud   C. John Barrymore   D. Edwin Booth

13) *The Woman's Prize*, written by John Fletcher in 1611, was a sequel to which of Shakespeare's plays?

    A. *All's Well That Ends Well*   B. *Love's Labor's Lost*
    C. *The Two Gentlemen of Verona*   D. *The Taming of the Shrew*

14) In 1974, British playwright Edward Bond wrote a play that speculates on how William Shakespeare's wealth and fame prevented him from fully loving both family members and humanity. What was the name of this play?

    A. *New Place Blues*   B. *Swan's Song*   C. *Bingo*   D. *Revels End*

15) Which of the following is the author of *Rosencrantz and Guildenstern Are Dead*, a look at the *Hamlet* story through the eyes of these two rather minor, and possibly misunderstood, characters.

    A. Neil Simon   B. Sam Shepherd   C. Edward Albee   D. Tom Stoppard

16) What is the name of the London tavern where some allege that Shakespeare regularly drank with a group of fellow writers?

    A. Mermaid   B. Wild Goose   C. Bell and Whistle   D. Anchor

17) William Davenant's 1662 *The Law Against Lovers* is an adaptation of which two of Shakespeare's plays?

    A. *Much Ado About Nothing* and *Measure for Measure*
    B. *The Taming of the Shrew* and *Love's Labor's Lost*
    C. *All's Well That Ends Well* and *The Two Gentlemen of Verona*
    D. *As You Like It* and *Twelfth Night*

18) Which of the following plays inspired the most ballets of all Shakespeare's plays?

    A. *The Winter's Tale*   B. *Romeo and Juliet*

    C. *A Midsummer Night's Dream*   D. *The Tempest*

19) Which two characters quote the Bible most often?

    A. Hamlet and King Lear   B. Desdemona and Rosalind

    C. Henry VI and Richard III   D. Henry V and King John

20) The Romantic poet Percy Bysshe Shelley drowned while sailing in a small boat with the same name as one of Shakespeare's characters. Which one?

    A. Ariel   B. Rosalind   C. Caliban   D. Orlando

21) Which famous Shakespearean character's real historical name was Gruoch?

    A. The Queen in *Cymbeline*   B. Antiochus's daughter in *Pericles*

    C. Mortimer's wife in *1 Henry IV*   D. Lady Macbeth in *Macbeth*

22) Which character's last words are "I'll be reveng'd on the whole pack of you!"

    A. Duke Frederick in *As You Like It*   B. Caliban in *The Tempest*

    C. Don John in *Much Ado About Nothing*   D. Malvolio in *Twelfth Night*

23) Which of the following characters did the German writer Goethe describe as "an oak tree planted in a costly jar"?

    A. Othello   B. King Lear   C. Hamlet   D. Macbeth

24) Which Shakespearean character owns a grey horse called "Capilet"?

    A. Dogberry   B. Sir Andrew Aguecheek

    C. Bassanio   D. Sir John Falstaff

25) In which play will you find a stepbrother and stepsister combination?

    A. *Hamlet*   B. *Cymbeline*   C. *Pericles*   D. *Coriolanus*

Quiz 90

Let's Set Our Men in Order: Put Kings in Chronological Order

Although not all have plays named after them, Shakespeare's plays show us the reigns of a number of English kings. These 10 kings are listed in alphabetical order. Put them in the correct chronological order, by numbering them 1–10, from earliest to latest, according to the year(s) they ruled.

____ Edward IV   ____ Henry VII

____ Edward V   ____ Henry VIII

____ Henry IV   ____ John

____ Henry V   ____ Richard II

____ Henry VI   ____ Richard III

Quiz 91

Mince Not the General Tongue: Unscramble the Play Titles

Unscramble the anagrams to form the titles of some of Shakespeare's plays.

1) FOG THEM WHEN HIS TREAT

2) HOLE LOT

3) OH AT A BUM DO NOT CHUG IN

4) ELK IN RAG

5) MICE CAN'T VENT HER OF HE

6) CAB THEM

7) PET HEM TEST

8) JAIL US SAUCER

9) AYE LOUIS KIT

10) TOUR MAN JOEL DIE

11) METER MAIDS DRUM SANG HIM

12) CLEAN PARTY TOAD ANON

13) WE LET THE RATS IN

14) OF TIN ON THAMES

15) LOANS CURIO

16) USE RARE FUSE ME ROAM

17) VALOR BELT SO LOSS

18) HEED FOR ME SORRY COT

19) TANGLE ME FOOT WHERE VENT ON

20) VIEW FIRM ROSS THEN DOWERY

21) SEER CLIP

22) THEN SELL TALL LEWD LAWS

23) MY LICE BEN

24) I STAIN ROUND CUTS

25) SAIL DREAD CUTS OR SIN

Quiz 92

What's in a Name?, Part I: Unscramble Female Character Names

Unscramble the anagrams to form the names of some of Shakespeare's female characters.

1) HOPI ALE

2) ED MADE SON

3) TOP CAR ALE

4) ACE TRIBE

5) LIAR CODE

6) SIN OR LAD

7) HA KNIT ERA

8) I AT A TIN

9) IRAN DAM

10) SIN OR ALE

11) ABLE SAIL

12) SIR SANE

13) HAPPY TOIL

14) SIDE CARS

15) IN A RAM

16) VAIN AIL

17) I A MILE

18) RAM OAT

19) DEAR PIT

20) LONE RIG

21) LANE HE

22) I GNOME

23) TREED RUG

24) MINE HERO

25) HI MARE

Quiz 93

What's in a Name?, Part II: Unscramble Male Character Names

Unscramble the anagrams to form the names of some Shakespeare's male characters.

1) RIPE TOUCH

2) MEET US RID

3) DINNER FAD

4) CAB THEM

5) SHOE INTRO

6) A NO LORD

7) CAB NAIL

8) OR GO RIDE

9) CURIO MET

10) REAL SET

11) TEN LIE VAN

12) ATE LOON

13) RAGED

14) AS TAME PUN

15) PRO PROSE

16) BAR TERM

17) NUN CAD

18) IS AN BEAST

19) CAN FEEL

20) NO BAND AIL

21) SEER CLIP

22) RUST OIL

23) BOLD HARP

24) OX PENS LIE

25) ROE NOB

Quiz 94

My Nearest Dearest Enemy: Find the Rivals Word Search

In many of Shakespeare's plays, there is considerable tension and rivalry between some of the characters. For each character listed, write the name of his rival in the space provided, then find the rival's name in the word search. Some characters have more than one rival, of course, but only one rival for each can be found in the puzzle. Answers can be found horizontally, vertically, diagonally, forward, and backward.

```
A X I N E R S U M T P O L I X E N E S C
P Z F E J I B O S U N A L O I R O C D I
K A B E A T R I C E L U M A W V A S T A
E C L I R S U D H R S O H Q U A X E C G
C R E A L I T E P A N I R E H T A K O O
S O E O M B U R E C U Q I R E N L G E N
U S F H I O S I W E R O C T A V I U S A
I K E A R G N W N O E N A I S E T Q O S
D A O N V S W I T H S I R E S F O P A E
U T M E H U T O D A F O V O F I R Z U P
A H I A S N I R L L O Y E A R E H B Y I
L O H A E N C S O D E P T P I S A T H S
C R C L S E D T H I J S I L C R N O P A
H O A G J M I R U W L E F J B I T E R I
A V I T I T A N I A R U H P X S O G V D
C Y D A N O P C F G V I S O P T N M E N
R E W I L B E A D O P J U U L W I R G U
A L F C P S G E H U D L R A N C O R A M
E D E M E T R I U S F S I F Y L P B N D
V I S A U O Y Q W O T F R E V I L O H E
```

1) Arcite _____	11) Oberon _____
2) Benedick _____	12) Orlando _____
3) Diomedes _____	13) Othello _____
4) Edgar _____	14) Petruchio _____
5) Hamlet _____	15) Posthumus _____
6) Julius Caesar _____	16) Prince Hal _____
7) Leontes _____	17) Proteus _____
8) Lysander _____	18) Shallow _____
9) Macbeth _____	19) Shylock _____
10) Mark Antony _____	20) Tullus Aufidius _____

Quiz 95

I of These Will Wrest an Alphabet: Shakespeare A–Z Crossword Puzzle

In this crossword puzzle, the first letter of each correct response will correspond to a letter of the alphabet, from A to Z (but not in alphabetical order). Every letter of the alphabet begins only one answer each.

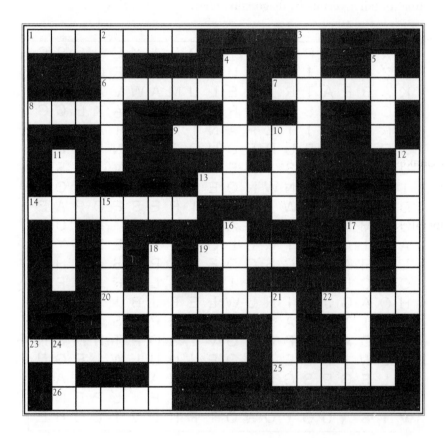

ACROSS

1. Honest, old counselor in *The Tempest*

6. Attends Hero in *Much Ado About Nothing*

7. Corrupt, doomed advisor of Henry VIII

8. Director of Royal Shakespeare Company

9. Planned to mourn dead brother for seven years in *Twelfth Night*

13. The shrew

14. Hostess of the Boar's Head Tavern

19. Opponent to Lancaster

20. Loves Hermia in *A Midsummer Night's Dream*

22. The _____ Lady of the Sonnets

23. Wife of Socrates—the only "X" word used by Shakespeare

25. Lear's good son

26. City where *The Taming of the Shrew* primarily takes place

DOWN

2. Shakespeare would say this, rather than "God's wounds"

3. In love with Orsino in *Twelfth Night*

4. Daughter of Pericles

5. Loves Claudio in *Much Ado About Nothing*

10. Kills the rebel Jack Cade in *2 Henry VI*

11. Mark Antony called him "the noblest Roman of them all"

12. Demands a pound of flesh

15. Juliet's surname

16. A merry wife with a jealous husband

17. The Fairy Queen in *A Midsummer Night's Dream*

18. Shylock's daughter

21. *The _____ of Lucrece*

24. Killed Cleopatra

Answer Key

Grading Scales

For 20-question quizzes:

17–20 A true Shakespeare scholar.
"An excellent unmatch'd wit and judgment..." (*Henry VIII*)

13–16 Your knowledge of Shakespeare is impressive.
"You are full of pretty answers..." (*As You Like It*)

9–12 No stranger to Shakespeare, but room for improvement.
"I will hope of better deeds tomorrow..." (*Antony and Cleopatra*)

5–8 Your Shakespeare knowledge is seriously lacking.
"I prithee, let me be better acquainted with you..." (*As You Like It*)

0–4 You urgently need to brush up on William Shakespeare.

"Get thee to a nunnery..." (*Hamlet*)

For 25-question quizzes:

21–25 A true Shakespeare scholar.
"An excellent unmatch'd wit and judgment..." (*Henry VIII*)

16–20 Your knowledge of Shakespeare is impressive.
"You are full of pretty answers..." (*As You Like It*)

11–15 No stranger to Shakespeare, but room for improvement.
"I will hope of better deeds tomorrow..." (*Antony and Cleopatra*)

6–10 Your Shakespeare knowledge is seriously lacking.
"I prithee, let me be better acquainted with you..." (*As You Like It*)

0–5 You urgently need to brush up on William Shakespeare.

"Get thee to a nunnery..." (*Hamlet*)

For Quiz 90:

9–10 A true Shakespeare scholar.
"An excellent unmatch'd wit and judgment..." (*Henry VIII*)

7–8 Your knowledge of Shakespeare is impressive.
"You are full of pretty answers..." (*As You Like It*)

5–6 No stranger to Shakespeare, but room for improvement.
"I will hope of better deeds tomorrow..." (*Antony and Cleopatra*)

3–4 Your Shakespeare knowledge is seriously lacking.
"I prithee, let me be better acquainted with you..." (*As You Like It*)

0–2 You urgently need to brush up on William Shakespeare.

"Get thee to a nunnery..." (*Hamlet*)

Quiz 1

1) *Hamlet* (Barnardo)
2) *Merchant* (Antonio)
3) *Henry V* (Chorus)
4) *Twelfth N* (Orsino)
5) *Macbeth* (Witch)
6) *Merry Wives* (Shallow)
7) *Love's LL* (Ferdinand)
8) *Titus* (Saturnius)
9) *Othello* (Roderigo)
10) *Richard III* (Richard III)
11) *Lear* (Kent)
12) *1 Henry IV* (King Henry IV)
13) *Tempest* (Shipmaster)
14) *Com Err* (Egeon)
15) *MN Dream* (Theseus)
16) *Tam Shrew* (Sly)
17) *3 Henry VI* (Warwick)
18) *Ant & Cleo* (Philo)
19) *Much Ado* (Leonato)
20) *J. Caesar* (Flavius)
21) *Tr & Cr* (Prologue)
22) *All's Well* (Countess of Rossillion)
23) *Measure* (Duke Vincentio)
24) *1 Henry VI* (Duke of Bedford)
25) *Rom & Juliet* (Chorus)

Quiz 2

1) *Henry V* (3.1.1—Henry V, as he leads his troops into battle)

2) *J. Caesar* (1.2.13—the Soothsayer's warning to Caesar)

3) *John* (3.4.93—Constance is lamenting the death of her son, Prince Arthur. It is believed that Shakespeare's son, Hamnet, died about the time he wrote this play and that this speech may reflect his personal anguish.)

4) *Othello* (3.3.165—Iago is manipulating Othello [and everyone else].)

5) *Richard III* (5.4.7—Richard III's famous cry of desperation on the battlefield)

6) *Rom & Jul* (2.2.184—Juliet)

7) *Tempest* (4.1.156—Prospero)

8) *Twelfth N* (2.5.144—Malvolio, reading a letter which will dupe him into ridicule)

9) *Hamlet* (1.5.106—Hamlet, after his first visit with the ghost of his father)

10) *1 Henry VI* (2.4.124—Richard Neville, the Earl of Warwick, is foreshadowing what would evolve into the Wars of the Roses.)

11) *Macbeth* (5.5.24—Macbeth is meditating on life, after learning of the death of his wife.)

12) *Merchant* (4.1.184—Portia)

13) *MN Dream* (3.2.115—the mischievous Puck's famous comment on humanity)

14) *Lear* (4.6.182—a typically depressing comment from Lear)

15) *2 Henry VI* (4.2.76—Dick the butcher comments on what he feels is the first step the new government under the rebel Jack Cade should take.)

16) *Richard II* (2.1.40—uttered by John of Gaunt; a great quote, especially if you're English)

17) *Merry Wives* (4.2.105—This statement, by Mistress Page, really was too easy, I'm afraid.)

18) *Tam Shrew* (3.2.229—Petruchio's view on women; thankfully not a popular opinion today)

19) *As You* (2.7.12—Jaques, after his encounter with Touchstone)

20) *Ant & Cleo* (1.1.33—Antony)

21) *Love's LL* (4.3.347—the witty Berowne)

22) *Win Tale* (1.2.67—Polixenes, as he reflects on his long friendship with Leontes)

23) *Much Ado* (1.1.199—Benedick's lament)

24) *1 Henry IV* (1.2.59—Falstaff, to Prince Hal)

25) *Measure* (2.1.1—Angelo, expressing his philosophy of law and governing)

Quiz 3

1) *Hamlet* (1.2.146)
2) *Love's LL* (5.1.36)
3) *As You* (3.5.52)
4) *Measure* (3.2.110)
5) *Lear* (4.2.30)
6) *Tam Shrew* (4.1.26)
7) *Richard III* (1.2.57)
8) *Coriolanus* (2.1.94)
9) *Win Tale* (2.1.173)
10) *Tr & Cr* (5.1.52)
11) *All's Well* (3.6.9)
12) *Henry V* (3.2.40)
13) *Merry Wives* (5.5.83)
14) *1 Henry IV* (3.3.24)
15) *J. Caesar* (1.1.35)
16) *Two Gents* (2.4.41)
17) *John* (4.3.123)
18) *Timon* (3.4.219)
19) *Much Ado* (2.1.3)
20) *Cymbeline* (1.2.29)
21) *Pericles* (4.6.168)
22) *Merchant* (1.2.88)
23) *2 Henry IV* (1.2.20)
24) *Rom & Jul* (3.1.22)
25) *Twelfth N* (3.2.81)

Quiz 4

1) *Hamlet* (1.3.78)
2) *All's Well* (4.3.71)
3) *MN Dream* (1.1.149)
4) *Ant & Cleo* (2.5.77)
5) *Two Gents* (1.3.22)
6) *1 Henry IV* (5.4.119)
7) *Love's LL* (4.3.213)
8) *Merchant* (3.2.74)
9) *Henry VIII* (1.1.140)
10) *Othello* (1.3.204)
11) *Twelfth N* (2.3.114)
12) *Merry Wives* (5.3.9)
13) *Pericles* (1.2.79)
14) *Macbeth* (1.4.11)
15) *Measure* (2.1.17)
16) *Tempest* (2.2.39)
17) *John* (4.2.219)
18) *Rom & Jul* (3.3.16)
19) *Richard II* (1.1.182)
20) *As You* (1.3.11)
21) *2 Henry IV* (2.4.108)
22) *Tr & Cr* (2.2.15)
23) *Much Ado* (5.1.35)
24) *Lear* (3.4.96)
25) *J. Caesar* (2.1.18)

Quiz 5

1) *Tr & Cr* (3.2.84)
2) *MN Dream* (1.1.134)
3) *Lear* (1.1.62)
4) *Two Gents* (4.4.183)
5) *Love's LL* (1.2.172)
6) *2 Henry IV* (2.4.260)
7) *J. Caesar* (4.2.20)
8) *Othello* (2.1.215)
9) *Merchant* (2.6.36)
10) *All's Well* (1.1.64)
11) *Much Ado* (2.1.175)
12) *Measure* (1.3.2)
13) *3 Henry VI* (4.1.18)
14) *Henry VIII* (3.2.443)
15) *Twelfth N* (1.1.9)
16) *As You* (3.2.400)
17) *Hamlet* (4.7.114)
18) *Win Tale* (4.4.573)
19) *Tr & Cr* (3.2.157)
20) *Rom & Jul* (2.2.67)
21) *Love's LL* (4.3.331)
22) *Much Ado* (2.1.177)
23) *As You* (3.4.57)
24) *Twelfth N* (3.1.156)
25) *Tam Shrew* (4.2.41)

Quiz 6

1) fly
2) say
3) skill
4) woe
5) side
6) bones
7) kings
8) undone
9) light
10) light
11) trust
12) delight
13) dust
14) sport
15) need
16) France
17) suddenly
18) so
19) endure
20) ended
21) renown
22) conscience
23) mine
24) meets
25) gain

Quiz 7

1) sun
2) marriage
3) child
4) sinners
5) wink
6) feast
7) mind
8) oyster
9) wicked
10) friends
11) mind
12) candle
13) safety
14) patient
15) mercy
16) hat
17) pride
18) winter
19) salad
20) fool
21) ambition
22) friends
23) god
24) slept
25) child

Quiz 8

1) kind
2) lender
3) philosophy
4) love
5) discretion
6) wit
7) art
8) honest
9) thinking
10) dreams
11) man
12) child
13) whipping
14) conscience
15) nunnery
16) fashion
17) sleep
18) mystery
19) pipe
20) virtue
21) battalions
22) remembrance
23) axe
24) divinity
25) angels

Quiz 9

1) mind
2) arrows
3) sea
4) shocks
5) Devoutly
6) coil
7) calamity
8) whips
9) pangs
10) patient
11) bare
12) sweat
13) dread
14) traveler
15) ills
16) hue
17) thought
18) enterprises
19) currents
20) action

Quiz 10

1) players
2) time
3) ages
4) puking
5) snail
6) Sighing
7) oaths
8) Jealous
9) bubble
10) justice
11) belly
12) eyes
13) modern
14) pantaloon
15) pouch
16) shrunk
17) scene
18) strange
19) childishness
20) taste

Quiz 11

1) sun
2) clouds
3) ocean
4) brows
5) merry
6) war
7) souls
8) lute
9) tricks
10) court
11) strut
12) feature
13) world
14) halt
15) weak
16) shadow
17) deformity
18) entertain
19) villain
20) idle

Quiz 12

1) heir	10) ignorance	19) reign
2) rhyme	11) devise	20) crime
3) thee	12) wrong	21) compare
4) heart	13) weeds	22) Will
5) stronger	14) play	23) pain
6) kings	15) praise	24) then
7) end	16) spent	25) night
8) green	17) breast	
9) yore	18) dead	

Quiz 13

1) *Merchant*	10) *Macbeth*	19) *Hamlet*
2) *J. Caesar*	11) *John*	20) *Macbeth*
3) *Merry Wives*	12) *John*	21) *Othello*
4) *2 Henry IV*	13) *Tempest*	22) *Coriolanus*
5) *As You*	14) *Othello*	23) *J. Caesar*
6) *Rom & Jul*	15) *Hamlet*	24) *1 Henry IV*
7) *Two Gents*	16) *John*	25) *Com Err*
8) *Hamlet*	17) *As You*	
9) *Merry Wives*	18) *Richard II*	

Quiz 14

1) *Merchant* (Gratiano)	14) *Com Err* (Dromio of Ephesus)
2) *Tam Shrew* (Lucentio)	15) *Much Ado* (Benedick)
3) *MN Dream* (Puck)	16) *Love's LL* (Don Adriano)
4) *Twelfth N* (Feste)	17) *Coriolanus* (Tullus Aufidius)
5) *2 Henry IV* (Epilogue)	18) *Win Tale* (Leontes)
6) *Othello* (Lodovico)	19) *John* (Philip the Bastard)
7) *Hamlet* (Fortinbras)	20) *Richard II* (Henry IV/Bolingbroke)
8) *Lear* (Edgar)	21) *Cymbeline* (Cymbeline)
9) *Richard III* (Richmond)	22) *J. Caesar* (Octavius Caesar)
10) *As You* (Rosalind)	23) *1 Henry IV* (Henry IV)
11) *Tempest* (Prospero)	24) *3 Henry VI* (Edward IV)
12) *Two Gents* (Valentine)	25) *Macbeth* (Malcolm)
13) *Measure* (Vincentio)	

Quiz 15

1) Rosalind (*As You*)
2) Beatrice (*Much Ado*)
3) Katherina (*Tam Shrew*)
4) Helena (*All's Well*)
5) Julia (*Two Gents*)
6) Mariana (*Measure*)
7) Emilia (*Othello*)
8) Viola (*Twelfth N*)
9) Hermia (*MN Dream*)
10) Silvia (*Two Gents*)
11) Gertrude (*Hamlet*)
12) Audrey (*As You*)
13) Bianca (*Tam Shrew*)
14) Lavinia (*Titus*)
15) Imogen (*Cymbeline*)
16) Anne Page (*Merry Wives*)
17) Olivia (*Twelfth N*)
18) Desdemona (*Othello*)
19) Nerissa (*Merchant*)
20) Hero (*Much Ado*)
21) Portia (*Merchant*)
22) Paulina (*Win Tale*)
23) Miranda (*Tempest*)
24) Celia (*As You*)
25) Hermione (*Win Tale*)

Quiz 16

1) *As You*
2) *Twelfth N*
3) *Merchant*
4) *Two Gents*
5) *MN Dream*
6) *Much Ado*
7) *All's Well*
8) *Measure*
9) *Tempest*
10) *Love's LL*
11) *Tr & Cr*
12) *Hamlet*
13) *Macbeth*
14) *Com Err*
15) *Two Gents*
16) *All's Well*
17) *Tam Shrew*
18) *Merry Wives*
19) *Measure*
20) *Love's LL*

Quiz 17

1) Bertram
2) Orlando
3) Coriolanus
4) Imogen
5) Ophelia
6) Cordelia
7) Malcolm
8) Jessica
9) Hermia
10) Hero
11) Desdemona
12) Marina
13) Katherina
14) Ferdinand
15) Lavinia
16) Proteus
17) Troilus
18) Perdita
19) Antipholus
20) Hamlet
21) Lucentio
22) Cressida
23) Florizel
24) Fleance
25) Miranda

Quiz 18

1) Measure
2) MN Dream
3) Rom & Jul
4) 2 Henry VI
5) 2 Henry IV
6) Twelfth N
7) Merchant
8) Timon
9) Win Tale

10) Much Ado
11) Love's LL
12) Com Err
13) 2 Henry IV
14) Measure
15) Twelfth N
16) Merry Wives
17) 2 Henry IV, Henry V
18) Much Ado

19) Tempest
20) MN Dream
21) Measure
22) Merry Wives, Henry V
23) 2 Henry IV
24) Romeo
25) Com Err

Quiz 19

1) Com Err and Measure
2) Merchant, Much Ado, Tempest, Twelfth N, and Two Gents
3) Othello and Tam Shrew
4) Measure and Much Ado
5) Hamlet and J. Caesar
6) Ant & Cleo, MN Dream, and Titus
7) Com Err, Othello, Win Tale, and Two Noble (sometimes spelled "Aemelia")
8) Measure and Rom & Jul
9) Hamlet and Tempest
10) Othello and Merchant (sometimes spelled "Graziano")
11) All's Well and MN Dream
12) Measure and Rom & Jul (duh!)
13) Cymbeline, J. Caesar, Timon, and Titus (In Titus it is both the name of Titus's eldest son and his grandson, Young Lucius.)
14) Love's LL and Twelfth N
15) All's Well and Measure
16) J. Caesar and Merchant
17) Tempest and Twelfth N
18) Merchant and Tempest (sometimes spelled "Stefano")
19) Two Gents, Titus, and Twelfth N
20) Measure and Tam Shrew

Quiz 20

1) Bertram
2) Solinus
3) Cymbeline
4) Fortinbras
5) Ferdinand
6) Macbeth
7) Don Pedro
8) Pericles
9) Alonso
10) Escalus
11) Tamora
12) Orsino
13) Leontes
14) Macduff
15) Oberon
16) Theseus
17) Leonato
18) Antiochus
19) Gertrude
20) Prospero
21) Hippolyta
22) Vincentio
23) Priam
24) Titania
25) Polixenes

Quiz 21

1) *MN Dream*
2) *1 Henry IV*
3) *Henry V*
4) *All's Well*
5) *Twelfth N*
6) *Tam Shrew*
7) *Win Tale*
8) *Love's LL*
9) *Macbeth*
10) *Ant & Cleo*
11) *Measure*
12) *Othello*
13) *Merchant*
14) *Hamlet*
15) *Lear*
16) *Titus*
17) *Two Gents*
18) *Com Err*
19) *Much Ado*
20) *Pericles*
21) *As You*
22) *Henry VIII*
23) *Tr & Cr*
24) *Timon*
25) *Rom & Jul*

Quiz 22

1) Portia (*Merchant*)
2) Helena (*MN Dream*)
3) Beatrice (*Much Ado*)
4) Viola (*Twelfth N*)
5) Cleopatra (*Ant & Cleo*)
6) Imogen (*Cymbeline*)
7) Hermione (*Win Tale*)
8) Juliet (*Rom & Jul*)
9) Titania (*MN Dream*)
10) Katherina (*Tam Shrew*)
11) Cressida (*Tr & Cr*)
12) Perdita (*Win Tale*)
13) Maria (*Twelfth N*)
14) Rosalind (*As You*)
15) Adriana (*Com Err*)
16) Volumnia (*Coriolanus*)
17) Ophelia (*Hamlet*)
18) Julia (*Two Gents*)
19) Olivia (*Twelfth N*)
20) Lady Macbeth (*Macbeth*)
21) Desdemona (*Othello*)
22) Miranda (*Tempest*)
23) Isabella (*Measure*)
24) Tamora (*Titus*)
25) Gertrude (*Hamlet*)

Quiz 23

1) Hamlet (*Hamlet*)

2) Macbeth (*Macbeth*)

3) Petruchio (*Tam Shrew*)

4) Shylock (*Merchant*)

5) Puck (*MN Dream*)

6) Falstaff (*Merry Wives*)

7) Sir Toby Belch (*Twelfth N*)

8) Titus Andronicus (*Titus*)

9) Romeo (*Rom & Jul*)

10) Mark Antony (*Ant & Cleo*)

11) Troilus (*Tr & Cr*)

12) Angelo (*Measure*)

13) King Lear (*Lear*)

14) Othello (*Othello*)

15) Brutus (*J. Caesar*)

16) Timon (*Timon*)

17) Iago (*Othello*)

18) Posthumus (*Cymbeline*)

19) Coriolanus (*Coriolanus*)

20) Prospero (*Tempest*)

21) Touchstone (*As You*)

22) Bertram (*All's Well*)

23) Caliban (*Tempest*)

24) Feste (*Twelfth N*)

25) Polixenes (*Win Tale*)

Quiz 24

1) Cleopatra (getting ready to leave this earthly existence in *Ant & Cleo* [5.2.280])

2) Gertrude (Hamlet's mother in *Hamlet* [3.2.230])

3) Anne Bullen, (who will later change her mind and marry the king in *Henry VIII* [2.3.45]—and probably wish she had remembered this thought)

4) Juliet (*Rom & Jul* [1.5.138])

5) Katherina (the shrewish Katherina Minola in *Tam Shrew* [3.2.220])

6) Miranda (the naive and innocent daughter in *Tempest* [5.1.182])

7) Beatrice (the man-hater in *Much Ado* [1.1.131])

8) Titania (who has fallen in love with a "transformed" Nick Bottom in *MN Dream* [4.1.76])

9) Emilia (She has a rather negative view of men in *Othello* [3.4.103]. Then again, considering who her husband is, I guess we really can't blame the poor woman for this attitude.)

10) Lady Macbeth (guilt stricken in *Macbeth* [5.1.50])

11) Ophelia (in *Hamlet* [3.1.160])

12) Rosalind (in *As You* [3.5.72], trying to discourage a young shepherdess who thinks she is a man and is in love with her.)

13) Helena (Mightily abused in *All's Well* [1.1.85], she laments her love for Bertram, who she *thinks* is too good for her. Even Bertram's mother doesn't believe that!)

14) Isabella (in *Measure* [2.4.106])

15) Hermione (falsely accused in *Win Tale* [3.2.119])

16) Portia (who has to deal with her father's unusual will in *Merchant* [1.2.23])

17) Cordelia (the king's honest daughter in *Lear* [1.1.91])

18) Viola (who, in *Twelfth N* [2.2.33], has a situation similar to Rosalind in *As You*)

19) Calpurnia (trying to warn her husband Julius Caesar in *J. Caesar* [2.2.30])

20) Cressida (a kind of prophetic statement in *Tr & Cr* [3.2.82])

21) Volumnia (in *Coriolanus* [1.3.2])

22) Desdemona (with a bad premonition in *Othello* [4.3.26])

23) Julia (reading the riot act to Proteus in *Two Gents* [5.4.105])

24) Rosaline (giving Berowne an ultimatum in *Love's LL* [5.2.819])

25) Imogen (describing her unenviable plight in *Cymbeline* [1.6.1])

Quiz 25

1) Bertram (*All's Well* [3.2.57])

2) Orlando (*As You* [1.1.66])

3) Coriolanus (*Coriolanus* [3.3.133])

4) Hamlet (*Hamlet* [1.2.132])

5) Hotspur (*1 Henry IV* [1.3.201])

6) Wolsey (*Henry VIII* [3.2.455])

7) Julius Caesar (*J. Caesar* [3.1.60])

8) King Lear (*Lear* [3.2.59])

9) Puck (*MN Dream* [2.1.43])

10) Macbeth (*Macbeth* [2.1.33])

11) Shylock (*Merchant* [3.1.64])

12) Benedick (*Much Ado* [2.3.240])

13) Othello (*Othello* [5.2.341])

14) Richard II (*Richard II* [3.2.155])

15) Romeo (*Rom & Jul* [3.1.136])

16) Prospero (*Tempest* [1.2.09])

17) Timon (*Timon* [4.3.54])

18) Valentine (*Two Gents* [3.1.104])

19) Orsino (*Twelfth N* [2.4.93])

20) Horatio (*Hamlet* [5.2.359])

21) Falstaff (*2 Henry IV* [1.2.9])

22) Henry V (*Henry V* [4.3.60])

23) Mark Antony (*J. Caesar* [3.2.73])

24) Richard III (*Richard III* [5.3.193])

25) Petruchio (*Tam Shrew* [4.1.208])

Quiz 26

1) Hamlet (*Hamlet*)

2) Hotspur (*1 Henry IV*)

3) Othello (*Othello*)

4) Juliet (*Rom & Jul*)

5) Richard II (*Richard II*)

6) Aaron the Moor (*Titus*)

7) Brutus (*J. Caesar*)

8) Iago (*Othello*)

9) Queen Gertrude (*Hamlet*)

10) Antony (*Ant & Cleo*)

11) Lear (*Lear*)

12) John (*John*)

13) Richard III (*Richard III*)

14) Romeo (*Rom & Jul*)

15) King Claudius (*Hamlet*)

16) Desdemona (*Othello*)

17) King Henry IV (*2 Henry IV*)

18) Cleopatra (*Ant & Cleo*)

19) Mercutio (*Rom & Jul*)

20) Buckingham (*Richard III*)

21) Richard, Duke of York (*3 Henry VI*)

22) Macbeth (*Macbeth*)

23) Titus Andronicus (*Titus*)

24) Coriolanus (*Coriolanus*)

25) Jack Cade (*2 Henry VI*)

Quiz 27

1) Lady Macbeth (*Macbeth* [1.5.40])

2) King Claudius (*Hamlet* [3.3.36])

3) Aaron (*Titus* [5.1.141])

4) Iachimo (*Cymbeline* [1.4.127])

5) Duke Frederick (*As You* [3.1.5])

6) Angelo (*Measure* [2.4.163])

7) Duke of Cornwall (*Lear* [3.7.83])

8) Don John (*Much Ado* [1.3.31])

9) Iago (*Othello* [1.1.60])

10) Richard, Duke of Gloucester, later Richard III, (*Richard III* [1.1.28])

11) King Antiochus (*Pericles* [1.1.143])

12) Tybalt (*Rom & Jul* [1.5.89])

13) Cloten (*Cymbeline* [3.5.137])

14) Caliban (*Tempest* [1.2.363])

15) Macbeth (*Macbeth* [3.4.134])

16) Shylock (*Merchant* [1.3.42])

17) Tamora (*Titus* [2.3.188])

18) King Leontes (*Win Tale* [2.3.174])

19) Antonio (*Tempest* [2.1.280])

20) Edmund (*Lear* [5.1.55])

Quiz 28

1) C. John

2) A. Richard II

3) D. Henry VI

4) B. Edward IV

5) D. Edward V (one of the famous princes in the Tower that Richard III is commonly believed to have had murdered; Richard's own 12-year-old nephew)

6) C. Anne Neville

7) C. Henry VII (previously Henry Tudor, the Earl of Richmond; founder of the Tudor line.)

8) C. Katherine of Aragon

9) A. Edward IV

10) B. Elizabeth Woodville (the wife of Edward IV)

11) D. John

12) B. Richard III (the last English king to die in battle)

13) A. Henry IV

14) C. Richard II

15) A. Henry IV

16) C. Margaret of Anjou (as described by her archenemy, Richard, Duke of York, right before she kills him in *3 Henry VI*)

17) C. Duchess of York

18) B. Richard I (Faulconbridge delights in the fact and uses the situation to ingratiate himself with Richard's brother [King John] and mother [Queen Eleanor].)

19) B. Richard III (He died at 33. Henry V died at 35, Edward IV at 41, and King John at 49.)

20) B. Richard III (His father, Richard, Duke of York, desperately wanted to be king, but failed in his attempts to replace the weak Henry VI. However, two of his sons become king: Edward IV and the infamous Richard III.)

Quiz 29

1) Brutus (Mark Antony makes this statement in *J. Caesar* [5.5.73].)

2) Falstaff (Henry V says this in *2 Henry IV* [5.5.47].)

3) Polonius (Hamlet makes this statement in *Hamlet* [3.4.31] after mistaking him for Claudius and killing him. Oops.)

4) Earl of Warwick (This statement is made by the future Edward IV to Richard Neville, Earl of Warwick, who is known as "The Kingmaker" in *3 Henry VI* [2.3.37].)

5) Cleopatra (in *Ant & Cleo* [2.2.234])

6) Macbeth (Lady Macbeth makes this statement about her husband, as she fears he may not have what it takes to kill the king and seize the throne [1.5.16].)

7) Hermia (described by her once and future friend, Helena [3.2.323])

8) Coriolanus (This statement is made by Cominius in *Coriolanus* [2.2.109].)

9) Beatrice (Benedick makes this rather unflattering statement in *Much Ado* [2.1.247].)

10) Juliet (Romeo is smitten with her [1.5.45], and we all know how *that* turns out.)

11) Prince Hal (Henry IV is referring to his son, the future Henry V, in *1 Henry IV* [3.2.123].)

12) Richard III (Margaret of Anjou is speaking about Richard Gloucester, later Richard III, in *Richard III* [1.3.288]. She certainly should know, considering Richard killed her husband and only son.)

13) Pinch (This description of the quack doctor is in *Com Err* [5.1.238].)

14) Proteus (*Sluggardized?* Well, anyway, Valentine is speaking, in *Two Gents* [1.1.5].)

15) King Lear (Honest Cordelia makes this statement to her father [5.3.3].)

16) Desdemona (Othello speaks of his courtship with her [1.3.167].)

17) Hamlet (Gertrude says this to her son, who is grieving over the death of his father and the lust of his mother [1.1.70].)

18) Ophelia (spoken by Hamlet [3.1.120])

19) Katherina (Hortensio says this to the shrewish woman in *Tam Shrew* [1.1.59].)

20) Anne Neville (in *Richard III* [1.2.227], Richard Gloucester, later Richard III, is a bit surprised over his successful attempt to woo her over the coffin of her husband, who Richard admittedly killed.)

Quiz 30

1) *MN Dream* (Used by Oberon and Puck, it causes great comic confusion.)

2) *Merry Wives* (Falstaff hides in it to escape a jealous husband.)

3) *Macbeth* (Macbeth imagines he sees it immediately before murdering Duncan.)

4) *Hamlet* (Hamlet ruminates over it in a graveyard.)

5) *Othello* (It was Othello's first gift to Desdemona.)

6) *Twelfth N* (Malvolio is deceived into wearing these in a misguided attempt to woo Olivia.)

7) *3 Henry VI* (Richard, Duke of York, has a paper crown placed on his head by his murderers, Lord Clifford and Queen Margaret.)

8) *Tempest*

9) *Merchant* (A suitor must correctly choose the lead one to win Portia.)

10) *Henry V* (They are an insulting gift sent to Henry V by the Dauphin of France.)

11) *As You* (They are nailed up in the Forest of Arden by Orlando.)

12) *Ant & Cleo* (Cleopatra has the snake smuggled in to commit suicide.)

13) *Two Gents* (Valentine plans to use it to elope with Sylvia, but he is caught in the act.)

14) *Titus* (Lavinia uses it to reveal the identities of her attackers.)

15) *Com Err* (The goldsmith Angelo delivers it to the wrong Antipholus twin.)

16) *Cymbeline* (Iachimo hides in the trunk to observe Imogen sleeping in her bedroom. His knowledge of this mark "proves" to Posthumus that he had an affair with her.)

17) *Pericles* (Thaisa, thought to be dead, is placed in the chest to be buried at sea.)

18) *Tr & Cr* (They are exchanged by the title characters.)

19) *Two Noble* (Arcite delivers these to Palamon prior to their duel.)

20) *Tam Shrew* (It is broken over the head of Hortensio by Kate.)

Quiz 31

1) *Com Err*

2) *Merchant* (Portia, Nerissa, and Jessica dress as men.)

3) *Othello* (Othello and Iago)

4) *Tempest* (Miranda)

5) *Cymbeline* (the unnamed Queen)

6) *Win Tale* (Hermione is the daughter of the Emperor of Russia.)

7) *Richard III* (Edward IV is the king when the play opens, and he is succeeded briefly by his son, Edward V. The young king is displaced by Richard III, and Richard is overthrown and replaced by Henry VII at the very end of the play.)

8) *Merry Wives*

9) *Henry V*

10) *All's Well* (Helena)

11) *Measure*

12) *Two Gents* (Julia)

13) *Rom & Jul* (Romeo wishes he was a glove so he could touch the cheek of Juliet.)

14) *Love's LL* (Berowne and his buddies)

15) *Tam Shrew* (Petruchio)

16) *As You* (Duke Senior)

17) *John* (King John sings as he lies dying, probably in delirium.)

18) *Ant & Cleo*

19) *Pericles*

20) *1 Henry VI*

Quiz 32

1) *Love's LL*	10) *Tempest*	19) *Richard III*
2) *Com Err*	11) *J. Caesar*	20) *1 Henry IV*
3) *Hamlet*	12) *Henry V*	21) *Much Ado*
4) *Othello*	13) *MN Dream*	22) *1 Henry VI*
5) *Two Gents*	14) *Tam Shrew*	23) *Coriolanus*
6) *Titus*	15) *All's Well*	24) *As You*
7) *Richard II*	16) *Macbeth*	25) *Lear*
8) *Measure*	17) *Twelfth N*	
9) *Merchant*	18) *Ant & Cleo*	

Quiz 33

1) *Hamlet*	8) *Rom & Jul*	15) *Macbeth*
2) *MN Dream*	9) *Othello*	16) *J. Caesar*
3) *Timon*	10) *Lear*	17) *Richard III*
4) *Two Noble*	11) *Much Ado*	18) *Twelfth N*
5) *Henry V*	12) *Merry Wives*	19) *Pericles*
6) *1 Henry IV*	13) *1 Henry VI*	20) *Ant & Cleo*
7) *Win Tale*	14) *Merchant*	

Quiz 34

1) D. *The Merry Wives of Windsor*

2) B. *Love's Labor's Lost* (Rosaline makes this demand of the wisecracking Berowne, in an effort to make him more serious.)

3) C. *The Taming of the Shrew* (Tranio disguises himself as Vincentio, the father of his master, Lucentio.)

4) B. *The Comedy of Errors* (Both the Antipholus twins and the Dromio twins are separated and reunited after a series of comic misadventures. They are reunited with their parents in the end, as well.)

5) A. *Measure for Measure* and *All's Well That Ends Well*

6) C. Proteus and Valentine (They are the two gentlemen of Verona.)

7) B. *The Merry Wives of Windsor* (One story is that Queen Elizabeth asked Shakespeare to write a play in which Falstaff, a comic character in the *Henry IV* plays, is in love. This is the result, according to legend.)

8) D. Vincentio

9) A. *A Midsummer Night's Dream*

10) A. *Measure for Measure* (The Duke punishes Lucio in this manner.)

11) C. *Twelfth Night*

12) B. *Love's Labor's Lost*

13) C. *The Merry Wives of Windsor*

14) D. *Twelfth Night* (It has 10 songs.)

15) A. *The Comedy of Errors*

16) C. Hugh Evans

17) B. Shylock in *The Merchant of Venice* (She is his deceased wife.)

18) B. *The Comedy of Errors* (2.2.80)

19) D. Antonio

20) A. *The Merry Wives of Windsor*

21) C. *Love's Labor's Lost* (It was spoken by the clown Costard to ridicule the pedant Holofernes, the curate Nathaniel, and the braggart Armado.)

22) A. *Measure for Measure*

23) C. *As You Like It*

24) B. *The Comedy of Errors*

25) D. *The Merry Wives of Windsor*

Quiz 35

1) A. Juliet

2) B. Juliet in *Romeo and Juliet* (She kills herself with a dagger.)

3) D. Coriolanus

4) A. Othello

5) C. Fulvia

6) B. Portia in *Julius Caesar*

7) D. Iago

8) A. Ovid's *Metamorphosis*

9) A. *King Lear*

10) D. *Antony and Cleopatra*

11) C. Titus in *Titus Andronicus* (He kills his son Mutius.)

12) C. *Romeo and Juliet*

13) B. *King Lear*

14) D. *Macbeth*

15) A. *Romeo and Juliet*

16) A. Titus in *Titus Andronicus* (Unfortunately for him—and his sons—his severed hand is returned to him, along with the heads of the two sons he hoped to ransom.)

17) C. Coriolanus

18) B. Timon (He declares his hatred for mankind in the play that bears his name.)

19) D. Julius Caesar (He doesn't have much to say until he is knocked off in Act 3, scene 1.)

20) C. *Titus Andronicus* (A drawing by one Henry Peacham shows the entrance of Tamora with actors in a mix of Roman and Renaissance dress.)

21) A. *Macbeth* (King James VI of Scotland became King James I of England and Scotland after the death of Elizabeth in 1603. *Macbeth* is set in Scotland and some speculate the play may have been written for festivities celebrating the visit of King Christian of Denmark, James's brother-in-law.)

22) B. 6 (all but *Hamlet, Macbeth, Lear,* and *Timon*)

23) D. *Hamlet* (Hamlet instructs the traveling players who are to perform before the court. It gives us a fascinating perspective into what Shakespeare may have thought about the craft of acting.)

24) C. *Othello* (There are "only" five: Brabantio, Roderigo, Emilia, Desdemona, and Othello. Iago is condemned to die a tortuous death, but he is still alive at the end of the play. *King Lear* has the most with nine deaths.)

25) C. Tamora in *Titus Andronicus*

Quiz 36

1) A. Britain

2) A. *Pericles*

3) C. *The Tempest*

4) B. *The Tempest*

5) D. *The Two Noble Kinsmen* (It's a retelling of Chaucer's "Knight's Tale.")

6) A. *Cymbeline* (Cornelius gives it to the Queen who wishes to use it to kill Imogen.)

7) C. *The Winter's Tale*

8) D. *Cymbeline*

9) D. Palamon

10) D. Emilia in *The Two Noble Kinsmen*

11) B. *Pericles*

12) C. *The Tempest* (Antonio conspires to kill his brother Prospero, and Sebastian conspires to kill his brother Alonso.)

13) A. *The Winter's Tale* (Shakespeare refers to him as "that rare Italian master.")

14) C. *The Two Noble Kinsmen* (Theseus and Hippolyta both also appear in *A Midsummer Night's Dream.*)

15) B. *Cymbeline*

16) B. *The Winter's Tale*

17) A. *The Two Noble Kinsmen*

18) D. *Pericles* (Marina endures these indignities.)

19) C. *Cymbeline* (The nasty villain gets his just reward—his head chopped off.)

20) B. *The Winter's Tale*

Quiz 37

1) B. *Henry VI, Part One* (Joan is depicted to be more of a crazed whore than a saint.)

2) A. *Henry V* (In this battle, Henry's sick and badly outnumbered army won an incredible victory against the over-confidant French.)

3) D. *Richard II*

4) B. *Henry V*

5) B. *Henry VI, Part Three*

6) D. *Henry VI, Part One*

7) A. *Richard III*

8) B. *Henry VI, Part Two* (He appears briefly at the end and immediately establishes his evil character.)

9) D. *Henry IV, Part Two* (Henry IV dies in this room. An earlier prophecy had predicted that he would die in Jerusalem, but he had interpreted it at the time to be the city of Jerusalem. Surprise!)

10) C. *Richard II* (This scene was banned from performance during Shakespeare's life and his company almost got in serious trouble for privately performing it as a "pep rally" for supporters of the Earl of Essex before his abortive attempt to overthrow Queen Elizabeth I.)

11) C. Bardolph

12) B. Richard, Duke of Gloucester (later, Richard III)

13) A. Edward

14) A. *King John*

15) B. *Henry V*

16) D. Lancaster

17) A. Elizabeth (daughter of Henry VIII and the unfortunate Anne Boleyn)

18) B. *Richard II*

19) C. *Henry V*

20) A. *Richard II* (Bolingbroke—the future Henry IV—is banished.)

21) A. *Henry IV, Part One*

22) C. *Henry VI, Part Two*

23) D. John

24) D. *Henry VIII*

25) B. Richard Neville, Earl of Warwick (His influence helped Edward IV and Henry VI to the throne.)

Quiz 38

1) A. *Venus and Adonis*

2) C. *Titus Andronicus*

3) A. *Love's Labor's Lost* (in 1598)

4) D. *Titus Andronicus*

5) B. Robert Greene ([1558–1592]; He was a minor Elizabethan dramatist [*Friar Bacon and Friar Bungay*]. His famous criticism of Shakespeare as an "upstart crow" proves that Shakespeare had become well established in the London theater world by the year 1592.)

6) C. *The Tempest* (listed first and categorized as a comedy in The First Folio)

7) A. *As You Like It* (He starred as Orlando. Before he obtained this role, he believed that Shakespeare could not be performed adequately on film.)

8) B. Sarah Bernhardt (She was 55 years old when she was filmed in the final duel scene between Hamlet and Laertes, which was first shown at the Paris Exhibition of 1900. It is believed the film no longer exists.)

9) D. *The Taming of the Shrew* (Sam Taylor's 1929 film adaptation)

10) D. *Richard III* (Made in 1912 and rediscovered in 1996, it was officially titled *The Life and Death of Richard III*.)

11) C. King John (Herbert Beerbohm Tree directed and starred in a 4-minute silent version in 1899.)

12) A. *Hamlet*

13) B. Desdemona (It was in Thomas Killigrew's production of *Othello*. Incidentally, she was the mistress of Prince Rupert, and bore his illegitimate child.)

14) C. King Lear (in 1983; directed by Michael Eliot)

15) B. *The Tempest*

16) D. *Measure for Measure*

17) C. Delia Bacon (She wrote an obtuse book advocating the theory, *The Philosophy of the Plays of Shakespeare Unfolded* (1857), and actually received some encouragement from highly regarded literary figures such as Emerson and Hawthorne. She died in a mental institution in 1859.)

18) C. *Henry VIII*

19) A. *Hamlet*

20) B. 1769 (The Jubilee was a three-day festival that received tremendous publicity and helped establish Shakespeare as a cultural icon and Stratford as a sacred site. The festivities were greatly disrupted by heavy rains, and Garrick lost a great deal of money.)

21) D. *Henry VIII* (The play also went by the title *All is True*, and was being performed on June 29, 1613, when sparks from simulated cannon fire set the thatch roof on fire. Miraculously, no one was injured, but the theatre itself burned to the ground. A second Globe was quickly rebuilt on the same site by 1614.)

22) C. *Henry V*

23) A. Nicholas Rowe ([1674–1718]; modernized the spelling and punctuation of the plays, divided the plays into acts and scenes, regularized entrances and exits of the characters, and attached a dramatis personae to each play for the first time)

24) B. Richard Burbage (a friend of Shakespeare's [he left Burbage money in his will], the leading actor of Shakespeare's company, and a part owner of the Globe and the company)

25) C. *Julius Caesar* (a modern-dress production, enhanced by newsreel footage)

Quiz 39

1) *Titus* (This befalls the evil Tamora.)

2) *Lear* (The Earl of Gloucester is blinded by the Duke of Cornwall.)

3) *Win Tale* (Leontes orders this nasty deed because he mistakenly believes the child is illegitimate.)

4) *J. Caesar* (Portia, the wife of Brutus, commits suicide in this fashion.)

5) *Richard III* (Clarence is murdered under order of his brother, Richard.)

6) *Macbeth* (King Duncan's horses engage in this unnatural behavior.)

7) *Titus* (Poor Lavinia, the daughter of Titus, is subjected to this brutality.)

8) *John* (Arthur, the nephew of King John, dies trying to escape.)

9) *Ant & Cleo* (Cleopatra and Charmian commit suicide rather than be subjected to Octavius Caesar.)

10) *Win Tale* (Poor Antigonus meets this fate.)

11) *J. Caesar* (Julius Caesar is stabbed repeatedly by the conspirators.)

12) *Hamlet* (The ghost of Hamlet's father drops this little bombshell.)

13) *Titus* (Titus still has four left, but no—wait—he kills one himself soon after the death of the others.)

14) *Othello* (Under the influence of the nefarious Iago, the gullible Othello kills Desdemona.)

15) *Macbeth* (The family of Macduff is ordered murdered by Macbeth.)

16) *1 Henry VI* (Joan of Arc is executed in this way.)

17) *3 Henry VI*

18) *Pericles* (Antiochus is the perverted king.)

19) *Tr & Cr* (The noble Hector's body undergoes this shame because of Achilles.)

20) *Tempest* (Caliban leads the drunken Trinculo and Stephano in an attempt to murder Prospero.)

Quiz 40

1) *Macbeth* (She appears to scold the witches.)

2) *Richard III* (There are 11 ghosts in this play).

3) *Tempest*

4) *MN Dream* (The adventures of Oberon, Titania, and Puck cause great fun.)

5) *Macbeth* (And Macbeth drinks it, too!)

6) *Richard III* (The ghost of Anne Neville haunts Richard III.)

7) *J. Caesar* (The ghost of Julius Caesar promises to meet Brutus.)

8) *2 Henry VI*

9) *Pericles* (The incestuous Antiochus and his daughter meet this fate.)

10) *Tempest*

11) *As You* (Incidentally, Hymen also appears in *Two Noble*.)

12) *1 Henry VI*

13) *Pericles* (Diana appears to Pericles in a vision.)

14) *Tempest* (Ariel is freed by Prospero.)

15) *Win Tale* (The oracle reports that Hermione is faithful, but Leontes still does not believe it.)

16) *MN Dream* (Puck puts a spell on the foolish but loveable Nick Bottom.)

17) *2 Henry VI* (Roger Bolingbroke and Margery Jordan conjure up Asnath.)

18) *Richard III* (Richard, Duke of Gloucester, soon to be King Richard III, makes this ridiculous claim.)

19) *Cymbeline* (Jupiter gives Posthumus the tablet.)

20) *Macbeth* (Banquo's ghost appears to Macbeth.)

Quiz 41

1) Elsinore	8) Messina	15) Egypt
2) Forest of Arden	9) Cyprus	16) Vienna
3) Illyria	10) Verona	17) Belmont
4) Scotland	11) Padua	18) Bohemia
5) Navarre	12) Phillipi	19) Milan
6) Athens	13) Agincourt	20) An unnamed island
7) Troy	14) Ephesus	

Quiz 42

1) B. Card game (It is also the game Shakespeare has Henry VIII and the Duke of Suffolk play in *Henry III* [5.1], as they await the birth of Anne Bullen's child, the future Queen Elizabeth I.)

2) D. Bowling. (A *rub* is an obstacle that disrupts the path of the ball.)

3) C. *The Tempest* (Miranda and Ferdinand are observed playing chess.)

4) C. Tennis balls (The implication is that Henry is more fit for games than kingship.)

5) A. *As You Like It* (Charles is defeated in the match by Orlando.)

6) D. *The Merry Wives of Windsor* (Although it really has nothing to do with sport other than his name, John Rugby is the servant of the foolish Dr. Caius.)

7) B. *Antony and Cleopatra* (Pining for her absent Antony, Cleopatra suggests playing billiards with Charmian [2.5.3.].)

8) C. Bear-baiting (Sackerson was a well-known bear who is mentioned by name in *The Merry Wives of Windsor*.)

9) A. Dice

10) C. Fencing

11) B. Mark Antony (described in this way by Brutus in *Julius Caesar* [2.1.189].)

12) B. *King Lear* (Kent makes this comment to Oswald [1.4.86]. Football was considered a lower-class diversion in Shakespeare's time.)

13) A. Backgammon (Berowne mentions the game in *Love's Labor's Lost* [5.2.326].)

14) D. Loggats

15) B. Fishing (Octavius says, "From Alexandria/This is our news: he fishes, drinks, and wastes/The lamps of night in revels..." [1.4.4].)

16) D. *Hamlet* (King Claudius and Laertes plot to murder Hamlet and make it seem as if it were a fencing accident. However, their plan is foiled, and virtually all characters of note end up dead. Just another typical day in a Shakespearean tragedy!)

17) C. Dice

18) C. Masques (In *A Midsummer Night's Dream* [5.1.39], Duke Theseus says, "What abridgement have you for this evening?/ What masque? what music? How shall we beguile/ The lazy time, if not with some delight?" In *Henry VIII* [1.4], an actual royal masque of 1527 is reenacted.)

19) A. Hunting (4.6.85)

20) B. Backgammon (Scored by means of pegs set into holes, the game lends itself easily to a comparison with sexual intercourse.)

Quiz 43

1) B. Boar	8) D. Rere-mice	14) A. Trout
2) D. Monkey	(*MN Dream* [2.2.4])	15) A. Serpent
3) A. Elephant	9) D. Crow	16) D. Crocodile
4) C. Jackass	10) B. Mole	17) B. Sparrow
5) C. Lion	11) C. Bear	18) C. Apes
6) B. Cat	12) A. Falcon	19) D. Hawk
7) A. Basilisk	13) B. Honeybees	20) C. Tiger

Quiz 44

1) Comfit-maker	8) Collier	15) Cobbler
2) Fuller	9) Mercer	16) Sawyer
3) Steward	10) Drawer	17) Ostler
4) Miller	11) Brazier	18) Drovier
5) Apothecary	12) Cutler	19) Tinker
6) Provost	13) Joiner	20) Chandler
7) Warrener	14) Milliner	

Quiz 45

1) Icarus	10) Prometheus	19) Phaethon
2) Pegasus	11) Amazon	20) Charon
3) Argus	12) Leander	21) Proteus
4) Thisbe	13) Ariachne	22) Nemesis
5) Narcissus	14) Pygmalion	23) Tarquin
6) Hymen	15) Centaurs	24) Bacchus
7) Cerberus	16) Mercury	25) Janus
8) Minerva	17) Hydra	
9) Diana	18) Niobe	

Quiz 46

1) Romeo (*Rom & Jul* [5.1.6])

2) Cinna (*J. Caesar* [3.3.1])

3) Banquo (*Macbeth* [2.1.20])

4) Hermia (*MN Dream* [2.2.147])

5) Andromache (*Tr & Cr* [5.3.10])

6) Caliban (*Tempest* [3.2.137])

7) Tullus Aufidius (*Coriolanus* [4.5.121])

8) Shylock (*Merchant* [2.5.16])

9) George, Duke of Clarence
(*Richard III* [1.2.3-4, 24-25])

10) Cardinal Beauford (*2 Henry VI* [3.2.31])

11) Nick Bottom (*MN Dream* [4.1.205])

12) Balthasar (*Rom & Jul* [5.3.137])

13) Posthumus (*Cymbeline* [5.4.123])

14) Humphrey (*2 Henry VI* [1.2.22])

15) Cleopatra (*Ant & Cleo* [5.2.76])

16) Titania (*MN Dream* [4.1.76])

17) Antigonus (*Win Tale* [3.3.15])

18) Lady Macbeth (*Macbeth* [5.1])

19) Calpurnia (*Julius Caesar* [2.2])

20) Brabantio (Desdemona's father in *Othello* [1.1])

Quiz 47

1) *Two Gents*	8) *Win Tale*	15) *Much Ado*
2) *Love's LL*	9) *Tempest*	16) *Twelfth N*
3) *MN Dream*	10) *Henry VIII*	17) *Tempest*
4) *As You*	11) *Two Noble*	18) *As You*
5) *Twelfth N*	12) *Merchant*	19) *Cymbeline*
6) *Measure*	13) *Othello*	20) *Much Ado*
7) *Cymbeline*	14) *Hamlet*	

Quiz 48

1) B. His son-in-law John Hall (Hall married Shakespeare's eldest child, Susanna.)

2) D. *Rom & Jul*

3) C. Helena in *All's Well*

4) C. Julius Caesar (Although no actual historian records this defect, Shakespeare has Caesar tell Mark Antony that he is deaf in his left ear [1.2.213].)

5) A. King Lear

6) B. Malvolio in *Twelfth N*

7) A. *Pericles* (Cerimon is a wise and noble doctor and scientist.)

8) D. *Merry Wives* (Caius is the only doctor that Shakespeare holds up to ridicule in his plays.)

9) D. Henry VIII

10) C. *Macbeth* (An English doctor and a Scottish doctor both appear.)

11) B. *Cymbeline*

12) C. Liver (Mentioned in many quotes by Shakespeare that allude to courage and cowardice, the liver was associated with love and other emotions, as well.)

13) D. Administering enemas

14) A. *Tr & Cr* (Pandarus makes this less than generous bequest. Considering the pessimistic nature of this "comedy," we shouldn't be all that surprised.)

15) C. *Timon* (another one of Shakespeare's pessimistic gems.)

16) B. Scrofula (referred to in *Macbeth* [4.3.146])

17) A. Julius Caesar

18) D. King Lear (He utters this vicious curse against his daughter, Goneril.)

19) B. Mistress Quickly in *Henry V* (The death is reported by her husband, Pistol [5.1.77].)

20) C. Plague

21) B. *All's Well* (The King of France is cured by Helena.)

22) A. Blood (Earth was represented by black bile, water by phlegm, and fire by yellow bile.)

23) C. Toothache (He lies to Othello that he was kept awake by a "raging tooth.")

24) D. Spleen (mentioned in many of Shakespeare's works.)

25) B. Syphilis (one of many names for the disease.)

Quiz 49

1) B. *Macbeth*

2) B. *Henry V* (Olivier directed it and starred in the title role.)

3) C. *Chimes at Midnight*

4) D. Playboy Pictures

5) D. Donalbain (the younger brother of Malcolm seems ready to recycle the ambition of Macbeth and destroy the promise of restored order that Shakespeare provides in his play.)

6) A. Olivier's (1948)

7) B. Micheal Machiammoir (who played the role of Iago in the film)

8) B. *A Midsummer Night's Dream* (Allen's film was called *A Midsummer Night's Sex Comedy.*)

9) C. Christopher Marlowe

10) A. *A Midsummer Night's Dream*

11) D. Richard Burbage

12) D. Richard III

13) A. *Julius Caesar*

14) B. *Hamlet* (He quoted "To be, or not to be....")

15) C. *Romeo and Juliet*

16) A. *Hamlet*

17) B. *Othello*

18) A. *Hamlet*

19) D. *The Two Gentlemen of Verona*

20) C. Welles's *Macbeth* (1948)

21) C. Playwright (His plays are known for their blood and gore, and his most famous works are *The Duchess of Malfi* and *The White Devil.*)

22) B. *Romeo and Juliet*

23) D. Vincent Price (Diana Rigg starred as his daughter.)

24) A. 35%

25) A. India

Quiz 50

1) A. Jean Simmons

2) D. Mark Antony (It was the third consecutive year he had been nominated.)

3) A. Franco Zeffirelli (who has also directed film adaptations of *Hamlet* and *The Taming of the Shrew*)

4) D. Olivier's 1948 *Hamlet*

5) C. Orson Welles's 1948 *Macbeth*

6) C. *Henry V*

7) B. 7 (It was nominated for 13 and won 7, including Best Picture.)

8) A. Gwyneth Paltrow

9) D. Basil Rathbone (Probably best known for his portrayals of Sherlock Holmes, he earned his first nomination, although he did not win.)

10) C. Judi Dench (She won the Oscar for her 8-minute on-screen performance.)

11) C. 4 (although it did not win any)

12) B. Norma Shearer (Then 36, she earned her 5th nomination starring opposite the Romeo of 40-year-old Leslie Howard.)

13) B. Best Costume Design

14) A. *As You Like It*

15) C. Othello (He becomes increasingly jealous of his ex-wife, who is playing the role of Desdemona.)

16) D. Frank Findlay

17) B. Best Cinematography and Best Film Editing

18) D. Maggie Smith

19) C. Geoffrey Rush (although he did not win an Oscar for his portrayal of theater owner Phillip Henslowe.)

20) B. Best Director (John Madden's first Academy Award nomination did not result in an Oscar.)

21) A. *Ran* (an adaptation of *King Lear*)

22) C. Franco Zeffirelli's 1966 *The Taming of the Shrew* (It was nominated but did not win for Art Direction, Set Decoration, and Costume Design. The others received no nominations.)

23) C. Richard III

24) D. Stuart Burge's 1970 *Julius Caesar* (*Titus* was nominated for Best Costume Design; *Richard III* for Art Direction and Costume Design; and *Hamlet* was nominated in four categories. None of the nominations resulted in winners, however.)

25) B. Stuart Burge's 1965 *Othello* (Olivier, Best Actor; Frank Findlay, Best Supporting Actor; and Maggie Smith and Joyce Redmond, Best Supporting Actress)

Quiz 51

1) A. Mickey Rooney (Rooney broke his leg during filming, and was wheeled around behind bushes on a bicycle during filming.)

2) B. Leslie Howard (He was the 3rd choice for the part after Clark Gable and Laurence Olivier, who turned it down saying that Shakespeare was not conducive to film.)

3) A. Lysander

4) C. Roddy McDowell

5) D. Peter Cushing (who would go on to have a successful and long career playing Sherlock Holmes and roles in numerous horror films, among other things)

6) A. John Gielgud

7) B. Ralph Richardson

8) B. Lucentio

9) C. Falstaff (the favorite Shakespearean role of Orson Welles)

10) D. Laurence Olivier

11) A. Anthony Hopkins (in the role that some may consider a fitting precursor to that of his later portrayal of Hannibal Lechter)

12) C. Charlton Heston

13) A. Jon Finch

14) D. John Hurt

15) A. Derek Jacobi

16) B. Ghost

17) D. John Gielgud

18) C. Denzil Washington

19) B. Laurence Fishburne

20) D. Billy Crystal

21) B. Feste

22) B. Joseph Fiennes

23) A. Kevin Kline

24) C. Costard

25) A. Ethan Hawke

Quiz 52

1) B. Douglas Fairbanks	10) A. Shylock	19) A. John Leguizamo
2) C. Nick Bottom	11) A. Richard Johnson	20) D. Kevin Spacey
3) D. Mercutio	12) D. King of France	21) C. Nigel Hawthorne
4) A. Basil Sydney	13) B. Alan Bates	22) A. Ben Affleck
5) D. Marlon Brando	14) C. Michael Keaton	23) A. Anthony Hopkins
6) B. King Edward IV	15) B. Kenneth Branagh	24) C. Oberon
7) C. Henry IV	16) C. Earl Rivers	25) B. Bill Murray
8) C. Leonard Whiting	17) C. Osric	
9) B. Jason Robards	18) D. Jack Lemmon	

Quiz 53

1) A. Mary Pickford	10) C. Diana Rigg	19) A. Kate Winslet
2) B. Elisabeth Bergner	11) C. Francesca Annis	20) C. Winona Ryder
3) C. Eileen Herlie	12) A. Joan Plowright	21) A. Claire Danes
4) C. Jeanette Nolan	13) B. Anna Calder-Marshall	22) D. Helena Bonham Carter
5) B. Greer Garson	14) A. Judi Dench	23) B. Jessica Lange
6) D. Claire Bloom	15) D. Helen Bonham-Carter	24) B. Michelle Pfeiffer
7) B. Jeanne Moreau	16) B. Isabelle Pasco	25) C. Julia Stiles
8) B. Olivia Hussey	17) D. Emma Thompson	
9) C. Marianne Faithfull	18) C. Kristin Scott Thomas	

Quiz 54

1) D. Olivia de Havilland

2) B. Sophie Stewart

3) C. Norma Shearer (The 35-year-old actress played the role of the 13-year-old Juliet.)

4) A. Freda Jackson

5) C. Jean Simmons

6) D. Suzanne Cloutier

7) B. Deborah Kerr

8) D. Maggie Smith

9) C. Elizabeth Taylor

10) B. Natasha Pyne

11) D. Estelle Parsons

12) A. Judy Parfitt

13) A. Irene Worth

14) C. Hildegarde Neil

15) D. Judi Dench

16) B. Emma Thompson (Branagh's wife at the time)

17) C. Glenn Close

18) D. Kate Beckinsale

19) B. Irene Jacob

20) D. Annette Bening

21) A. Imogen Stubbs

22) B. Julie Christie

23) C. Laura Fraser

24) C. Helena

25) A. Alicia Silverstone

Quiz 55

1) D. *Othello*

2) D. *The Tempest*

3) C. *The Taming of the Shrew*

4) A. *The Tempest*

5) B. *King Lear*

6) D. *Macbeth*

7) B. *Hamlet*

8) A. *Othello*

9) D. *The Comedy of Errors* (It is a tale of two sets of identical twins who are separated at birth until a business conflict brings them together.)

10) A. *King Lear*

11) C. *My Own Private Idaho* (a 1991 film starring Keanu Reeves and River Phoenix)

12) A. *Hamlet*

13) D. *Julius Caesar* (turned into a tale of the ruthless business world)

14) D. *King Lear*

15) C. *Othello*

16) C. *King Lear*

17) B. Peter Sellars

18) A. Gary Oldman

19) B. *Macbeth* (Directed by Adrezej Wajda, this offshoot is also known as *Siberian Lady Macbeth*.)

20) C. *Hamlet*

Quiz 56

1) B. *The Comedy of Errors* (It ran for 235 performances and starred Eddie Albert and Burl Ives.)

2) C. Richard Burton

3) D. Carol Lawrence (in the play that opened at the Winter Garden Theatre on September 26, 1957 and ran for 732 performances)

4) A. Leonard Bernstein and Stephen Sondheim

5) D. Peggy Ashcroft

6) A. Richard III (Stepping in for his ill father, Junius, he played the role of Richard III. Of course, his younger brother John Wilkes Booth was Lincoln's assassin.)

7) C. Meryl Streep

8) A. Orson Welles

9) D. Ira Aldridge (in the mid-19th century)

10) B. Peggy Ashcroft (who was made a Dame of the British Empire in 1956 and played most of the major Shakespearean roles for women)

11) C. *Macbeth* (If an actor says the name of the play, he is cast out of the dressing room, must turn around three times, spit, and recite the line from *The Merry Wives of Windsor*: "Fair thoughts and happy hours attend on you." Then he must knock on the door and beg to be readmitted.)

12) A. Louis Armstrong

13) B. Richard III

14) B. Henry Irving

15) D. Katherina in *The Taming of the Shrew*

16) A. *Timon of Athens*

17) C. Edmund Kean ([1787–1833], noted for portrayals of Shylock, Richard III, and Othello)

18) C. *Twelfth Night* (It is set in Manhattan Island, Illyria where Orson is a theatrical agent, Olivia is the operator of a discotheque, and Viola and Sebastian are rock singers.)

19) B. *A Midsummer Night's Dream* (The play focuses on the six lowly workers due to perform before Duke Theseus on his wedding day.)

20) B. Ellen Terry

21) A. *The Taming of the Shrew*

22) D. David Garrick

23) D. Shylock (He was the first to give dignity to the part of Shylock, who had previously been crudely played as a laughingstock.)

24) C. Charles Dickens (who played the role of Justice Shallow in the production that toured England and Scotland.)

25) B. Joseph Papp (Since 1962, the festival has offered free summer performances in the Delacorte Theatre in New York's Central Park.)

Quiz 57

1) A. William Shatner

2) D. Patrick Stewart

3) A. *Hamlet* (1.4.39)

4) C. *Macbeth*

5) B. *Hamlet*

6) C. *Macbeth*

7) D. *The Winter's Tale* (5.2.110)

8) A. "Shall I Compare Thee to a Summer's Day?" (#18)

9) B. *Macbeth*

10) B. *The Taming of the Shrew*

11) D. Leak (Oh, that Data!)

12) C. The scene in *Henry V* where Henry mingles with troops before the battle of Agincourt

13) C. *The Merchant of Venice* (The statement is also found in the Bible.)

14) A. *Hamlet* (Hamlet makes this comment about his late father [1.2.187].)

15) B. *Othello* (5.2.13)

16) C. *A Midsummer Night's Dream* (Riker reads Oberon, Data reads Puck, Crusher reads the first fairy, and the landlady reads Titania.)

17) D. *The Tempest*

18) D. *Henry V* (3.1.1)

19) B. *Twelfth Night* (3.4.201)

20) A. *Hamlet* (3.1.66)

21) C. *Hamlet* (3.1.78)

22) D. *Romeo and Juliet* (2.2.184)

23) B. *Julius Caesar* (3.1.273)

24) A. *Hamlet* (5.1.163)

25) C. *Richard II* (3.2.155)

Quiz 58

1) *Twice Told Tales* was used as a title by at least two major authors, Nathaniel Hawthorne and Charles Dickens.

2) *Rosencrantz and Guildenstern Are Dead*, a play by Tom Stoppard

3) *Something Wicked This Way Comes* by Ray Bradbury

4) *The Weaker Vessel* by Antonia Fraser

5) *Words of Love* by Pearl S. Buck

6) *The Winter of Our Discontent* by John Steinbeck

7) *Not So Deep as a Well* by Dorothy Parker

8) *Brave New World* by Aldous Huxley

9) *In Cold Blood* by Truman Capote

10) *Cakes and Ale* by Somerset Maugham

11) *The Quality of Mercy* by William Dean Howells

12) *And Be a Villain* by Rex Stout

13) *The Moon is Down* by John Steinbeck

14) *Under the Greenwood Tree* by Thomas Hardy

15) *Bottom's Dream* by John Updike

16) *New Heaven, New Earth* by Joyce Carol Oates

17) *Sad Cyprus* by Agatha Christie

18) *Nothing Like the Sun* by Anthony Burgess (a novel about the love life of Shakespeare)

19) *The Razor's Edge* by Somerset Maugham

20) *The Sound and the Fury* by William Faulkner

Quiz 59

1) Alfred Lord Tennyson, *The Idylls of the King*

2) John Milton, *Paradise Lost*

3) Shakespeare, *The Comedy of Errors* (3.1.26)

4) Shakespeare, *Titus Andronicus* (1.1.390)

5) Shakespeare, *The Merchant of Venice* (1.3.179)

6) Benjamin Franklin, *Poor Richard's Almanack* [sic]

7) Shakespeare, *Macbeth* (3.2.11)

8) Miquel de Cervantes, *Don Quixote del la Mancha*

9) Shakespeare, *King Lear* (1.4.346)

10) Sir Walter Scott, *Marmion*

11) Shakespeare, *Hamlet* (4.7.128)

12) Christopher Marlowe, *The Tragical History of Doctor Faustus*

13) Shakespeare, *Cymbeline* (3.3.79)

14) Shakespeare, *Othello* (2.3.370)

15) Shakespeare, *Macbeth* (5.5.23)

16) John Donne, *Devotions Upon Emergent Occasions*

17) John Dryden, *Alexander's Feast*

18) Francis Bacon, *Meditationes Sacrae*

19) Shakespeare, *As You Like It* (4.1.106)

20) Shakespeare, *Othello* (3.3.157)

21) Alexander Pope, *An Essay on Criticism*

22) Shakespeare, *Romeo and Juliet* (2.6.9)

23) Shakespeare, *Henry V* (4.1.1)

24) John Keats, *Ode to a Nightingale*

25) Charles Dickens, *A Tale of Two Cities*

Quiz 60

1) Shakespeare (*Richard III* [1.2.71])

2) Bible (Job 32:9)

3) Bible (Proverbs 23:7)

4) Shakespeare (*The Two Gentlemen of Verona* [3.2.71])

5) Shakespeare (*Timon of Athens* [1.1.107])

6) Shakespeare (*Coriolanus* [3.1.198])

7) Bible (Romans 4:15)

8) Shakespeare (*The Winter's Tale* [2.3.115])

9) Shakespeare (*A Midsummer Night's Dream* [5.1.120])

10) Bible (Ecclesiastes 4:13)

11) Bible (Matthew 6:28)

12) Shakespeare (*Hamlet* [3.4.178])

13) Bible (Hosea 8:7)

14) Shakespeare (*Henry V* [4.1.176])

15) Shakespeare (*King Lear* [4.2.38])

16) Bible (John 15:13)

17) Bible (Luke 4:23)

18) Bible (Romans 6:9)

19) Shakespeare (*Troilus and Cressida* [2.3.154])

20) Bible (Matthew 22:14)

21) Shakespeare (*Love's Labor's Lost* [1.1.77])

22) Bible (Isaiah 22:13)

23) Shakespeare (*The Taming of the Shrew* [4.3.172])

24) Bible (Isaiah 8:7)

25) Shakespeare (*Richard II* [3.2.54])

Quiz 61

1) Ben Jonson	8) Virginia Woolf	15) Leo Tolstoy
2) Voltaire	9) Charles Dickens	16) Matthew Arnold
3) John Dryden	10) Samuel Pepys	17) John Keats
4) Mickey Spillane	11) Samuel Johnson	18) D.H. Lawrence
5) T.S. Eliot	12) Henry Miller	19) Robert Graves
6) William Hazlitt	13) George Bernard Shaw	20) Mark Twain
7) James Barrie	14) Samuel Coleridge	

Quiz 62

1) Philip Henslowe	8) Thomas Kyd	15) Edward Alleyn
2) Richard Burbage	9) John Webster	16) Sir Philip Sidney
3) William Kempe	10) Francis Langley	17) Robert Armin
4) Edmund Tilney	11) Edmund Spenser	18) Christopher Marlowe
5) John Fletcher	12) Francis Beaumont	19) John Heminges
6) Ben Jonson	13) Raphael Holinshed	20) Francis Bacon
7) Henry Condell	14) Henry Cary	

Quiz 63

1) D. Mr. Ed (Walter Brooks created the stories of the hard-drinking, Shakespeare-quoting horse. The TV show was made possible by the support of George Burns.)

2) B. Batman (When the button was pushed it opened a secret sliding door, behind which were the Batpoles that led to the Bat Cave.)

3) C. Lyndon Johnson (Macbird [Macbeth] is the Johnson character, John Ken O'Duncs [Duncan] represents John Kennedy, and Lady Macbird [Lady Macbeth] characterizes Lady Bird Johnson.)

4) C. *The Taming of the Shrew* (David [Willis] continually quotes from other Shakespeare plays and is repeatedly admonished by the rest of the cast, and at one point, Maddie [Shepherd] blurts out "Goest thou to Hell!")

5) A. *Hamlet* (Believe it or not, the episode was named by TV Guide as one of the 100 greatest TV episodes of all time.)

6) D. Neil Gaiman ("A Midsummer Night's Dream" won a 1991 World Fantasy Award for Gaiman.)

7) B. *Much Apu About Nothing* (When an anti-immigrant law is put into effect, Apu risks being deported as an illegal alien, and Homer attempts to help him get fake papers [May 5, 1996].)

8) D. Steve Allen (The conversations contained many rhymed couplets and Shakespearean quotes.)

9) A. *Macbeth* (Superman also rescues Shakespeare from the wrath of an angry nobleman, who was lampooned in *The Merry Wives of Windsor*.)

10) C. Beany and Cecil (In the episode "Never Eat Quackers in Bed," William Shakespeare Wolf captures a little duckling named Graham Quacker and tries to eat the little bird, but he is foiled in the end.)

11) B. Earl of Oxford (In this episode, which has some resemblance to events in the widely popular film *Shakespeare in Love*, Mr. Peabody suggests Juliet as an alternative to Zelda.)

12) A. *Julius Caesar* (Plummer is a noted Shakespearean actor, and at the end of the show, Theo and Cockroach perform Antony's funeral oration in rap.)

13) C. *The Postman* (He acts out some scenes with his donkey.)

14) D. *Hamlet* (It centers around activities in the Elsinore Brewery, and a song from the soundtrack is "Shakespeare Horked Our Script." We can only wish that he did.)

15) D. Macbeth (Goober was a skinny dog who turned invisible when he was frightened, and only his hat would show. He was accompanied by a group of youngsters, including members of the Partridge Family singing group, who investigated paranormal activity. Luckily for children everywhere, it produced episodes for only one season.)

16) B. The Puzzler (Evans played a Riddler wanna-be and quoted plentifully from *Hamlet* and *Macbeth*.)

17) A. *Shylock's Daughter* (Yes, *that* Erica Jong. You remember *Fear of Flying*, don't you?)

18) C. *Kiss Me, Kate* (It was sung by two mobsters, and many consider it to be the highlight of the show.)

19) C. A set of cocktail napkins featuring humorous cartoons and Shakespearean quotes

20) D. John Updike (The novel attempts to fill in the gaps of Shakespeare's play, and in doing so, gives interesting perspectives to many of the characters, most notably the usually maligned Gertrude and Claudius.)

Quiz 64

1) A. Lepidus

2) C. Fulvia

3) D. Julius Caesar

4) D. Mardian

5) A. His love for Cleopatra is interfering with his duties as a Roman leader.

6) B. Fulvia

7) A. A pearl

8) A. Agrippa

9) C. Charmian

10) B. Send him word that she has killed herself

11) A. Menas

12) A. As long as Antony remains in Rome, he will be overshadowed by Caesar.

13) A. A fleet of 60 ships

14) D. He blames himself for corrupting Enobarbus.

15) B. He follows her and leads his troops in a retreat.

16) C. To be allowed to live in Egypt with Cleopatra

17) D. Eros (who refuses and kills himself rather than Antony)

18) B. Keep her on display in Rome

19) D. She lets herself be bitten by poisonous snakes.

20) C. Dolabella

Quiz 65

1) B. France (Spelled "Arden" in the Folio text, the Forest of Ardenne is in France.)

2) C. Adam

3) A. Oliver ignores the provisions for Orlando in their late father's will.

4) C. Niece

5) D. Jaques

6) D. Charles

7) B. Necklace

8) C. Oliver

9) A. Ganymede

10) D. He pins love poems to the trees in the forest.

11) C. Jaques

12) B. Phebe

13) B. She will pretend to be his love and reject his courtship.

14) C. Vicar

15) D. Lioness

16) C. Duke Frederick (He decides to restore the dukedom to its rightful ruler, Duke Senior, and then "put on a religious life" as a hermit. Jaques then decides to join him.)

17) A. Jaques (a different Jaques than the melancholy attendant to Duke Senior)

18) A. Audrey

19) B. Silvius (The shepherd marries the shepherdess Phebe. Fitting, isn't it?)

20) C. Rosalind

Quiz 66

1) C. Because Imogen has married Posthumus Leonatus

2) D. Stepbrother

3) A. Cornelius

4) C. Poison (She plans to use it to have Cymbeline killed.)

5) B. His father died before he was born (a common Roman custom of the time)

6) B. Bracelet (Imogen gives Posthumus a diamond ring as a parting gift.)

7) D. Italy

8) D. Belarius (He kidnapped Cymbeline's sons because of his unjust exile.)

9) C. Iachimo

10) A. Cymbeline refused to pay tribute to Rome.

11) A. He hides in a trunk that he has delivered to her room.

12) C. Breast

13) B. Milford Haven

14) D. Pisanio (the well-known servant type of folklore character who serves his master best by disobeying him)

15) A. Fidele

16) C. He is killed and beheaded by Guiderius.

17) C. Arviragus (He and Guiderius are the sons of Cymbeline, kidnapped by Belarius.)

18) B. His father, mother, and brothers

19) A. Cymbeline

20) D. Cymbeline announces an alliance with the Romans once again.

Quiz 67

1) D. Reynaldo

2) B. Hebona (The ghost tells Hamlet that Claudius "With juice of cursed hebona in a vial,/ And in the porches of my ears did pour/ The leprous distillment..." [1.5.62].)

3) B. Wittenberg

4) C. 3 (The ghost appears once to the guards and Horatio [1.1]; again before the Guards, Horatio, and Hamlet [1.4-5]; and finally before Hamlet in Gertrude's bedroom [2.4].)

5) C. France

6) A. Julius Caesar

7) D. *The Murder of Gonzago*

8) B. *The Mousetrap*

9) A. Norway

10) D. Love (He's ordered Ophelia to reject Hamlet's advances so he thinks it's unrequited love.)

11) C. Yorick (When the gravedigger tells him whose skull it is, Hamlet utters the famous line, "Alas, poor Yorick! I knew him, Horatio..." [5.1.184].)

12) B. Gertrude (in the bedroom scene [3.4.178].)

13) D. England (Claudius puts him on a ship, accompanied by Rosencrantz and Guildenstern, who bear letters asking the English to execute Hamlet.)

14) D. Drowns

15) B. Osric

16) C. 8 (Polonius, Rosencrantz, Guildenstern, Ophelia, Gertrude, Laertes, Claudius, and Hamlet)

17) A. 3 (Hamlet kills Polonius, Laertes, and Claudius.)

18) A. Pearl

19) D. Hamlet

20) C. Fortinbras

Quiz 68

1) D. The Boar's Head

2) B. Shrewsbury

3) B. Richard II

4) A. To lower expectations, so that when he becomes king, he will be more impressive

5) A. Henry Percy (Actually, we would call him Henry Percy, Jr. today, because his father had the same name.)

6) C. Younger brother (John of Lancaster is known for his serious nature, unlike Hal.)

7) D. Welsh

8) B. Prince Hal and Henry IV

9) D. They say that Henry is ungrateful for their role in helping him attain the throne.

10) B. Bardolph

11) A. Glendower (who is ridiculed by Hotspur for making this claim)

12) C. Poins

13) C. Hotspur was his son instead of Prince Hal

14) B. A crusade to the Holy Land (Henry wanted to engage in a crusade to atone for deposing the previous king of his throne.)

15) A. Mortimer

16) D. Mistress Quickly

17) D. Kate

18) B. Glendower

19) C. He was too ill.

20) C. A bottle of wine (which Hal is disgusted to find)

Quiz 69

1) D. Humphrey, Duke of Gloucester

2) A. Duke of Exeter

3) C. Sir John Bates

4) B. Nym

5) C. Lieutenant

6) A. After becoming king, Henry V rejected him.

7) D. Mountjoy

8) C. Tennis balls

9) D. Charles VI

10) B. Harfleur

11) B. Fluellen

12) A. Alice

13) C. Bardolph

14) D. Mocking contempt

15) C. His father usurping the throne from Richard II.

16) A. Earl of Westmoreland

17) B. Duke of York

18) D. The English pages guarding the luggage are murdered.

19) D. Edward, Duke of York

20) C. Become a thief and a pimp

Quiz 70

1) A. Sons of Pompey

2) C. March 15 (In the ancient Roman calendar, the "ides" was the 15th day of March, May, July, and October, and the 13th day of the other months.)

3) D. Calpurnia

4) C. Lupercalia (The predecessor of St. Valentine's Day, it was one of the most famous of all Roman Festivals. Selected Romans performed sacrificial rituals and ran a race in the city, whipping those in their way. Being whipped was thought to enhance conception.)

5) B. Flavius

6) D. Adopted heir (Octavius was the son of Caesar's niece, Atia.)

7) B. Epilepsy (Julius Caesar has an epileptic fit, as reported by Casca [1.2.248]. Brutus calls it "the falling sickness" [1.2.254].)

8) B. Fear that Caesar will become king and abuse his power

9) A. Brothers-in-law (Cassius married the sister of Brutus.)

10) C. Cassius (who tells this story to Brutus [1.2.100])

11) C. Decius Brutus

12) D. Artemidorus (3.1.3)

13) A. Cicero (When he is suggested as a possible conspirator, Brutus rejects his inclusion.)

14) B. Casca

15) A. Publius

16) D. Cassius

17) C. Honorable

18) C. Strato (who agrees to do this after others refuse)

19) B. Philippi (in Macedonia)

20) D. Mark Antony

Quiz 71

1) B. She refuses to express her love for Lear as strongly as her sisters.

2) C. France

3) B. Edmund

4) A. Kent

5) A. Burgundy

6) C. Duke of Albany

7) D. He is placed in the stocks.

8) D. Beggar

9) A. Because Gloucester helped Lear escape him

10) B. One of his servants (who dies trying to stop the blinding of Gloucester but mortally wounds Cornwall in the process)

11) C. Devils

12) A. Goneril (who wants her husband dead so she will be free to marry Edmund)

13) C. Poisoned by Goneril (Yes, she poisons her sister because Regan also wants to marry Edmund.)

14) B. Suicide by stabbing

15) A. Edgar (Of course, Edmund is lying, and Edgar is planning no such treachery.)

16) D. Regan and Goneril

17) D. 80 (5.7.60)

18) C. To save Cordelia and Lear from death

19) D. Caius (The name is mentioned only once, near the very end of the play.)

20) B. Edgar (Albany offers shared rule to Kent and Edgar, but Kent declines.)

Quiz 72

1) B. Norway

2) B. Thane of Cawdor (Duncan gives the title of the treasonous thane to Macbeth.)

3) D. Sinel

4) B. Macduff

5) C. Macdonwald (The bloody sergeant makes this report to Duncan [1.1.22].)

6) A. Banquo (his friend and fellow general)

7) D. Inverness

8) A. A floating dagger (Macbeth sees it right before he murders Duncan in Act II.)

9) C. Macduff

10) B. Diamond

11) C. Fleance

12) C. Ireland (and Malcolm goes to England)

13) D. Scone

14) A. A sailor's thumb (It is used by the witches to make a spell in Act I.)

15) A. 8 (the last, holding a glass [mirror] in his hand)

16) B. Seyton

17) C. Birnam

18) D. Macduff (Evidently his mother had a C-section.)

19) C. Young Siward (As he dies, Macbeth sarcastically states, "Thou wast born of woman" [5.7.11].)

20) A. Malcolm

Quiz 73

1) C. He says he does not know why he is sad. (Some believe he is depressed over his homoerotic feelings for Bassanio.)

2) A. His extravagant lifestyle.

3) B. Antonio was rude to Shylock's wife before her death.

4) A. It was a condition of the will of Portia's recently deceased father.

5) D. To donate a large sum to an Italian orphanage

6) B. "Who chooseth me shall get as much as he deserves."

7) A. Prince of Morocco

8) D. Bassanio

9) B. Tubal

10) C. Gratiano

11) A. 3,000 (for a term of 3 months)

12) A. Jessica

13) D. Lorenzo

14) B. Bellario

15) C. He displays resigned acceptance of his fate.

16) B. The bond allows for a pound of flesh but does not allow for any blood to be taken.

17) D. Half his estate goes to Antonio, and he must pay a fine and become a Christian.

18) A. He says he does not feel well and asks to leave.

19) C. The ring that Portia gave him.

20) A. Three of the ships that were thought to have been lost have arrived in port.

Quiz 74

1) C. Egeus (who is angry that his daughter Hermia refuses to marry Demetrius, his choice for her husband)

2) C. Helena (who does this to try to get in the good graces of Demetrius, with whom she is in love)

3) B. Amazons (the fierce race of warrior women)

4) A. An Indian boy (His deceased mother was of Titania's order. Oberon wants him to be his "henchman.")

5) C. Robin Goodfellow

6) D. Hobnail

7) B. Lysander

8) C. Height

9) A. Philostrate (a rather humorless Master of the Revels for Theseus)

10) D. Weaver

11) C. Peter Quince

12) A. Nick Bottom

13) B. She thinks they are both mocking her.

14) C. Have Quince write a ballad about it

15) B. Snout

16) A. Hippolyta

17) D. He thinks it's badly performed.

18) D. Pyramus and Thisbe

19) B. Dance (A Bergomask is a rustic dance taking its name from Bergamo, in Italy.)

20) C. Puck

Quiz 75

1) C. Cousins

2) D. Sicily (It takes place in Messina on the island of Sicily.)

3) A. Prince of Arragon

4) A. Don Pedro

5) B. Half brother (Throughout the play, Don John is referred to as "the bastard.")

6) C. He tries to convince Claudio that Don Pedro is wooing Hero for himself.

7) A. Malapropisms (such as this statement made to Borachio: "O villain! thou wilt be condemn'd into everlasting redemption for this" [4.2.56], which adds great humor to the play)

8) C. Verges (Dogberry's primary "straight man")

9) D. Conrade (4.2.73)

10) D. Borachio

11) C. To pretend that Hero is dead until they can reveal her innocence

12) B. Dogberry's watchmen

13) D. Leonato banishes Margaret for her role in Don John's plan to discredit Hero.

14) A. Dogberry (who wouldn't understand the plan even if he knew it)

15) C. Benedick and Claudio fight a duel in which Claudio is wounded.

16) B. Borachio

17) D. To agree never to marry and spend his life praying for Hero

18) C. Kill Claudio

19) C. Francis

20) A. Love poems they wrote for one another

Quiz 76

1) B. 28 (Iago says, "I have looked upon the world for four times seven years..." [1.3.311]. Of course, Iago is certainly not one of the world's more truthful fellows, so who knows?)

2) A. Senator

3) D. Gratiano

4) C. Montano

5) C. Cyprus (where the rest of the play takes place)

6) B. Emilia

7) A. Ensign

8) D. Bianca

9) C. Jealousy

10) C. Brabantio

11) A. Othello gave Cassio a promotion that Iago desired. (Although there is evidence that responses B and C are also true, the only reason Iago gives Roderigo is that Othello gave Cassio a promotion he desired.)

12) B. Roderigo and Emilia (his dupe and his own wife)

13) B. An Egyptian charmer (who told her it would keep her husband faithful)

14) C. Turkey

15) D. Sagittary

16) D. Emilia

17) A. Smother her in bed

18) C. Iago saw a love letter Cassio had written to Desdemona.

19) B. Roderigo

20) A. Honorable

Quiz 77

1) A. Duke of Gloucester

2) C. Anne Neville

3) A. Earl Rivers (Anthony Woodville)

4) D. Edward and Richard

5) B. Sir James Tyrrel (who is hired by Richard, and then "subcontracts" Dighton and Forrest to actually commit the murders)

6) B. Duke of Buckingham

7) A. Queen Margaret

8) C. Jane Shore (the openly acknowledged mistress of Edward IV)

9) C. Strawberries

10) C. Lord Stanley (The allegiance of the other three to Richard is evident in a doggerel of the time: "the cat [Catesby], the rat [Ratcliffe] and Lovell our dog,/rule all England under a hog [Richard].")

11) D. Marquess of Dorset

12) B. He arranges that the heirs of Edward are declared illegitimate.

13) B. Elizabeth York, daughter Edward (his neice)

14) A. Jane Shore

15) C. King Henry VI

16) A. Earl of Richmond (who plans to "unite the White Rose and the Red")

17) B. King Edward IV

18) C. Lord Stanley (However, at the crucial moment in the battle, Stanley withholds his aid.)

19) B. Earl of Richmond

20) D. 1485

Quiz 78

1) B. 13 (She was two weeks away from her 14th birthday.)

2) D. Rosaline (until he falls in love, at first sight, with Juliet)

3) B. Tybalt

4) A. Paris

5) C. John

6) A. Mantua

7) B. 5 days

8) D. Lord Capulet (about his daughter, Juliet)

9) D. Paris

10) A. He is offended that Romeo shows up at the Capulet ball.

11) C. Mercutio (1.4.53)

12) C. Benvolio

13) A. Juliet

14) D. Prince Escalus

15) B. They will erect golden statues of the young lovers.

16) B. Dagger (in the event the potion does not work and her father tries to force her to marry the man of his choice.)

17) A. Friar Laurence

18) C. She died with grief over Romeo's exile.

19) D. 42 (4.1.105)

20) D. Balthasar

Quiz 79

1) D. 12 years

2) D. Gonzalo (who provided them with food, water, books, and other necessaries [1.2.160])

3) A. Alonso

4) B. Milan

5) C. Antonio

6) C. Alonso

7) B. In a cloven pine

8) A. Claribel

9) D. Fish

10) B. Stephano (Alonso's drunken butler)

11) C. Sebastian (Ariel foils the plan by singing a song and waking Gonzalo.)

12) A. Caliban tried to rape Miranda.

13) B. Trinculo (the jester)

14) A. 3 years old

15) D. Harpy

16) B. Sycorax

17) A. Stephano and Triculo engage in a drunken duel, and Triculo is wounded.

18) C. To provide calm seas for the return of the ships to Italy

19) C. Gonzalo decides to stay on the island and form a utopian community there.

20) B. Prospero (Some scholars interpret the passage to be Shakespeare's farewell to the theater, as was mentioned in the introduction to this quiz.)

Quiz 80

1) A. Messaline (There is no such city, so either Shakespeare made it up or it is a printer's error.)

2) B. She and her brother are shipwrecked and separated.

3) C. Uncle

4) B. Steward

5) D. Alcoholic beverages

6) A. Fabian (He serves Olivia.)

7) D. She mourns her brother, when he's in heaven.

8) D. Olivia's father

9) C. He committed piracy against Illyria.

10) B. Maria

11) A. His purse

12) B. When she sends "Cesario" the ring

13) C. Sir Andrew

14) C. Red velvet, plumed hat

15) A. Curate (and goes by the name of Sir Topas)

16) D. Fabian

17) D. Sir Toby

18) A. Sebastian

19) C. Antonio

20) A. "The rain it raineth every day"

Quiz 81

1) D. Leontes is king of Sicilia, and Polixenes is king of Bohemia.

2) C. Visiting, because they have been friends since childhood

3) B. Mamillius

4) A. Antigonus

5) D. 9 months

6) A. Camillo

7) C. Apollo

8) C. She says that the child physically resembles Leontes.

9) B. Cleomenes and Dion

10) B. "Hermione will sleep, and her daughter will be lost."

11) D. Hermione

12) A. Killed by a bear

13) C. 16

14) D. A shepherd

15) B. Doricles

16) C. Autolycus

17) A. Camillo

18) D. Autolycus

19) B. Paulina

20) D. Camillo

Quiz 82

1) C. Dunce	10) A. Foolishness	19) C. Great
2) B. Dagger	11) D. Taste	20) A. Informer
3) A. Sky	12) D. Elf	21) D. A top
4) D. Ruby	13) A. Song	22) A. Portion
5) D. Burden	14) C. Goblin	23) C. Person
6) B. Truth	15) B. Perhaps	24) C. Morning
7) C. Thief	16) A. Coward	25) B. Since
8) B. Gallows	17) B. Thank you	
9) D. Rude person	18) C. Jury	

Quiz 83

1) Invective	8) Chiasmus	15) Paradox
2) Simile	9) Prolepsis	16) Metaphor
3) Oxymoron	10) Synecdoche	17) Soliloquy
4) Hyperbole	11) Dramatic irony	18) Allusion
5) Doggerel	12) Caesura	19) Anagnorisis
6) Onomatopoeia	13) Alliteration	20) Metonymy
7) Blazon	14) Anachronism	

Quiz 84

1) D. Stratford

2) B. Hathaway

3) A. Arden

4) D. 8 (William was the third child; the two sisters born before William seemed to have died in infancy.)

5) C. 3 (Susanna was born in 1583, and twins—Hamnet and Judith—were born in 1585.)

6) D. 1564

7) B. 1616 (It is believed by many that he died on his birthday and was exactly 52 years old at the time of his death.)

8) A. Avon

9) A. April 23

10) C. 2 (His two daughters survived him. Hamnet died at age 11, in 1596, of unknown causes, possibly the plague.)

11) C. His wife (Anne died in 1623.)

12) C. Glover (He also brokered in wool and was elected alderman and later bailiff [mayor] for Stratford.)

13) A. The second best bed (This may not be the insult some perceive it to be today—according to ancient custom, she was entitled to 1/3 of his estate.)

14) D. 6

15) B. John Heminges and Henry Condell (They were evidently good friends of Shakespeare's. They refer to him glowingly in the introduction to The First Folio, and Shakespeare left them money in his will to buy memorial rings.)

16) A. 4 (Elizabeth was the only daughter of Susanna. Three boys—Shaksper, Richard, and Thomas—were the offspring of Judith, and none had children of their own.)

17) C. Martin Droeshout (His flawed portrait, with the head too large in relation to the torso, is the most famous portrait of Shakespeare and believed to be—along with the sculpture on his tomb—the most accurate depiction of his looks.)

18) B. William D'avenant (His parents ran an inn in Oxford, between London and Stratford, where Shakespeare reportedly stayed on occasion.)

19) D. Henley Street

20) B. Actor (Record of his burial lists him as "a player"—an actor.)

21) C. Medical doctor

22) A. Holy Trinity (in Stratford)

23) A. He was a witness in a lawsuit (May 1612, involving his former landlord in London, Christopher Mountjoy, a wig-maker, sued by his son-in-law and former apprentice, Stephen Belott)

24) C. Alice

25) B. Thomas Quiney (He was the husband of Shakespeare's daughter, Judith. Shortly after the marriage, Quiney was punished by the town for fornication, which occurred before the wedding with another woman, who died in childbirth. Shakespeare was evidently not pleased, and shortly before his death, he changed his will to protect Judith from Quiney.)

Quiz 85

1) B. Italy

2) B. 154

3) A. 14

4) D. Iambic pentameter

5) B. 10

6) C. ABAB CDCD EFEF GG

7) A. Mr. W.H.

8) C. A child

9) A. Me ("Me" is used 10 times and "thee" is used 8 times.)

10) B. *Romeo and Juliet*

11) D. Queen Elizabeth

12) D. William Wordsworth

13) C. *A Lover's Complaint*

14) A. *Venus and Adonis*

15) B. *The Phoenix and the Turtle* (It has 67 lines, while *A Lover's Complaint* has 329, *Venus and Adonis* has 1,194, and *The Rape of Lucrece* has 1,856.)

16) A. Henry Wriothesley, Earl of Southampton

17) A. Gored by the tusk of a boar

18) D. A purple flower

19) C. Doves

20) C. *A Lover's Complaint*

21) D. *The Passionate Pilgrim*

22) A. Rhyme royal

23) A. Tarquin

24) B. Collatine

25) C. Commits suicide by stabbing herself

Quiz 86

1) B. *Hamlet* (It has 4,042 lines. *Coriolanus* is second with 3,752 lines, *Cymbeline* is next with 3,707, and *Richard III* has 3,667.)

2) C. *Com Err* (It is the shortest of all the plays with 1,787 lines, followed by *MN Dream* with 2,192. *Tempest* has 2,283 and *Two Gents* has 2,288.)

3) D. Richard III in *Richard III*

4) A. *Othello* (Iago speaks 1,097 lines while Othello has "only" 860.)

5) B. Rosalind in *As You* (668 lines)

6) A. Cleopatra in *Ant & Cleo* (She has 622. Portia, with 562, and Juliet, with 509, are next.)

7) D. *Macbeth* (It has 2,349 lines. The next shortest is *Timon* at 2,488.)

8) B. *Merry Wives* (Only 12% of its lines are written in verse.)

9) A. 10%

10) C. Cleopatra in *Ant & Cleo* (She speaks 4,066 words, but Antony speaks 4,484 words.)

11) C. 65%

12) B. *Love' s LL* (1,150 rhyming lines out of a total of 1,734 lines for 66%)

13) A. 36 (Most modern scholars now accept *Pericles* and *Two Noble*, both likely late collaborative efforts, which the editors left out.)

14) D. 18 (If not for The First Folio, plays such as *Macbeth*, *As You*, *Tempest*, *Twelfth N*, and 14 others likely would have been lost.)

15) C. *Ant & Cleo* (It is divided into 42 scenes. No other play has as many as 30.)

16) B. Henry V in *Henry V*

17) D. *Rom & Jul* (18% of its lines rhyme. *Lear* has 7%, *Hamlet*, 5%, and *Othello*, 4%.)

18) D. *Hamlet* (It has 4,686 unique words.)

19) C. 29,066 (To demonstrate how incredible this vocabulary is, compare it to the vocabularies of the following authors: Petrarch, 4,491; Marlowe, 11,448; and Dante, 14,822.)

20) D. 42 (19 from the Old and New Testaments, 6 from the Apocrypha)

Quiz 87

1) D. Red Lion (Although the Red Lion [1567] is now believed to be technically the first, the Theatre [1576], was really the first substantial purpose-built London playhouse.)

2) B. Southwark (on the south bank of the Thames River.)

3) D. Groundlings

4) B. 2,500

5) C. 1599

6) C. Swan

7) B. The Theatre

8) A. Peter Street

9) A. Blackfriars (A replica of it opened in Staunton, Virginia, in 2001.)

10) C. Dr. Simon Forman (He recorded observations about three of Shakespeare's plays that he saw performed at the Globe Theatre: *Macbeth*, *The Winter's Tale*, and *Cymbeline*.)

11) D. Hell

12) A. Rose (which housed the Admiral's Men—the chief rival to Shakespeare's company)

13) C. Tiring house

14) C. 2 p.m.

15) B. *Henry VIII* (then known as *All Is True*; during a performance, staged cannon fire [1.4.49] ignited the thatched roof—there were no injuries, and the Globe was rebuilt within a year)

16) D. 1 penny (That was for your basic standing room only. Once in the playhouse, a person could pay more to proceed into other areas that offered seating.)

17) C. He held the prompt-book to remind actors of their lines.

18) A. 10% (He was part of a syndicate which included Richard and Cuthbert Burbage, who held 50% of the shares, and Shakespeare split the remaining 50% with John Heminges, William Kemp, Augustine Phillips, and Thomas Pope.)

19) B. 1644

20) C. 1924 (by W.W. Braines)

21) D. 20

22) C. Sam Wanamaker

23) C. *Henry V* (Shakespeare's Globe opened with a performance starring artistic director Mark Rylance in the title role.)

24) A. Blackfriars (It became the indoor home of Shakespeare's company and they would spend the winter season there and go to the outdoor Globe for the other times of the year.)

25) B. The Lord Chamberlain's Men (When James I took the throne in 1603, he became their patron, and they become The King's Men.)

Quiz 88

1) D. *The Twilight Zone* (Shakespeare becomes disgruntled and returns to wherever he came from when TV executives makes changes in his script.)

2) A. *Macbeth* (It is said he read passages from the play aloud to friends mere days before his death.)

3) B. Ulysses S. Grant (while serving in the Fourth Infantry Regiment in 1845 in Corpus Christi, Texas)

4) A. *The Tempest*

5) C. Point

6) B. 230

7) A. Richard II

8) D. Chaucer (The Queen Mab speech in *Romeo and Juliet* was influenced by *Parliament of Fowles*, and "The Knight's Tale" influenced *The Two Kinsmen* and *A Midsummer Night's Dream*.)

9) D. Uranus

10) A. Hector Berlioz (a French composer who wrote numerous works inspired by Shakespeare)

11) C. *Titus Andronicus*

12) D. Walter Matthau

13) B. George Bernard Shaw

14) C. William Henry Ireland (He even forged a play that had a one night stand and was essentially laughed off the stage. The others are highly regarded critics and editors of Shakespeare's works.)

15) A. Bardolph and Margaret of Anjou (However, the ghost of Henry VI appears in *Richard III*, and if you add that to his appearance in the three *Henry VI* plays, he also appears in four plays.)

16) B. Anthony Burgess (in *Nothing Like the Sun*)

17) D. *Timon of Athens*

18) A. Washington, D.C.

19) A. Keats (In a letter to Benjamin Robert Haydon dated May 10, 1817, Keats wrote: "I remember your saying that you had notions of a good Genius presiding over you. I have of late had the same thought—for things which I do half at Random are afterwards confirmed by my judgment in a dozen features of Propriety. Is it too daring to fancy Shakespeare this Presider?")

20) C. *Hamlet* (Holden also refers to Hamlet as "a sad, screwed-up type of guy.")

21) B. Cymbeline

22) D. *Pericles*

23) B. *Troilus and Cressida*

24) D. *Much Ado About Nothing* and *Romeo and Juliet* (Friar Francis orchestrates the "death" of Hero, and Friar Lawrence does the same for Juliet.)

25) C. Triolus (mentioned in [4.1.150])

Quiz 89

1) A. Voltaire (the pen name of Francois Marie Arouet, one of France's greatest writers and philosophers)

2) A. Charles and Mary Lamb

3) C. *Othello* (The version Dickens penned was *O'Thello* [1834].)

4) B. Mark Twain

5) B. Hotspur

6) C. *Twelfth Night* (January 6 commemorates the first appearance of the Christ child to the Magi, the three Wise Men of the East. In the Renaissance, it marked the final day of Christmas revelry.)

7) D. Thomas Bowdler (His work appeared in 10 volumes [in 1818] and was extremely popular and reprinted many times. His work created a new word that is still in use: *bowdlerize*, which means to censor by omitting vulgar language.)

8) C. Paris Gardens

9) C. Sir John Oldcastle (However, this name offended the influential descendants of a man with that name, so it was changed to Falstaff, and a disclaimer was even later inserted.)

10) A. King James Bible (Some feel that Psalm 46 may have been translated by Shakespeare. The King James version of the Bible was printed when Shakespeare was 46 years old. Moreover, the 46th word from the beginning of the psalm is "shake" and the 46th word from the end of the psalm is "spear.")

11) B. *3 Henry VI*

12) B. John Gielgud

13) D. *The Taming of the Shrew* (Subtitled *The Tamer Tamed*, it took place after the death of Katherina and involves Petruchio being tamed by his second wife.)

14) C. *Bingo* (Bond portrays Shakespeare as a wealthy landowner and often absent father having difficulties with his daughter, Judith.)

15) D. Tom Stoppard (who later collaborated with Marc Norman to write a screenplay for the widely popular 1998 film *Shakespeare in Love*)

16) A. The Mermaid (It was a tavern on Bread Street in Cheapside, where aristocrats and intellectuals would gather the first Friday of each month. Shakespeare had ties to the proprietor of this tavern and the story goes that "Many were the wit-combats betwixt him and Ben Jonson.")

17) A. *Much Ado About Nothing* and *Measure for Measure*

18) B. *Romeo and Juliet*

19) C. Henry VI and Richard III

20) A. Ariel (originally named Don Juan.)

21) D. Lady Macbeth in *Macbeth*

22) D. Malvolio in *Twelfth Night* (5.1.378)

23) C. Hamlet

24) B. Sir Andrew Aguecheek (in *Twelfth Night*)

25) B. *Cymbeline* (Imogen and Cloten)

Quiz 90

1) John
2) Richard II
3) Henry IV
4) Henry V
5) Henry VI
6) Edward IV
7) Edward V
8) Richard III
9) Henry VII
10) Henry VIII

Quiz 91

1) THE TAMING OF THE SHREW
2) OTHELLO
3) MUCH ADO ABOUT NOTHING
4) KING LEAR
5) THE MERCHANT OF VENICE
6) MACBETH
7) THE TEMPEST
8) JULIUS CAESAR
9) AS YOU LIKE IT
10) ROMEO AND JULIET
11) A MIDSUMMER NIGHT'S DREAM
12) ANTONY AND CLEOPATRA
13) THE WINTER'S TALE
14) TIMON OF ATHENS
15) CORIOLANUS
16) MEASURE FOR MEASURE
17) LOVE'S LABOR'S LOST
18) THE COMEDY OF ERRORS
19) THE TWO GENTLEMEN OF VERONA
20) THE MERRY WIVES OF WINDSOR
21) PERICLES
22) ALL'S WELL THAT ENDS WELL
23) CYMBELINE
24) TITUS ANDRONICUS
25) TROILUS AND CRESSIDA

Quiz 92

1) OPHELIA
2) DESDEMONA
3) CLEOPATRA
4) BEATRICE
5) CORDELIA
6) ROSALIND
7) KATHERINA
8) TITANIA
9) MIRANDA
10) ROSALINE
11) ISABELLA
12) NERISSA
13) HIPPOLYTA
14) CRESSIDA
15) MARINA
16) LAVINIA
17) EMILIA
18) TAMORA
19) PERDITA
20) GONERIL
21) HELENA
22) IMOGEN
23) GERTRUDE
24) HERMIONE
25) HERMIA

Quiz 93

1) PETRUCHIO	10) LAERTES	19) FLEANCE
2) DEMETRIUS	11) VALENTINE	20) DONALBAIN
3) FERDINAND	12) LEONATO	21) PERICLES
4) MACBETH	13) EDGAR	22) TRIOLUS
5) HORTENSIO	14) APEMANTUS	23) BARDOLPH
6) ORLANDO	15) PROSPERO	24) POLIXENES
7) CALIBAN	16) BERTRAM	25) OBERON
8) RODERIGO	17) DUNCAN	
9) MERCUTIO	18) SEBASTIAN	

Quiz 94

1) Arcite's rival is **Palamon** in *The Two Noble Kinsmen*.

2) Benedick's rival, and later his wife, is **Beatrice** in *Much Ado About Nothing*.

3) Diomedes is the rival of **Troilus** for the love of Cressida in *Troilus and Cressida*.

4) Edgar is the rival of his bastard brother, **Edmund** in *Lear*.

5) Hamlet's rival is his uncle, **Claudius**, the man who killed his father and married his mother.

6) Julius Caesar's rival is **Brutus**, among others, in *Julius Caesar*.

7) In *The Winter's Tale*, Leontes believed his rival was **Polixenes**, but later finds this to be untrue.

8) Lysander rivals **Demetrius** for the love of Hermia in *A Midsummer Night's Dream*.

9) Macbeth's rival is **Macduff**.

10) Mark Antony's main rival in *Antony and Cleopatra* is **Octavius**.

11) Oberon is having problems with his fairy queen, **Titania**, in *A Midsummer Night's Dream*.

12) Orlando's rival is his older brother, **Oliver**.

13) Othello's rival is **Iago**, but unfortunately, he doesn't know it for most of the play.

14) Petruchio's rival is the shrewish **Katherina**, who is later his obedient? wife.

15) Posthumus's rival in *Cymbeline* is **Iachimo**.

16) Prince Hal's main rival in *1Henry IV* is the appropriately named **Hotspur**.

17) Proteus rivals **Valentine** for the love of Sylvia in *The Two Gentlemen of Verona*.

18) Shallow's rival is **Falstaff** in *The Merry Wives of Windsor*.

19) Shylock wants to cut out a pound of flesh from **Antonio** in *The Merchant of Venice*. That qualifies him as a rival.

20) Tullus Aufidius's rival is **Coriolanus**.

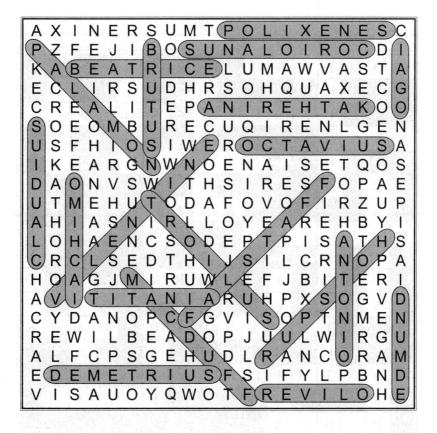

Quiz 95

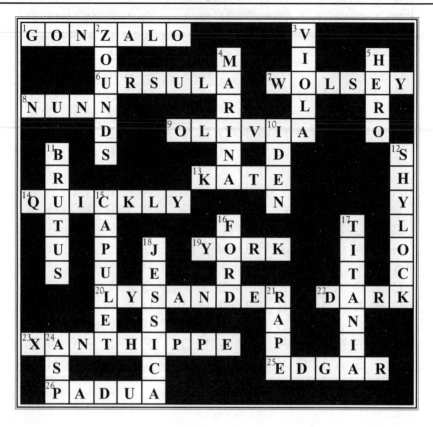

Bibliography

Bloom, Harold. *Shakespeare: The Invention of the Human*. New York: Riverhead Books, 1998.

Burgess, Anthony. *Shakespeare*. New York: A.A. Knopf, 1970.

Evans, G. Blakemore, ed., *The Riverside Shakespeare*. Boston: Houghton Mifflin, 1974.

Levin, Bernard. From *The Story of English*. Robert McCrum, William Cran, and Robert MacNeil. New York: Viking, 1986.

Wells, Stanley. *Shakespeare: For All Time*. Oxford: Oxford University Press, 2003.

About the Author

Thomas Delise has taught Shakespeare in high school for more than 25 years. He organizes numerous Shakespeare workshops and festivals every year for high schools, middle schools, and elementary schools, and he regularly conducts workshops for teachers on how to teach Shakespeare through performance. At Century High School in Sykesville, Maryland, he is the cofounder of both *The Shakespeare Factory*, a multifaceted approach to infusing Shakespeare study into schools and the community, and *The Rude Mechanicals*, Century's Shakespeare acting troupe. He has directed high-school performances of *The Tempest, Romeo and Juliet, A Midsummer Night's Dream, Twelfth Night*, and *Henry IV, Part One*, and he has had work published in *Shakespeare Magazine*. He lives in Baltimore, Maryland with his wife, Christine, his dog, Preakness, and his cat, Ophelia.